THE CORNISH WITCH

ELENA COLLINS

B
Boldwood

First published in Great Britain in 2025 by Boldwood Books Ltd.

Copyright © Elena Collins, 2025

Cover Design by Alice Moore Design

Cover Images: Shutterstock and iStock

The moral right of Elena Collins to be identified as the author of this work has been asserted in accordance with the Copyright, Designs and Patents Act 1988.

All rights reserved. No part of this book may be reproduced in any form or by any electronic or mechanical means, including information storage and retrieval systems, without written permission from the author, except for the use of brief quotations in a book review. This book is a work of fiction and, except in the case of historical fact, any resemblance to actual persons, living or dead, is purely coincidental.

Every effort has been made to obtain the necessary permissions with reference to copyright material, both illustrative and quoted. We apologise for any omissions in this respect and will be pleased to make the appropriate acknowledgements in any future edition.

A CIP catalogue record for this book is available from the British Library.

Paperback ISBN 978-1-78513-179-0

Large Print ISBN 978-1-78513-180-6

Hardback ISBN 978-1-78513-178-3

Ebook ISBN 978-1-78513-181-3

Kindle ISBN 978-1-78513-182-0

Audio CD ISBN 978-1-78513-173-8

MP3 CD ISBN 978-1-78513-174-5

Digital audio download ISBN 978-1-78513-176-9

This book is printed on certified sustainable paper. Boldwood Books is dedicated to putting sustainability at the heart of our business. For more information please visit https://www.boldwoodbooks.com/about-us/sustainability/

Boldwood Books Ltd, 23 Bowerdean Street, London, SW6 3TN

www.boldwoodbooks.com

For Sarah R.

THE WITCH'S KISS
A CORNISH SEA SHANTY

Early in the morn, on the clifftop, all alone
A Cornish maid stands waiting, her locks all long and blown.
Her face is wet with tears, me boys, and I can tell you true,
She's searching for a fishing boat lost in the ocean blue.

Let's hear it for the Cornish boy who sails the salty brine.
And for the maid who waits alone upon the dark shoreline.

The maid was watching the long day, she watched all through the night
But ne'er a ship did sail her way, it ne'er filled her sight.
Her heart was broke in twain because her love was far away
And, oh me boys, the maid still waits, she waits until this day.

Let's hear it for the Cornish boy who sails the salty brine.
And for the maid who waits alone upon the dark shoreline.

And others saw to tell the tale, who heard her softly moan.
They begged her stint, to leave the cliffs, return unto her home.
But still she watched, in winds and rain, each day became the night

And still she watched, as storms did cease, at th' early dawning light.

Let's hear it for the Cornish boy who sails the salty brine.
And for the maid who waits alone upon the dark shoreline.

She loved him with a love so strong, her eyes upon the sea
Until her flesh did melt away and soon all bones was she
Until the last breath left her lips, his name was just a sigh
And now she'll wait for evermore, his ship will ne'er draw nigh.

Let's hear it for the Cornish boy who sails the salty brine.
And for the maid who waits alone upon the dark shoreline.

The years have gone and much is changed, the fishing boats still roam
And in the wind they say, some nights, you still can hear her moan.
Oft times you'll see her on the shore, pale in the gliding moon
Weeping for the boy who stole her heart, but he will ne'er return.

Let's hear it for the Cornish boy who sails the salty brine.
And for the maid who waits alone upon the dark shoreline.

So when you walk the cliffs, me boys, and stand upon the beach
She'll be watching there behind you, better pray you're far from reach.
Her lips will brush against your face and rest assured of this
No man has never lived who felt the Waiting Witch's kiss.

Let's hear it for the Cornish boy who sails the salty brine.
And for the maid who waits alone upon the dark shoreline.

— WORDS BY JUDY. MUSIC WRITTEN BY HILLSTREET (TONY & IVOR)

The sea shanty is available on YouTube: https://youtube.com/watch?v=tNv-XZFX7Zjw&feature=shared

Would you learn the secret of the sea?
 Only those who brave its dangers comprehend its mystery!

— HENRY WADSWORTH LONGFELLOW

You can't stop the waves but you can learn how to surf.

— HAWAIIAN PROVERB

The witch knows nothing in this world is supernatural. It is all natural.

— LAURIE CABOT

GLOSSARY

Chawk – an old Cornish word for jackdaw
Caul – afterbirth
Croust – an early Cornish pasty, filled with meat or fish, onion, swede, turnip and carrot
Cunning – Cunning folk were practitioners of folk medicine or healing. Their services often included thwarting witches. Early fourteenth century: conning, 'learned, skilful, possessing knowledge', present participle of connen, cunnen 'to know', from Old English cunnan. Wortcunning is a knowledge of herbs or plants.
Jangling – gossiping, telling tales
Kicky-wicky – slang word for wife or girlfriend
Pellar – a wise man or woman in Cornish, a healer
Pickthanks – gossips who tell tales to curry favour
Poppet – small doll figure of a human being used in witchcraft
Simples – single herbs used as remedies
Swill belly – drunkard

PROLOGUE
SEVERAL MONTHS AGO, ST MAWGEN COVE, CORNWALL

The man with the beard, dressed in jeans and T-shirt, hooked himself over the bar of The Ship Inn, a dingy hostelry that had been built for fishermen years ago, near the harbour of St Mawgen Cove.

'Rum. Double,' he said in a metallic voice.

The bleary-eyed barman refilled his glass and set it down with a clunk, then he moved back to his own tumbler of whisky. His wife was hanging glasses on a rack. Darkness clung to the room; there was no sound except the crackle of dry twigs burning in the inglenook. The lone drinker's eyes were dull as he cranked his arm upwards and tipped the rum into his mouth. He placed the empty tumbler soundlessly on the bar.

'Thank 'ee.'

'G'night, John.' The barman didn't look up. He was trapped in his own thoughts, staring towards the ruddy glow of the fire where a moth hovered.

John hunched his shoulders and gazed around. He was the last customer; it was past closing time. He made for the door, pushing it ajar. The hinges creaked like an ache. He stepped into the darkness and looked down the hill towards the twinkling harbour lights. The pub sign swung overhead; the 'For Sale' board on the white wall now read 'Sold'.

The man lurched towards home, smelling of sweat and rum, mumbling beneath his breath. It had been a long day. On either side of the road, a few shroud-pale cottages huddled. Moonlight glinted on the water. A ship shifted; a mast groaned. He forced his stare ahead as he turned the corner – it was folly to look back.

A breeze puffed against his face, filtering through the thin cotton of his T-shirt, and made his skin gooseflesh. He quickened his pace. Beyond, the grey cliffs were jagged as rotten teeth. John could still taste the sharp spirit on his tongue. He'd be home soon, back in his little cottage with his lovely wife. The sooner the better.

The moon slipped behind a stray cloud and the air became colder. John glanced over his shoulder without intending to, then hurried on. His feet crunched against rough gravel; he pushed his hands deeper into his pockets to keep the blast of the wind away.

Then he heard a whisper on the breeze.

'*I'm here.*'

He stared towards the cliffs and fear gripped him. She was there, on the summit. He was sure: a figure, wraith-like, dressed in translucent white. He couldn't look away from the flowing hair, the way her body leaned towards the sea, the wind tugging her shift, blowing through it. He heard the sound of her whisper.

'*I'm here.*'

Someone was behind him, the tingling closeness of another person at his shoulder. He daren't turn. He knew only too well the old rhyme that had passed from father to son over many generations:

> *If she walk behind ye, fear*
> *in case she come too near.*
> *If ye ever hear her call*
> *Then that same moment, ye shall fall.*

She was there, so close he could feel her breath on his neck. He heard the faint breathing.

'*I'm here.*'

Then she said the single syllable of his name.

He wasn't sure what happened next. Cold fingers touched the back of his neck. Her arms embraced him and he wheezed beneath her stifling clutch.

Her long fingers felt deep into his heart. Perhaps it was his imagination, the woman clinging to him, but a searing pain engulfed his chest, squeezing, as if the last breath was being forced from his lungs.

Her voice came again.

'*One breath, one kiss... you are mine.*'

He stumbled, sprawling on the stony ground, groaning, then he exhaled. His eyes were still open. The last thing he felt was the cold touch of her lips against his.

'*One kiss...*'

She was gone.

The following morning, someone found him on the ground, his eyes wide open, and said he'd died of a heart attack. Or perhaps he'd tripped on the way home after he'd had one drink too many.

But many folk in St Mawgen Cove believed otherwise. They knew it was the Waiting Witch.

1

THE PRESENT, MINEHEAD, SOMERSET

It was a day that would change their lives for ever. And like any such day, it began with no sign of it being anything special.

Megan woke early, as she usually did on Mondays, showered and pulled on thick clothes. It was early September, the fourth, but a chilly autumn wind already hovered over the sea and funnelled down the Esplanade. Wriggling into a jacket and a woollen hat, she needed to be warm. She hurried down the stairs from the flat to the main street where her car was parked outside her shop, Earthbound Essentials. Megan started the engine of the battered old VW Beetle. She always felt a moment of relief to hear the throaty clatter once the key was turned, as if she expected it to fail.

In her head, she could hear her mother laughing kindly: 'How does that old thing ever get through an MOT? You should treat yourself to something reliable.'

'We go back a long way, me and my Beetle. We're used to each other,' Megan would always say, and her mother would reply, 'Just like me and your dad.'

Megan clutched the wheel with cold hands. The heating in the car didn't work properly; it tended to come on at full force during a summer heatwave and blow out cold air when the weather was icy. She drove along Townsend

Road, smiling as she passed the primary school. They had a new head-teacher now. Her father had retired and not a day too soon. These days he spent his life tending to the garden instead of burying his head in Annual Improvement Plans, strategic leadership and reporting to parents. He enjoyed growing potatoes instead.

Megan headed along the road, Dunster Castle to her right, and into Carhampton, turning up Hill View Road, towards Park Lane. She was on autopilot; she made the journey twice a day, five times a week. Her mother, Jackie, didn't like driving now, but they shared the shop, one of them selling herbal remedies, essential oils and gifts out front while the other provided healing treatments at the back. Her mother offered reflexology; Megan gave reiki and aromatherapy massages.

Megan wondered if her mother might want to reduce her hours now that her dad had retired. She could run the shop by herself easily, but having some company during the day was always nicer. It was autumn and business was quiet now the holidaymakers had gone. The regulars would come in as usual, but she'd miss the friendly faces and the different regional accents of the visitors.

She parked the VW outside her parents' house, a neat three-bedroomed semi with a tidy privet hedge, woodlands to the rear. As she locked the car, a cheery voice greeted her.

'Morning, Megan. I could set my clock by you.'

'Morning, Shaun.' Megan glanced at the postman who stood on the pavement. He was wide awake and chirpy, with a gap-toothed grin. They'd been at the same secondary school and he'd been a postie since he'd left at eighteen. He was two years older than her – he'd be thirty now – but they went back a long way.

'It's all right for some, cadging breakfast from the parents again.' He paused, handing her several letters. 'Give these to your dad, can you? It'll save my aching legs a journey down the path.'

'I will. Have a nice day,' Megan said, watching him stride away in perennial grey shorts, his muscly legs hardened against all weathers.

'You stole my line,' Shaun called as he dragged open the gate to the house next door. 'Now, you take care.'

His next words were lost over the lively barking of a dog, then he called out, 'Hello, Freya. No. No. There's a good girl.'

Megan made for the front door and her mother was there, smiling. 'Breakfast's on the table.'

Megan followed her mother into the house, smelling toast and coffee. She was used to the morning ritual at her parents' home, but it was nice to see her father sitting at the table in jeans and an old shirt, slippers on his feet. In term time, he'd normally have left already in a suit and tie. As headteacher, he'd always made sure he was in school by half past seven.

Megan plonked herself at the table and looked from one parent to the other. 'How are you both?'

'We can't grumble.' Jackie Hammond was pouring coffee, arranging toast in a rack. In her late fifties, she still had the bustling air of someone whose priority was to fuss over her family. Generous, always cheerful. Megan was an extrovert like her mother, but she looked like her father, with dark curly hair and an easy smile. Bill Hammond stretched his legs as if to prove that he was relaxed nowadays.

'This is the life.'

He brought his cup to his lips and Megan thought he seemed a little lost. She hoped retirement wouldn't mean he'd be at home each day doing nothing.

Bill gave a quiet sigh. 'Well, normally I'd be welcoming the teachers into the newly polished hall for training.' He seemed a little sad. 'They'd have suntans from their holidays and be chatting happily. Then by coffee time they'd be wondering where the summer had gone. We'd sit through a Power Point for three hours and by four o'clock, it'd feel like a long time till Christmas.'

'It's time for someone else to do the work.' Megan hugged him. 'Have you and Mum thought about what I was saying about taking a holiday?'

'We've talked about it. I'd love to go somewhere in January.' Jackie plonked a plate of toast in front of her daughter. 'Your father can't make his mind up. I think he just likes pottering in the shed.'

'You need a holiday yourself, Megan,' Bill said. 'When was the last time you went away?'

Megan knew when it had been, and an awkward silence sat at the table with them for a moment. Two years ago, she'd been camping with Jay. They'd both been living in the flat above Earthbound Essentials, planning a future. For the whole of August, they'd taken the blue VW Beetle everywhere, spending an idyllic month swimming, surfing, scuba diving, going from one coastal resort to another: Somerset, Devon, Cornwall. Then it had finished abruptly, a year ago. Megan didn't really talk about it now: no one did. He hadn't treated her fairly. She hadn't seen it coming.

Jackie guessed her thoughts. 'You need a break, Megan. It'd do you good.'

'Maybe.' Megan concentrated on chewing her toast. Then she remembered. 'Oh, Dad, these came. They are addressed to you.'

She picked the three letters from the table, passing them over. Two were bills, which he set aside immediately. The third was a creamy envelope, addressed in round black handwriting. He opened it carefully and scanned the contents.

Megan noticed the change in him immediately. He was absolutely still for a moment, then his hand shook. His face held an expression she'd never seen before. The skin on his face was taut, the colour draining away. As if he was haunted.

Jackie was oblivious, bustling around, checking her handbag. 'I don't want to be late this morning, Megan. I've got a nine thirty reflexology with Mrs Downes. Her blood pressure's sky high again.'

Megan watched her father. His brow knitted; he was reading each word again, concentrating. He shook his head, as if in disbelief.

'Then I have a twelve o'clock with a new client. I booked it over the phone on Friday. She's called Jennifer. She sounds nice.'

'Ah, good, yes.' Bill folded the letter deliberately and pushed it into his shirt pocket. 'Excuse me a minute, Jackie. I've just remembered something.'

'Oh?' Jackie gave him her attention at last. 'What's the matter?'

'I left a book upstairs.' Bill shuffled towards the door and was gone, Megan staring after him, wondering what was happening.

'Is Dad all right?'

'I suppose he's finding it hard to adjust. To be honest, I worry about him being here all day. He could've stayed on until he was sixty-five, but the job was getting too much.' Jackie's forehead wrinkled with concern. 'I hope he'll get used to things now. A holiday might be a good idea.'

'It might be. And you should spend more time together; go out.'

'I should but...' Jackie patted Megan's arm confidentially. 'I do love being in the shop. Just having people to talk to. Your dad likes his shed and his books. I'd be by myself most of the time if I retired.'

'You should travel, make memories.'

'So should you, love.' Jackie looked even more anxious. 'I worry about you, working so hard. You need to have fun.'

'I've got my swimming, and I meet Amy and the others in the pub.'

'That's no life.' Jackie made a muffled noise of disapproval. 'The problem with living in Minehead is that it's very beautiful, but it's isolated. The winters can be lonely. And I think of you in the flat, by yourself.'

Megan knew what her mother was getting at. She forced a laugh. 'Don't worry, Mum. One morning you'll come into the shop and I'll have packed my bag and be heading off to Bangkok to find myself.'

Jackie was aghast. 'Oh, I didn't mean you should give everything up.'

'Nor did I.' Megan laughed to break the tension. 'I'm fine. Yes, there are times when I fancy a change, but I'll get there, when I'm ready.'

'You've always been the same. When you were a baby, all the ordinary things, crawling, talking, reading, you were late with them all and then, whoosh, you suddenly caught up. You take your time and do everything at your own pace, either too slow and hesitant or madly impulsive. No middle way.'

'But here I am now, crawling, talking and reading,' Megan joked. She paused, wondering about her father. He was upstairs, possibly clutching the letter, his face frozen in an expression of – what was it? Dismay? Horror? She ought to go up and ask him if he was all right.

'We should get off.' Jackie was on her feet. 'I'll leave the dishes for Bill. He'll need something to occupy him.'

'Shall I pop up and say goodbye?' Megan asked.

'I'll just yell up the stairs.' Jackie reached for her jacket, scurrying into the hall, shouting, 'See you later, Bill. I'll be back before five.'

Megan heard a low sound, Bill's attempt at a reply. His thoughts were clearly elsewhere. She was surprised that her mother hadn't noticed. That's thirty years of married life for you, she told herself cynically. Then she rallied and called, 'See you, Dad.' There would be time to find out what was in the letter later.

Her mother had reached the gate as Megan closed the front door. Jackie turned round, her expression already disappointed. 'Oh, this old boneshaker.' She indicated the blue VW. 'I know it's only ten minutes into Minehead, but it sets my nerves jangling. And it's colder inside the car than out. I'll be a bag of nerves by the time we start work.'

2

For the next couple of days, in the private environment of the shop, Megan asked her mother how her father was feeling, only to be told that he was all right, his usual quiet self. One thing was clear: Jackie didn't share Megan's concern. She was oblivious to the letter and he clearly hadn't told her anything about it.

On the spur of the moment, Megan phoned him after the shop closed on Wednesday. Bill sounded pleased to hear from her, but he was lost in his thoughts, not really listening. Megan was so concerned, she invited herself round on Friday evening when her mother went to her weekly reading group.

Her father was still on her mind on Thursday when she went swimming in St Michael's Pool after work. She changed into her swimsuit and dived beneath the surface, enjoying the way her arms sliced through the water, propelling herself forward. She loved the pool, the friendly atmosphere. It was here she'd met Jay four years ago. They'd both been local, and keen swimmers. She recalled their first tentative glances at the edge of the pool, and brief exchange of words. Their romance had been inevitable. They had shared a first date, kisses, they'd fallen in love, then he'd moved into the flat with her. They had been happy. She'd believed it would last and last.

Then one evening in September last year, he'd spoken casually to a woman at the bar in The Old Ship Aground, and Megan knew immediately that it was over. There was something in the way their eye contact held. He left Megan a fortnight later to take up with Annelise. She was the new love of his life, he'd said; he was sorry, but their time together had come to a natural end. Besides, he knew what real love was now. Megan had let him go and pretended that it didn't hurt.

She kicked her feet against the side of the pool, turning, diving deeper, changing direction. Her father's face came back to her, the moment he'd looked at the letter. It had to be bad news, she was certain: she'd never seen him react with such fear. By the time Megan completed the tenth length, she was worried about his health. By the time she had finished her usual fifty lengths, she was convinced he'd been sent death threats. She would ask him tomorrow. She had to know.

By seven thirty, she was driving to Williton to spend the evening with her old school friend Amy, who arrived at the door damp from the shower, baby Leo wriggling under her arm. Amy waved Megan inside, where the living room was warm and the lamps golden. Several crystals hung from the ceiling, all bought from Megan's shop. Amy deposited Leo in a playpen where he picked up a Jellycat Fuddlewuddle, chewed the ear and threw it out onto the carpet. Amy beamed as though he'd performed a miracle. She handed Megan a glass of Coke and a plate of nibbles.

'I'm in charge of a six-month-old and you're driving. We're strictly off alcohol tonight.'

'Where's Ross?'

'He's gone to The Masons. It'll do him good to have a night away from me and Leo. We never get any sleep. Teething's torture, although the chamomile spray you gave me helps tons, and it's better than drinking gallons of disgusting chamomile tea.'

'You look well,' Megan said. Amy's eyes sparkled despite the dark circles, and little Leo was full of beans.

'So.' Amy made one of those concerned faces that showed far more compassion than was needed. 'How are things, Meg?'

Megan avoided the sympathy look. 'I'm fine. Work's dropping off now the holidaymakers have gone. I'm trying to persuade Mum and Dad to go on holiday. They need some fun.'

'You need some fun too. When did you last take a break?' Amy persisted, gazing over her shoulder to check on Leo. He was sucking a soft fabric cube with a giraffe printed on it. Amy tugged it from his mouth and his face crumpled. He began to yell at such a volume that Megan wondered how mothers coped. Amy stood up and walked zombie-like to the kitchen, opening the fridge, returning with a beaker of cooled water. The baby took it, sipped once and flung it away. Amy plucked him from the cot. She looked at Megan hopefully.

'Do you want to hold him?'

Megan held out her arms for a hug and Amy handed him over gratefully. Leo immediately tried to grab Megan's hair. She tucked dark curls behind her ears and he lunged for her nose with sticky fingers.

'He's so clever,' Amy said fondly. 'You know, Meg, I never thought I'd be the first to start a family. You were more popular with boys.'

'Was I?' Megan asked. That wasn't how she remembered it.

Amy began to fold clean baby clothes. 'Ross and I said we'd wait until we'd done the house up but accidents happen.'

Megan smiled indulgently, removing the little 'accident' from where he was trying to eat the toggle of her hoodie. She felt the marshmallow softness of his cheek, inhaling the sweet baby smell.

'He's adorable, but it must be tough. Babies are all right as long as you can hand them back.'

Amy clearly didn't want Leo back yet. 'Oh, I adore him to bits, but he's hell at three in the morning.' She scrutinised her friend's expression. 'Meg, are you sure everything's all right? You don't seem your bubbly self.'

Megan was secretly impressed. Amy had been her best friend since they were eleven-year-olds. They'd shared ups and downs, secrets and heartbreaks, and even now, up to her ears in motherhood, Amy was still able to read Megan's face.

'I'm not sure,' she said. 'Ask me at the weekend. I'll have a better idea then. Dad's a bit unhappy. I'm going to see him tomorrow.'

'Maybe retirement blues have kicked in?'

'Retirement blues? Is there such a thing?'

'I'd love to retire right now. Every day's full-on. What I'd do for sunshine, a beach, cocktails. Or even a part-time job.' Amy suddenly had an idea. 'Oh, I know, I'll get Ross to babysit on Saturday and come to you. We can go to the pub and I can pretend I'm normal. I can't tell you how much I need time with people who aren't mums.' She made a disapproving face. 'Does that make me a crap parent?'

'No, the pub's exactly what we both need.' Megan offered Leo to his mother, who whisked him into her arms and blew raspberries on his belly, making him chortle.

She was beginning to feel lighter, although it might have been the relief of handing the wriggling baby back. Her mind was already on Friday evening and what she'd say to her father.

* * *

Megan bumped into her mother as she was leaving the house on Friday evening. Jackie was carrying her handbag and a bottle of wine, several books tucked beneath one arm.

'A bottle of red and a few murders. It'll be a lively night at the reading group,' Megan said.

'We're still discussing cosy crime – Ann Cleeves' latest,' Jackie said, as if that explained her hurry to leave. She gave her daughter a quick hug. 'I hope it doesn't put me in the mood for murder, though. I could have killed your father earlier on. He hardly spoke at dinner. I even suggested he ask for his old job back. He's been miserable all week.'

'What's wrong?'

Jackie had no idea. 'I offered him some reflexology to sort out his mood swings. I said we needed to talk and he just snapped at me. Can you believe it? And then he had the cheek to tell me I should stop pestering him. Of course, that's your father all over, hiding his feelings. But it's not like him to be confrontational.'

'Poor Dad,' Megan said. 'Poor you, too.'

'I hope you can cheer him up, love.' Jackie's eyes widened with worry. 'I wonder if he's pining for something.'

'I'll see what I can do,' Megan said.

Jackie was already halfway down the path. 'He'll probably tell you it's nothing, but if anyone can find out, it's you.' She waved. 'I'm over at Jan's, if you need anything. I'll be back by ten.'

Megan watched her go, then she walked into the hall, closing the door behind her. She called cheerily, 'Dad?'

The silence in the hall told her he was not downstairs so Megan hurried upstairs, into her parents' bedroom. The room was neat, the bed made, the duvet smooth. A top window was open; a light breeze billowing the curtains. Several photos stood tidily on the dressing table: a wedding photo from 1993, a few photos of Megan as a smiling child, a frowning teenager. A jug of water and a bottle of tablets sat on the bedside cabinet, her father's blood pressure medication. But the house seemed eerily empty.

She called again, 'Dad?' Her voice echoed, then there was silence.

Megan padded downstairs into the living room. The French doors were open; her father would be in the garden. She stepped outside onto the patio, following the path, rose bushes and shrubs on either side, the fishpond full of flickering koi.

She kept her voice low. 'Dad?' There was still no reply.

Beyond the apple and pear trees was the potting shed behind which the freshly painted fence gave way to woodland. The door was ajar. Her father would surely be inside, arranging apples in boxes for the winter. She pushed the door wide and gazed in.

Her father's back was to her. He was leaning against a bench, hunched over, his head down on his arms. He appeared to be doing nothing at all. Megan watched him: he was not moving, as if he was propped up. His back was curved awkwardly; he looked uncomfortable. For a second, she wondered if he'd had a heart attack and died where he'd stood. She couldn't help the fear in her voice.

'Dad?'

Bill turned round slowly, as if in pain, and faced her. He held the cream envelope in his hands, clutched in twisted fingers. He met her eyes, and his own were raw and wet. His face shone with tears.

Then he said, 'Oh, Megan, I'm so sorry.' And she heard the sadness in his voice, as if he had done something dreadful and the whole world was about to come to a sudden and terrible end.

3

'Dad?'

Megan threw her arms around her father, her cheek against the rough knit of his sweater. She could smell the lavender of her mother's soap powder as a deep sigh shuddered from beneath.

'I'm sorry, Megan. I've let everyone down.'

'No, you haven't.' Megan held her father at arm's length. 'You're not ill, are you? I mean, there's nothing wrong?'

'No, no, it's not that. It's...' Bill looked at the ceiling, away, keeping his gaze from Megan. 'There's something I should have...'

'Is it to do with the letter?' Megan asked.

He nodded.

'Is it bad news?'

He nodded again, then shook his head.

'I can't tell Jackie. She can't know.'

Megan took a breath. 'Can you tell me?'

Bill stared, not knowing how to answer. Then he said, 'It's difficult.'

She gripped his arm. 'Let's go in and get a hot drink. Then you can tell me.'

He shook his head. 'I don't know.'

'You need to share this. I mean, it's clearly hurting you.'

He nodded, but didn't move.

'A problem shared, Dad,' Megan insisted.

Bill moved his head almost imperceptibly again. Then he allowed her to lead him into the kitchen, where he slumped at the table, the letter still pressed between his fingers like a crushed butterfly. He stared at it, as if stunned. Megan busied herself with making tea, watching him all the time. He looked miserable.

She placed a steaming mug in front of him, sitting opposite, and grabbed his hand. 'Now, what's happened?'

Bill exhaled wearily. 'The past has come back. It's like being haunted.'

'Dad?'

Bill said nothing for a moment, then he whispered, 'She's called Emma now.'

'Who is?'

'Baby Sarah Jane.'

'Who?'

Bill's hand trembled and Megan gripped it tighter. 'She's written to me. Emma Davey, she's called now. She's forty-three years old.'

'Who is she?'

Bill reached for his tea. 'She's my daughter.'

It was Megan's turn to be lost for words. Her mind raced: the letter was from a woman called Emma who was forty-three, her father's daughter. That made her a half-sister. She did the maths: her father would have been eighteen.

She said, 'What happened to her?'

'We gave her up for adoption.'

'Who did?'

'Me and Chrissie.' Bill closed his eyes. 'Chrissie and I had been together since we were fifteen years old. We were at school, in Taunton. Then during A levels, she became...'

'Pregnant?' Megan helped him out.

Bill nodded slowly. 'Chrissie and I, you know, we were young, in love. We thought we'd stay together. Of course, it all went sour. Her parents were furious. I took the brunt. They wouldn't let me see her. Or the baby.'

'You never saw your daughter?'

'No.' Bill paused, as if he was remembering. 'I heard Chrissie had called her Sarah Jane. But she gave her up, straight after birth. A nurse took her away. A couple in Cornwall adopted her.'

'How did you feel, Dad?'

'As if I'd done wrong. As if I had no say in the matter. As if I'd been removed from the child's life without even the chance to see her, to say, "Hello, I'm your dad."' There was a tremor in his voice. 'When you were born, I cried. Mostly because I felt so much love, because you were my baby, mine and Jackie's. But I cried for Sarah Jane, too. And for all the hurt I'd caused.'

'That's so unfair, Dad. On all of you.'

'And now she's found me. She got this address. In the letter, she asks if I'm the man who's named as her father on the birth certificate: William John Hammond. She wants to get to know me.'

Megan took a breath. 'And what do you want to do?'

'I don't know. I'm terrified.'

'Why?'

'Because it's been so long. Because I feel guilty. Because I neglected her. Because I have my own life and she's not a part of it.'

'And Mum?'

'She can't know.' Bill's eyes filled with tears again. 'I can't tell her.'

'Why not?' Megan frowned. 'Mum would understand.'

'No, no.' Bill shook his head vigorously. 'She wanted more children after you, but none came. Then... you know about the hysterectomy.'

'So what will you do? Will you write back to Emma Davey? Or will you, you know, let sleeping dogs lie?' She leaned towards him. 'It's your choice.'

'She didn't give me her home address, although she says she lives in Cornwall. Just an email.' Bill took a breath. 'I can't tell Jackie. But then if I don't reply, I'm abandoning her all over again.'

'And what happened to Chrissie?'

'Her family moved away after the baby. Somewhere up north, Yorkshire, I think. She didn't keep in touch.'

'That must have been so tough.' Megan met her father's brown eyes. He looked tired. 'What are you thinking?'

'I'm frightened.'

'Frightened?'

'Of hurting Jackie. Of rocking the boat. Of meeting Emma. Of what happens if I don't.'

'Right,' Megan said, her voice determined. 'This is what I suggest.'

Her father looked suddenly hopeful and Megan's heart went out to him. He needed her to be strong, to help him make decisions. She squeezed his hand again. 'This is our secret for a while. We don't have to rush or say anything to anyone. We'll wait for the dust to settle. Then...'

Bill met her gaze quickly, anxiously.

'Then we'll go for a walk at the weekend, me and you, on Sunday morning when Mum's doing her crossword and Sudoku.'

Bill forced a laugh. 'She says it keeps her mind active.'

'We'll talk it through. There are several options. You can do nothing. You can write back to Emma and say you aren't the right person. Of course, that would be a lie and a bit unfair, but if it keeps you safe I'll support you. Or you could reply and say yes, you're her dad, but you don't want to meet her. Or you can just say yes and see what happens. Where in Cornwall does she live?'

'St Mawgen. I don't know where that is.'

'I'll google it,' Megan said firmly. 'You might want to talk to Mum. It'll be hard to keep it a secret.'

'It's been difficult all these years, more than you'd realise.' Bill's voice cracked with sadness.

'Then maybe it's better out in the open. But it's your choice, Dad, and whatever you decide, I'll support you.'

'I have the best daughter in the world,' Bill said.

Megan couldn't help herself. 'Perhaps you have the two best daughters.'

Again, Bill looked stunned. 'It's hard to take in. I'd assumed it was a secret I'd never have to deal with again.'

'It's tough,' Megan agreed.

'We'll go to Dunkery Beacon,' Bill suggested. 'Come for Sunday lunch.' He closed his eyes. 'I feel so dishonest, keeping this from Jackie, but the alternative's unthinkable.'

'Dad, you've had forty-three years of sadness. It can't have been easy. But you've told me. That wasn't too bad, was it?'

'You're not...' Bill searched for the right words. 'Shocked? Ashamed of me?'

'No, not at all,' Megan said. 'I'm proud you're my dad. And I'm proud of the young man you were when, you know, the baby was born.'

'I offered to step up. I'd have done anything: given up sixth form, got a job, brought the baby up.'

'I know,' Megan soothed. 'We'll work it out. Now, Mum'll be home in a couple of hours. How about we look for a good film or a documentary on TV and see if there's any cake?'

* * *

Megan thought about little else for the whole of the next day. How lost her father must have felt at eighteen. She imagined his young girlfriend, Chrissie, and the baby she'd named Sarah Jane. But she put it from her thoughts and managed to be bubbly as she chatted to her mother in the shop. Jackie had no idea that Megan's mind was a jumble of thoughts about a half-sister called Emma.

That evening, Megan went out with Amy and some friends in The Old Ship Aground, making her glass of wine last for two hours while Amy threw back four gin and tonics and gushed about how wonderful it was to have an evening away from Ross and Leo, how Megan had no idea how dreadful it was washing sick from baby clothes twenty-four seven, but she wouldn't change it for the world. Three times she said she was desperate to get a job just to get out of the house. Megan put her into a taxi at eleven o'clock, waved her off affectionately, then rushed back to her flat above Earthbound Essentials. She had something she wanted to do.

She already had some chamomile oil and a leaflet about magnesium-rich foods to help her father rest. But it didn't seem like enough: he was hurting and she wanted to show him she cared. So she turned to something else that she believed might help. She laid out several semi-precious stones on the table: rose quartz to mend heartbreak, a beautiful pink stone, cool and smooth to the touch; amethyst to ease the sadness; obsidian to help him stay grounded. Finally, she added her own favourite stone, blue chrysocolla, representing life lessons and wisdom. Megan threaded the beads on strong stretchy cord into a bracelet. She'd give it to her father during their walk.

She wondered how he'd react. He wasn't the sort of man who'd take herbal remedies and wear bracelets, and there was every chance he'd refuse it or leave it in a drawer, but Megan wanted to show her support. She imagined her father at eighteen, shut out of the birth of his baby. It must have been heartbreaking for Chrissie, feeling alone at the birth, saying goodbye to her baby immediately afterwards. Megan wondered if she'd held little Sarah Jane in her arms, if she'd had the chance to whisper words of love before the baby was whisked away. She threaded more beads onto the cord and thought of Sarah Jane, now renamed Emma who, at forty-three, had never met her father.

Her thoughts moved to her mum, oblivious that her husband had a grown-up child, living in Cornwall. The truth might break her heart and shake her trust in the man she'd loved for thirty years.

Megan tied the bracelet in a firm knot and thought of Bill, Jackie, Emma Davey and herself. She hoped with all her heart that they'd all come through this difficult time unscathed.

4

ST MAWGEN COVE, CORNWALL, 1625

Susanna Boram sat by the hearth on a three-legged stool, watching the orange firelight flicker on her daughter's face. There was no sound in the darkened room other than the crackling twigs. Her daughter, Katel, was staring into the flames, occasionally peering up the chimney as smoke curled and drifted away. Susanna glanced at the table where a basket of summer herbs had been placed ready to be dried. There were two empty bowls smeared with the last of the pottage, and half-eaten hunks of coarse bread. In the corner stood the old chest containing herbs and potions, and flagons of liquor. A jar held several marigold flowers in bloom: the petals were useful to colour and flavour food. Susanna thought of the work she had to do: an ointment of marigolds would help a nursing mother, soothing cracked or tender nipples. The juice from the leaves would remove warts; eating the raw leaves in a salad would treat a child's cough and swellings in the neck.

Susanna glanced back to the hearth, where more bunches of herbs hung from the blackened beam and hot water bubbled in a pot over the fire. Occasionally, splashes would spit over the rim, hissing on the glowing twigs. Katel was still hypnotised by the flickering light. Susanna put out a hand and stroked her long fair hair, feeling the thick silky coil of it in her hand. She sighed, the deep sound of a mother who loved her daughter too much, who was afraid for her future. Katel was seventeen, but she had the innocent eyes of a child. She was sweet natured and far too trusting.

Susanna worried about her all the time. There was no father or brother in the home to look out for her, although her uncle Samuel lived next door. He'd promised Susanna to keep a watchful eye for Katel at the harbour after a haul had come in, when most of the village was gutting and salting fish for storage. Young fishermen already glanced her way when she was about her work. Susanna was all too aware that her pretty child had become a beautiful young woman, and it made her afraid. She'd made mistakes she didn't want her daughter to make. She touched her smooth cheek.

'I'm ready for my bed, child. Will you come up with me now?'

'In a while. I want to wash first with some hot water. I hate the smell of the fish on my skin.'

'It's been a long day. There was a good haul in the bay. Samuel says we'll be eating well for the rest of the summer, God be praised.'

Katel turned to her mother. 'Aunt Annie's big now. How is it with her?'

'You know her time's near,' Susanna said.

'And will you help with the birthing?'

'I will.'

Katel grabbed her mother's hands in a swift movement. 'Your hands are rough like mine. Will you not hurt the baby?'

'No, I know to take care. Yours are dry from gutting the fish but I have some cream that will soothe them.'

'What did you make it from?'

'Old lard and oil from flowers. It makes the skin soft. I can teach you how to prepare it.'

'Perhaps you can.' Katel looked away towards the chimney. 'I have much to learn about these things.'

'I want to help you. You can become a pellar like me.'

'Could I become a great pellar?' Katel's face was earnest. 'I don't want to gut fish for ever, although it pays well. I might be the best cunning woman in Cornwall one day, one who knows everything about how to make people well.'

Susanna hugged her daughter. 'The idea fills me with happiness.'

'I'll learn from others who share their cunning with me.' Katel wrapped her arms around her knees, her face dreamy. 'Tedda Lobb from the cove says I learn fast.'

Susanna was suddenly serious. 'You might be wise to have less to do with Tedda. I trust her as much as I would a rat in a barn.'

'I saw her today when I was down at the harbour. She whispered something.'

Susanna sat up straight, her brow furrowed. 'What did she whisper, child?'

'*Gura da. Rag ta honan te ya gura.*' Katel's voice was low.

'Do good. It is for thyself thou doest it.' Susanna frowned. 'What does she mean by that? She shouldn't be talking to you in the old Cornish tongue, speaking of the old ways.'

'She smiled at me, Mother, with her two remaining teeth, as if she meant me no ill. I'd profit much from her knowledge.'

'Don't think so.' Susanna stood up, smoothing her apron. 'Healing's done for the good of others, Katel, not for pride or for our own gain.'

'But Tedda likes me.'

'Poor Tedda has no child of her own. She lost all of them, five babies in childbirth and it's made her bitter. She wants to make a daughter of you, I think.'

'But she's kind, and I like her.'

'She's not to be trusted, as I've said. Now will you come up to bed? I'm weary.'

'No, I'll wash myself, then I'll sleep by the fireside,' Katel said determinedly.

'Very well.' Susanna reached for a candle. 'I'll see you on the morrow. Sleep well, child.'

'And you too, Mother.' Katel's voice was almost inaudible. She was staring at the coiled smoke, straining to see up the chimney.

Susanna climbed the narrow staircase to the one room above, to her straw-stuffed mattress on the floor. Kneeling by the bed, she clasped her hands together, whispering, 'O My God, I love Thee with all my heart. Pardon me for the evil I have done this day; and if I have done any good, deign to accept it. Watch over me while I rest, and deliver me from danger. May Thy grace be always with me. Amen.'

She paused for a moment, wondering if Katel was praying too. There was magic power in spoken words. Susanna listened carefully but no sound came from downstairs. Katel must have fallen asleep. Susanna combed and braided her hair, then cleaned her teeth with a toothpick. She tugged off her clothes, struggled into a nightshift and huddled under a rough woollen blanket. Despite it being July, the room was cold. She would normally snuggle up with Katel, breathe in the soft warmth of her skin as she slumbered. It had always been that way since she was a baby.

But today Katel had made a choice. She was ready to separate herself from her mother.

Things were changing. Perhaps Katel would find a husband, as all young women did, and there would be marriage and babies. Susanna would be alone in the tiny cottage for the remainder of her days. She thought briefly about Katel's father, his strong arms, his bold promises. It had all been a long time ago; she'd been seventeen. Katel was born from their single passionate encounter and Susanna found it painful to remember it now. The name of Katel's father would never escape her lips: she'd sworn it to herself as the birth pangs gripped her on the same mattress she slept on now. No one knew, not even Katel, and it would stay that way until her last breath. Susanna listened to the wind moan through the straw roof and saw the image one last time, recalling how the man she'd given her heart to had whispered words of undying love into her hair. The next day, they had not spoken of what passed between them.

She closed her eyes and let sleep come.

The following morning, the sound of a chattering jackdaw woke her. It was cawing from the roof, as if urging her to get out of bed. Susanna pulled on her shift, skirt, neckerchief, a cap and her apron and hurried downstairs. Katel was at the table, cutting bread, slicing hunks of cheese, filling cups with warm ale.

'Can you hear Master Jack, Mother? He's making a fuss this morning.'

'He is.' Susanna accepted the cup gratefully. 'He's up with the dawn.'

'Do you believe chawks can talk to us?'

Susanna was surprised to hear her daughter use the old Cornish word for jackdaw. 'Some folk say they can understand the language of crows and the like. I think the birds shriek because they're happy to be alive.' She took a thirsty gulp from her cup. 'As I am, each day. It's a joy to welcome another dawn.'

'It is,' Katel agreed. 'I shall head down to the harbour bright and early to finish salting pilchards. I'll bring some home for supper, and perhaps a crab, if I can get one.'

'Samuel will bring fish for us.' Susanna frowned. 'There's no need for you to chatter idly to fishermen.'

Katel looked away. 'But I might bring the biggest crab for our pot.'

Susanna covered her mouth with her hand. Instead of snapping about her daughter coming home with more than she'd bargained for, Susanna said quietly, 'Be wary of some men, child. Behind the kindest word often lies a selfish heart.'

'The fishermen are pleasant to me, some especially so.' Katel paused, holding a piece of bread away from her lips. 'A selfish heart? Do you mean a man like my father?'

'Perhaps.'

'You never speak of him.'

'There's nothing to be said, Katel.'

Katel met her eyes and Susanna saw something there she'd never seen before: determination, boldness. 'Except for his name. You could tell me that.'

'I've told you never to ask.'

'But I want to know. You were my age when you birthed me. Is he a local man? Does he see me in the village? Why doesn't he call me daughter?'

'It's a memory I wish to forget.'

'But what if I want to have a father like others do?'

'Peace, Katel, ask me no more.'

'A father might keep me from harm.'

'Katel.'

'But—'

'No more!' Susanna raised her voice, something she seldom did. 'Now let's eat quietly. Then we must begin our day's toil. I'll call in on Annie next door and see how she fares. I want to see how low the baby lies.'

'Pray all will be well. I like Annie,' Katel said. 'I like everyone in the cove but for Beaten Gilbert, who was gutting fish with me yesterday. I don't like her at all.'

'What's amiss with Beaten?' Susanna asked. 'Gilberts have lived in St Mawgen Cove for years. I sometimes treat her father for pains in his hands. Hedyn Gilbert's an honest man. There's no mother in the house. Beaten must be your age. She has a brother too, a strong young man.'

'Merryn Gilbert. He's not like Beaten. He's polite and pleasant. Beaten looks at me strangely. She has cold eyes, like a fish's when you gut it.'

'It's wrong to dislike people. It's not God's way,' Susanna said sternly. 'Look into your heart and find some kindness for Beaten. Perhaps she needs a friend.'

Katel reached for her shawl. 'Beaten hates me because I'm pretty and she's plain. She looks at me with envy because the fishermen say I'm lithe as a mermaid and she's so ill-favoured, no man will ever want her as his kicky-wicky.'

'Katel, don't speak so.'

'Beaten smells of fish while I wash myself daily. Her skin's scaly and when she stands next to me to prate and prate, which she does all the long day if I don't tell her to stint, her breath's bitter like salt.'

'I bid you, be kind to her,' Susanna said gently.

Katel was suddenly more biddable. 'Very well, I'll try.' She kissed her mother's cheek. 'Now I must to work, although I hope to see Tedda today. She says I'm meant for fine things.' She gave a graceful curtsy, as if to prove her point. 'Good day to you, Mother.'

'May God give you a good day,' Susanna said quietly, but Katel had already dashed across the earth floor and made for the door out into bright sunlight, her hair flowing.

Susanna stared after her for a moment, deep in thought. She didn't like to hear her daughter speak so rudely about Beaten, who was sweet natured and dutiful. Susanna knew the Gilbert family well: they were down-to-earth people with good hearts. Tedda Lobb was not a good influence on Katel. Tedda reminded Susanna of a snake. Her eyes were furtive, her tongue flickered across her lips as if she was about to strike a poisonous blow. And she was bitter, which drove her to say unpleasant things.

Susanna checked herself, stopping any unkind thoughts. Tedda was simply a sad and strange woman who had lost her children and kept herself to herself, that was all. Everyone in the cove knew how dangerous idle talk was. Susanna's mother had warned her about it years ago, when she was fourteen years of age. A year later she, and then Susanna's father, had died of cholera. Her parents never knew that she'd got herself with child by the time she was seventeen. Susanna remembered her mother's words exactly.

'Tittle-tattle is the curse of every village. For who knows what a wagging tongue in the morning will bring home to roost by nightfall?'

5

Megan arrived at her parents' house on Sunday morning, her walking boots and cagoule in the back of the Beetle. Her mother was bustling in the kitchen while her father sat at the table, his nose in the paper. He glanced up as she walked in and she saw the anxiety in his eyes. She kept her voice light.

'Hi, Dad. It's a perfect day for a walk.' She hugged her mother. 'And then lunch. I'm looking forward to it, Mum.'

Jackie was delighted. 'I'll do Yorkshires too. What time shall I expect you back?'

'Two o'clock?' Megan suggested.

'That'll give me time to sit down with the crossword. And I want to have a look at the herb garden, do a bit of weeding.'

Megan winked in her father's direction. 'Shall we go, Dad?'

'Have you taken your Prinivil?' Jackie asked anxiously. 'You don't want to be walking on the Beacon and remember you haven't taken them.'

'I took them first thing.' Bill didn't look up from the *Observer*.

'You probably ought to make an appointment with Dr Gladstone and get a check-up,' Jackie said. 'It's been a while.'

'My heart's fine. My blood pressure's normal now.' Bill turned a page a little too enthusiastically.

'Right, shall we go?' Megan noticed the stiffness between her parents. 'We can take the Beetle. It's only—'

'I suggest you take the Rover, Bill,' Jackie interrupted. 'It's more comfortable.'

'I'm ready.' Bill stood up abruptly. 'I'll get my jacket and we'll take the Rover.' He shuffled towards Jackie and pecked her cheek. 'We'll see you later, love.'

'Two o'clock sharp, not a moment later,' Jackie said, turning back to the cooker, wiping a cloth across the surface.

Megan kissed her mother. 'See you soon.'

'Have a good time,' Jackie said chirpily. Then she lowered her voice. 'Keep an eye on your dad, love. He's definitely not his usual self.'

'I will. Don't worry, Mum.'

Megan settled herself into the passenger seat of Bill's car, her walking boots, waterproofs and bottled water by her feet. Bill started the engine, a smooth rumble compared to the rattle of the Beetle.

'Mum's a bit tense.'

Bill shook his head. 'She does go on sometimes. That business about the blood pressure tablets has started to get on my nerves.'

'Have you been arguing?'

'It's not her fault. It's me,' Bill said. 'She keeps asking if I'm sleeping well, do I need to see Dr Gladstone.' His eyes were still on the road. 'My mind's been on the letter. On Emma. Jackie's picked up on my edginess.'

'You *both* need a break. I keep saying you should take a trip.'

'Maybe.' Bill turned left, watching the steady stream of Sunday traffic heading in the other direction, towards the coast and Dunster Castle. 'But I need to decide what to do about the letter first.'

Megan patted his arm. 'We'll work it out. Meanwhile, let's check out all the deer on the Beacon.'

'It'll be swarming with Sunday walkers,' Bill said. 'People who come out occasionally, just like me. Oh, it's good to get outside, though. It's lifting my mood already. Jackie's had to suffer my grumpiness all week. I'll buy her flowers on the way home, as an apology.'

'Good idea.' Megan's fingers touched the tissue paper in her pocket. She'd wrapped her father's bracelet, ready to give it to him when the time was right.

An hour later, in sturdy boots, Megan and her father strode along the path, flanked by scrubby yellow gorse and a patchwork of green fields. The sky was filled with creamy clouds and there was a stiff breeze from the coast, but Megan was snug inside her jacket, the cagoule in her backpack in case it rained.

Bill had been silent for a while, then he said, 'I can't help imagining being here with Emma. I wonder if she's the outdoor type.'

Megan thought her father must have made the decision to meet Emma but she wouldn't ask, not yet. Instead, she said, 'I wonder what she looks like.'

'Like me, perhaps, dark hair. Or like Chrissie, who was fair, short-sighted, slim. Who knows?' Bill seemed lost in thought.

Megan considered Emma for a moment, imagining her looking just like her father, but with long hair. 'She's my big sister.'

Bill's stride slowed down, then he stopped. 'I still can't decide what to do.'

'I understand that,' Megan said kindly. 'It's been a long time.'

'I'd like to meet her. I owe her that much.' Bill started to walk slowly, staring ahead. 'But I owe Jackie so much more.'

'Mum might like to meet Emma. She'd be a stepdaughter,' Megan said.

'I should have told Jackie when we first met.'

'Why didn't you?'

'I just didn't. I left it. Talking about myself isn't a strong point. Then I suppose it was too late, we'd married, and then we had you. I pushed it to the back of my mind.'

'You could send Emma an email, Dad.'

'I'd be doing it behind Jackie's back. That's dishonest.'

'Then talk to Mum.'

'And say what? "Here's your cup of tea, love, and by the way, I have a daughter I've never met." Oh, Megan. It's such a mess.'

Megan decided it was time. She plunged her hand into her pocket and held out the bracelet wrapped in tissue and some chamomile. 'I brought you these, Dad.'

He took the little bottle of chamomile oil. She watched him open the tissue carefully and examine the bracelet. Any moment now he'd ask what it was for. Megan said, 'It's to help you think things through.'

To her surprise, Bill slipped the oil into his pocket and the bracelet over his hand.

'Do you like it?' Megan asked.

His look was pure affection. 'I'll treasure it. I'm making a big decision, a life-changing one. You're supporting me the best way you know.' He pecked her cheek. His lips were cold.

'So, why don't you put the letter away for a while, Dad? Give it time.'

'I'd feel disrespectful to Emma. That's the problem. Either I hurt your mother, which I won't do, or I hurt my daughter, whom I've neglected her entire life.'

'Then tell Mum.'

'I'm afraid to, Megan.' He met her eyes. 'Does that make me cowardly?'

'No, it means you don't know how Mum will react. I get that.'

'I wouldn't hurt her for the world.'

'So is there a middle way?' Megan asked. 'What about if *I* send Emma an email and say I'm her half-sister? Or I could give her my address.'

'Would you do that?'

'Of course,' Megan said.

'But we don't know what floodgates that might open. What if she drove up here and demanded to see me? What if she's angry?'

'Did she sound angry in the letter?'

'It was very formal,' Bill said. 'If she is angry, she didn't let it show.'

'So we need to find out more about her?'

'But we can't,' Bill said.

'There might be a way,' Megan insisted. 'I looked up St Mawgen Cove. It's on the southern tip of Cornwall. It's very remote. It would take Emma at least three and a half hours to drive here.'

'If she has a car. Perhaps she doesn't,' Bill said. 'The train would only get her as far as Taunton and then it's a long bus ride.'

'So, Dad.' Megan gave him a quizzical look. 'What does your heart say? Just forget about Mum's and Emma's feelings for a moment.'

'And yours too?' Bill added. 'It must have been a shock.'

'But leave that to one side, Dad. How do *you* feel? Your heart, not your head.'

'I want to meet her,' Bill said.

'Right. So the answer is simple. We just need to find a way to make Mum happy and then you can meet Emma.'

'I wish it was that easy.'

'It'll come to us.' Megan strode on. Then she stopped dead and pointed. 'Look – Porlock. And the sea.'

Megan and Bill stared towards the horizon, the ocean glistening in sunlight, merging with the speckled blue of the sky.

'It's so beautiful,' Megan said. 'The perfect place to think. We'll make the right decision, you'll see.'

Bill wrapped an arm around her. 'You're the best daughter.' Then he was quiet, suddenly aware what he'd said.

'We'll be fine, Dad,' Megan said quietly. 'We're a strong family. We'll get through this and come out closer than ever, me, you and Mum.' She leaned against his shoulder, buffeting him with her head. 'And Emma, too.'

* * *

Megan was still thinking about her father as she drove back to her flat. It had been a lovely family meal. Bill had kissed his wife's cheek and given her the flowers, telling her that the walk had done him good; that he'd found it difficult adjusting to retirement but he'd be fine now. He'd settle to a routine and in January they'd go somewhere warm. Megan noticed the twinkle in his eyes.

Back at the flat, she sat at the laptop and brought up the map of St Mawgen Cove. The drive was three hours and thirty-four minutes. Megan could be there and back in a day, but it would be a tiring journey, and the Beetle might not be up to it. Her fingers tapped keys: places to stay at St Mawgen Cove.

Straight away, a picture flashed up of an old white building with a thatched roof, leaded-light windows, heavy hanging baskets crammed with blooms. The Ship Inn. Built in the 1500s for local fishermen and workers who had been modernising the nearby thirteenth-century church. The accommodation was an old extension, which had been fishermen's cottages in the seventeenth century, with stone and cobb walls and a black front door. There were other photos taken inside the inn, and Megan got an impression of low ceilings, dark beams, dim lighting. She researched the four bedrooms. They looked clean and quaint, each with an ensuite bathroom and standard pine furniture. Bed and breakfast was reasonably priced.

Megan scanned the reviews – the average rating of 3.7 out of 5 stars was interesting. Visitors either gave the place five stars and were exuberant about the warm welcome and the delicious meals, or they'd left only one star, with brief comments like, 'I wouldn't come here again' and, 'Avoid at all costs.'

But St Mawgen Cove was where Emma lived, and The Ship seemed like Megan's best option for somewhere to stay in the village.

The owner was a Mr Julien Fontaine. There was a phone number: Megan picked up her mobile and dialled. She was just making enquiries, nothing more.

6

Susanna wrapped her shawl tightly against the sea breeze, picked up her basket of herbs and stepped outside into bright sunlight. She could smell the sharpness of fish in the air; yesterday's catch was in the salt cellars and smokehouses, being baulked – the locals' word for salting – before being packed in hogsheads and pressed to remove the oil. The fish would be stored, some to be sold, some for the villagers in the winter. Hogsheads of pilchards would find their way to the inn, stacked in the cellars. Yowann Hicks owned The Ship, and the little fishermen's cottages that Susanna and Samuel lived in, attached to the back of the inn. He owned many of the fishing boats, the seine nets – most of the local fishermen in St Mawgen Cove worked for him. He lived in the biggest house in the village with his wife, Eliza.

Susanna shuddered: Yowann Hicks took whatever he wanted, whoever he wanted. She felt sorry for Eliza, his long-suffering wife. Susanna made a mental note to visit her soon. She had so many ailments: chilblains in winter, aches in her fingers and constant shortness of breath. She was a phlegmatic person, always in her husband's shadow. Susanna had mixed a potion of barley, aniseed and fennel to help her breathing, but that was the least of Eliza's problems.

Susanna's first call of the day was to Anne, her brother's wife. Her need was greater. Susanna rapped at the old wooden door and called, 'It's just me, Annie.'

Anne Boram stood in the dark room, leaning on her besom broom, the twigs bending against the earthen floor. She eased herself upright, rubbing her back, grateful for a reason to rest. Her round face was flushed with the effort but her voice was filled with warmth. 'Come in, Susanna. Sit yourself down. I'll get you something to quench your thirst.' She moved slowly, a ship in motion, as she poured from a jug. Her belly strained against the cloth of her apron, her hair spilling from beneath her cap.

'How are you feeling?' Susanna asked cheerily.

'Very good, I have to say. I was up with the lark this morning. I'd been properly tired and my back still aches something terrible. But today I have more energy.'

'The little one won't be long now.' Susanna knew the signs. 'Come sit a while.'

Anne handed Susanna a cup and plonked herself in her chair by the fire. She placed a hand over her belly. 'The child moves around less. These last few mornings, he's been quiet.'

'He's getting ready to meet you,' Susanna explained. 'You must both rest while you can.'

'I'm so afraid of birthing that I can't sleep,' Anne admitted quietly. 'Samuel's afeared too, although he'd never say it. He watches me and I sense his thoughts. He's worried I might die, as some women do, and he'll be left alone with the child.'

'Samuel's just a husband,' Susanna said. 'Men know nothing of these things. They think it's women's work and keep themselves apart. In truth, childbearing is only a baby struggling into the world and his mother working hard to bring him there. Praise God, all will be well.'

'I hope so.' Anne fanned herself with her hand. Susanna didn't think it was warm in the room despite the roaring fire. The little cottage was slightly larger than her own, one room upstairs, one down, but it would be cramped when the baby started to grow.

Anne was staring into the flames, thoughtfully. 'Is birthing very bad?'

'It's bearable,' Susanna replied. 'I have some ergot ready for the labour. It'll ease the pain.'

'The parson on Sundays says that pain is the Lord's just punishment for Eve's sin,' Anne said.

'The parson's a man. He has no idea of what he speaks,' Susanna said quietly. 'Childbearing is what we are born to do. And the time we spend in our childbed is not so long that we remember it after labour is done. We women help each other. If we lived in a larger place, you'd bring forth your child in a room full of gossips who'd wait on you.'

Anne touched her arm. 'I often think of you, all alone, birthing Katel. You had no mother to help you, no wise woman. And you were but a child yourself.'

'I was seventeen,' Susanna said determinedly. 'I'd learned about birthing from my mother when I was young, visiting women in their childbeds. I wasn't afraid, although during the birth I called upon God several times to save my soul.' She laughed. 'And I'm here to tell of it. Katel was born whole and well.'

'She's such a pretty child, with her fair hair and cornflower eyes.' Anne looked away for a moment. 'She's not dark like you and Samuel.'

'People always ask who her father was,' Susanna said, her chin high. 'But I won't tell. Don't ask it of me, Annie.'

'Should the child not know? Samuel thinks it bad that she has no father named.'

'It's not Samuel's place to say so,' Susanna said.

Anne lowered her voice. 'But many people in the cove speak among themselves. They think that you were some man's whore. And Samuel doesn't like them to speak this way of his sister. You know he has a temper on him and he'd fight them because of a single word.'

'My life's my affair, not my brother's, and what I do is of no consequence to the villagers,' Susanna said firmly. 'Katel and I need nothing from those who wag their tongues.'

'Oh, I didn't mean to offend.' Anne put a hand to her mouth. 'You're a wonderful healer. Indeed, people say they'll have no one but you. Tedda Lobb's not so gentle, and her eyesight's poor. In truth, I fear her, and others say the same. She mutters under her breath and sometimes she speaks ill. It's whispered in the village that her fingers often make mischief.'

'Don't listen to tittle-tattle.' Susanna placed a hand over Anne's, folded in her lap below the baby bump. 'And don't be afraid, Annie. When the time comes for this little one to show himself, I'll be beside you and, God willing, we'll bring him safely into the world with a lusty cry.'

'Samuel wishes for a boy.' Anne's eyes gleamed. 'He'd have another fisherman in the family. But I'd like a girl, a gentle soul who'll help me with the household chores.'

'A girl's good company,' Susanna agreed, although she was thinking of Katel's increasingly wilful ways. 'Who knows what will be?' She stood quickly, kissing Anne's cheek. 'I must leave you now. I've a call to make to someone who needs a potion and a prayer. But I'll come this evening.'

Anne stayed sitting down, her face suddenly fretful. 'You'll not be far?'

'I promise,' Susanna soothed, and picked up her basket. 'Meanwhile, I've brought you some pennyroyal to drink with water, and you must keep the house warm. Wash your hands often and eat some milky frumenty with honey. It'll make you strong for the birthing.'

Anne nodded, but her thoughts were far away: Susanna sensed that her time was near. She kissed her sister-in-law's cheek again and whispered a hurried goodbye, then she was on her way up the path towards the cliff where Yowann Hicks lived. She hoped he wouldn't be at home. It was Eliza she wanted to see, not her husband.

It was a short walk to reach the Hickses' house, a timber frame filled in with wattle and daub, with three rooms downstairs and three more upstairs, a cellar below. Susanna always marvelled at the lattice windows, filled with small pieces of glass held together with lead. The Hicks family were the only people in St Mawgen who had glass. Everyone else made do with linen soaked in linseed oil.

She knocked and was relieved to see Eliza who waved her inside. She stepped into the living room onto a small mat of woven reeds. 'How are you feeling today, Eliza? When will someone be here to help you?'

'Beaten Gilbert comes most evenings after work to clean and wash clothes. I don't know how I'd manage without her. I wish Yowann would take her on full time, but he says I should make his meals and keep house myself. He doesn't believe that I'm unwell.' Eliza gave a rasping cough. She was small inside her pale linen shift, neat and tidy, wearing a perfectly clean white cap.

Susanna was conscious of her own brown fustian shift, her apron washed with urine and wood ash to take away the stains. The Hickses' house smelled strongly of rosemary; sprigs of it lay on the floor, more rosemary burned in the hearth. Eliza smelled of the herb too; her skin was scented with oil.

Susanna breathed it in and sighed. 'The place smells so sweet. It clears the lungs.'

Eliza looked anxious. 'You told me that rosemary would ease my mind from troubled thoughts and that it would...' She lowered her voice. 'It would attract love.' She paused, embarrassed. 'I also heard that it puts off any demons that might be nearby.'

Susanna pressed Eliza's hand. 'They say rosemary's good for the liver. I've brought a potion for your breathing too, with fennel and aniseed. And you must avoid eating cheese and drinking milk. They'll make your breathing worse.'

'Yowann mocks me for it,' Eliza said humbly, and Susanna could see in her face that she was used to being criticised. 'He likes cheese, oily fish, red wine. He says he enjoys the fine things in life.' She paused for a moment. 'He has little time for me.'

Susanna had no comment to make. Instead, she said, 'You must put yourself first.'

'He doesn't respect me because I can't give him a child. It's too late now. My time for birthing is past. He married me for a good match. My father was a wealthy man over in Perranporth.'

'I've heard people say so.' Susanna sensed that Eliza was lonely and needed to talk.

'We've been married for fifteen years. Yowann's almost forty years old now and I three years older.' Eliza's eyes were nervous, like a small animal's. 'I believe he has children in St Mawgen with other women. Yowann's a difficult man to refuse.'

'I don't listen to idle gossip,' Susanna began.

'I forget myself. Let me offer you refreshment,' Eliza said quickly. 'I seldom venture outside, and your company cheers me. Will you stay awhile?'

Susanna knew that spending time with Eliza would lift the lonely woman's spirit, but she was anxious to avoid her husband. Yowann made her feel uncomfortable: he had a way of standing too close, speaking to her as if she had no choice but to agree with him.

Eliza took her hand earnestly. 'In truth, I envy you, Susanna. You have a daughter to keep you company and no husband to despise you. I wish it were that way with me. I would give up all I have to live as you do in a small cottage with people who care for me.' She put a hand to her throat. 'It's loneliness that chokes my breath. And my fingers ache so, especially at night and when I wake.'

'I'll bring rue soaked in water and vinegar for you to drink. It may ease the pain.'

'Yowann tells me that bloodletting will cure me. Do you think so?'

'It's used too often and to no avail,' Susanna said, realising that Eliza trusted her husband completely. 'Rue's hard to take, but it will help over time.'

'I'll try it.' Eliza turned round, eyes on Susanna. 'You're the best pellar in St Mawgen and I thank you. Here.' Eliza pressed a coin into Susanna's palm. 'Don't tell my husband I pay you.' She was suddenly nervy. 'Yowann will be here soon, wanting food and drink and I must get to it. Then Beaten will clear it all away.'

'I bid you a good day.' Susanna watched Eliza scuttle to the kitchen.

She hurried towards the door, basket in hand, hugging her shawl. Yowann was barring her way. He was not particularly tall; his thick fair hair gave him a youthful appearance, but the way he stood, feet apart, hands on hips, showed that he had authority. She nodded briefly to hide how nervous he made her feel.

'Yowann.'

His voice was suddenly gentle. 'Susanna. Good day to you. How are you? Well, I hope?'

'I am, thanking you.' Susanna glanced towards the door, which was ajar. She wondered if she could squeeze past Yowann and make an escape.

'And how's Katel?'

'She fares well. She's working at the harbour.'

'I saw her this morning, salting fish.'

'Your wife waits for you in the kitchen,' Susanna said quickly. Yowann's eyes were examining her face, but he said nothing. She tried again. 'I've much to do.'

'Then I'll call upon you soon.'

'There's no need.' Susanna made to go, but he caught her wrist.

'The cottage belongs to me. Your daughter works for me.'

'I know.' She wriggled from his grasp.

'Besides, it's always pleasant to see you.' Yowann placed a hand on her shoulder where it lay heavily. 'You're pretty as ever.'

'I must take my leave.' Susanna took a deep breath to calm her thumping heart and pushed past him, running out into the street. She glanced down the hill towards the harbour where the haul of fish was being packed, then she was on her way towards The Ship Inn and her tiny cottage.

As she walked along the dirt track, she reminded herself that she still needed to collect some rue for Eliza. In that moment, she recalled that rue was a symbol for adultery, for repentance of all women's transgressions, for everlasting suffering. Rue was a bitter herb, difficult to swallow, just like a woman's lot in life: love, childbirth, the yoke of marriage.

She'd loved Yowann once, she'd loved him too much. He still made her heart beat fast. Even now, she was afraid to spend a long time in his company. The power of his blue eyes, his crushing embrace, his overwhelming passion for her made her weak.

She gave a short laugh to lighten her feelings and said a quiet charm to herself, promising to protect Katel from the trials faced by women, and from the influence of selfish men such as Yowann Hicks.

7

As Megan came out of the therapy room on Tuesday morning with her client, Jackie was leaning against the counter, staring through the window at the bleak sky. Megan helped her visitor into a light jacket. 'I hope you're feeling refreshed, Lin. Now, don't forget to drink plenty of water.'

'I always feel great after a massage. I wish the effects would last for ever.' Lin, a woman in her forties, flourished her card to pay. 'What oils did you use for my arthritis, Megan?'

'Lavender, chamomile, eucalyptus and nutmeg. I have turmeric capsules to help with the inflammation too.'

Jackie inhaled deeply. 'I can smell the nutmeg. It takes me back to my mother's egg custards.'

'Scents always bring back memories,' Megan said.

'Yes, please to the turmeric,' Lin said. 'I'll stock up on scented soap while I'm here. I'm off to Greece for a fortnight to catch the last of the sunshine.'

'Lovely,' Jackie said. 'We all need a dose of vitamin D, especially as the days get shorter. I'm always telling Bill he looks peaky.'

Megan finished serving Lin while Jackie pottered around the shop tidying the displays, and finally Lin left with a large paper carrier of goodies, pulling the door behind her with a 'ting' of the bell.

'Is Dad all right?' Megan asked quickly.

'He's fine,' Jackie said. 'I keep nagging him to have a break. It's so quiet here now. We could just open three days a week through winter, like we did last year.'

'It makes sense.'

'It'd free me up to spend time with your dad,' Jackie said.

'Well, here's a thought,' Megan said. 'I could take a week or two off, be back for the beginning of October and run the shop by myself until the spring. You'd have some time with Dad.'

'That's a good idea,' Jackie said. 'Where would you go?'

'Cornwall,' Megan said. 'I could swim, dive, do some surfing.'

'Who with?' Jackie asked, surprised.

'I'll just head off by myself,' Megan said. 'I don't know anyone who could get time off at short notice, but I'll meet the last of the surfers. I'll soon make friends.'

'Won't you be lonely?'

'If I am, I'll move on or come home. There's going to be an Indian summer, according to the forecasts.' Megan was really excited by the idea now. 'What do you think, Mum? I'll have two weeks' break, you cover the shop, water my plants in the flat, then you take the winter off.'

'Apart from the run up to Christmas, when the shop's always busy.'

'Right. The cinnamon and orange candles go like hotcakes.' Megan wrapped an arm around her mother. 'What do you think?'

Jackie's eyes twinkled. 'It's a great idea. But are you sure you won't be lonely?'

'Surfers meet up, talk, hang out. I'll be fine.'

'And you'd be safe in the sea? I'm not saying you're not a strong swimmer or an experienced surfer but...'

'I'll be up at dawn enjoying the rad barrels, partying until four in the morning with the bros.' Megan hugged her mother harder. 'Right, Mum. I'll book some accommodation and leave after work on Saturday.'

'Why don't you go on Friday evening? I mean, I wouldn't want you to miss the "rad barrels at dawn patrol" on Saturday,' Jackie said, using the only surfing language she'd picked up from her daughter.

'Friday night it is,' Megan said. She wondered if The Ship Inn at St

Mawgen still had a room available. They weren't fully booked when she'd rung. She'd phone them again at lunchtime.

* * *

It was past five. Megan's mother had just left to catch the bus back to Carhampton; Megan had time to phone her father. He picked up straight away.

'Dad?'

'Is everything all right?' Bill's voice was suddenly alarmed.

'Mum's on her way home. I wanted a quick chat.'

'What can I do for you?' He sounded calmer.

'Well, it's about what I might do for you.' Megan took a deep breath. 'I've booked a room in The Ship Inn at St Mawgen for ten days.'

'Oh?' Bill sounded confused, then the penny dropped. 'St Mawgen? Where Emma lives?'

'I thought I'd check the place out, report back.'

'Are you going to meet her and tell her who you are?'

'I just thought I'd have a holiday, do some swimming and surfing, you know, a preliminary visit. Maybe I'll pick up some information about the Davey family. I don't want to snoop, though.'

'So I'd have more information?'

'Exactly. Emma might be a busy woman with six kids.'

'But then I'd have grandchildren.'

'You would,' Megan said. 'She might be a multimillionaire, or she might spend all her time in her garden like Mum does, or she might be a teacher.'

'I'd definitely want to meet her.'

'Or she might be lonely. St Mawgen Cove looks quite isolated.'

Bill was quiet for a moment. 'I think it's a good idea, Megan. Even if you don't discover anything, you can tell me about the place. And you'll get a holiday, too.'

'We have a plan,' Megan said. 'I'll keep it low key and stay in touch. And send photos of the cove.'

'Thanks.' Then Bill's voice rose. 'Oh, the bake might be ready. I can smell burning cheese. I'd better go.'

'We'll speak soon. Bye, Dad.'

* * *

On Friday, Megan drove down to Cornwall, two holdalls and a surfboard in her car. By the time she passed Bodmin on the A30, the sky was dark except for a few shreds of grey clouds. It would take another hour to reach St Mawgen Cove and she hoped she'd arrive before the inn closed. She'd spoken to Julien Fontaine, one of the co-owners, when she'd made her reservation. He sounded French or Belgian, although his English was good, and he seemed friendly. He assured her that she'd been given the prettiest room, number three, on the ground floor, and she was welcome to book an evening meal in advance. She'd said no because she knew she'd be late, but an early breakfast on Saturday morning would be perfect. Then she planned to get her bearings, wander around the cove and check the surf times.

Julien had said that there was a surf-wear shop just a stone's throw from the inn, and the owner would tell Megan about local groups. She was excited: this time of year was perfect for the consistent, bigger waves that would last throughout the winter, ideal for experienced surfers. Megan was looking forward to it. The last two times she'd been away on a long surfing break, she'd been with Jay. They'd surfed and scuba dived. She'd been really good at it. Now she intended to take full advantage of her independence: she'd eat alone, surf alone, get her rusty diving skills back. It was an opportunity to take time for herself.

She thought about the stone she was wearing on a silver pendant chain, a smooth tiger's eye, which was supposed to combat fear. She was ready to go on holiday by herself. And she hoped she'd find out something about Emma. The prospect of a half-sister filled her with both delight and trepidation.

The traffic had lightened. At Bodmin there had been signposts to the brooding moors, to the old jail. She knew a little about the area: Jamaica Inn was nearby, made famous in the novel by Daphne du Maurier. It was an eighteenth-century coaching house with a history of smugglers and a reputation for strange sightings in haunted rooms.

She shivered, already nervous about going to St Mawgen. It felt somehow like a place that still belonged to the past.

She was deep into Cornwall now, and as she drove into the night she had the feeling of being steeped in history, a county that held itself separate from the rest of England. It had its own identity, Celtic roots, its own language, and the people were fiercely proud and independent. She knew there had been a great deal of poverty in its history, workers in tin mines, fishermen and their families struggling to survive. But Megan loved the green coastline, miles of beaches, crystal waters and rolling surf. She was looking forward to a holiday, to arriving at The Ship Inn and falling asleep in a comfortable room with a feather-soft bed.

The final part of the journey made her realise just how isolated the cove was. She drove down narrow roads where rabbits leaped in front of the headlights and a badger crawled into a hedge. Trees hung low and the darkness was intense. There were no houses, no streetlights, and at times she worried that Google Maps was leading her the wrong way. There was a creepily abandoned atmosphere to the countryside, as if time had stood still. She expected torrential rain to fall at any moment and a cloaked figure waving a scythe to step from the hedge.

Megan was on holiday alone. She'd need to keep her imagination in check.

She turned a corner and finally came into St Mawgen. Even in misty darkness, it was a picturesque village, with white-painted houses and a small parade of shops. There was a sign indicating the inn to the right, and she thankfully pulled into a large car park, where just three other vehicles remained in shadows. A few dim lights gleamed orange inside The Ship Inn and Megan grabbed her handbag and holdalls, glancing at the roof rack on the Beetle where her surfboard was secured. She'd go in first, ask to be shown her room, and then collect the rest of her things. She was tired but she was on holiday – she'd driven a long way. If the owners were friendly, it would be nice to sit in the bar and enjoy a glass of wine.

Then she'd turn in for the night and sleep like a log.

8

Susanna wandered past The Ship Inn on her way to Bylen woods. She'd call on Anne later to check her progress. The baby would be a boy, she was sure; she could tell by the way Anne's face had become ruddy. Heat in the womb meant a male child, but there was another test she'd done once or twice when a woman wanted desperately to know about her baby before it was born. A drop of blood or milk taken from the right side of the mother, placed in clear water from a pure fountain, would always give a true answer. If the drop sank to the bottom, the child would be male; if it remained on the top, the child would be female.

Susanna glanced back towards The Ship Inn. It was quiet now, but it would be busy later when the fishermen came up to fill their bellies with ale. Colan Stephens and his young wife, Joan, were preparing for the evening rush. Susanna imagined Colan bringing up a barrel from the cellar; there would be more room down there for Yowann Hicks's hogsheads of pilchards.

Susanna's mind filled with thoughts of Colan Stephens. She'd known him all her life, trusted him like a brother. No, not like a brother. He'd always been so much more. With his light hair and cornflower-blue eyes, lean and tall, Colan was still attractive in his mid-thirties. Susanna pushed the thought away; she mustn't think of him that way now. He had married three years ago. Joan was ten years younger, a hopeful young woman who idolised him.

Susanna could see from the way her eyes shone that Joan adored Colan. The fishermen in the inn would tease her as she served them ale, calling for a kiss and a kind word, but Joan was faithful. And she baked a good croust, a favourite of the customers, who'd demand it with a cup of ale. Joan's croust was filled with beef or fish and crammed with onion and swede. Many of the fishermen claimed Colan had married his wife because her crousts were so tasty.

Susanna continued on towards Bylen woods. There was a good crop of chickweed and mallow. She wanted to fill her basket with meadowsweet, which would be good for Eliza Hicks's breathing difficulties and the pains in her fingers. Yarrow would stem bleeding: it might be useful during Anne's birthing. It could treat fevers too. Susanna hoped Anne wouldn't develop a chill in her childbed.

She hurried along the narrow dirt track towards the woods, intending to be back before Katel arrived home. There was already a pot of water boiling over the fire for her bath. Susanna knew her daughter liked to wash her skin clean of all traces of fish. She liked her clothes washed often and complained constantly about the smells in the streets, the horse manure, the sweat of the women who salted fish. Susanna made oil from lavender, which Katel could rub on her skin to soothe and scent it, and she demanded a constant supply.

The woods were dense, crammed with bushes and plants. Susanna began to gather herbs, moving deftly towards the darkest place where many grew in abundance. There was always a sense of foreboding there, where the sun seldom filtered onto the grass. It was quiet, no birdsong.

She bent to look for black cohosh, which grew nearby. It was good for childbirth, menstrual cramps and delayed menstruation, but it had to be used with care. A cold breeze blew between the tree trunks and made her shiver. Bylen was a word seldom uttered by locals. It meant evil and referred to a creature that was reputed to haunt the woodlands after dark. As a result, many locals refused to venture there. There had been a murder many years ago, one fisherman killing another with a fishhook over the love of a woman.

Susanna continued to fill her basket. She gathered lady's mantle, which she'd make into a tisane for women who came to her with cramps, and for men too, who had problems digesting food after eating too much.

Susanna stopped; someone was behind her, watching. She knew it. She stood slowly, clutching her basket, and said, 'Good day to you, Tedda.'

'*Durdatha whye!*' The greeting was returned in the Cornish language.

She turned slowly. A little woman dressed in black was watching her with eyes like stones. She cackled, a grating sound like a crow's caw. 'You'm got eyes on the back of your head, Susanna Boram.'

'I could smell your old clay pipe.'

Tedda didn't move. 'I likes a smoke of baccy, and I likes to keep a bit in my jaw to chew.' Her eyes flickered to Susanna's basket. 'You'm got enough herbs there for the whole cove. You'm getting ready for your Samuel's wife's birthing, I see.'

'I am.'

'She'll bring forth a girl,' Tedda said. 'She's carrying it high.'

Susanna said nothing. She glanced at Tedda's basket and breathed in nervously. She had picked a bundle of deadly nightshade.

'There's a lot of belladonna in your basket, Tedda. Do you know how dangerous it can be?'

'You'm able to tell me what it can do?' Tedda's gaze held hers.

'It causes eyes to blur, a rash to develop, then headaches. Anyone who swallows the nightshade has slurred speech, convulsions and will eventually die.'

'There's some call for it in the cove,' Tedda replied. 'Used by a proper pellar, it can ease agues, cure a child's cough, stop the sickness and the palsy.' She narrowed her eyes. 'But only a true pellar can use it to cure ailments.'

'I bid you good day.' Susanna turned abruptly. Tedda's level expression unnerved her, as if she was hiding bad thoughts.

'Tarry,' Tedda called, and Susanna paused. 'You need to know about that daughter of yours.'

'I think not,' Susanna said. 'I've no intention of listening to gossip.'

'She's a beauty. Just coming into flower. And some men are taking more than a proper interest.'

'Katel's a good child.' Susanna lifted her basket.

'Like her mother was?' Tedda's voice was a croak, but the mockery was clear. 'Your belly was full at seventeen and no one knows who put the whelp there.'

'Enough, Tedda.' Susanna took several steps away, walking through long grass.

Tedda called after her, 'Katel asked me for crushed worms mixed with powdered periwinkle.'

'A love potion?' Susanna felt her heart lurch. 'Why would she do that?'

'You'm no idea where that maid's eyes have found their mark. She has a young man in her sights, I'll wager.' Tedda chuckled.

'And did you give her the potion?' Susanna wanted to know.

'I told the maid that if she comes round to my cottage, I'll teach her how to make one. Or as many as she needs to put in the ale of a fine young man.' Tedda hugged her basket of nightshade close to her frail body possessively. 'If she were my maid, I'd keep a watchful eye on her, Susanna Boram. She'll come to no good, mark my words. *Tereba nessa.*'

'Until next time,' Susanna translated, and walked away briskly towards the light. She wouldn't give Tedda any more of her time. Besides, if she was quick, she'd be home before Katel came back. There were a few questions she wanted to ask her. She didn't believe Tedda's accusations, but Susanna felt consumed with anxiety for her child. It was unwise to ask Tedda for potions. The rumours were that she practised all kinds of dangerous magic. Susanna didn't want Katel's name linked with Tedda's.

As she passed The Ship Inn, the bubble of male voices burst through the windows, fishermen supping ale, demanding a croust to stop their hunger. Susanna scurried to the little cottage and pushed open the door. Katel was by the fire, rubbing salve on her hands. She whirled round, her long hair flying.

'I'm here early, Mother, and I've brought supper. See?' She pointed to the table where a large white fish lay. Susanna planted her basket next to it.

'It's indeed a fine fish. A hake. Where did you get it?' Susanna eyed it suspiciously.

'A fisherman gave it to me.' Katel made her skirts twirl. 'Is it not the best hake, fit for a princess?'

'You're in a merry mood.' Susanna feared the worst.

'And why not, pray? I've salted a whole hogshead of fish, and I heard Yowann Hicks say each hogshead contains up to three thousand fishes! I've been paid well for it. Now I plan to wash and oil my skin with lavender. Oh

—' Katel remembered something. 'Beaten may come to see you. She's afflicted with warts.'

'She can cure warts herself. She must take a small piece of meat, rub the wart with it and then bury the meat. As the meat decays, the wart will disappear.'

Katel was not listening. 'The warts are on her chin. She has red pustules on her face too.'

'She has an imbalance of humours then. I'll mix a cream of lemon, honey and sulphur.'

Katel gave a small laugh. 'She thinks it's because she has impure thoughts.'

'Why would Beaten think that?'

'I told her so.' Katel's eyes danced with mischief.

'Then you're unkind, Katel.' Susanna looked at the fish again. 'Who gave you this?'

'A handsome fisherman.' Katel swung her skirts again.

'You mustn't accept gifts from strangers.'

'He's no stranger. He lives by the harbour. He likes me.'

'And do you like him?'

'I care not a jot for him. Tedda says I can have my pick of men.'

Susanna sighed deeply. 'Katel, you mustn't spend time with Tedda Lobb. You know how people's tongues wag. I fear for you.'

'She's promised to teach me cunning skills, not just healing the sick as you do, but a more gainful trade to tell fortunes, and procure love. She says she can identify a witch and defeat her by her own counterspells.'

'She can't do that, Katel. Few people have such a skill. I saw her in Bylen woods when I was gathering simples.' Susanna placed her hand on her hips, recalling the bundle of nightshade. 'She told me you'd asked for a love potion.'

'That's not true, Mother.' Katel met her gaze. 'Besides, I know how to make one if I wish to, from worms and powder of periwinkle. But I've no need of love potions.'

Susanna was immediately suspicious. 'Why's that?'

'The fishermen flock to me like gulls to a crumb. I may choose whom I wish.' Katel noticed her mother's troubled expression. 'But I wish for no ordinary man from St Mawgen Cove. One day a fine prince will come from a land far away, speaking in tongues of gold, and he'll choose me.'

'And you believe this?' Susanna asked, her brow furrowed.

'I heard it while I slept,' Katel said simply. 'I'll be the finest of princesses. I asked Tedda if it was true and she said yes. A passing bird whispered it in my ear.'

'Katel.' Susanna felt instantly troubled. Katel was naïve. 'Don't speak of such things, I pray you. If someone should hear, they may think that the evil one has visited you in your sleep.'

Katel laughed as if her mother was being foolish. 'I'm not afraid of people in the cove. But I'll tell no one. It will come to pass, you'll see.'

9

Megan sat in the dining room of The Ship Inn at breakfast time, directly opposite the bar. The air was cold – the whole inn was cold – but the food looked appetising. It would make up for the icy rooms. She was staring at the dish Julien had placed in front of her.

'It looks incredible.' She meant it, too; she wasn't sure she could get it all down, but she was going surfing later, and it would provide energy.

Julien filled her coffee cup from a cafetière. He was a tall man with neat dark hair and a smooth face. Megan assumed he was a few years older than her.

'Claude likes to make a French breakfast for guests. This is a croque madame.' He indicated the huge sandwich on her plate. 'It's a lightly toasted sandwich made with soft sweet brioche bread, filled with cheese and ham in a rich bechamel sauce, all crowned with a fried egg. This *petit déjeuner* will last you until lunchtime.' He winked. 'I notice you've brought your board.'

'I'm just going to get my bearings this morning.' Megan sipped her coffee. 'So, are you and Claude the owners?'

'We are. We came from Brittany a few months ago. This place was doing badly – just a few locals, no food customers, not many visitors. We're trying to make a go of it, though.'

Megan glanced around. A middle-aged couple sat at the table near the door, holding hands, drinking coffee. Their plates were empty, everything eaten. There were no other guests. Low dark beams hung overhead. The walls were dotted with sepia pictures showing historical scenes of the cove.

Julien noticed her straying gaze and said, 'This winter, we plan to give the place a facelift, bring it into the twenty-first century, but keep the traditional features. This pub's been here for hundreds of years. Your room was the living room of a fisherman's cottage.'

'Oh.' Megan was lost in thought, imagining her room hundreds of years ago. Right now it was untidy, her clothes strewn across the floor, her surfboard against the wall. The sash windows, with their billowing curtains, were huge and everything seemed bright and modern. But Julien was right, the place would benefit from a fresh coat of paint and some tasteful décor hinting at the inn's history.

'So business isn't booming?'

'Claude's food is bringing people in. He's a great chef. And I do bookings, work behind the bar.' Julien bit his lip. 'But we may have a quiet winter. Hey-ho. It's our chance to decorate, to advertise. The surf crowd will be our target, young people, holidaymakers. The cove's filled with mystery.'

'You sound like a travel brochure,' Megan said. She was still wondering how to attack the huge croque madame.

'The locals come in sometimes, but nobody wants to work here. The place has a history.'

'Oh?' Megan was interested.

'I'm new to it all. I used to be a civil servant in France.' Julien shook his head. 'St Mawgen has many old tales – do you say old wives' tales?'

'Yes. Or fishermen's yarns.'

'Stories from history.' Julien suddenly straightened. 'I'll be back later to refill your cup. Then you have a choice of homemade viennoiseries or fruit if you wish.'

'Oh, fruit please – no more carbs on top of that croque.'

Julien nodded. 'I've put the heating on. It's always cold here and worse in the bedrooms. Let me know if you need it turned up.'

'OK.' Megan frowned; it was as cold inside as outside.

'Enjoy your croque. And if there's anything you need, anything at all,' Julien said kindly, 'just ask me or Claude. You'll meet him tonight.'

'Thanks, Julien.'

Megan picked up her phone and checked her messages. There was one from her mum, fretting because Megan hadn't called last night. One from her dad telling her to enjoy her stay. And of course she read between the lines immediately. He was looking forward to hearing anything about Emma. There were three messages from Amy, asking her to send photos of the scenery and the beach, and to update her on any fit Cornishmen she might meet while 'getting barrelled'.

Megan imagined herself and a handsome surfer balancing on their boards beneath a huge arc of water, covered by a barrelling wave. It was the ultimate feeling of exhilaration.

Jay came into her head, his tousled hair, his laugh, and she told the memory to leave immediately. She had no intention of being hurt again. She was on holiday alone. It was going to be a holiday for herself, not just to find out about Emma. She badly needed the break. But she didn't need her heart broken again. That wasn't going to happen. She was the new, independent Megan now.

She thumbed replies to the messages, promising to phone in the evening, then she picked up her knife and fork and dug in heartily.

* * *

An hour later, she was walking down to the cove, past a surfing shop that, according to the note on the door, didn't open until eleven on a Saturday. It was called Unravel the Ocean and the window was a rainbow array of boards, bodywear and bright shirts. She peered at the notice board for surf activities, clubs or meetings and there was a colourful poster offering lessons in July and August, but nothing current. She decided to pop back later and chat to the owner, to ask whether she should travel up the coast where the surf might be better.

She passed a tiny convenience store, the outside painted sea blue, the windows crammed with everything from alcohol to breakfast cereals and postcards. She made a mental note to buy some cards to send back home. A little further on, she noticed a group of houses. She paused outside a double-fronted shop, a hearse parked outside and a sign in the window depicting a colourful surfboard above the words 'Catch the Last Wave – Tom Hocking, Funeral Director'. Megan wondered if it was a joke. Some surfers drove hearses because they were big enough to keep surfboards, sleeping bags and camping equipment in. However, this one was fitted with some clips on top so that a surfboard could be fixed like a fish's fin. It seemed as though it belonged to a real undertaker with a gimmick and a questionable sense of humour. She gazed up at the sky, azure blue with high clouds. Beyond, the road twisted down the hill towards the harbour, the indigo line of the ocean in the distance, tall cliffs rising on both sides. Her step quickened before she became aware of it, the power of the sea tugging her along.

She walked past a few more shops and an old church. There was an artist's studio with oil paintings of the harbour in the window, a ceramic shop and a gift shop, the window crammed with gaudy items for the beach. All the shops were closed. Further down, there was a B & B, a chip shop and several small cottages. Megan passed a pretty white building called Anchor Cottage, with a 'For Sale' sign outside, and another predictably called Ocean View. There was a third, with a blue door, the garden a tangle of flowers, and a distressed beechwood sign proclaiming Surf's Up!

She wondered if Emma Davey lived in one of them.

At the bottom of the hill, the harbour wall rose on three sides. There was a warning sign with an old black-and-white photograph of the sea hurling itself over the wall; high winds meant high waves, and that could be dangerous. To the right, there was a small café with a sign: a cocktail glass, a pineapple and the words Afterdune Delight. The café door was open, advertising Cornish cream teas, and there was a hatch where people could buy coffee, pasties and ice creams to go. A young woman was buying a lolly for a child in a pushchair. Megan glanced in her direction, wondering if she was Emma Davey.

Megan strolled down to the harbour wall, past a white, three-storey block of flats, towards the railings that overlooked the ocean. The harbour was deserted. There was a small beach, accessed by steep steps, the waves pulling away from the sand, leaving a frothy streak. She tasted the salt in the wind's bite as it tugged at her hair and lifted coils of it. There was a winding path leading to the top of the cliffs, which she resolved to climb during her stay; there would be an incredible view. The cliffs were rocky, topped with scrubby grasses, looming over the ocean like watching giants. A bird circled before swooping back to the clifftop, a black-backed gull or a kittiwake. Megan shivered without knowing why. The atmosphere of the cove was filled with something strange she couldn't put a name to.

She decided to take a dip later and surf tomorrow morning before breakfast. The best time of day would be around sunrise or sunset when there was a swell in the water and light offshore winds. She'd check with the owner of the surf shop. She didn't want to miss the surf 'firing,' and the locals would always know the best times and places.

She looked out to sea, imagining what St Mawgen Cove had been like hundreds of years ago. Probably little had changed. She wondered if tall ships had sailed into the harbour, bringing salt, taking away hauls of packed fish to ports around the country. She found herself trying to picture what the locals' lives were like. It was easy to imagine small-boned women in fustian frocks, aprons and bonnets cooking over a pot at the fireside in the smoky little fishermen's cottages on dark nights, as the rain lashed the windows. Their lives must have been hard.

She was still staring out into the ocean, her eyes watering with the whip of the wind. In the distance, the water was darker, deeper. Something rose to the surface and ducked beneath again. Megan narrowed her eyes. It was a seal, perhaps: she'd heard dolphins and whales were often spotted around the Cornish coastline, porpoises, even a basking shark. She'd read that people swam in the waters with whales. There had been many sightings reported along the coast, and the best advice was to put one's engine in neutral and give the approaching creatures a wide berth, especially if there were calves present. But it would be wonderful to swim with whales and dolphins watching.

There it was again! A smooth-headed seal, rising to the surface. Megan glimpsed an arm, a hand. It had a long body, a mask, a snorkel. It was a diver. Megan watched again, as the diver came up for air, bobbing on the surface for a moment, before disappearing beneath the water again. The last thing she saw was a long leg in a wetsuit and a stray flipper. She wondered what the diver was looking for: coral fish, underwater rock formations, wrecked ships? Her mind filled with images of lost treasure and sunken hulls. Perhaps she'd be able to go scuba diving while she was here.

She wandered back towards the café where there was a queue at the hatch now, a bustle of visitors chatting loudly, selecting ice creams, and continued towards the hill. She recalled seeing a gift shop on her way into St Mawgen last night, which she would browse in later in the week, buy something for her mother. She passed the small cottages, Anchor Cottage, with its 'For Sale' sign, Ocean View Cottage, Surf's Up! It occurred to her to knock on the door of one of them and ask about Emma, but Megan wanted to be more subtle in her approach. She'd take her time, find her bearings first.

She drew level with the hearse, the bright painting of a surfboard in the window and the sign, 'Catch the Last Wave – Tom Hocking, Funeral Director'. She thought about taking a photo and sending it to Amy. She stared at the funeral director's parlour. The premises extended back a long way, with living accommodation to the side. The front door opened and a man in a parka jacket came out, his hood up, revealing steely eyes and a bushy grey beard. He approached the car and opened the door before noticing Megan.

He nodded a greeting. 'Morning, maid.'

'Hello,' Megan said.

'I was just about to move the hearse round the back. Today's a quiet day.'

'Oh. I was admiring the surf sign over your window.'

'You're not from round here?'

Megan tried a casual conversation opener. 'I'm on holiday. Are there any good barrels out there?'

'Dawn patrol,' the man replied. 'Ankle slappers during the day, nothing but chunder. Last thing at night's not bad.'

'Do you surf much?' Megan asked.

'I used to, a lot. I still get out from time to time. I'm sixty-four,' the man replied. 'If you don't use it, you lose it.'

'I bet.' Megan wanted to keep him talking. 'So, is that a real hearse or...?'

He held out a hand. 'It's real all right. So am I. Tom Hocking, undertaker.' Megan shook it; he had a grip like iron. 'I take it you're looking to surf – and not for an undertaker.'

'That's right. I'm Megan Hammond,' Megan said. 'I didn't mean to be rude. It's just so...'

'Unusual?' He laughed. 'People in the cove can be a bit eccentric, if you know what I mean. I've adapted the hearse to carry a surfboard coffin, if that's what people want, or back to the regular version for non-surfers.'

'Clever.' Megan thought that he was obviously a canny businessman.

'Business has been good these past few months in the dispatch trade,' Tom Hocking said, with a single laugh. 'But when it isn't, I offer the limo out with ribbons on for weddings and parties. That's parked round the back, where this one should be.'

'That's a good idea,' said Megan. 'It's nice to meet someone from the cove who surfs—'

Tom narrowed his eyes. 'Are you staying at The Ship?'

'Yes.'

'Two French chaps have just taken it over, haven't they? One's the chef, the other does all the stuff out front?'

'That's right.' Megan wondered if she was being indiscreet, but it was too late now.

'And which room did they put you in?'

Megan hesitated. It was a strange question. 'Why?'

'As long as you're in number three, you'll be all right.'

'What's wrong with the other rooms?'

'Haunted as sin,' Tom replied as if it was quite normal.

'Haunted?' Megan forced a laugh to dispel the shiver that wriggled up her spine.

'It's true,' Tom said in a matter-of-fact way. 'There's some history in that pub and the ghosts trouble visitors from time to time.'

'Have you seen them?' Megan asked, feeling uncomfortable.

Tom shook his head. 'I smelled one once. An overpowering salty smell.' He pulled a face. 'And I've heard the other one. Oh, you don't want to hear her, I can tell you.'

Megan was aware of a prickling sensation on her skin. 'Really?'

'St Mawgen's full of stories. Lots of places around here are haunted by one ghost or another. There have been Hockings in the cove for generations so tales have been passed down. There's a house down by the seafront, Anchor Cottage, that had a family tragedy and their presence has been felt around the harbour. But that's nothing compared to the one who haunts the cove. I won't tell you what happens if a man sees the witch standing on the clifftops when the moon comes out.'

'It's probably hearsay.' Megan's teeth chattered despite the warmth in the air.

'Ah, no.' Tom shook his head. 'The last man to see her – let me see – it must have been about four months ago, I reckon. I should know. I organised his funeral. Anyway, I'd better get off. I've got things to do.' Tom turned to go. 'Talk to any of the locals about the ghosts in The Ship. They'll tell you. But don't ask about the witch's kiss. It's bad luck to bring it up here in St Mawgen. She isn't seen often, but you never know when she'll appear. I won't say any more. Enjoy your holiday, Megan. Surf's good.' Tom ambled away, tugging his parka hood over his ears. He called over his shoulder, 'Folks are very welcoming in St Mawgen. Just stay away from the cliffs.'

Megan watched him walk back towards the hearse and clamber inside. A sudden chill took her and she began to tremble.

10

The fish had been baked, the dishes scraped, washed with lye soap scented with lemon balm, scalded and put away. Susanna and Katel settled down by the fire to drink warm ale from pewter beakers. It was silent in the little cottage but for the creaking roof. The only light was the orange glow from the hearth and the flickering tallow candle that hung on the wall in a wooden box, away from hungry mice.

Susanna yawned. 'It's time for my bed. Will you come up?'

Katel closed her eyes. 'I like it best by the fireside.'

'I must put a straw mattress near the hearth then, so that you'll be comfortable when you sleep.'

'I have the sweetest dreams here. The fire soothes me. And I often hear a voice from the chimney.'

'A voice?' Susanna was suddenly awake. 'It's your imagination.'

'No, it is Master Jack the chawk, on the roof.' Katel shook her long hair. 'He tells me what will come to pass.'

'It's a dream,' Susanna said, her voice filled with warning. 'Jackdaws' talk is not for you and me.'

'I understand what Master Jack says. He's my friend,' Katel said quietly. 'Some nights he tells me how beautiful the moon is, and the stars, and that I should go outside and look at them.'

'It's not wise to go outside after dark.' Susanna's eyes shone in the firelight. 'Some fishermen drink too much and they come out of The Ship with their minds raddled.'

'I hear them often, singing and caterwauling,' Katel agreed. 'But Uncle Samuel's next door, and he looks after me, and Colan Stephens from the inn keeps an eye on you all the time too. He likes you well, I think.'

'Colan and I have known each other since we were children,' Susanna said. 'We're friends.'

'Indeed, but he looks on you with soft eyes. I've seen him do it.'

'He's married, Katel. Joan is a good woman.'

'He turned to her because you refused him,' Katel insisted. 'You know that's true.'

'It's not something we should speak of,' Susanna said patiently.

'But people say he would've married you, Mother. He would've been a father to me. Indeed, many believe that he is my father.'

'Stop your prattling,' Susanna said quickly.

'Tedda told me he has the same eyes as me, blue as a cornflower.'

'Enough,' Susanna said gently. 'It's time for bed.'

'I wish he was my father; he's kind and sweet natured.' Katel's face crumpled. 'I long for a father.'

'Colan's a good man. But think not of him, Katel.'

Katel stared into the flames. 'I hope my father's not Yowann Hicks. People at the harbour call him a beard splitter.'

Susanna caught her breath with shock. She'd never heard her daughter use such bad language. She said, 'Do you know what that means, child?'

Katel's eyes shone in the firelight. 'I've heard the fishermen say it. It means a careless man who enjoys many women but loves none of them.' She shrugged as if it was nothing. 'Yowann comes down to the harbour and speaks to the fishwives, calling some of them pretty names. He says to me, "How do you fare today, Mistress Boram?" and he makes to chuck my chin or pinch my cheeks. After he has passed, I call him an arse-worm.'

'That's another coarse word the fishwives say. You shouldn't use it,' Susanna said. 'Let's talk no more. It's time for sleep. I'm weary to my bones.'

'But I'm wide awake,' Katel said. 'I enjoy our time together, Mother, but it pains me to ask again of my father. I wish I had one.'

'I wish it too, for your sake.' Susanna smoothed her daughter's hair. 'But Uncle Samuel's next door, always watchful.'

'He's the best uncle.' Katel stretched her arms carelessly. 'When you go upstairs, I may wash my hair. It needs a good comb too; Beaten's hair is full of lice and when she stands next to me, my head itches. I can't abide it.'

Susanna kissed Katel's cheek. 'I bid you good night. Sleep well and don't chatter to Master Jack. You'll be tired in the morning.'

Katel looked as if she was about to speak, then she thought better of it. 'Very well. Good night, Mother.'

Susanna moved to the narrow staircase. She was about to go up when there was a sudden rapping at the door. She frowned. 'It's late. Who can that be?'

The tapping became louder and a husky voice called, 'Susanna.'

'It's Samuel,' Susanna said, suddenly wide awake again as she rushed to let him in. He stood in the doorway, his breath smelling of ale, his pale linen shirt dishevelled.

'I just came from The Ship.' He clutched Susanna's hand. 'I found Annie on her hands and knees, lowing like a cow. I've no idea how to help her. You must come.'

'The baby's on his way, that is all.' Susanna disentangled herself from her brother and picked up her shawl and basket, which she had ready with extra linen and the herbs and tinctures she would need. 'I'll tend to your wife. You go upstairs, Samuel, and lie down. You need to sleep.'

'I will.' Samuel was already on his way towards the stairs on unsteady legs. 'I'll leave you to your work. Birthing's women's business.'

Susanna stood at the door. 'Do you want to help me, Katel?'

Katel shook her head. 'I hate the blood and the wailing a woman makes as she travails.'

Susanna noticed her brother had become pale. His hand that held the stair rail shook. She spoke kindly. 'Don't fret, Samuel. I'll take good care of your Annie. You rest and I'll call you when it's done. Praise God, you'll be able to kiss your happy wife and your newborn son tomorrow morning.'

* * *

Susanna walked into Samuel's cottage to find Anne on her knees, her face contorted in agony. She was breathing heavily as she gasped, 'Come quickly, Susanna, and help me, or I'll die.'

'You will not,' Susanna said, her voice reassuring. 'It's the time for your travail. Every woman knows she must do it, because God told Adam and Eve to be fruitful and multiply.'

Anne groaned again, her eyes bulging with the sudden shock of the pain, and Susanna recalled her own labour and how afraid she'd been at first, before her body took over.

She knelt beside her, taking both her hands. 'Don't fear, Annie. We shall go through this, and each step of the way I'll explain what we'll do and how close we are to the baby being born. Listen carefully, do as I bid, and ask me if you don't understand. Then all will be well. Is it agreed?'

'It is.' Anne nodded anxiously. 'Thank you.'

'Thank me when you're holding your baby in your arms and kissing his brow. In a moment, I'll see how well you progress. But first, I must make sure that everything's clean.'

'I swept the floor this afternoon.' Anne caught her breath again. 'I washed myself as you bade me.'

'Well done. Patience awhile, then we will see how you fare. First, I need to cover the windows with curtains, block the keyhole, keep any foul air outside. Then I'll make sure the fire is well stoked. I'll need hot water and clean linen.' Susanna stood up, bustling around the room, moving a small stool to the centre. 'We'll make sure you're nourished. I have some warm caudle for you with sugar, spices and eggs.' Susanna removed several items from her basket, placing a cup in Anne's hands. 'Drink. You'll need to be strong.'

Anne sipped loudly, then another moan escaped her lips. Susanna busied herself lighting tallow candles, placing them in their baskets on the wall. 'How long have the gripping pains been with you?'

'I can't be sure.' Anne shrugged. 'All day my back ached, then at lunchtime I doubled over with it. This afternoon, they came faster but now they don't cease, not even so I can catch my breath.'

'I'm pleased to hear it,' Susanna said lightly. 'All's well. I'll need to lift your shift and examine how your baby does.' She took Anne's hand. 'If you sit on the stool, before long I may see the baby's head appear, and I can help you to push him out into the world.'

Anne caught her breath as another pain came. Susanna led her to the stool and eased her to a crouching position. Anne's lips were dry. Susanna stroked her hair, whispering soothing words, and fetched more water in a cup, urging her to drink in small sips. Anne whimpered again and Susanna spoke quietly.

'Now listen, Annie. I'm going to rub your belly with an eagle stone to hasten the baby's birth. Then I'll use some sweet almond oil and some herbal tinctures to keep you calm.'

Anne stared in front of her as if in a trance. She was panting lightly. Susanna's voice was gentle as she worked, her fingers light.

'The baby will soon come. You'll need to sit forward on the stool and do as I bid. Breathe lightly. Push hard to expel the child when I say it. All will be well.'

Anne closed her eyes, blocking the pain. Then when she opened them again, they were filled with gratitude. 'Thank you, Susanna. You're a true sister.' She took a light breath. 'The pains grip me again. I'm ready.'

'And so is the little one. A wise doctor once called women's labouring "exquisite torment". I think once your child's born, you'll understand his words as well as I do.'

* * *

It was almost dawn. Anne sat on the stool clutching her son in her arms, smiling into his round eyes. Susanna had tied and cut the cord, washed the baby and swaddled him in clean linen to make sure his limbs grew straight. She finished tidying the room, hiding all signs of birthing so that Samuel could be fetched from his slumbers. Anne's face shone with love. Susanna moved swiftly to her side, helping the new mother to put the baby to her breast. 'It is good to let him suckle now. He will be hungry. I'll prepare more caudle for you.'

'Thank you.' Anne was tired but her eyes sparkled. 'Samuel and I have decided we'll call him Bartholomew.'

'After my father?' Susanna said. 'I like it well.'

Anne gazed fondly at her baby. 'Is he not the most beautiful child ever born?'

'He's your first,' Susanna said. 'He has the face of an angel.'

'I'll have more babies. I want a girl. I'll call her Susanna,' Anne said. 'And then I'll have another son. Samuel wants many sons.'

Susanna laughed. 'Your swill-belly husband knows nothing of women's toils. His own part in it all took but a short while.'

'It did.' Anne began to laugh. 'And now he's slumbering in his pit without a care in the world.'

Susanna moved to where Anne sat, cradling her baby. She wrapped an arm around her. 'It's time for me to take you upstairs to your mattress where you and Bartholomew can rest. You must lie there until you feel well enough to rise. Samuel can take his food in my cottage, and I'll make sure your home is warm and clean and that you have nourishment.'

'Thank you,' Anne said, full of gratitude.

'You'll be a good mother, Annie,' Susanna said encouragingly. 'Now let's get you upstairs and later we'll call on that slug-a-bed husband of yours to greet his new son. It's Sunday morning, so he can get himself to church to thank the Lord for your safe delivery, and then to The Ship Inn, where the fishermen of St Mawgen will drink to the baby's health and chirp merrily until they fall into a stupor.'

11

It seemed a long walk back up the hill towards the surf shop. Megan was lost in thought: Tom Hocking's ghost stories had rattled her, and the witch who haunted the cliffs sounded the most chilling of all. Megan's room had felt safe. It had been a little cold, the modern furniture out of place against the uneven walls and low beams, but she'd slept soundly enough. Perhaps Tom had been joking. Perhaps it was a local custom, to scare visitors. Or Tom was just superstitious. She'd ask Julien about the ghosts at dinner.

She reached Unravel the Ocean, where the doors were wide open and music was playing loudly. Megan recognised Los Relámpagos's rendition of 'Misirlou'. She strolled inside, looking at the shirts on a rail, a row of bright bikinis, a tall stand of sunglasses. She selected a polarised pair with a ventilated frame to reduce fog. Buying something would be a good way into a conversation. She took the glasses to the counter where a young woman was drinking coffee. She was wearing a rainbow T-shirt; she had tanned arms and tousled blond hair, long on top and short at the sides. There was a tiny diamond stud in her nose. Megan put the sunglasses on the counter.

'I'll have these please.'

'Nice choice,' the woman said, offering the card machine.

Megan presented her card. 'So, is the surfing good here?'

'It can be, especially early mornings. Or, if you don't mind driving over to the north coast, Polzeath's good, if you're a learner.' She looked at Megan with interest for the first time. 'While you're over that side, Perranporth's nice. Fistral's my favourite.'

'Do you surf in St Mawgen?'

'Most mornings, before the shop opens. I get up at the crack of dawn. Best time.'

'Right.'

'I'm closing the shop for the winter in October and heading off to Peniche in Portugal. That's the best place in the world to surf.'

'I'm here for a little over a week,' Megan said. She didn't want the conversation to end yet. 'I want to surf, do a bit of swimming or diving. I'm based at The Ship.'

'Oh, nice,' the woman said. Megan examined her expression to see if there was any evidence of the hauntings she'd just heard about, but she seemed unmoved. Megan thought she'd ask. 'I've just been talking to the undertaker.'

'Tom Hocking? Did you see his longboard hearse?' the woman asked. 'He's a good surfer.'

'He was telling me there are ghosts at The Ship.'

'Wouldn't be surprised. The whole cove is Ghost Central,' the woman said. 'St Mawgen's steeped in haunted houses and moaning souls wailing in the moonlight. I don't really listen. I'm from Winchester originally. I run the shop during the summer then I head to Portugal until spring.'

'Right, well, I'm here to surf.' Megan looked at the woman hopefully, as if more recommendations might be forthcoming.

'I hope you enjoy it.'

'I will,' Megan said, picking up the sunglasses. 'I might pop back and treat myself to a new bikini.'

'It's the end of season. I'll do you some deals,' the woman said. 'I'm Carly, by the way.'

'Megan,' Megan said. 'I'll pop in on Monday.'

'Great. Or I'll see you down the beach first thing.' Carly ruffled her tangled fringe. 'Enjoy your day.'

'I will,' Megan called back as she walked to the exit. She was feeling pleased with herself. Carly's local knowledge might be useful. Perhaps she'd get to know her well enough to ask about Emma Davey. Megan decided to head back to the inn, have a look at the map and check out the beaches Carly had recommended: Polzeath, Perranporth, Fistral. Then she'd grab her wetsuit and go for a swim. She wondered if she'd meet the diver she'd seen earlier. The idea of exploring beneath the waves really appealed to her.

* * *

That evening, as Megan was on her way to dinner, her hair still damp from the shower, she bumped into the man she'd seen with his wife at breakfast. He held the front door open for her, a case in his hand.

Megan said, 'Hi. How are you enjoying it here?'

'It's all right for one night,' he said flatly. Megan thought he seemed a little brusque. 'My wife and I are spending a few days in Cornwall. This is our first time in St Mawgen. The cove's pretty, but there's not much to do.'

'I swam this afternoon,' Megan said.

'I imagine the water's cold.' The man shuffled his feet. 'Our room isn't very warm either.' The man paused as if he was about to say something else. 'My wife's picked out a spa hotel in Falmouth. It's a bit more upmarket.'

'Sounds lovely,' Megan said politely. 'I'm off to dinner.'

'By yourself?' the man asked.

'Yes.'

He shook his head. 'I wouldn't want to be on holiday by myself. And I certainly wouldn't stay here more than one night.'

'Why not?' Megan asked brightly.

'Oh, these old places...' The man looked down at his case. 'Well, I'd better get on. My wife's upstairs. I don't want to leave her too long.' He gave a quick smile that disappeared just as rapidly. 'Enjoy your dinner.'

'Thanks.' Megan asked herself what his words meant. He and his wife must be looking for a bit of luxury. The inn was basic and a bit chilly, but for her that was part of its charm. As Julien had said, it just needed a lick of paint and a better heating system.

A small table had been reserved for her in a quiet part of the inn. She could hear the bustle of locals gathering to drink their way through Saturday evening. Julien brought her a glass of crisp white wine and hurried away as she picked up the menu. Another man arrived at her elbow in chef's whites. He was lean, almost gangly, with fair hair and a sweeping fringe. He held out a hand.

'I'm Claude, the chef.'

Megan took in the French accent. She thought Julien's English was a little more confident. Claude had kind eyes and a gentle voice.

'Hi, Claude. I just wanted to say, breakfast was great this morning.'

'Thank you.' Claude gave the tiniest of bows. 'I like to bring the taste of Brittany. The menu you have there is the usual type of thing, the spaghetti Bolognese, the gourmet burger, the fish and chips, but...' He clasped his hands, looking intensely at her. 'Do you want lunch tomorrow?'

'Oh, I'll probably just grab something. I'll be out most of the time.'

'We offer lunch for residents and non-residents. It was quite busy during the summer but' – Claude looked dejected – 'it's quiet now. Even for Sunday lunches we're only half full, a few regulars.'

'I'll be back for dinner,' Megan said reassuringly.

'That's good. I'll make something special tonight, not on the menu. Crab linguine with cucumber salad, my own recipe. Would you like to try?'

'Ooh, thanks very much,' Megan said. 'I love seafood.'

'The crab's locally sourced. The cove's famous for its fish. Pilchards, crab, bass, whiting, pollack, mackerel.'

Megan met his eyes. 'Do you know much about the history of the inn?'

'I do. When we bought this place, a few documents came with it,' Claude said. 'In the seventeenth century, it was attached to two small fishermen's cottages. They were turned into the accommodation where you are staying.' He leaned forward. 'Julien and I want to bring the inn back to its traditional state. I've got big plans for the future.'

Megan almost asked him about the ghosts, but instead she said, 'I'm sure you will. It's beautiful.'

'I adore it here,' Claude agreed. 'The people in the cove are nice and one day, Julien and I will make the pub famous. Then four rooms will not be enough.' His eyes gleamed. 'I know we can do it.'

'I hope so,' Megan said kindly.

'Julien tells me you're here to enjoy the surf, but anything you need, please ask.' Claude gave another almost imperceptible bow. 'Now I cook your linguine.'

'Thanks,' Megan called after him, then she reached for her wine and paused, listening. Music came from the bar area, the gentle squashy sound of a concertina, the light nasal fluttering of a pipe. The locals were singing sea shanties. A gravelly male voice led the song, a chorus swelling in response. She listened to several more songs; everyone in the bar seemed to be joining in. There was a repeated theme in the lyrics: the call of the sea. Megan felt herself swaying along with the music and for a moment, she wished her table was in the bar area, so that she could be part of the communal singing. Then Julien arrived holding a bowl of pasta, garnished with herbs, placing it before her with a flourish.

'Here we are. *Linguine au crabe, sauce à la crème, haricots verts et salade de concombre.* Claude has made it with love.'

'That looks great.' Megan smiled with delight. 'And I love the music. Does the singing happen every night?'

'Not always,' Julien replied. 'It depends who comes in. Local musicians are a great crowd puller with holidaymakers. They like traditional songs.' He paused, listening. A woman was crooning in a plaintive voice. Megan could make out some of the words.

> And this is my Cornwall, I'll tell you all why,
> For here I was born and here I shall die.

Megan took a breath. 'She has a beautiful voice.'

'So many shanties are about lost love, death, sailors going missing in their ships,' Julien said. 'For a reason I can't understand, people prefer them to the ones about drinking too much.'

'Maybe it's human nature to enjoy a good tragedy.' Megan ate a forkful of linguine. 'This is delicious.' She sensed Julien was hovering to find out what she thought of Claude's dish. He indicated her almost empty wine glass.

'Another *vin blanc*?'

'I usually don't have more than one.' Then she relented. 'But I'm on holiday, so let's push the boat out.'

She and Julien both stopped to listen again.

Push the boat me hearties, push the boat,
Heely-ho boys, let her go, let her go.

'Right on cue, and not a sign of tragedy,' Megan said. 'Yes, I'll have another – whatever it was.'

'Chenin blanc, to go with the fish.' Julien turned to go. 'Claude will be delighted you like his food.'

'Mm.' Megan forked another mouthful of pasta, chewing and listening. Another woman was singing now, her voice reedy and high. The song was about lost love, a maid deserted. Megan thought with a sigh that she knew that feeling only too well, being abandoned, hurt.

But here she was in St Mawgen by herself, tucking into a delicious meal.

Julien arrived with another glass of wine; then, as he whirled away, a man struck up in a hearty voice about the Cornish boys who fought for the king. Megan decided to stay and listen for a while longer, have a dessert and a coffee. Tomorrow morning she wanted to go surfing at dawn and come back in time for breakfast.

Her mood lifted. This break was turning out to be just what she needed.

12

Susanna was busy the next morning. She visited Anne first, bringing her food and a liquor of fennel root to help her milk flow. While Anne was resting, she'd make sure Samuel had meals ready when he came home, and that his house was clean. In the afternoon, she returned from Eliza Hicks's house, where she'd delivered garlands of rosemary to keep her nightmares away.

On her way home, Susanna saw Tedda Lobb, who greeted her with her almost toothless grin and swore that she'd told Susanna in Bylen woods that Anne Boram would give birth to a boy: she'd never made a mistake in her life when predicting a baby's sex. Susanna walked away without a word.

Then, in the late afternoon, as the sun sank low behind the cove, she stood in front of the fire, tending to the pottage of fish and vegetables. Katel was late. On the table, the basket was piled with foxgloves to treat maladies of the heart, and a bundle of lady's bedstraw with its dark green leaves and spikes of yellow flowers. Susanna had found it growing on the side of the cliff.

She said softly to herself, 'This is a good herb. I'll use some for Annie to stay her bleeding. The ointment's good for burns and it'll break a kidney stone. A decoction will help with Eliza's joints. And I'll stuff the dried flowers in a mattress for Katel. It keeps the lice away.'

She busied herself, tying bundles to be dried. Her heart lifted as she thought of Anne's baby, Bartholomew. Her beloved father would have been happy to know that his grandson bore his name.

There was a light rap at the door, then a tentative voice. 'Susanna?'

Susanna recognised the voice. 'Joan. Yes, come inside, I pray you.'

Joan Stephens peered round the door. She was young, in her mid-twenties, with the loose limbs of a colt and chestnut hair that held a reddish glow beneath her cap. Susanna thought her very pretty. Colan had made a good match. He had chosen a sweet woman who worked hard, cooked the best crousts and kept the drunken fishermen at bay with her good-tempered wit. But there was a sadness in her face, as if she had a secret she couldn't share. Susanna took her hand. Her fingers were cold, despite the heat outside.

'How are you? Is Colan well?'

'He's setting barrels of ale in the cellar,' Joan replied and there was a silence between the two women. Joan hadn't answered the question and Susanna guessed what was on her mind. For a moment, they made small talk.

Joan said, 'I hear Annie's delivered of a son. I hope they're both hearty.'

'They are. The baby's called Bartholomew. Annie's recovering.'

'And...' Joan took a breath. 'Samuel's well? Katel?'

'Indeed,' Susanna said. It occurred to her that Samuel's cottage was joined to the inn, she knew his family thrived, but Joan was here on another matter. This was not a social call.

Susanna said, 'What can I do for you?' She looked into Joan's eyes to see if she was pregnant. Susanna could usually detect changes, but there was no better test than scrying urine. She asked, 'Are you feeling well?'

'I'm a little melancholy.' Joan looked away. 'Yowann called around to see Colan this morning. I think he wants to hide more goods in the cellar, but Colan says I shouldn't speak of it. Yowann can do as he wishes. He comes in during the evenings to meet with strangers. Often silks, tea, tobacco and barrels of brandy come into his hands from the French ships.'

Susanna nodded. 'I've heard it.'

'But this morning he spent an hour with me, drinking ale, and he said things that made me uncomfortable.'

'What did he say?'

'That Colan owes him money. That I'm a pretty dimpled maid. That I could do much to pay off Colan's debts if I chose to do so.' Joan looked at her hands. 'I didn't know how to reply. But I asked him not to say such things.'

'You did well,' Susanna said. She wondered if Joan had come to ask for a charm, something to keep Yowann at a distance. Susanna didn't dabble in magic. She understood wortcunning, she knew herbs well, but cursing and spells were more Tedda's business, if the rumours were true.

'Susanna, I want to ask you something about Colan.' Joan took a breath to steady herself.

Susanna felt suddenly uncomfortable. 'What is it?'

'You've known him since you were children. You and he were close.'

'It was many years ago.'

'Colan's a proper man, kind.'

'He is.'

'And people in the cove were surprised when he married me. They thought he would be a bachelor all his days.'

'It's good that he's wed. You're a fine match.'

'And he's highly thought of by all who know him.'

'So how can I help you, Joan?'

'I fear he doesn't truly love me in his heart,' Joan said. 'When we lie together, he doesn't speak my name or utter words of endearment. It's as if he is imagining I'm someone else.'

'That can't be,' Susanna soothed, her heart heavy. She knew there was some truth in Joan's words. 'You're sweet natured, pretty. He must love you.'

'I can't get with child.'

'You have plenty of time.'

'It's because he doesn't love me. If I could make Colan love me the way he loves...' Joan's voice trailed off.

'In time he will.'

'But I fear he loves another.'

Susanna knew who Joan was referring to. But she was determined to do her best for her. 'You're fretting needlessly, I'm sure.'

Joan closed her eyes for a moment. When she opened them, she said, 'Please help me. I beg you.'

'I deal only in herbs and tinctures,' Susanna said uneasily. She wasn't sure what Joan wanted, but she noticed the desperation in her expression.

'Tedda Lobb makes a love charm from dried periwinkle and worms that you can put in his ale.'

'I don't trust Tedda. But I trust you. Susanna, can you talk to Colan for me?'

'Talk to him? What should I say?' Susanna imagined trying to speak to Colan on his wife's behalf. It would be awkward.

Joan took a shuddering breath. 'That you don't love him. That he should care for his wife who loves him more than life itself.'

'Joan.' Susanna thought how to frame her words. 'I'll talk to him as a friend, if you wish it. I'll tell him that he has a wonderful wife who's deserving of his heart.'

Joan grasped her hand. 'Would you say that?'

'He's indeed fortunate. Yes, I'll say that.'

'Perhaps then he may turn to me.'

Susanna felt a rush of sympathy. 'I'll do my best to help you, Joan, I swear it.'

Joan wrapped her arms around Susanna. 'Thank you.' She was suddenly anxious. 'I ought to go back. The fishermen will be asking for crousts.' She touched Susanna's fingers gently. 'I'll bring some round later, for Samuel and Annie.'

'That's kind,' Susanna said, feeling grateful, and glad that she and Joan had cleared the air. 'I promise, I'll talk to your husband.' She paused; there were loud voices outside in the street. Both women listened a moment. A man raised his voice harshly, shouting, 'Go to your mother, and quickly.' It was Samuel's voice.

Susanna stiffened with fear as she heard Katel reply, 'You're not my father. It's no business of yours.'

Susanna pushed the door open and tried to make sense of the scene in front of her. Samuel held Katel by the shoulder. His face was red and he was hissing, 'I think only of your reputation. Once lost, it'll not return.'

'I have no need of...' Katel turned anxiously, noticing her mother.

'What's all this noise?' Susanna said to Samuel. 'Why do you shout?'

'Katel does not behave in a way that befits...' Samuel paused as Joan appeared behind Susanna.

She looked at each face awkwardly and said, 'I'll return home. My husband waits,' and she was gone in a rustle of her skirt.

Susanna waved a hand, ushering Samuel and Katel into the cottage. 'Let us go inside.' She followed them in, closing the door. 'So, why do you shout in the street for all to hear?'

Samuel was furious. 'Susanna, I may be younger than you, but I must intervene. This child has no father to control her.'

'I'm not a child,' Katel spat, and Susanna noticed her fierce expression. She had never seen her look so wild.

'What's happened?' Susanna turned from her daughter to her brother. 'Samuel?'

Samuel put his hands on his hips and took a breath. 'I saw Katel – consorting – with one of the fishermen.'

'Consorting?' Katel laughed loudly, as if he had lost his mind. 'We were simply talking. He asked me if I would like a fish to bring home for supper and—'

'In exchange for a kiss,' Samuel shouted.

'A kiss is just for a moment,' Katel argued. 'Besides, he likes me.'

'Who wanted to kiss you, Katel?' Susanna asked quietly, doing her best to stay calm.

'Merryn Gilbert,' Katel said smugly. 'He stares at me all the time. This afternoon he told me I was the most enchanting creature.'

'Enchanting?' Susanna found the word troubling. It was a word local people used for magic.

'And in full view of all the people in the cove, Katel allowed this man to put his arm around her waist and—' Samuel's fists balled. 'I won't allow her to bring shame on the name our father gave us, Susanna.'

Susanna wanted to calm him but her own heart was beating too fast. 'Thank you, Samuel. Please, let me talk to Katel. You've worked hard today. Perhaps you would like to spend an hour in The Ship and take a draught of ale? I have food ready for your supper and we can take some to Annie and see how she and little Bartholomew fare.'

'Katel must learn—'

'Indeed she must,' Susanna said gently. 'I thank you for bringing her home.'

Samuel's cheeks were still flushed. He seemed about to say something, then he changed his mind, strode quickly to the door and opened it. 'We'll talk of this later,' he said, and was gone.

Katel laughed. 'My uncle's face flares like a flame. I've never seen him in such a choler.'

'You mustn't mock him.' Susanna frowned.

'And he shouldn't drag me home by my arm,' Katel countered. 'I was talking to Merryn, who's kind and means me no ill. But Uncle Samuel was suddenly shouting and accusing.'

'I understand that he has vexed you.' Susanna drew a deep breath to calm herself. 'But, Katel, you need to be careful when young men talk to you in the harbour. They may not have good intentions.'

'Intentions?' Katel trilled a laugh. 'I jest with them, that's all. Like a kitten with a mouse. I merely play with their affections. I'm not seeking a husband.'

Susanna sighed. 'You must be modest in your behaviour. It's not good to allow a public show of affection to a man you're not promised to.'

'I don't care what people think.' Katel looked away. 'I've told you what the chawk says to me at night. He whispers down the chimney. I won't marry a man from St Mawgen Cove, a fisherman whose hands are rough and stink of the sea. A prince will come, speaking in tongues of gold.'

'Do you believe this?'

'I do, Mother. Tedda tells me that Master Jack foretells what will come.' Katel's eyes were wide. 'That is why I can talk to Merryn Gilbert and anyone who gazes fondly at me. I know I'm waiting for someone better.'

'I don't like this.' Susanna frowned again. 'I pray, say nothing to anyone. People in the cove like to wag their tongues and I know what trouble it may bring. I don't want your name on people's lips. A maid who talks to chawks...'

'I care not what others say.' Katel stretched her arms. 'I'm weary now. And I hate the reek the salt leaves on my skin. So, I'll take some of the hot water and wash myself, then we'll eat a pleasant supper. Afterwards, let's go and see Aunt Annie's baby.' She kissed Susanna's cheek lightly. 'You wait and see. A man will be here in a boat and I'll become a princess. Oh, and have you washed my best shift and dried it well? And is there lemon balm oil to rub on my skin? I want to smell sweet.'

Katel whirled towards the fireplace where the hot water was bubbling over the flames. She paused for a moment, as if listening, then her voice was hushed. 'By the way, Mother, the nets will need to be out early tomorrow. The huer will shout from his hut on the clifftop that there are shoals of fish in the cove and St Mawgen will have its biggest haul ever.'

'How do you know this, child?' Susanna said, her expression troubled.

'Master Jack whispered it in my ear.'

Susanna shivered as Katel started to draw water from the pot, humming lightly, in a merry mood now. As she watched her daughter, her brow clouded.

Katel was changing. The strange things she said disturbed Susanna. Her instincts cried out that listening to the talk of the jackdaw would bring bad luck. She wanted more than anything to keep her child safe. She did not want her name to be on people's lips. She knew what they would say about her.

And she knew well that, once invited into the house, ill fortune would not go away.

13

Megan opened her eyes to stare into darkness. The room was quiet now, but she was sure she'd heard a dull noise from the bedroom above. She'd slept deeply since coming back from dinner, her head buzzing with the squeezebox sound of sea shanties and the soothing effect of two glasses of wine. The St Mawgen sea air had filled her lungs like a sigh and she'd fallen asleep quickly, but the sudden bumping sound had woken her. Footsteps? She was fully alert now, her ears straining.

She huddled beneath the warmth of the duvet. There were shapes in the shadows: the mountain of the dressing table, the television on top like a crouching sprite. The ensuite door gaped wide open and she could see the pale glow of the shower screen. Beyond the window a light glowed. Megan listened for the noise. It must have been her imagination.

She rolled over and closed her eyes. There it was again: a single thump, like something being moved in the room above. She sat up, listening hard.

Silence.

She glanced at her phone on the table by the bed and picked it up. It was twenty past three. A message had come in from her mother, just a few words asking when they could next chat – she was missing her. Even though they'd talked before dinner, Megan knew that Jackie worried. She'd call her briefly after breakfast. She intended to get up in a couple of hours' time, pull on her wetsuit and go down to the beach. She closed her eyes, rolling into the warmest space.

She had just started to snooze when she heard a harsh thud above, followed by another. Her eyes still closed, she concentrated on listening. Perhaps the couple in the room upstairs were lumbering about, or having an argument. She recalled meeting the man on the way to dinner. What had he said? They intended to try out a spa hotel in Falmouth. She recalled the edge to his voice when he said he wouldn't want to stay long in The Ship.

She snuggled deeper into the warmth of the bed. There was a noise again, this time louder. A creaking sound, over and over, like a chair rocking. There was a pause. Then another longer sound, like something being dragged along the floor. Megan wondered if the couple were packing to leave before daylight. She could smell something too, a strange earthy odour that clung to the air like damp. Her sense of smell had always been keen, and it was definitely a pungent stink, like rotting wood.

The sound came again, a low scraping, as if a bed was being tugged above, or a chair. Then there was a loud bump, before silence. Nothing but an eerie stillness.

A shiver tingled down her spine. The banging noises weren't the noises of residents at this time of night, surely? Megan felt suddenly alone and anxious. She took a deep breath, concentrating on the thought of white waves rolling onto the bay and the crystal curve of the surf at dawn, the sky mottled indigo and red. She was looking forward to being there. She exhaled slowly and let sleep come.

She woke with a start and sat up. Beyond the curtains, daylight was dazzlingly white. She reached for her phone and groaned. It was almost nine o'clock. She'd slept in and missed the morning surf. She imagined Carly on the beach as dawn broke, the crumpled sea still pink from the rising sun, grumbling about lightweight holidaymakers before launching herself and her board into the sea. Megan promised herself she wouldn't miss it tomorrow.

But what to do today?

The room was cold. Megan hurried to the window and pulled back the curtains, gazing out onto a patch of garden that contained huge umbrella-leafed plants that looked like giant rhubarb. The sky was azure, cloudless. It was an exploring day, she decided. She'd have a swim in the cove, maybe drive to one of the nearby beaches and check out the surf there. Then tonight she'd have dinner at the inn again – perhaps she could ask for a table nearer the bar so that she could see the musicians singing shanties. She hoped they'd be back. The chill on the air made her shiver. She reached for her vitamins and a bottle of water.

Twenty minutes later, she was sitting at her usual table in the small dining room and Julien was pouring coffee and offering a selection of croissants, pastries and jams. There was far too much food; Megan wondered what happened to all the leftovers. She was surprised that she was the only one in the breakfast room: none of the three other tables was set with plates and cutlery. It was cold in there today, despite the bright sunlight outside, and she reached for her steaming coffee eagerly.

Julien appeared distracted as he returned with a small jug of orange juice. He asked, 'Did you enjoy your meal last night?'

'It was lovely,' Megan enthused. 'And the music was fantastic.'

'It's nice when the locals come in to sing,' Julien agreed.

He was about to go when Megan asked, 'Where's everyone this morning?'

'There's no one here now. They've all gone,' Julien said. 'Normally, someone arrives, they stop for one night and the next day they're off again.' He looked relieved. 'It feels like you're a regular already. Claude was delighted you enjoyed his linguine. He's asked me to ask if you'd like *moules marinière* this evening?'

'Oh, I'd love that. And can I move closer to the bar so that I can watch the musicians?'

'Consider it done,' Julien said kindly. 'And as for the *moules* – the *marinière* sauce is white wine, shallots, parsley and butter. But if you'd prefer a cream sauce, he can do that.'

'*Marinière* is great.' Megan pulled a croissant apart. 'Thanks, Julien. I feel really spoiled.'

'We want to spoil our customers. I just wish we had more of them.' He looked sad for a moment and turned to go. Megan wondered what was bothering him.

She couldn't help herself. 'Is everything all right?'

Julien glanced over his shoulder, walking away slowly. 'Oh, it's fine – enjoy your breakfast.'

Megan thought she noticed tears in his eyes and she called again. 'Julien?'

He paused. 'How can I help?'

'Grab a cup and join me?' Megan suggested. 'A problem shared.'

Julien gave a shrug, picked a coffee cup from a cupboard and sat opposite her, refilling her cup from the cafetière and then filling his own. She watched as he plopped three sugar cubes in with shaking fingers.

'You need the sugar rush?'

'I do. Claude tells me I must watch my figure, but I need some energy.' He sighed. 'I want to make a success of The Ship.'

'And you will,' Megan said. 'I run my own shop back in Minehead.' She was surprised she hadn't thought of Earthbound Essentials for a while. 'I know how tough it is to make a business work.'

'What do you sell?' Julien asked.

'Oh, what they call new-age stuff, though it's really as old as the hills: herbal remedies, essential oils, a range of gift items. Plus we do massage therapies, my mum and me.'

Julien said, 'Do you have herbal potions that relieve stress?'

'Yes,' Megan said. 'Ashwagandha capsules have had amazing results. I did a course a few years ago on Ayurvedic medication.' She studied his worried face.

Julien gave a short laugh. 'Will it help with my staff problems?'

'Who knows?' Megan said. 'It might. Why?'

'Josh, my barman, handed in his notice last night. He wants to move away from St Mawgen. He says it's a backwater.'

'That's what's so nice about it. It has such a sense of community.'

'And my gem of a cleaner will go on leave soon, too. She'll be hard to replace. There's a limit to how many jobs I can do myself.'

'Could Claude help with the cleaning when he's not cooking?'

'Claude?' Julien gave a cynical laugh. 'It's the one thing he and I argue about. All he wants to do is cook. He's an ambitious chef, always going over budget buying exotic ingredients. And he spends time making beautiful things just for the pleasure of it. We have to eat them ourselves. No wonder I'm putting on the kilos.'

'So you're in charge of everything else?'

'I'm the only one with any business sense,' Julien said. 'And I'm beginning to realise I've – what is the expression? – bitten off more than I can chew.'

'Can't you advertise?' Megan asked simply.

'I'll try.' Julien sighed as if he was already defeated.

Megan said, 'Is Claude optimistic?'

'Oh, he's in love with the pub,' Julien said. 'We came here from Crozon, a beautiful part of Brittany, and thought we could make it special. As long as he's cooking, Claude's happy. He doesn't worry – he leaves that to me. But, of course, we need customers, and they don't come.'

'I'm sure they will,' Megan said encouragingly. 'This inn's gorgeous. You just need to get through the winter and wait for the holidaymakers to rush in when the weather improves.'

'I wish it was that simple. If it was just the change of seasons, all would be well, but being here has its own special problems.' Julien finished his coffee. 'I'm sorry to talk of such depressing things. I should ask instead. Did you catch the surf at dawn?'

'I slept in. I heard the people in the room above bumping about in the night and there was this strange damp smell.'

Julien tensed. 'What did you do?'

'I just fell asleep again. I'll go for a swim later and catch the evening surf.' Megan noticed Julien staring. 'What did I say?'

'Nothing. Everything's good.' Julien tried to pull himself together. 'Well, I hope you have a great day and this evening there will be a special table for you near the bar.' He stood slowly. 'Thanks for listening. I'm sorry to tell you all my problems, and you're right – I'll advertise for a new bartender and a temporary cleaner and in the spring, the guests will come rushing through the door.' He said, 'Tonight's first glass of wine will be on the house.'

He gave a complicit wink and was gone.

Megan finished her croissant, brushed crumbs from her T-shirt and made for the exit. She reminded herself to ring her mother and ask her to put some herbal remedies in the post tomorrow. And she'd thought of a special stone that she wanted Julien and Claude to have: she'd ask for that too. That might cheer them up.

As she burst through the door, she almost bumped into a woman who had her back to her, an unusually long dark ponytail to her waist. The woman was dressed in a floral skirt and she held a mop, dunking it in a bucket with a clatter. As she turned, Megan noticed that she was heavily pregnant. She had a soft local accent.

'Oh, I'm sorry. I'm in the way.'

'Not at all,' Megan said. 'I'm just grabbing my stuff and then I'm off.'

'Lovely day, though,' the woman said. 'You're staying in room three?'

'Yes.'

'I'll just give it a quick vacuum once you've gone,' the cleaner said, and turned back to her mop.

'Thanks.' Megan pushed her key into the door lock, then she asked, 'I didn't see the couple who stayed upstairs at breakfast.'

'They left yesterday evening,' the cleaner replied, still mopping.

Megan recalled meeting the man at the front door last night, the case in his hand. 'Oh yes, they said they were off to Falmouth. So, who's in there now?'

'Nobody.' The cleaner spoke as she worked. 'There's just you.'

'Oh, thanks.' Megan stepped inside her room and shivered. Despite the warm air, she felt suddenly intensely cold. The woman's words had hit her like the slap of icy water.

If the room upstairs was unoccupied, then who had been bumping around during the night?

14

The cry from the hut on the clifftop came early, as the sun dappled the skies pink and blue. The huer waved branches and shouted, 'Hevva, hevva!' then blew a blasting trumpet note to alert everyone that the seas were full of pilchards ready to be hauled in. People shuffled from their homes tiredly and boats were pushed out to sea. Then a wall of small-mesh nets was cast in a horseshoe. Colan and Joan Stephens were preparing the cellar of The Ship Inn, making space to store the fish. Yowann Hicks, in a smart white shirt and dark breeches, strode around barking orders, organising the activity. Everyone from the cove was there, fishermen in crews of four oarsmen and a cox.

Susanna emerged from her front door, wrapped in a warm shawl. She watched as the men threw nets from heavy double-ended seine boats, dragging in their catch of pilchards. Shore-based capstans hauled in the net. Then the rest of the villagers, women and children, rushed into action to baulk the fish, cutting and salting them, pressing them in hogsheads to expel the oil.

Anne came to stand beside her clutching baby Bartholomew. Katel was already amidst the throng on the harbour, her limbs moving lightly, lifting pilchards into a hogshead. Beaten Gilbert, who often helped Eliza Hicks with her chores, was working next to her and even from a distance, Susanna could see the tension between the two young women. Katel chattered gaily to everyone around her, deliberately excluding Beaten, who looked on awkwardly, hoping to join in. Tedda Lobb, swathed in a black shawl, hovered at Katel's elbow. She gazed towards Susanna cunningly, and Susanna looked away.

'It's a big haul, this one, Annie,' Susanna said. 'It'll feed the cove well.'

'It will,' Anne agreed, pulling the baby to her, covering his head with her shawl against the sea breeze. 'And Yowann will export much of it to distant places: Spain, France and Gascony. Will you look at the big fishing boat where Samuel is cox? There's Merryn Gilbert, rowing with mighty muscles, big as kegs of ale. Look how he pulls the oars.' She finally made her point. 'Samuel says he's becoming foolishly fond of Katel.'

'I don't think she has eyes for Merryn,' Susanna said quickly.

'But he'd make a good husband. And she's of an age.'

Susanna knew that Anne was thinking about her baby, her family, and she wished all women the same happiness as she held Bartholomew to her breast.

'We'll see,' Susanna suggested enigmatically.

'She's a pretty maid,' Anne persisted. 'Not like poor Beaten Gilbert. Have you seen her face? Working with oily fish has given her a bad complexion. I feel sorry for her.'

'I'll seek her out and give her some witch hazel and calendula.'

'I've heard that Tedda Lobb tells young girls to wash their faces in their morning urine and that will greatly improve their skin.' Anne's expression showed that she too had been given the same advice.

'Urine's an astringent, but a plant tincture will soothe and heal the skin.' Susanna was still gazing towards the harbour where Yowann was shouting at the capstans to haul the nets faster. He turned and caught Susanna's eye, then he doffed his cap and gave an elaborate bow. Susanna responded with a curt nod, raised her chin and looked away.

Anne cupped a hand around Bartholomew's head and turned back towards her cottage. 'I'll take him inside now. There's a breeze blowing in. Besides' – she lowered her voice – 'Yowann Hicks would surely have me packing sardines, babe in arms.' She brushed Susanna's cheek with her lips. 'I'll make supper for Samuel today. I feel stronger now, thanks to the herbs you've given me.' Her expression was one of gratitude. 'Thank you, Susanna.'

Anne slipped away and Susanna was conscious of someone watching her. Colan Stephens stood in the doorway of The Ship Inn, his arms folded. He inclined his head towards her. 'Susanna.'

'Good day to you, Colan,' Susanna said, feeling the familiar tingle of warmth she had always felt towards him. 'It's a big haul. This afternoon, the fishermen will be demanding ale to celebrate. And your cellars will be full.'

'Indeed,' Colan said quietly. 'Joan's baking crousts to fill their bellies.'

Susanna remembered the conversation she'd had with Joan the previous day. She turned to Colan. 'I wonder if I may have a word?'

'Come inside.' Colan led the way into the inn, where tallow candles glimmered on the walls below dark beams. In the corner, a hearth blazed. Colan asked, 'Can I get you a cup of something?'

'No, thank you.' Susanna looked around to make sure no one was listening. She wasn't sure how to approach the subject so she said, 'Colan, you have a good wife.'

'Joan works hard.'

Susanna said, 'I think she's lonely.'

'How can she be lonely?' Colan's brow furrowed and Susanna was reminded of him as a young boy, how he would look at her quizzically to puzzle out her feelings before speaking to her, as if making her happy was his only concern. She'd loved that, the way he was so considerate. In a flash, the warm feelings came back, the flood of affection, and she pushed them away.

He took a breath. 'Joan's busy all day and at night she's weary. She has no time for loneliness.'

'She needs love, Colan.'

He met her eyes, a direct gaze filled with sadness. 'I need love, too.'

'Then talk to your wife.'

'I try, Susanna. I'm not a bad man.'

'I know.'

'But I'm not the best husband for Joan.'

'I think you are. You're a kind person, gentle. Show her that you care.'

Colan sighed. 'I try. When I married her, it was because an innkeeper needs a wife.'

'Everyone needs to be loved.'

'But what of you? You're alone – you have no one.'

'I have Katel.'

'I waited and waited for you, Susanna.' Colan's voice was hushed. 'I asked you to marry me many times.'

Susanna felt her pulse thud. She had explained the same thing to him so often: it was difficult for her too. She still felt a surge of affection. Much more than that. 'You know I have a daughter. She has no father named. I couldn't agree to marry you. People would have talked. They would call you bad names and I couldn't have allowed that to happen.'

'I would have treated her as my own. Perhaps she is mine.'

'Colan.' Susanna wanted to say that she had once loved him. That, in truth, she still thought of him tenderly. But she had to make the situation clear now, for Joan's sake. 'Think of your wife. Your future is with her.'

'How can I give her my heart when I've already given it to you? I cannot take it back.'

'You must,' Susanna insisted.

'You loved me once. Since we were children, we've loved each other. All our lives.'

'It's true,' Susanna admitted, feeling her eyes fill. 'And it breaks my heart to remember it. But I can't have soft thoughts for you again. Our love must be a sweet thing of the past. I'll stay as I am. You'll go to your wife, treat her kindly.' Susanna grasped his hand. 'Have children, be happy.'

A moment took them both and stretched, as their gaze held. Susanna wanted to reach out her hand, to pull him to her in an embrace, but it would end badly. She felt the same surge of love they'd shared as teenagers. She recalled the question in his eyes when he discovered she was with child, her stubborn refusal to name the man who had left her this way. He placed a hand against her cheek.

'There's only ever been you. There will be no one else.' He moved closer. 'I know you feel the same way, Susanna. When we're together, we both know it's true. There will always be a bond between us, a love stronger than time, than—'

'Please don't,' Susanna whispered. She was trembling. 'We've chosen our own paths. I'm a mother; I heal people. You must be the best person you can for Joan. Have a family of your own.'

'But you and I care for each other deeply. That will never change. You know it—'

'We mustn't speak of it. Think of Joan.'

'I think only of you.' His lips brushed hers and Susanna took a step back as if she had been stung.

'Colan.' Susanna held her breath. There was a noise behind her, someone moving away with a rustle of skirts. She gasped. 'Look to your wife.'

She rushed to the doorway, leaving him staring after her, and out into the bright sunshine. She tugged her shawl around her shoulders and smelled the heavy aroma of tobacco. She shuddered. Tedda Lobb stood a few feet away. She spat on the ground, a huge gobbet of chewed tobacco.

'*Metten daa.*' Her voice was a crackle as she gave the Cornish greeting. 'You'm look as if you'm been affrighted, Susanna Boram.' Her eyes gleamed like beads beneath matted hair and a grey cap. 'Or is it Joan Stephens who caught a fright with what she has seen? She knows her husband will never love anyone but you.' She pointed a skinny finger. 'Will you betray her one day, Susanna, or will you betray your own heart?'

'I've no idea what you speak of.' Susanna lifted her chin and hurried towards her door.

'It's no matter,' Tedda called after her. 'Things will come to pass soon in St Mawgen Cove that will change our lives. Today the biggest haul of fish was caught and your daughter knew that it would happen. She heard it from the chawk who called down the chimney. Many of the fishermen heard her predict it. They were surprised that she foretold it to them. They talk now as if she's my daughter, not your'n.'

'Leave Katel alone,' Susanna said over her shoulder. 'Stay away from her, Tedda. She's not your child.'

'She'll be mine one day. But for now she's your'n and someone else's, who'll never be named. You'm said it many times. But you and I both know who he is. She's his image.'

Susanna hurried inside the cottage, slamming the door behind her, doing her best to make the leering Tedda disappear. She shouted, 'Go away.' But Tedda's voice could still be heard outside, a low uttering.

'Katel longs to learn the old ways. She learns fast. One day, she may be rewarded for her skills, Susanna. And you'll witness it. As will everyone in the cove. The future can't be stopped.'

Susanna ignored her, her breath coming fast in her throat, until she was finally sure Tedda had gone away. She moved to the table, lifting herbs from the basket, inhaling their sweet perfume.

She set about cleaning ceramic bottles and containers for the mixture. She had some henbane in the basket, a herb that she treated with extra care when she prepared it as a medicine. Mixed with a little claret wine, it was useful in counteracting fever and helping a person to sleep, but in larger doses it could cause the skin to become cold as ice, then death would come. Susanna was confident that she could use a small amount of henbane to help Eliza Hicks rest at night.

She approached the hearth, warming her hands, inspecting the pot of willow bark that simmered gently. She shook her head, dispelling fond thoughts of Colan Stephens, but she still felt his rough hand against her face, the scent of his skin as she stood too close. She often wished she'd been able to put away her stubbornness and accept him as her husband.

The truth was, she loved him more than any man. But Katel came between them. She'd been born out of wedlock from one brief tangled moment, and there was no going back. Susanna would at least save him from the gossip of the cove.

The willow bark was ready to be cooled and turned into a tincture. With a little honey Susanna could make cordials and syrups, easy for a patient to swallow and to digest. She reached up to lift the pot from its hook and bring it away from the heat, when something caught her eye, high up in the chimney. It was pale, almost gleaming. Susanna grasped it in warm fingers and tugged it down.

She cried out in fear.

It was a little doll, made of cloth. The mouth was a stitched line and the eyes were two tiny buttons. Susanna frowned, wondering who had put it there. She shifted away from the fire to the tallow candlelight and inspected it more closely, holding it to her nose, inhaling the musty stench of mouse urine. She recognised the scent. It was poisonous hemlock but that was not what worried her most.

Strands of human hair had been wrapped around the head: whoever had made the doll had attached someone's hair to it. Several pins had been pushed into the face, looking like raised acne. Susanna knew at once who the poppet was made for, and what harm it was intended to do. It was working its bad magic well.

Susanna trembled with terror. What was Katel doing? And who had guided her hand? When her daughter came home, she would have some searching questions for her.

She knew exactly what she would ask. And the answer Katel might give made her feel more afraid than she ever had.

15

Megan drove down to the cove in the noisy Beetle, her clothes over her wetsuit, towels in the back, music blaring from the tinny radio. She was looking forward to a swim. She passed the premises belonging to Tom Hocking. There was no hearse outside so Megan assumed he was out on business. Or perhaps it was parked round the back?

She passed the three cottages on the left, Anchor Cottage, Ocean View and Surf's Up! and her mind drifted to Emma Davey. It felt strange to think of her as a half-sister, but that's what she was. Her father's daughter by another woman, Chrissie. Megan imagined herself knocking at a door, a young woman emerging with the same dark hair and eyes as she had.

What would she say? How would she introduce herself? The idea seemed almost unreal. She thought about how to contact Emma as she parked the Beetle next to an old Suzuki Jimny. By the look of the stickers in the window, it was owned by a surfer.

She clambered out and gazed towards the ocean where the waves sparkled blindingly in the sunlight. She reached onto the dashboard for her new sunglasses. The cove seemed quiet, although the café was open and doing reasonable Sunday business with parents with children buying ice creams from the hatch. The cliffs loomed dark against the bright sky and Megan looked up, watching a walker with a dog hiking along the path. The air was cool from a buffeting sea breeze, but the wetsuit would keep her warm enough in the water. She was ready for a dip.

A movement in the water caught her eye as a snorkel appeared, a round head, a face mask. Then he was striding towards the beach, a scuba diver, sleek in black. He had something in his hand but Megan couldn't see what it was. She watched him pause in the shallow water, tugging off flippers, hauling off his diving cylinder, his face mask. He ruffled his hair, which might have been blond had it not been wet, and unzipped his wetsuit, wriggling out of the top half, exposing tanned flesh.

Megan looked away, across the sea, but there were no other swimmers. Then her gaze returned to the diver, his wetsuit pulled down to his waist. He was muscular, probably her age. She thought about walking down to the beach so she could talk to him. He might be local and she could ask him questions about the swimming conditions, and life in the cove. But something held her back. The diver had an aloofness about him.

A light pressure on her arm made her jump and she turned round to see Carly, clutching a cardboard cup, a coffee to go. Her hair was wet, and she ran a hand through it, laughing as she did so. 'You're late.'

'I slept in,' Megan said. 'I'm a lightweight.'

'Didn't you sleep well?' Carly asked, and an awkward moment passed between the two women, Megan thinking about the noises that came from the empty bedroom above. She broke the silence.

'I stayed on for breakfast. I thought I'd go for a swim instead.' She glanced down towards the beach. The diver had disappeared. She scanned the paths that led away from the sea, but he was nowhere to be seen.

'Are you busy for the rest of the day?' Carly asked.

'No, I'm just checking the cove out.'

'Then why don't we go to Gunwalloe? Swimming's really good there. Apparently there's a seventeenth-century ship still visible that was lost offshore.'

'Have you seen it?' Megan asked.

'No. Cornwall's full of wrecked ships, though.' Carly shook her head. Drops of water flew everywhere. 'But the water's clear and the beaches are sandy. Shall we go in my old banger?' She indicated the yellow Jimny with an expression that suggested the car had seen better days.

'Let me grab my stuff.' Megan reached into the Beetle for her bag, then she clambered into the Jimny. 'Thanks, Carly. I'm sorry I was late this morning.'

'The surf was good, too,' Carly said.

'Tomorrow's on, definitely,' Megan promised.

'Today's a swimming day,' Carly said. 'And if you like, we can bomb around this part of Cornwall. It's my favourite place for water sports. Except for Peniche. Have you been to Portugal?'

'No,' Megan said.

'You should go. It's the best place in the world for surfing – and surfers.' Carly started the engine. 'So what do you do when you're not on holiday, getting up too late to catch the surf?'

Megan laughed. 'I have a shop in Somerset. I sell herbal remedies, essential oils and stuff, and do massages.'

'Oh, you'd do great business here in the summer,' Carly said. She was zooming up the hill, past the undertaker's, past The Ship and out of St Mawgen. 'We get some interesting dudes here, mostly for the surfing. A lot of them camp out or do Airbnb. Not many people stay at The Ship. It used to be owned by a couple who were quite antisocial but they sold it to the French couple. They're hoping to turn trade round but they won't find it easy.'

'Oh?' Megan wondered if Carly would tell her more about the pub's reputation, but she changed the subject.

'I'm thinking of stocking crystals in Unravel the Ocean. Surfers can be superstitious – they love all that. What would you recommend?'

'Any quartz is good. But surfers need stones that won't be damaged in the water. As long as you avoid crystals like black tourmaline. And haematite will rust.'

Carly shot her a glance. 'You know your stuff.'

'I make up a surfer balm for chapped lips, and I do one for bruises and rashes from comfrey and calendula. They sell like hotcakes in the summer,' Megan said. 'I've had the shop for ten years.'

'Don't you get bored, stuck in one place?' Carly turned left and headed down an open road. 'I love it here in the summer but by the autumn, I'm ready to head south.'

'Minehead's quiet in the winter,' Megan agreed. 'I must say, heading off towards the sun does sound good.'

'St Mawgen's lovely until September,' Carly said. 'I spend most week days in the shop and I meet loads of people. There are parties on the beach every night. It's not a bad life.'

'Great.' Megan wondered how long it would take her to get tired of surfing and spontaneous parties. It occurred to her that she didn't know what she wanted. 'Do you ever go to The Ship?'

'Not often,' Carly said. 'It pulls in the sea-shanty crowd.'

'I heard them last night. It was lovely.'

'They're mostly locals. I call this place St Ghost's Cove – there's talk about hauntings everywhere. The locals like to tell a lot of old wives' tales.' Carly left the sentence in the air. She turned another corner, the Jimny bouncing downhill over uneven ground. 'You'll love Gunwalloe. It's one of my favourite places to swim.'

Megan wondered whether to mention the blond diver she'd seen on the beach, to find out if he was a local, but Carly switched the radio on and music blared through the speakers. She raised her voice over the sound. 'I just love Weezer, don't you?'

'Definitely.' Megan listened to the jangly guitars and rocking bass lines as Carly drove along a winding road. The sea came in sight, a glorious ribbon of azure beyond the village ahead, and Megan felt her spirits lift.

'We're almost here.' Carly beamed. 'Ready for a dip in the clearest waters in Cornwall?'

'I was born ready,' Megan said. Suddenly, she felt as if she really was on holiday. Thoughts of haunted rooms at the inn and finding her half-sister were distant. Right now, she just wanted to enjoy herself.

They swam in the sea for twenty minutes, came out for a breather and braved the cold waves again for another fifteen. Megan was exhilarated; she wondered why she didn't do this every day. She loved the swimming baths in Minehead, but here in the sea, the experience was thrilling. She ran onto the beach, shivering, her hair dripping.

'Let's get ourselves dry and then we'll hit the town,' Carly suggested.

Megan looked round the little cove. There were a few shops, cafés, bars but it was all very quiet. 'Where do you suggest?'

'Do they have cream teas in Minehead?' Carly asked.

'Yes.'

'I'll treat you to a Cornish one. Lashings of strawberry jam, dollops of Cornish clotted cream.' Carly winked. 'The good thing about sea swimming is that we need the calories. And there's a lovely little teashop that's open on a Sunday that serves cream teas all day.'

Megan was impressed. 'You must've been here so many times.'

'A group of us hang out here during the summer. And, once upon a time, I used to come here with my other half for a swim.' Carly pulled a cynical face. 'I had a relationship that lasted five years. We ran the shop together, but last year I bought him out. I surf solo now.'

'I'm sorry,' Megan said sympathetically. She was about to add that she'd been in a similar situation with Jay, but the hurt still stuck in her throat and stopped her speaking about it.

'Being single's the best way. No one'll break my heart again.' Carly gave Megan a brief hug, an arm wrapped momentarily around her shoulders. It felt good to share the empathy of a kindred spirit.

They reached the doorway of the café, A Slice of Kernow, the sign proclaiming the cream teas to be the best in the world. Megan led the way in and was immediately ushered to a table by a small woman with black-framed glasses, smooth white hair and dimples. She wore a white apron over a black dress. There was no one else in the café apart from an older man with a newspaper sitting by the window, with a teapot, cup and saucer in front of him.

'Are you on holiday?' the waitress asked in a soft Cornish accent, looking at Megan.

'Yes.'

'We're from St Mawgen,' Carly replied, her eyes twinkling.

The woman laughed. 'Not with that accent you're not. I been here all my life. I know Cornish from emmets.'

'I own the surf shop in St Mawgen Cove.' Carly took up the bait.

'You weren't born there, though.' The waitress raised an eyebrow.

'I'm from Winchester,' Carly said. 'I'm a child of the universe.'

'I see.' The waitress was amused. 'And what would a child of the universe want to eat and drink today?'

'Two of the best cream teas in the world, please.' Carly didn't miss a beat.

'And what tea would you like to drink with that?' the waitress asked.

'Earl Grey,' Carly replied.

'Can I have Cornish tea?' Megan asked.

The waitress turned to Carly, her voice dismissive. 'This young lady knows what's what. Proper Cornish tea's the best choice. But I'll bring you a pot of Earl Grey as well. Right.' She turned, speaking as she walked towards the kitchen. 'It'll be with you dreckly.'

Megan met Carly's eyes anxiously. 'Did we upset her?'

'No, not at all.' Carly shook her damp hair. 'She's famous for it. All the surfers come here. She gives them a hard time and they lap it up and give the banter back. A good time's had by all.'

'She's not grumpy, then?'

'No, she loves a joke. Bless her, she has a heart of gold. She pretends to be miserable as sin. And guess what? She's called Joy.' Carly stifled a laugh.

Megan looked around at the simple décor: the wooden floorboards, the chintzy wallpaper and white curtains. She wondered if the owners of the café found it hard to make a living during the winter months too.

There was the sound of feet padding on the wood and Joy was back with a tray. 'Here you are,' she said briskly, placing pots of tea, cream, jam, cups and a cake stand piled with scones. 'The proper job.' She eyed Carly, pretending to be furious. 'You won't get a cream tea like that in Winchester.'

'It looks gorgeous.' Megan reached for a teapot.

'You're not from these parts either,' Joy commented.

'I'm from Somerset. I'm on holiday, staying at The Ship in St Mawgen.'

Joy took a step back. 'The Ship? Whatever made you want to stay there?'

Megan searched for what to say. 'It's old. It has a great atmosphere.'

'Atmosphere? I've never heard it called that before,' Joy said. 'There are ghosts all over St Mawgen. It's haunted by the past. But The Ship's the worst place.'

Megan remembered the noises in the room above and her skin prickled. She shook the thought away. 'I'm not sure I believe it.'

Carly laughed. 'Everywhere's haunted in St Mawgen's Cove. I've heard about a cottage near the beach that won't sell because of its ghosts, and lost souls of drowned sailors moaning on the beach.'

Joy ignored her. 'How long are you stopping?'

'A week, maybe more,' Megan began.

'They've got you in room three, I suppose.'

Megan was astonished. 'How do you know that?' She remembered Tom Hocking had said something similar.

'You haven't left,' Joy said with a telling look.

Carly reached for a scone. 'It's just local gossip.'

'It certainly is not.' Joy folded her arms. 'I went to The Ship once. The atmosphere's like ice. No warmth comes into that place. I know the history. It used to be an old pub and two cottages. Now it's been knocked into one. Everyone in these parts knows what happened there in the sixteen hundreds. It's common knowledge, passed down for generations.'

'What happened?' Megan asked. Her whole body was suddenly cold.

'You ask anyone in the cove about the Drenched Man. Or the Weeping Woman. The place is haunted by them. People will tell you tales that'll make your skin crawl.'

'It's just local myth,' Carly said, spooning jam onto a scone.

'It's no myth. The stories are all connected to that woman who stands on the clifftop, watching.' Joy made a low ominous sound. 'You won't need to ask anybody, though. You'll know soon enough.'

'What happened there?' Megan wasn't sure if she should speak of it. Tom had said something about it.

Carly glanced at Joy. 'You shouldn't scare her.'

'I'm not scaring anybody. I just say it as it is.' Joy's eyes gleamed. 'You can't stay in The Ship and not notice its history. It's always there, in the walls, under the floorboards, wherever you look, you can smell it, the damage that was done, the evil.'

'What evil?' Megan asked, really nervous now. She glanced at Carly for support. Joy's words had really shaken her.

'Witchcraft,' Joy said simply. She picked up the tray and turned to go. 'Enjoy your cream tea.'

16

Katel returned just as Susanna finished preparing the herbs. She burst through the door in a fine mood.

'I'm exhausted, Mother. I've never seen so many fish. But I've been paid well. I might ask for a new frock, a pretty one with brocade, dyed with lavender. We packed many hogsheads of pilchards. The salt cellars and smoking houses are full. I reek of the ocean. Is there any hot water to wash in? The dry salted fish will stay in the fish palace for a month, so there will be work to last the year. We'll eat well. The fumador pilchards are in the smoking houses. Half the village are at work there. You can smell the fish smoking from here. What a catch, though. Yowann Hicks is like a cockerel, strutting round, pleased with himself.' She paused. 'What is it? Why do you look at me so crossly?'

Susanna held out the stitched poppet.

'What's that?' Katel's face was far too innocent.

'You know very well what it is.' Susanna's breath came fast. 'How did you make it? Who showed you?'

'It wasn't me.' Katel opened her eyes wide, protesting her innocence. 'Where did you find it?'

'You know where, Katel. You put it inside the chimney.'

'I've never seen it.'

'It has her hair. And pins in the face.' Susanna lowered her voice. 'Katel, this is dangerous.'

'It wasn't me.' Katel's face was pale. She was lying. Susanna felt her temper rise.

'Did Tedda Lobb give it to you?'

'I tell you, I've never seen it.'

'Katel.' Susanna stepped forward, lifting the poppet above her head. She was shaking with fury. 'You will not lie to me.'

'I know nothing of it.'

'No wonder Beaten is afflicted with a livid pox on her face. Look.' Susanna shook the doll. 'I know you don't like Beaten, Katel, but this is an evil thing.'

Katel took a step back and whispered, 'Tedda showed me how to do it. I thought it was a game. I wanted to see if it would work. Beaten can be spiteful. She's jealous.'

'This is wrong, Katel.' Susanna's eyes glinted. 'And dangerous. Do you know what will happen if people hear of this?'

Katel shook her head. 'It wasn't meant to cause harm. Tedda said…'

Susanna took her daughter by the shoulder firmly. 'Have you not heard of Mother Chattox and Old Demdike? Did I never tell you what happened to them? It was a few years ago, when you were a child. You could have been no more than five years old.'

Katel met her mother's eyes. 'I haven't heard.'

'It was in the north country, a place called Pendle, far away. Old Demdike and Chattox and many other women confessed to selling their souls to the devil. Mother Chattox's daughter created clay figures and they were all arrested and accused of terrible things.'

Katel's mouth was open. 'What became of them?'

'Old Demdike never reached trial; the dank dungeon she was kept in killed her. Many of the eleven accused were widows. Only one was set free.'

'And the others?'

'People spoke bad things about them and they came to a terrible end,' Susanna whispered. 'Once a woman's accused, there are many others prepared to give evidence, even against their own families. You need to take care.'

'But Tedda's kind to me. She tells me to dream of wonderful things.'

'Don't be fooled by pretty words.' Susanna pushed the poppet into her daughter's hand. 'Here. Take this back. Tell Tedda that you will have none of her bad magic.'

'But I can't.' Katel looked at the doll. 'She told me to keep it here.'

'It's dangerous,' Susanna said quietly. 'Many women cure ailments with herbs and stones. But Tedda seeks to do harm.'

'She told me you'd say that.' Katel was suddenly sulky. 'She warned me that you're jealous.'

'Me?'

'Tedda's older than you, wiser. She says she's the best pellar in the cove and you envy her.'

'I do not,' Susanna said, exasperated. 'Katel, go now. Give her back the poppet. Tell her you will not visit her again.'

'No, she told me I couldn't take the magic back.' Katel grasped the doll in her hand. 'Tedda sent the chawk to me. Master Jack tells me that I—'

'Take the poppet back to her.'

'I won't.'

'You'll take it.' Susanna glared. 'Or I'll take you to her house and we'll talk to her together. I won't have you—'

'I won't take it back.'

'You'll do as I say.'

Katel bared her teeth. The poppet was clutched in her fist. She hissed, 'You can't tell me what I should do.' She rushed to the fire and hurled the doll on the flames where it crackled and singed.

Susanna smelled burning hair. She rushed to the hearth and tugged it out, catching her fingers in the flame. She whirled round. 'What have you done?'

'Nothing.' Katel pouted. 'I was afraid.'

Susanna took a step back. Her hand tingled as she clutched the charred doll. Her voice was low with fear. 'Wash yourself, then we'll eat. After that, you'll settle down to sleep. We'll talk of this tomorrow.'

Katel said something beneath her breath and Susanna was sure she'd said that she'd do just as she wished.

For the rest of the evening, her daughter avoided her eyes and neither of them spoke a word, but Susanna brooded. Her mind was full of worries.

* * *

The news came the next day. It was early in the morning, as Susanna placed bread on the table for breakfast and began to slice it. Katel was asleep in front of the fire, her hair tousled, her mouth open. Susanna was about to wake her when there was a loud rapping on the door.

A male voice called urgently, 'Mistress Boram, come quickly. I've much need of your skills.'

Susanna opened the door to see Merryn Gilbert outside, dressed in a pale shirt and breeches. His handsome face was anxious as he pushed a hand through rough curls. 'Susanna, please. There's been an accident.'

'What has befallen your father? Is Hedyn well? Is it the pains in his fingers?'

'It's Beaten. She's hurt. She came back from working at the Hickses' house late last night. She was tired out. This morning she fell into the hearth when she was cooking our breakfast and...'

Susanna knew at once. 'Is she badly burned?'

Merryn stepped inside. His eyes strayed to Katel, who was awake now, stretching like a sleepy cat by the fire. He took a deep breath. 'I fear she is. She's in much pain. Her hands—'

'Wait, I'll fetch what I need and come with you.'

Susanna rushed around the room, collecting ointments and tinctures. 'Here, I have some lady's bedstraw. The ointment helps with burns. And I will bring poultices – plasters, I call them – Beaten will need a soothing salve, and henbane and hemlock to ease the pain.' She lifted her basket. 'I have all I need here. Let's go quickly, Merryn.'

Merryn peered towards Katel again and Susanna noticed her daughter smile in his direction.

Susanna touched his arm urgently. 'Make haste. Your sister needs our help.'

They hurried down the hill towards the fisherman's cottage at the bottom, pausing at a small door with the words Anchor Cottage above it. Susanna could hear Beaten's screams even from outside. Her white-haired father, his fingers twisted by rheumatism, knelt behind her, bathing her face and hands with water.

Susanna took in the scene and was shocked by what she saw. Beaten's palms were livid red, her hands blackened at the back. The burns continued up her arms. Patches of her hair had been singed, the skin beneath raised and blistered. Her face was red and puffed, soot-blackened in places, but beneath it, the flesh had been burned away.

Susanna turned to Merryn quickly. 'Fetch me some wine, if you have it, ale if you don't, in a cup.' She knelt next to Beaten, who was still screaming, sobbing, catching her breath and then groaning. She was trembling, shaking her hands. Susanna grasped her elbow to steady and comfort her and to inspect the hands. She turned to Hedyn.

'Tell me exactly what has befallen her. Did she scald herself or fall in the flames?'

'It happened quickly.' Hedyn was breathing rapidly, in shock. 'One minute, Beaten was stooping over the fire, then she fell headfirst, arms out, into the flames as if she had been pushed.'

'I felt it behind me. Something pushed me,' Beaten sobbed.

'You were tired, Beaten. Yesterday was a long working day.' Susanna applied salve liberally to the girl's hands, taking care not to break the skin. Next, she turned her attention to Beaten's face. Where the acne had been, the skin was peeling and red. Susanna carefully smeared poultice across the weals of scorched skin. 'This will help.'

Merryn was at her elbow, holding a cup. 'Here, a little wine.'

Susanna reached into her basket, bringing out a jar of powder. Carefully, she dropped a sprinkling into the cup and held it to Beaten's mouth. 'Drink this slowly. It will deaden the pain.'

'What will happen now?' Hedyn asked anxiously. 'Will she recover?'

'I'll come back each day and tend her wounds.' Susanna smeared the last of the salve. 'We'll soothe the pain and help the skin grow back.' She turned to Beaten. 'I want you to lie down and rest. The mixture I've given will help you sleep.'

'Who'll make our food?' Hedyn asked. 'We depend on Beaten. I have no wife now.'

'You have neighbours,' Susanna said quickly. 'Poor Beaten must rest and recover. You're to let her stay in her bed. She'll heal best if allowed to rest. I'll dress her burns and keep them clean.'

'Thank you, Susanna,' Hedyn said quickly. 'Beaten's a good girl; she works hard. It pains me to see her this way.'

Beaten sobbed. 'I've no idea what happened. I haven't tumbled before. I felt a hand on my back pressing me into the flames.'

'You must be exhausted,' Susanna said. 'Let me take you up the stairs and put you in your bed.'

Susanna led Beaten up the narrow wooden staircase into the smallest of two bedrooms where a straw mattress lay on the floor. She helped her off with her cap, apron, dress and neckerchief, leaving her shivering in her shift.

Beaten said, 'I grow cold now.'

'It's the shock,' Susanna explained gently. 'Are you drowsy, Beaten?'

'I am.'

'Then let us lay you down and you can sleep. I'll come back later today to see how you fare. And I will bring more salve, and something else for the pain.'

Beaten crumpled onto the mattress, trembling as Susanna covered her with a woollen rug. 'Will I recover?'

'I'll do my best for you.'

'Will I be ugly?' Beaten's lip trembled, and tears fell from her eyes, mixing with the creamy salve. 'My face will be scarred. No one will want me.'

'Shush now,' Susanna soothed. 'Let's make you better.'

Beaten met Susanna's eyes, her own glazing, filled with pain and fear. 'Thank you.'

Susanna touched her hair gently, avoiding the scorched places, the blisters beneath. 'Rest and heal, Beaten. And may God bless you.'

'Amen,' Beaten whispered through dry lips. Her eyelids were drooping, and she was almost asleep.

Susanna tiptoed downstairs to find Hedyn and Merryn waiting for her, both in the same position, standing awkwardly, their faces twisted with anxiety.

'How fares my daughter?' Hedyn asked.

'She'll sleep now,' Susanna said quietly. 'I'll return later.'

'Will Katel come too?' Merryn asked. He was suddenly embarrassed. 'I mean, will she assist you?'

'I don't know.' Susanna thought of her conversation with Katel the previous evening, of their argument. She had much more she needed to say to her daughter now. 'We'll see.'

'Will my sister be well?'

Susanna gave him an encouraging look. 'Pray God.' She turned to Hedyn. 'I must go.'

'I'll pay you when you return,' Hedyn said. 'Susanna, Beaten said she was pushed.'

'How can that be?' Susanna felt her heartbeat quicken. 'It's not possible.'

'Yet.' Hedyn frowned. 'I was watching my daughter as she prepared the food over the fireplace, and when she fell it was indeed as if an unseen hand had forced her forwards.'

'You imagined it,' Susanna began.

'I saw her fall, I swear it.' Hedyn looked afraid. 'It was for all the world like the hand of the devil shoved her into the flames.'

17

Megan stood in her room, listening, but everywhere was silent. It was almost seven o'clock. There was no sound from above; the upstairs room was empty and she was the only resident in the hotel now. She was thinking about what Joy had said in the café about the other three rooms being haunted. As Joy had taken their empty plates away, she'd been chirpier, but she'd reminded Megan that she was staying in the only 'safe' room. The other three had bad reputations. The inn's accommodation had been two cottages once upon a time. The upstairs bedroom in the middle cottage and both rooms in the end one were the site of some terrible tragedy. Joy had said the rooms were – what word did she use? – *chilling*.

Megan understood the meaning of the word. She felt cold now. Julien had said the heating wasn't very good, but this was a different type of cold. It was bone-achingly cold. The ice cold of fear.

She decided to ask Julien if he knew about the inn's reputation. She wondered if, later tonight, there might be more sounds coming from the room overhead. As she gazed up towards the ceiling, the thought made her tremble.

No, she needed to get a grip. She wanted to sleep well. There was no way she'd be late for the early morning surf again. She told herself that room three was fine, that she didn't really believe in ghosts anyway.

Certainly, Carly didn't. She lived in the small flat above the surf shop that had been an old cottage dating back hundreds of years, and she'd said jokingly, as she'd driven back to the cove, that she'd never heard any moaning sailors on the beach when she went surfing and if she did, she'd tell them where to get off. Megan believed she was made of the same strong stuff. She'd come on holiday alone: she was doing fine. No, she wouldn't worry about superstition. St Mawgen Cove probably thrived on ghost stories, tales of pirates and smuggling and romance, just like in the sea shanties. It was simply a local superstition.

She showered and changed, shivering worse than before in the cold room, pulling on a warm top, and jeans, then she rinsed out her swimming gear, hanging it over the shower rail to dry. Claude was cooking *moules* tonight and she was suddenly determined to have a nice evening and sleep like a log after all the sea air.

A small table near the bar had been prepared for her. The inn was empty apart from a grey-bearded man drinking from a pewter jug in the corner. Megan studied him and wondered if he was a ghost, he was sitting so still. What did Joy call one of the ghosts? The Drenched Man. She imagined what his story might be. And Joy had mentioned the Weeping Woman. Megan wondered if their lives were connected.

Julien interrupted her thoughts as he appeared with a glass of Chablis. 'Your first drink is on the house. I promised.'

'You've no idea how much I've been looking forward to this.'

'Busy day?' Julien asked.

'Oh, yes. I went swimming at Gunwalloe, then I had a cream tea in a lovely café called A Slice of Kernow.' Megan wondered whether to tell him about what Joy had said. She'd leave it until later. Instead, she said, 'I'm looking forward to dinner.'

'Claude says the *moules* are fresh.'

'Great.' Megan peered into the bar. 'Where are the musicians?'

'Sunday night can be quiet,' Julien explained. 'They don't come in every night.'

Megan was disappointed. 'I hope I see them again before I go.'

'There will be singers in during the week, I'm sure,' Julien said. 'The locals seem to need to sing about their history.'

'Oh?' Megan took the opportunity. 'Tell me about the history.'

'Well,' Julien said, 'apparently, the cellar was used for storing smuggled goods in past times. And when I'm down there sometimes, changing the barrels, I can smell fish, and something else, like a burned smell. They say direst deeds were done here. Contraband.'

'So there were smugglers?'

'Yes, the locals like to sing about smugglers and shipwrecks.'

'I bet.'

'There was even a witch in the village hundreds of years ago.'

Megan leaned forward, interested. 'What happened to her?'

Julien didn't know. 'I expect she came to a sticky end. Witches usually do.'

'Did you know this place had a reputation before you came?' Megan asked.

'No.' Julien seemed sad. 'We bought it because it was so beautiful. We're romantics. The previous owners were not doing good business. Of course, we got a bargain price and we didn't think to ask why. I was sure that when people tried Claude's cooking, everyone would want to eat here. The Ship would become special.'

'And it will,' Megan said chirpily. 'I'm sure no one believes tales about witches and suchlike.'

'Apparently it's all true.' Julien frowned. 'The local people pass the stories down in their songs. St Mawgen's full of superstition. It's a shame.'

'Why's that?'

'It doesn't help tourism.' Julien paused. 'Stories of men being kissed by witches and dropping dead is enough to put anyone off. But never mind.' He forced himself to stand taller. 'I'll fetch your *moules*.'

* * *

Susanna stood on the beach, looking for the pebbles she needed. She'd been busy for half an hour, sifting misshapen stones: she needed to collect eleven with natural holes, to thread them on cord and hang them inside the chimney. Already, she'd found seven. Bending down, picking up a small brown mineral stone with a gap through the middle, she dropped it into her basket. Straightening slowly, she glanced up towards the cove, where the fishermen were busy with the boats. Merryn Gilbert would be there. She felt an immediate jolt when she thought of Beaten, and a sinking anxiety. The story of unseen hands shoving her into the fire would reach the cove gossips. It wouldn't be long before someone was blamed.

Then there was the matter of the burned poppet that still lay on her table. It had been charmed, and Susanna had no idea how to dispose of it without doing harm to Beaten. She wondered if she could clean it, wrap it in cotton and keep it somewhere safe.

She picked up another stone, rounder than the others and with a perfect hole. Two more and she would have enough to make a hag-stone charm that would keep witches away. Tedda had bewitched her daughter. Perhaps she had spoken to Katel when she was asleep, whispered magic in her ear, or she'd flown down the chimney in the shape of a jackdaw, telling imaginary stories to enchant her.

Katel was at risk from Tedda's bad magic. The hag-stones had protective powers. They would protect Katel against Tedda.

Susanna bent down again for another stone, rough, with a slight sheen to it. She needed one more. There it was, within her reach. She stretched out an arm.

'Susanna.' A rough voice behind her made her stop, turning in alarm. She knew his tone, his smell. His presence troubled her before she saw his face.

'Yowann.'

'*Durdatha whye!*' He greeted her, handsome in dark breeches and a crisp white shirt. His brow was lined now and there were grey streaks in his fair hair, but he was still a striking man, and he knew the power he had over women. It was evident in the arrogance of his stride, the easy way he moved towards her. 'What are you doing on the beach?'

Susanna met his eyes, determined to hide her real intention. 'I'm looking for pretty stones to make a little border for my herb garden.'

Yowann was watching her intently. 'It's cold. Allow me to escort you home.'

'No, thank you,' Susanna said firmly. She gazed towards the harbour where the fishermen were mending nets. 'Yesterday was a good haul.'

'The best ever,' Yowann said. 'Last night friends sat at my table and drank brandy until the early hours.'

'Indeed.' Susanna knew the local men Yowann was referring to. They were surly, secretive men, many of them merchants from nearby villages who helped him wreck local ships by drawing them to shore with lights. When the ships ran aground, they stole the best of the cargo and hid it in The Ship Inn. She turned her face away. 'And does Eliza like the merry company you keep?'

'Eliza was sent to her bed,' Yowann said quickly. 'It matters not to her what company I keep.' He grabbed her arm. 'Eliza's no wife to me. She complains of aches and pains. And she's lazy. Not such a woman as you are, Susanna.'

Susanna stared at his hand on her arm. He let it drop. She turned her gaze to his face. 'I must go home.'

'I'll come with you,' Yowann said, his tone mock-gallant. 'We'll walk.'

'You misunderstand my meaning,' Susanna began, but he pulled her to him.

'You're often alone in your house. Do you not think my company would be pleasant? We could while away the lonely hours.'

'I'm not lonely.' Susanna glared at him, but she could not help the way her heart pounded. She felt her resolve weakening. She tried to replace soft feelings with anger. 'You should go home and give Eliza good cheer.'

He held her tighter. 'Are you not afraid of me, Susanna? A word from me and you could be cast onto the streets. Katel too.'

'No, I'm not afraid.' Susanna didn't move; she stared at him. 'You're a powerful man, Yowann Hicks, but there's a greater power in the air and the sea than you dream of.'

She saw him flinch. 'Do you mean witchcraft? I hear women can do strange things with their wortcunning—'

'I mean God.' Susanna's voice was quiet. 'I fear no man.'

'Susanna.' She noticed his face change. 'You know how I feel for you. I've always felt this way.' He pulled her against him. His breath was warm against her neck, and she felt her legs buckle.

'Let me go.'

He was fierce with sudden passion. 'I get whatever I want.'

She met his eyes again, her own filled with disdain. 'Not everything.'

'I own your house. St Mawgen Cove belongs to me.'

'I'm not your possession.' Susanna didn't move. 'You're full of self-importance, Yowann. I care nothing for that.'

'But I care for you.'

'You have a wife.'

'You cared for me once. You can't deny it.'

She took a deep breath to steady herself. She would not allow him to see the effect he had on her. 'I was mistaken. I saw the real person you are. Money is all that matters to you.'

'That's not true. If you gave me one chance.' Yowann pressed his lips against hers before muttering, 'You and I could have the world at our feet.'

'Go home to Eliza.' Susanna lingered in his embrace a moment too long, then she tugged away. Being out of his grasp meant she could think more clearly. 'Pay attention to your wife.'

Yowann stepped back as if he had been slapped. 'You'll regret refusing me.'

'I think I will not.' Susanna turned to go, stooping to pick up the final stone. She put it in her basket.

'Is it Colan Stephens who still stirs your heart? I can have him thrown out of The Ship in an instant.'

'Good day to you,' Susanna said, walking away.

'You've no idea of the power I wield,' Yowann called after her, but she continued to walk. 'I'll have my way, mark my words. You'll see...'

Susanna stared ahead, clambering from the beach, up the hill towards her cottage.

Yowann Hicks could go to hell. She'd loved him once, his closeness had always been intoxicating, and she had struggled to control her feelings for him. He had a power over her like no other man. But she knew him for who he was: arrogant, selfish. All that mattered to him was money.

Her mind was on the stones in her basket. Tied with cord and placed in the chimney, they'd keep Tedda Lobb at bay. Now she needed to speak to Katel, to talk sense to her. It was important that her daughter understood the grip Tedda had on her and that, if allowed, she would squeeze her until she was completely in her power.

Susanna would not allow it to happen.

18

Megan woke at five thirty to the buzzing of her phone alarm. She stared into darkness: she'd slept throughout the night without disturbance. Feeling pleased with herself, she switched on a light, stretched her limbs and struggled out of bed, reaching for a swimsuit, a warm jumper, jeans, shoving her wetsuit into a bag. The waves called to her, and with luck, the surf would be up.

She drove down to the cove in the dim light and parked next to the yellow Jimny where Carly was waiting, music blaring. She leaped out, pushing back her blond fringe, wide awake. 'You made it then?'

Megan was wriggling into her wetsuit. 'I wasn't going to miss out again.'

'The surf's looking good.' Carly whooped with excitement. 'Let's dive in.'

They hurried down to the beach, boards under their arms, and gazed at the ocean. Megan was aware of that familiar tingle that seemed to shudder throughout her body: she hadn't felt it in ages. Standing next to Carly, studying the swell of the waves in the distance, hearing the roar, she was reminded of the times she'd been in the water with Jay, the way the adrenalin rushed as the waves rose around her. Jay had been a good surfing buddy. At the beginning, he was more confident and skilful – he'd surfed all his life – but she'd been a quick learner and a better scuba diver. Now, standing by the seashore, her heart was pumping and she couldn't wait to be part of the waves. She turned to Carly, who was breathing deeply, her mouth open, and was sure she was thinking the same thing.

Megan said, 'Let's get in there.'

Moments later they were in the water on their boards, paddling long and slow, cranking it to second gear after a couple of strokes, then giving it all they had until they were right at the crest of the wave.

Megan felt the exhilarating speed, the wind in her face, the energy of the ocean beneath her feet through the surfboard as she skimmed along. She shifted her weight slightly and the board reacted, changing direction. Her heart thumped. The surfboard glided as Megan watched a wall of water stretch out in front of her, an ever-changing track that caused her to accelerate, although she was conscious that at any time it could send her plummeting to the sea bottom. The rumble of the water, the blinding colours, the taste of salt made her senses tingle. Her legs absorbed the sudden drop from height, then she felt the instant speed and made a lightning reaction to harness the energy for a high-g bottom turn.

The connection with the ocean was magical, challenging, an immediate and thrilling sensory overload. The wave rose before her and Megan began to accelerate down the face of it, like dropping down a giant vertical ramp at a skatepark.

Now!

She was riding the surf. Wind and spray buffeted her and she concentrated hard. The smallest change in weight or balance would quickly shoot her up or down the face of the wave. Everything was spraying white foam, splashing, a deafening crashing, then the sound blurred out into nothingness, a white noise of peace. Megan felt cleansed: her breathing was calm, she was alive, conscious of the moment, strong and surrounded by clear water.

Another surfer was in the corner of her vision, emerging from the same wave, and Megan glanced to one side. It wasn't Carly: she was behind, and the surfer close to her had different blond hair. She was aware of him leaning confidently into the rising arc of water, hovering forward like a sea sprite. Then he was gone, and the surf was rising again.

Later, as they paddled back to shore, Megan turned to Carly. 'That was amazing. Just the best thing I've done in ages. I'm coming back tomorrow for more.'

'Apart from the end. Did you see me fall off?' Carly asked.

'No. What happened?'

'I was watching the other surfer share your wave. My concentration went for a moment and that was it for me, the surf spat me out and then – wipeout.'

'I did see someone.' They had almost reached the shore and Megan looked about. 'He didn't hang around to say hi. Unless he's still in the water.'

'I've seen him before a few times. He's local. He's often diving, looking for old stuff.'

'Oh?' Megan remembered she'd seen a blond man before, scuba diving, standing on the beach taking off his wetsuit.

'He came here last spring, or the beginning of the summer. He lives in one of the cottages just up the road, Surf's Up!' Carly said. 'He comes into Unravel the Ocean to buy surfing stuff. I've spoken to him a few times. He knows what he's talking about. I think he's professional.'

'A professional surfer?'

Carly shook her head, droplets of water flying everywhere. 'Diver, I think. He has something to do with the university.' She shivered. 'Let's get back to the car, grab a towel.'

'I'd forgotten how good that felt,' Megan said as they hurried across the beach. 'It's been far too long.'

'Are we talking about surfing or surfers?' Carly gave her a knowing look.

'Surfing. I've missed it,' Megan said. 'The ocean's full of minerals and salts – magnesium, calcium and potassium – beneficial in so many ways.' She gave a laugh. 'That's more than I can say for men.'

They had reached the cars. Carly winked. 'Let's go back to mine, shall we, and you can grab a shower? I'll get us a hot drink – you'll still be back to the inn in time for breakfast – and you can tell me all about the man who broke your heart.'

* * *

Katel sat by the fire that evening, her face streaked with tears. A sob lifted like a hiccup in her chest, then another. 'I'm truly sorry.'

'I'm glad to hear it.' Susanna pressed her lips together, trying to be firm. 'When I called in on Beaten this afternoon, she was still in pain. Her hands will heal but her face will be scarred and I doubt that her hair will grow back.'

'And it's all because of the poppet Tedda gave me?'

'We can never speak of this,' Susanna whispered. 'There are plenty of pickthanks in the village who'll tell tales to gain favour. Your name mustn't ever be associated with Tedda's.'

'Yet she talks to others as if I'm her own child.' Katel looked afraid. 'I'll go to Beaten with you this evening, Mother. I'll make a friend of her and console her. But I can never make amends.'

Susanna stared into the fire. 'Beaten has paid a high price for your association with Tedda.'

'And what of the doll?' Katel was suddenly alarmed. 'We must bury it, or hide it.'

'Leave it with me. We may harm poor Beaten if we make a wrong choice.'

'I discovered that to her cost, and I'm sorry.' Katel wiped her face. 'What shall I do now? I'm afraid.'

'You could learn from me, discover the healing properties of simples, herbs and stones. You could become a pellar. It pays well.'

'Yowann pays me well too. And he likes me. The fishermen like me, and I enjoy spending time there. The work's hard but the company is pleasant.'

'You're young. I can understand you wanting to keep company with others. But Tedda has you in her sights. You're not safe.'

'I won't be in the cove for long. The chawk said my prince will come across the water, and then I'll be with him.'

Susanna sighed. 'Tedda told you that?'

'The chawk.'

'I fear Tedda assumes the shape of Master Jack to whisper these things to you.' Susanna could see the disappointment in Katel's face.

Katel shook her head determinedly. 'No, it's true what the chawk says. I believe it.'

'Do not, Katel. Tedda seeks to harm you.'

'But why?'

'Who knows, child? I suspect she wants you as one of her own. The ways of evil people are strange.'

'Perhaps if I married Merryn, I'd be Beaten's sister. I could live a good life, make amends.' The tears came again and Katel wiped her face with her hand. 'But I've set my heart upon the prince who speaks in a strange tongue. In my soul, I already love him.'

'It's Tedda's way. Her spells will ensnare you.' Susanna reached out and wrapped Katel in her arms, touching her cheek tenderly with her fingers, a gesture she had used since Katel was a baby. 'Heed my words. Tedda speaks nothing but lies and enchantment. Don't trust her.'

'I'm so confused. But I'll do as you say.' Katel laid her head against Susanna's shoulder and a sigh shuddered from her. 'Mother, I'll try my best.'

* * *

It was almost nine o'clock when Megan parked the Beetle in The Ship car park and hurried to her room to drop off her wetsuit. She was starving after the exhilaration of dawn surfing, and she couldn't wait to return tomorrow. Before she went to the dining room for one of Claude's special breakfast treats, there was just enough time to message Amy, to phone her parents, although she didn't want to mention Emma to her father. She had nothing to report, not yet.

Instead she'd tell them about surfing, how she'd made a friend from the surf shop. She'd spent an hour at Carly's, talking about their exes. Carly was adamant that her last relationship had put her off for life. She was independent now and that was how she intended to stay. Bernie, her ex, had been Australian, from Perth. Although they'd stayed together for five years, it had been nothing but arguments. Megan had listened sympathetically. She'd had no opportunity to mention anything about Jay except for his name and the fact that he'd been a good surfer.

As she pushed the key into the lock, the door opposite, to the other ground-floor bedroom, opened and a woman came out. She was silver-haired, smartly dressed and she was carrying a neat handbag. She glanced at Megan and smiled. 'Hello.'

'Hi. I'm in room three,' Megan said. 'How long are you staying?'

'A couple of days, for a reunion,' the woman explained. 'I'm meeting old friends in Penzance. St Mawgen's lovely.'

'It is,' Megan agreed.

'Have you been here long?' the woman asked.

'Since Friday,' Megan explained. 'I've been surfing this morning. Up at dawn.'

'How wonderful,' the woman said. 'It must be so nice to be sporty. In my youth I used to play tennis, but now I take things slowly. I'm a widow.'

'Oh?' Megan realised that the woman wanted to talk.

'Tim and I went everywhere together. He loved travelling and we both adored the English countryside. He died five years ago. I mean, he wasn't even sixty.' The woman's eyes were misty. 'It's so unfair.'

'I'm sorry,' Megan said.

The woman seemed to notice her properly. 'Are you on your own?'

'Yes.'

'It must be lonely, by yourself,' the woman said, her face sympathetic. 'At least I'm meeting friends.'

'Oh, you always meet people surfing.' Megan smiled. 'Will you be here for dinner tonight?'

'I don't think I'll be back until late,' the woman said. 'My friends and I are having the whole works today.'

'I hope you enjoy it,' Megan said.

'I will,' the woman said as she bustled away.

Megan pushed the door to her room and was about to step inside. She glanced back over her shoulder to the white door opposite, room number one, staring at it ominously, feeling anxious.

Joy in the teashop had said the accommodation had once been an old inn and two cottages. She'd mentioned that the locals believed there were two ghosts, the Drenched Man and the Weeping Woman.

Megan tried to remember if she'd said which one of them visited room number one.

19

It was not yet dusk. Susanna left Katel washing the dishes with hot water and lye soap. She would use the last of the water later to wash herself, using the liquor of rosemary water, nettles, mint and thyme on her hair. Often, as she was drying it, she'd rub in a little bacon fat mixed with liquorice root to make it shine.

'I'll be back soon,' Susanna called, wrapping herself in her shawl, hiding a small bottle beneath it, in her hand. 'Then you and I will call on Beaten and see how she fares.'

Katel said something in response, but she was absorbed with her work. Susanna slipped outside, hurrying past Samuel and Anne's cottage, where the baby could be heard crying. Bartholomew was hungry; Susanna knew the high-pitched sound well. She uttered a prayer for the family and hurried into The Ship.

The inn was full, smoky, dark beneath low beams. Many men were huddled at tables, their heads close, cups of ale or wine in their hands. There were low voices, muffled chuckles. Susanna squeezed past a table where a group of men leaned over a piece of paper. She noticed the rough drawing of a map, a large X marking a spot. Somebody whispered a strange word – *Bonaventure*. A hand reached out and grasped her wrist and she heard Yowann's voice, raised in greeting.

'Susanna, we don't see you here often. Come and sit awhile.'

There was a chorus of laughter, a rumble of agreement, an expletive. Susanna tugged her arm away.

'I'm here on business, Yowann.'

She heard a low comment from one of the men and ignored it. Yowann's eyes sparkled. 'When your business is finished, come back to me. I may have something for you.'

A man guffawed. 'And he keeps it warm in his breeches.'

Another growled, 'Yowann'll pay ye handsomely for it.'

'Leave her,' Yowann commanded. 'Susanna,' he spoke courteously. 'I meant you no harm. I apologise for these ruffians. They've no knowledge of how to treat a lady.'

'Lady?' one of the men said sarcastically beneath his breath. 'She has a child with no father.'

'I pray you, come and see me when you have more time,' Yowann said politely.

Susanna said something that she hoped was neither yes nor no, and hurried on. Colan Stephens was behind the bar, lifting a barrel. He paused and met her eyes.

'Susanna.'

'Good evening to you, Colan. I'm here to see Joan.'

'She's out back, baking.'

'Thank you.' Susanna decided it would not help to talk to him more. She pushed past him and into the kitchen, where a fire was blazing. Joan, in cap and apron, her kerchief loosened, was lifting her tray from the hearth. She turned suddenly, placing the crousts on the table. Susanna examined her face for emotion and found none there.

'I've brought something for you,' Susanna whispered.

Joan rushed over. 'Does Colan know you are here?'

'I passed him,' Susanna said quietly. 'You can tell him I brought some lavender ointment. Here.'

Joan took the small bottle, her face disappointed. 'Thank you. That's kind, and my skin will feel the benefit. But I'd hoped for—'

'Shush. Take this too.' Susanna slipped a second bottle into her hands.

'Mix this with a little ale and drink it each morning. It'll help you to get with child.'

'Thank you.' Joan's face glowed with relief and gratitude. 'What is it?'

'Chaste tree and red clover. Taken each day, it will work. As long as you and Colan do the rest.'

'I'll do my best.' Joan tucked the small ceramic bottles into her apron. 'He must never know.'

'He won't hear it from me.'

Joan took a step backwards. 'He loves you still, Susanna. He can't deny it.'

'I'm sorry for it.' Susanna was genuinely sad. 'My mother would have bid you make him a love cake. That was how she won my father.'

'How do I do that?' Joan was immediately serious.

'A woman bakes a cake naked for the man she desires to love her and rubs sweat from her body into the dough. When the man eats it, he will become hers entirely.'

'Have you ever made one?'

'No, in truth.'

'And you've never taken a potion to get with child?'

'No, but when I discovered that I was, I considered swallowing a tincture of savin and bay leaf, to start my monthly bleeding. But I didn't have the heart to do it. And now I'm glad.'

Joan was staring at her. 'You've never had need of a love cake or a charm to make a man love you. You're still fair.'

'As are you.' Susanna took Joan's hands in hers. 'And sweet and kind. Any man would easily love you.'

'Except for my husband, who gave his heart to his childhood sweetheart long ago.' Joan's face was filled with sadness. 'You know it's true.'

'Pray God a child will do the trick. Colan's a big-hearted man. He would love his children and you too, for bringing them into the world.'

'It's the only chance I have,' Joan said.

There was silence for a while, both women lost in their thoughts, then Susanna said, 'I must go to see Beaten. She needs help with the pains in her hands.'

'I heard she fell into the fire,' Joan said. 'The men in the pub were talking with Hedyn Gilbert. He was telling everyone that she was pushed.'

'That cannot be,' Susanna said, suddenly afraid.

Joan's eyes were wide with horror. 'Hedyn thinks she was cursed. It was the hand of the devil that shoved her into the flames. Everyone in the cove is talking of it.'

'Such tittle-tattle is dangerous,' Susanna said quickly. 'I'll go to make her better. Your crousts will get cold if we tarry, and the men at the tables are hungry.'

'They are.' Joan lifted a tray. 'The work of an innkeeper's wife is never done.'

'Then I'll leave you to do it,' Susanna said.

'Here.' Joan handed several crousts to Susanna. 'These are for Beaten and her family. I hope they'll bring them strength.' She gave her a jug of ale. 'Take this too.'

'Thank you. And I wish you luck with the potion. Let me know when your menses cease. Perhaps soon, the inn will have a lusty new pair of lungs to keep you busy.'

'I hope it may come to pass,' Joan said. Susanna turned quickly and rushed back through the inn, where the smoke was dense and the guttural conversations whispered were about ships being lured aground and plunder for the taking.

Half an hour later, as the sun sank behind the horizon, spattering the sea dark orange, Susanna and Katel walked down the hill towards Anchor Cottage, carrying a basket.

Katel tucked an arm nervously through her mother's. 'I'm afraid that Beaten won't speak to me. What if she knows about the poppet?'

'She won't know, Katel, and you must say nothing. We go to her to heal her wounds and to help her bear the pain of it, that's all.'

'But my heart's heavy.' Katel's small face creased with anxiety. 'I'm filled with sorrow.'

'Then you must stop thinking of yourself and think only of Beaten.' They had reached the little fisherman's cottage and Susanna knocked gently. 'I have salve in my basket for her burns. You can help me smear it on her hands and bind them against infection.'

'Is her face very burned?' Katel whispered quickly. 'Will I find it hard to look on her without crying out that it was all my fault?'

'Shh, child,' Susanna said quickly. The door opened. Merryn Gilbert filled the space, his eyes lingering on Katel. 'I thank you for coming, Susanna. My poor sister has need of you.'

Susanna stepped inside. Hedyn Gilbert was sitting close to the fire, rubbing his twisted fingers to warm them. He nodded in greeting. 'Susanna.'

'Beaten cries all the time,' Merryn explained.

'With pain?' Katel's voice was hushed.

Merryn shook his head. 'With sorrow. And I can't get her to eat.'

'Joan Stephens sent you these, with her good wishes.' Susanna lifted her basket, taking out the pottery jug of ale and the crousts filled with beef and swede, placing them on the table. She dug deeper into the basket, bringing out a plate covered with cloth. 'And I've brought bread for you, and a baked fish.'

'We haven't yet eaten,' Merryn said. 'We're used to Beaten making our food.'

'Then fill your bellies now and take some to Beaten when Katel and I have finished. Is she awake?'

'She can't sleep,' Merryn said.

'She groans and cries and calls upon her mother, who has been dead these ten years,' Hedyn said, gazing into the flames. 'I fear her spirit is heavy.'

'Let's go up to her, Katel.'

Susanna led the way to the narrow staircase. In the dim bedroom, Beaten was huddled on the bed, swathed in a woollen rag. As she approached, Susanna could see that she was shivering. She laid a gentle hand on her shoulder. 'Beaten, you're cold.'

Beaten rolled over. Her face was swollen and blotched, white blisters forming on the livid red burns. Susanna heard Katel catch her breath. She reached for the salve and began to apply it to Beaten's charred skin with the lightest touches of her fingers. Beaten flinched, whispering through dry lips, 'I shiver all day. My teeth chatter. And the pain's so bad that I wish I was dead. I wish my mother would come from heaven and take me.'

'Shush,' Susanna soothed. 'Today's the worst day. Tomorrow will be better. And the day after that, better again. The salve will cool the heat in your skin and help it to heal well.'

Beaten eased herself up in bed. Her hair was singed and stuck up in raw tufts; her face was swollen and misshapen. Susanna felt Katel stiffen in fear. She said, 'Apply the salve to her hands with the lightest touch.'

Katel sprang into action. 'I'm here, Beaten. I'm sorry for what has befallen you, but I promise I'll come every day.'

Beaten's voice was choked in her throat. 'Why would you do that, Katel?' Her eyes filled with tears. 'Have you come to gloat? You're beautiful, and I'm ugly. My skin will never be smooth.'

'I wish I could help.' Katel applied more cream. 'But if it cheers you, I'll come after work each day and tell you what's happened in the harbour.'

'Merryn could tell me, but he talks of nothing but you,' Beaten said bitterly. 'And now my hands are damaged, I won't be able to work and we'll have less money. My father's not quick now. His bones are full of aches. Merryn must bring in food for us all but I know he seeks to marry. He has someone he holds dear in his heart, who he'll ask to be his wife.' Beaten glanced from Katel to Susanna. 'And I'll become a burden.'

'Don't think it. You must get well. Drink this.' Susanna placed a cup to her lips, ale mixed with powdered herbs. 'It'll help you sleep. The pain will go, and tomorrow Katel and I will return. There's food downstairs. Katel, hurry down and bring a croust for Beaten, and some milk, if there is any.'

'I pray you, do not.' Beaten swallowed the ale and Susanna took the cup away. 'I want to sleep. It's too painful to be awake. My hands burn as if they're in the flames even now.'

'Then sleep,' Susanna soothed. 'You can eat tomorrow. Katel will call in before she goes to work and she'll bring you milk and cheese, a little fish.'

'Merryn will be glad to see her.' Beaten's eyes began to close. 'For my part, I hope that when the sun wakes tomorrow, I won't wake with it.'

'It's the pain that tortures you,' Susanna said. 'Soon, as you heal, things will become easier.'

'Heal?' Beaten's eyes glittered. 'How will I heal? To be a hideous monster, with a face that makes men turn away and children laugh?' She lay back on the pillow. Katel had found another woollen rug and Susanna tucked Beaten in.

Beaten groaned with pain. 'I'd be better dead.' Then her eyelids became heavy and she drifted off to sleep.

'Poor Beaten. It's worse than I imagined.' Katel grasped Susanna's arm, her face in shadow. 'Will she recover?'

Susanna led her to the top of the stairs and spoke as quietly as possible. 'The salve will help, but the skin will scar.' She shook her head. 'You must be her friend, Katel. Beaten's spirits are low.'

'I promise I will,' Katel said earnestly. She followed Susanna downstairs.

Hedyn was sitting by the fire, a mug of ale cupped in his hands. Merryn lit a tallow candle and placed it in the wooden box on the wall. Susanna moved to the table and began to cut bread, placing it next to a plate of cheese, the baked fish, a pottery jug of ale and the crousts Joan had sent. 'Now you can eat.'

'I'm hungry,' Hedyn admitted. 'I hadn't noticed how my belly growled. My thoughts are with poor Beaten.'

'How is she?' Merryn asked.

'Will her hands always be as they are?' Hedyn said anxiously.

'I'll do what I can,' Susanna promised.

Hedyn handed her a coin. 'I pray to God and give you thanks for your trouble.'

'Don't pay me today.' Susanna placed the coin on the table. 'It'll be soon enough when Beaten's back at work.'

'And if she can't work again?' Hedyn asked.

'Then keep your coins,' Susanna said. 'Come, Katel. It grows late and we must be up with the sun.' She moved to the door.

Merryn grasped Katel's hand, bringing it to his lips. 'Good night, Katel. Thank you for tending to my sister.'

Susanna noticed Katel's flirtatious expression as she dipped a curtsy before they stepped outside into the darkness.

Susanna asked, 'Do you love him, Katel?'

'You know I don't, Mother,' Katel said. 'I like how he looks at me. He thinks me the most beautiful creature and I like how that feels.'

'He wishes to marry you.'

'I will say nay,' Katel replied. 'The chawk tells me—'

'Don't speak of the chawk. I don't believe it, and nor should you,' Susanna said. 'Merryn's a good man. The Gilberts are a proper family. They've lived in the cove for years. You could do worse.'

'I don't care,' Katel said, swirling her skirts. 'My heart's already lost to a man I'll meet soon.'

'Katel, this is foolish.' Susanna took her arm. Then she froze. The smell of tobacco wafted through the air and she gazed towards the harbour. In the moonlight, she could see a figure standing, immobile, on the clifftop, overlooking the harbour.

'Who can that be?'

Susanna narrowed her eyes against the breeze that blew in from the sea and stared towards the ocean. On top of the cliff, a woman leaned forwards, a dark shadow, her arms out, as if trying to command the waves. The moon glinted on the water and the small figure turned, holding out a hand, pointing towards Susanna and Katel as the wind blew through her clothes.

A soft laugh lifted on the air and Susanna stared into the darkness towards the figure on the clifftop.

It was Tedda Lobb.

20

Megan was deep in sleep when she heard the piercing scream. She opened her eyes and sat up in the darkness. Her phone showed that it was past four o'clock. There it came again, a shriek splitting the silence, and seconds later, someone was thumping at her door. A voice yelled, 'Let me in, please.'

Megan leaped up and pulled on a dressing gown against the cold air. She flicked the light switch and opened the door. The light in the hall was bright; the woman whom she'd met yesterday was hugging herself in pyjamas, shivering.

'Are you all right?' Megan asked.

'No – no, I'm not. C-can I come in?' The woman was already in Megan's room. She gazed around anxiously, as if someone else might be there. Then she sat on the end of the bed, her arms wrapped tightly around her chest. 'I can't go back in that room.'

Megan frowned: she'd just woken up and nothing made any sense yet. 'What's happened?'

'There's someone in there.'

'What?' Megan wondered if it was a burglar, or someone had made a mistake and wandered in. 'Who?'

'I don't know.' The woman whispered, 'Something – eerie.'

Megan decided to give the woman time to calm down. She went over to the window where there were complimentary teabags, sachets of coffee and her box of herbal tea. 'Can I make you a drink?'

The woman didn't reply. She looked around again, as if she expected something terrifying to be lurking in the corner. Megan filled the kettle anyway and placed a teabag into a mug. Then she moved back to the bed, sitting next to the woman who was still in a state of shock. The best way forward was to be friendly and sympathetic, although Megan had to admit, she felt a little rattled by the woman's dramatic entrance. A few minutes ago, she'd been deeply asleep. 'So what happened? I'm Megan, by the way.'

'Theresa.' The woman hunched her shoulders. 'I'm not going back in there. I swear – it's horrible.'

'What is?' Megan kept her voice low. She was awake enough now to realise what had happened. Up until now she hadn't completely believed the rumours about hauntings, not seriously. She recalled the bumping she'd heard from the room overhead two nights ago and as she looked at the terrified woman now, the rumours were starting to feel real. 'What did you see?'

'I was asleep. I woke up all of a sudden,' Theresa said. 'As if someone had touched me. I felt cold fingers on my face. I could hear it, just inches from the bed.'

'Hear what?'

'Breathing. The sound of someone – in there.'

Megan had to ask. 'Are you sure? I mean, it wasn't your imagination?'

'No, it wasn't,' Theresa snapped. 'I knew they were there. Then I saw it.'

'Saw what?'

'A shape by the wall, crouching down. The face was turned away. But it was a woman, I'm sure.'

'You weren't dreaming?' Megan couldn't help fear rising in her chest.

'She was there, just like you are. I could see her: a pale figure, her head in her hands.'

Megan shivered. She got up, poured hot water into the mug and handed it to Theresa. 'Can you drink that? It'll steady your nerves. Then maybe we can go into your room together and check.'

'No.' Theresa gasped.

'We'll both go,' Megan said, but the thought terrified her. 'We'll put all the lights on and just look round, check that everything's fine.'

'I can't sleep in there,' Theresa insisted. 'Nothing will persuade me.'

'It's all right,' Megan said gently. She looked at Theresa's terrified face and she knew it wasn't.

Theresa was suddenly embarrassed. 'Do you think that I'm imagining it?'

'No, not at all.' Megan took a shaky breath. 'I don't think anything.'

'All my things are in there – my handbag, car keys, phone.' Theresa's eyes were wild. 'What am I going to do?'

'Drink your tea,' Megan suggested. 'Then we'll sort it out together.'

'I'll have to tell the owners. I can't stay in there. No one could. I'm sorry I woke you. It's an unearthly hour.' Theresa shuddered, as if the meaning of her words hit her.

Megan glanced towards the clear quartz stone she kept next to her bed. She was glad of its comforting presence now. She clutched it in her hand. 'It'll be all right, you'll see.'

Theresa gazed into her mug and hunched her shoulders. 'I want to go home.'

Megan thought quickly for a solution. 'Do you want to take my bed? You can sleep here and I'll sleep on the floor.' There was no way she intended to swap rooms.

'I can't go in there.'

'Then I'll get the pillows and duvet.'

'I just want to leave.' Theresa closed her eyes. 'I can't stay a moment longer.'

'Come on.' Megan said. 'Let's get your stuff, then we can decide.'

Theresa hesitated. 'You'll go in with me?'

'Let's do it.' Megan moved towards the door and felt her heart start to pound. 'A quick in-and-out.'

She stared into the bright hall, the single light blazing. Beyond, the door to room one gaped wide. It was shadowy inside.

Megan led the way, but Theresa hung back. She needed support; Megan told herself that there were two of them at the doorway – they'd be fine. She flicked the light on and gazed around the room. The duvet was on the floor, from Theresa making a quick escape. Megan walked into the room, leaving Theresa waiting in the doorway. She strode into the ensuite, glancing at the bath, the neatly folded towels, then back into the bedroom where Theresa stood, hands to her mouth.

'It all looks safe enough,' Megan said, her tone deliberately chirpy.

'I suppose you think I'm stupid?' Theresa asked.

'No.'

Theresa pointed towards the far wall, opposite the bed. 'It was there. I saw her. Crouching with her head down. I heard her breathing. It was really terrifying. Then she began to sob.'

Megan walked over to the wall. There was a low table, a suitcase placed on top and a handbag next to it. Theresa could have easily mistaken it for a crouching figure, but Megan didn't think so. The room was cold as a refrigerator. 'Everything seems fine,' she said optimistically, but she heard the concern in her own voice.

'Don't ask me to stay here,' Theresa said too loudly. 'I've never heard such terrible crying.'

'Bring your bedding. You can sleep in my room.'

'No.' Theresa's eyes were wide at the thought. 'I won't.' She rushed over to her case and stopped abruptly, standing absolutely still. 'Can you smell something odd?'

Megan sniffed the air. There was definitely a residual smell, the salt of the sea, an acrid aroma. 'Yes.'

'What is it?'

Megan shook her head. 'I've no idea. Something organic – the ocean?'

'It's horrible,' Theresa whispered, glancing over her shoulder to see if anyone was watching. Then she snatched up her handbag, grabbed her phone and hurried around the room, packing toiletries, stuffing them into her case. 'Can you wait?' There was fear in her voice as she took her clothes into the bathroom. She emerged a moment later fully dressed and breathed deeply. 'Thank you, Megan.'

Megan wasn't sure what to say. 'Are you feeling all right now?'

'They can't expect people to stay in a freezing cold place like this. The atmosphere's terrifying.' Theresa inspected every corner of the room for her belongings. 'I'm driving home now.'

Megan looked around. 'I think it's fine.'

'It's not,' Theresa snapped. 'If you'd been here, you'd have seen it. There was a definite presence. It was oppressive.' Her voice trailed off. She picked up her coat.

'Do you want me to walk to the car park with you?' Megan asked.

'No.' Theresa took a deep breath to try to restore calm. 'No, thank you. I just want to get home and...' She strode to the door.

'Right.' Megan felt uncomfortable.

'I'll be on my way.' Theresa pushed the key in the door. 'I don't intend to pay for the room.' Her eyes flew to Megan again. 'If anyone asks – it's up to you what you say. I know you're staying for a few days but I don't know how you can.'

'Well,' Megan began, but there was no way that she could explain that room three was the best of the four.

Theresa was already in the hall, tugging at the door that led to outside. 'I hope I haven't troubled you.'

'No.' Megan didn't know what else to say. 'Goodbye.'

Theresa had gone, and Megan felt a draught of cold air around her bare ankles that had seeped through the open door. She was alone now in Theresa's room, but fear quickly kept her company. She looked around, turned off the light and stepped into the corridor. The room was immediately filled with shadows.

As she was about to close the door, she heard a low noise, like a cry caught in someone's throat. A single sob.

There it was again. A soft moan. Then it stopped.

Megan froze in horror.

She stood in the corridor, shaking in the cold, listening hard.

There was nothing now, just silence.

As she pulled the door to with a sharp snap, it sprang back, wide open. She'd had enough. She fled to the warmth of her own room, turning the lock, clambering into bed, hunkering down.

She'd heard the Weeping Woman. A broken, grieving spirit whose soul ached with loss.

Feeling exhausted now, she closed her eyes, but she had no idea how she'd sleep. Despite the comforting hug of the duvet, Megan shook with fear.

21

It was almost five o'clock. There was no point trying to sleep. Megan had rolled over in bed countless times to calm her rushing thoughts, but the terrifying sob was still in her mind. She pictured a distraught woman, torn apart by grief. She wriggled out of bed, turned music on her phone loudly, pulled on her swimsuit, the wetsuit over the top, then a warm jumper. The sea was calling and the surf would help to clear her head. She needed to get out. To calm down.

For a moment, she recalled the two bracelets in her luggage, black tourmaline beads and smoky quartz, and the malachite pendant she had brought. They were the perfect crystals for protection, but she couldn't wear them in the water. Instead, she rummaged in one of the holdalls and found a tiger's eye necklace to boost her self-confidence. She slipped an amethyst pendant around her neck as well – she hoped it would bring calm. Right now she needed it more than she could say.

She collected the things she'd need in a bag: towel, clothes, shoes, her phone, and then her surfboard, and locked the door of room three behind her.

A moment later, she stood in the hall, listening. The door to Theresa's room was still ajar, so she approached it cautiously and pushed it wide. It gave a dull creak. There were no lights on: the gloom was crammed with shadows. It felt eerie and very cold. Megan leaned her board against the wall and hesitated in the doorway.

There was a stillness to the room she hadn't felt before, as if the darkness had inhaled and was holding its breath. She glanced across to where the low table was, where Theresa said she'd seen the huddled shape. It was the same place from which she'd heard the muffled sobs. There was nothing there now. Megan reached out and switched on the light. The room was suddenly illuminated, and everything was normal. She stepped inside. It was just a large, empty hotel room in a seventeenth-century inn, with rough walls, low ceilings, all traces of the past altered. The large window was framed by loose drapes; the furniture was modern and plain. Just like her own room. Megan sat on the edge of the bed and asked herself if room one did, in fact, feel as safe and comfortable as hers. She wasn't sure. It might be her imagination, but there was an odd feeling in here, as if she was being watched. As if she wasn't alone. She shuddered.

Megan tried to imagine the space as it might have been in the sixteen hundreds, when it was a tiny two-roomed cottage. It would have had the same low ceiling, exposed beams. A rickety door would have led to the street outside, which then led down the hill to the harbour. There would have been no glass in the small window. The holes would have been covered with animal hide, cloth, or wooden shutters. There would almost certainly have been a blackened inglenook fireplace, probably where the low table was. Perhaps it was still there, behind the plastered wall. A basic wooden table, chairs. In the corner, there would have been a staircase that led to a bedroom. Room two, upstairs.

She wondered what it was like up there, if room two had the same uneasy feeling. She imagined a family living in the cramped cottage centuries ago. There would have been no bathroom, no toilet – a chamber pot beneath the bed would have sufficed. She assumed that many of the local people would have worked at the harbour: fishermen perhaps. Their wives would have had a hard life making ends meet, cooking over a fire, washing clothes, sweeping a dirt floor clean. Megan imagined a woman in a cap wearing a muted-coloured dress, an apron tied around the waist, a long-sleeved linen under-dress. She'd be a fisherman's wife perhaps, bustling around the room, baking bread, making soup. Perhaps she had children, several little ones.

The door slammed with a loud crash. Megan almost jumped out of her skin. She looked up. The wind must have caught it and it banged shut. The room was suddenly icy with the chill of the breeze from the sea. She shivered with new fear. It was time to leave, to go down to the beach. She tugged out her phone and thumbed a message to Carly that she was on her way. Briefly, she wondered if there was someone she might talk to, who would know about the strange presence in the inn. Julien and Claude might not be the best people to ask.

She was still trembling. To calm herself, she tried to plan her day. After surfing, she'd come back for breakfast, then there was the matter of Emma Davey. She hadn't forgotten that she intended to find out about her half-sister. But there was plenty of time, it was only Tuesday. The room had grown even colder now, bone cold. Megan wondered if the heating would come on soon. Perhaps it was already on.

She shifted her bag onto her back and opened the door, hurrying outside, feeling a sense of relief. It closed behind her with a dull clunk.

**

It had been raining for a whole week. Susanna heard the dull patter of water against the shutters. She opened the door and peered out. There were puddles in the road, rivulets wide as streams running down the hill towards the harbour. A horse lumbered by, tugging a cart packed with hogsheads of fish. Its hoofs were spattered with mud. Katel was down at the harbour in the salt cellar, baulking sardines. Susanna would have time to visit Eliza before she came home. She reached for her shawl, then she remembered the poppet. She'd hidden it beneath her pillow, but she wanted to put it somewhere else, somewhere it would never be discovered, where it would do Beaten no more harm.

She rushed upstairs and came down with it in her hand. Tonight, when Katel was sleeping, she'd take it out the back of the house and bury it in the herb garden. Beaten's burns were healing slowly, but she was still in pain and she suffered from melancholy. Susanna had more salve to take to her tomorrow. For now, she wanted to hide the poppet. The hag-stones hung high in the chimney breast and, Susanna believed, they were doing their work.

Tedda had not spoken to her for several days now; perhaps the rain was keeping her away. She placed the doll in the chimney next to the stones hanging from their cord and reached for her basket, looping the shawl over her head against the teeming rain.

The rain had become heavier. Susanna scurried past Anne's cottage, head down. Anne would be busy with Bartholomew, but Susanna wanted to call in later to see how she was, to offer some gripe water she'd made from crushed fennel seeds and ginger root. It would soothe the baby and help him to sleep. She passed The Ship Inn. Joan was cooking – the smell of baking came from inside. Susanna wished from her heart that the chaste tree and red clover would work its magic and that Joan would soon be a happy mother. Then she began to ascend the path to Eliza's house. Susanna was always worried about Eliza, her aches and pains, her nervous disposition.

The driving rain in her eyes, her feet squelching mud, Susanna reached the largest house in the cove with its six rooms, a cellar below, and lattice windows. She knocked on the door and waited. There was no reply so she knocked again. The door was tugged open and Eliza stood inside. She looked frail, exhausted, and her forehead was damp. She whispered, 'I'm pleased to see you. Come inside.'

She led the way into the living room and sank down on a chair. 'I fear I'm unwell. I've been melancholy for days and now I can't sleep. I'm hot, then cold and shivering. My throat's swollen and I can't eat. And Beaten doesn't come to assist me. I've asked Yowann to get me a servant girl but he—'

'You need to lie down, Eliza,' Susanna said firmly.

'My limbs are racked with pain. I can hardly move, but I have to make sure Yowann has food ready when he arrives home.'

'I can do that,' Susanna soothed. 'Come, let's get you up to your room.'

'I'm weak,' Eliza moaned. Susanna placed a hand on her forehead, which was very hot. She touched Eliza's neck with light fingers; there was swelling on either side. Eliza's eyes were glazed, her breathing rapid. Susanna took her by the arm, coaxing her upstairs.

'How long have you been this way?'

'Days. The fever goes and then it returns.'

'Let me get you to your bed.'

'I must sleep in the smallest room.' Eliza wheezed and began coughing.

'It's cold there, but Yowann won't lie with me because I have the fever.' Her expression was terrified. 'Will I die?'

'I can make you well.' Susanna led her to the bedroom, helping her off with her dress, easing her to lie down in her shift, covering her with woollen blankets. 'You have influenza, I believe. If you rest for several days, you'll regain your strength.'

'I can't rest. I have a husband to care for, and no Beaten to tidy up after him.'

'I'll make something for you that you can easily digest. Then I'll leave food for him,' Susanna said grimly. 'Yowann won't starve. Besides, he can swill ale and eat Joan's food at The Ship.'

Eliza closed her eyes as her chest heaved and she coughed again. 'Are you sure I'll get well?'

'Yes.' Susanna lifted the cloth on her basket and reached inside. 'I have coriander here to reduce fever. I always carry it during weather like this. I can ease your lungs with a potion of liquorice and comfrey. There's some cough syrup here, a strong paste of honey and the seeds of parsley, anise and pepper. You must mix it with a little wine, to be used every morning and evening till you are whole again.'

'I'll try.' Eliza sighed deeply. 'Thank you, Susanna. I feared I would die.'

'I think not.' Susanna took her hand. She measured out a small amount of mixture from a small bottle with a spoon and mixed it in a cup. 'Let the herbs work their magic. Rest will help too.'

'I'm cursed,' Eliza began, then the coughing took over.

'No, Eliza, you're not.' Susanna eased her upright, then set about placing two bottles by the side of the bed, a cough mixture, and a green potion in a small bowl.

'Cursed in a bad marriage. Yowann wed me because my father was rich.'

Susanna rearranged the blankets. 'I'll bring you soup. I'll leave bread and cheese for Yowann, some fish, fruit.'

She was already descending the stairs when Eliza called out, 'He must have wine. He's angry if I forget to put it out.'

'Rest,' Susanna called back.

'There are coins on the table to pay you,' Eliza croaked, but Susanna was already by the fire, ladling thick fish soup from the bubbling pot into a bowl.

While it cooled, she placed a pottery tumbler and plate on the table. She found wine, cheese, a baked fish. Yowann could help himself when he came home.

Susanna placed extra wood on the fire, checked that hot water was boiling on the flame, and took the soup upstairs. Eliza was lying on her back, her eyes wide. For a second, Susanna wondered if she had died, she was so still. She raised Eliza's shoulders slightly, supporting her, easing spoonsful between her lips.

'You must take nourishment,' she coaxed, as Eliza did her best to swallow. 'There. Now sleep.'

'But Yowann will—'

'It's done. His food and drink are on the table.' Susanna placed a calming hand on Eliza's forehead. She knew the soothing, healing power of touch, skin against skin. She left her palm there and watched as Eliza's eyes grew heavy, and her breathing slowed. 'Sleep now. I will come by tomorrow.'

Eliza was almost asleep. Susanna hurried downstairs, towards the door. She was anxious not to meet Yowann. Moving quickly, she stepped out into the blinding rain and hurried towards her cottage. The rain pelted down, soaking her shawl, spattering her legs.

She opened the door to her cottage and froze. Someone was inside.

A small woman stood in the centre of the room, not moving. Susanna could smell tobacco.

'Tedda.'

Tedda's eyes glowed, pure malice. 'I've been waiting for you, Susanna.'

'You may not come into my house.'

'I'm here already.'

'What do you want?' Susanna said crossly.

Tedda watched her for a moment. '*Kows orthiv yn Kernewek.*'

'No, I won't speak to you in the old language.' Susanna crossed her arms. 'Now tell me what you want and then go.'

'You'm got it nice in here.' Tedda gazed around the cottage. 'You'm all scumped up cosy, like a hedgehog, you and that pretty maid you got.'

'Don't speak of Katel.' Susanna was gripped with the need to protect her child.

Tedda chuckled. 'Them hag-stones won't stop me, Susanna Boram. I got the old cunning. I know the ways.'

'It's time for you to leave.'

'Not till I've told you a few truths. Your brother lives next door with his nice little wife and babe, and at the weekend he goes to The Ship and gets drunk as forty cats. But he don't know what's a-coming to him.'

'Leave Samuel alone.'

'And that maid of yours, who talks to chawks.' Tedda shook her head. 'She's waiting for a prince to come. Ah, she might find him too, but she'll wait a long, long time after he's gone.'

'You leave her be, Tedda.' Susanna took a step forward, feeling anger mix with fear in her chest. 'Now get out or I'll throw you out into the rain.'

'You'm like a cat in a bonfire – don't know which way to turn, Susanna. I put the frights on you, for sure. I've always been the best pellar in the cove. You can't stop me, with your herbs and potions and your hag-stones. You wait and see. I got the measure of you.'

'I said get out.' Susanna took Tedda's arm and led her firmly to the door.

Tedda stood in the doorway and said something under her breath in Cornish. She spat a gobbet of tobacco onto the dirt floor. It landed at Susanna's feet in the shape of a crow, its mouth open to squawk.

'It's such a shame, what happened to Beaten Gilbert,' Tedda said craftily. 'You watch your back, Susanna. And watch out for those you keep close. 'Tis all I came to say to you. Good day, Mistress Boram. *Gorthuher da.*'

Susanna refused to wish her a good evening in Cornish. Tedda deliberately invoked the old ways, holding on to old magic, refusing to embrace new ideas. Susanna watched Tedda walk slowly into the rain, buffeted by gusts of wind as she drew her black shawl over her head and continued down towards the harbour until she was enveloped in a mist.

Susanna rushed to the fireplace. The hag-stones were scattered in the hearth, their cord broken. She searched for the poppet but it was missing. She gazed up the chimney for the little rag figure, but it was nowhere to be seen. She wondered for a moment if Tedda had taken it away with her.

Then she saw it on the table.

It was lying in a bowl of water, face down, floating on the surface.

22

Megan was euphoric after surfing, her hair and wetsuit dripping. She and Carly returned to the beach, reaching for towels, staring up at the sky. The orange, pink and blue blend of light arced over the deep indigo of the ocean.

Megan said, 'I think I'll have a quick swim. Are you coming in?'

Carly shook droplets of water from her fringe. 'No, I can't. I've got a shop to open. I'll head off. Is that OK?'

'Of course. I'll pop in later. I'm going to treat myself to something nice. I'm on holiday, after all.'

'See you then.' Carly lifted a hand.

Megan waved briefly and rushed back to the water, diving into the waves. She floated on her back, and her own words came back to her – *I'm on holiday*. The thought made her spirits lift. It was only Tuesday. She had the rest of the week left and then the weekend. There was so much she wanted to do. Surfing each morning was her priority now. She'd forgotten just how much energy it gave her, how empowered it made her feel.

She reminded herself that she ought to start asking in the cove about Emma Davey and she paused to think about how to do it. She didn't want to appear as if she was stalking her. She could always ask Julien, although he was relatively new to the area, and he probably wouldn't know her. Tom Hocking might, though. Or Carly. But a chance would surely come soon, before the end of the week. For the moment, the inn filled her thoughts and the surfing made her buzz with energy.

She was fascinated by the three haunted rooms, the ghost stories that seemed to start in the seventeenth century. She had to admit, room one had felt terrifyingly eerie as she'd sat on the bed. And she'd definitely heard noises above, in room four. She could ask Julien at breakfast, but he was invested in the pub being a viable business – ghostly tales wouldn't help. Megan wondered if there was a way of contacting the previous owners.

She swam out a little, calmer now, hoping she'd see some sea life. She'd heard that there were bottlenose dolphins in the ocean, often visible from spring until early autumn. There were porpoises, seals, sharks too. The idea of sharks alarmed her and she trod water for a moment, narrowing her eyes, staring out towards the horizon. It was cold now so she turned and swam back to shore.

On the sand again, she picked up her towel and surfboard, walking back over shingle and pebbles towards the car park. Someone was sauntering towards her as if he had all the time in the world. Megan recognised the diver, the same man she'd shared a wave with when surfing yesterday.

He was strolling down the hill; Megan could see the mane of blond hair, the dark wetsuit. He carried flippers and a mask in one hand, an underwater camera in the other, and there was an oxygen bottle strapped to his back. He wasn't making eye contact; he seemed miles away. She waited, her feet on shingle, fiddling with her towel, pretending to dry her hair.

The diver drew level, but he was still looking into the distance. He was so close, Megan noticed a chain around his neck, a little engraved bell, probably made of gold. She wondered if it was a good-luck charm.

She said, 'Good morning,' in her most friendly tone.

He met her eyes and looked away again without speaking. There was something of the Greek god about him, Megan thought – she'd done an A level in classical civilisation. He made a low noise then and carried on walking towards the waves. He was Poseidon, of course! Poseidon was the most bad-tempered, moody Greek god, the god of the sea. How fitting.

Megan thought about shouting after him, 'Have a nice bloody day,' but she was too polite. It was his loss.

She arrived back at her room, surfboard under her arm, around nine o'clock. The cleaner was already in room one, moving around, the door wide. A bucket had been left outside containing polish and cloths, and a vacuum was already plugged in. Megan was glad there was someone there to talk to.

She called out, 'Hi. You start early.'

'I do,' the woman called back, and she emerged, cloth in hand. She placed a hand on her rounded belly. 'I'm doing less hours now. Visitors are a bit thin on the ground.'

Megan took in the smiling face, the unusually long hair, now twisted in a plait. She asked, 'When's your baby due?'

'Just after Christmas,' the cleaner said nervously. 'It's my first. I wasn't going to have any kids – but here we are.'

'Well, congratulations,' Megan said cheerily. She took in her face and guessed she might be in her late thirties.

'Julien's terrified I'll leave once the baby's born.'

Megan had to ask. 'I suppose it would be hard to find someone to do your job. Some of these rooms are a bit creepy.'

'They are,' the cleaner said, and Megan noticed again the soft Cornish burr. The cleaner indicated room one with a nod of her head. 'I heard another visitor left during the early hours.'

'Does that happen often?' Megan was intrigued.

'Only when the Weeping Woman pays a visit.' She spoke as if it was normal. 'Or him upstairs, in room four.'

'Him upstairs?'

'The Drenched Man.'

'Have you seen them?'

'Oh, yes.' The cleaner frowned. 'Well, you smell the Drenched Man rather than see him. A lot of bumping and thumping.'

Megan knew. 'I heard him the other night.'

'Drenched man, room four – Weeping Woman room one and two, upstairs, because that was her cottage.'

'Do you know anything about them?'

She began vacuuming vigorously, her back to Megan, raising her voice over the whirr of the motor. 'Apparently, there was some argy-bargy in the cove back in the day.'

'Argy-bargy?'

'Who knows? Those were the times of smuggling and witchcraft.' She glanced over her shoulder. 'Sorry, no time to chat. Work to do.'

'Of course. But...' Megan felt a chill come over her. 'What's the story of the witch?'

The cleaner paused, clearly choosing her words carefully. 'It's not something we talk about.' She heaved her vacuum. 'Better get on. I'll give your room a quick once-over.'

'Thanks.' Megan was almost ready to offer to do it herself. She felt anxious for her, pregnant and still working at her arduous job. She pushed the key in her door.

The cleaner switched off the vacuum and called, 'If you're keen to find out about the history of the cove, pop in to see Tom Hocking.'

'Tom Hocking.' Megan remembered the funeral director, the huge hearse parked outside his premises. He'd spoken about hauntings as soon as she'd met him. 'Thanks.' Megan realised she hadn't introduced herself. But the cleaner was vacuuming again; she was clearly too busy to chat. Megan closed the door on the deafening noise, turned on the shower and began to peel off her wet clothes. She just wanted to feel warm again.

By half past nine, she was in the breakfast room, damp-haired, drinking hot coffee. Julien placed a plate of fruit in front of her. 'Nibbles – the last of the summer fruit – while you're waiting for the *galettes de sarrasin*.'

'Buckwheat crêpes.' Megan realised how hungry she was. 'Dawn surfing has given me an appetite. I'm starving.'

'I'm glad,' Julien said. 'We expected two of you for breakfast this morning, but the lady in room one has left early. Claude has made too much batter.' Megan watched him walk away. He looked sad and she wasn't surprised. He and Claude were clearly losing business. She helped herself to a banana and gazed around the dining room. Once it must have been part of The Ship Inn, perhaps a bar where men sat together drinking ale, plotting smuggling expeditions. She tried to imagine the scene then, and it wasn't difficult, with the low beams, dim lighting and small windows. She thought of men's faces lit by candlelight, a huge inglenook fireplace, logs burning, in the corner; a man and a woman serving ale behind the bar, the whoop of belly laughs, the whisper of scurrilous plans.

Julien was back with a package. 'This came for you.' He handed the parcel to Megan and turned to go. 'I'll bring your galettes.'

'Wait.' Megan held up the package. 'This is from my mother, bless her. I asked her to send it. Have you got a minute?'

'Of course.' Julien came back to the table, his face apologetic. 'Forgive me.'

'Not at all.' Megan unwrapped the package and tugged out a pale orange crystal and some herbal capsules. 'These are for you and Claude.'

Julien's face changed from miserable to happy. 'For us? Why?'

'This is a citrine stone. It'll hopefully bring you luck and wealth in your business. And here's the ayurvedic supplement to help you relax.'

Julien drew up a seat. 'This will bring better luck?'

Megan nodded. 'Citrine's known as the merchant's stone.'

'You've brought these things for us? For our business?' Julien was quite emotional. 'How much do I owe you?'

Megan laughed. 'Nothing – it's my way of saying thanks.'

Julien called over his shoulder, '*Claude, viens ici.*'

Claude bustled from the kitchen in chef's whites, a plate of crêpes in his hand. He placed them in front of Megan. '*Galettes de sarrasin* with cheese and herbs.'

'Thank you.'

'And what have we here?' Claude gazed as Julien held up the capsules and the crystal.

'Megan's a woman who heals people,' Julien explained. 'This stone is citrine. It's supposed to bring luck in business. And these capsules will make us less anxious. They are presents.'

Claude was perplexed. 'Will they work?'

'They have two chances,' Julien said cryptically. 'But we need all the help we can get. Another guest – what's the phrase they use here? – did a runner last night.'

Claude rolled his eyes. 'The ghost came again?' He indicated the plate. 'The galettes are best to eat warm.'

Megan took the hint and dug in. 'Will you both join me for a coffee?'

'Why not?' Julien said. 'I only have washing up to do – and the accounts. They can wait.'

Claude agreed. 'The accounts don't look good.'

Julien shrugged. 'We have only one room we can let, yours. The others – who knows what will happen when guests come to stay? Sometimes calm, sometimes things go bump in the night.' He poured coffee. 'As they say in Brittany, Claude, *c'est foutu!*'

'Totally messed up!' Claude took a sip of his coffee. 'I don't know what we'll do. Takings are low now.' He lifted his cup. 'But thank you, Megan. I hope this citrine will bring luck. I'll make you anything you want for dinner. Tell me, what's your favourite food?'

Megan knew at once. 'My mother used to make macaroni cheese for me when I was small – with a brown cheesy crust on top. That's my idea of heaven.'

'It'll be on your plate tonight – with a salad of dressed leaves and tomatoes,' Claude promised. 'But it will be my own version, with béchamel sauce, crème fraîche and Gruyère.'

Julien touched the stone thoughtfully. 'I hope this works. I need our luck to change.'

'This crêpe's divine, Claude.' Megan chewed a mouthful of galette. 'I've just had a thought. Have you heard of Jamaica Inn?'

Both men shook their heads.

'I passed it on the way down. It's an old smuggling inn on Bodmin Moor. It has its history in a famous book about ghosts and smugglers. It even has a gift shop.'

Julien nodded. 'Maybe we should go there, Claude – see if we can steal any good ideas.'

'I suppose it's worth a try,' Claude said.

'The thing is.' Megan was thoughtful for a moment. 'What if you incorporated the ghosts into your advertising?'

'Incorporate them how?' Julien was interested.

'Free spirits after closing time?' Claude joked.

'That's a great slogan.' Megan leaned forward excitedly. 'Well, you could either turn a liability into an asset and advertise The Ship Inn as a haunted inn – "Stay here if you dare" – or...'

'Or what?' asked Julien.

'Or you could try to help them find peace?' Megan said. 'I could ask around if you like. Tom Hocking might be a good place to start. He'll know stories that have been passed down the generations.'

'That sounds like a good move,' Claude said. 'If we help these spirits find some peace, then our clients can have some too.'

'You could have a range of T-shirts – you know the sort of thing – "I spent a whole night in The Ship" or a badge that says, "I slept with the Drenched Man". You could get a visitors' book to record ghostly experiences. Or – and this ties in with what you've told me about the pub – you could concentrate on the smuggling side of its history. It works for Jamaica Inn.'

'We could have themed evenings where everyone turns up dressed as a pirate.' Julien was excited now. 'Would that work?'

'What do we have to lose?' Claude asked. 'We need to update our website, in any case.'

Megan was on a roll. 'You could develop your website with smugglers' stories and maybe you make the history part of the décor.'

'That sounds good,' Claude said.

'Why not?' Julien agreed. 'You're so clever.'

'I've got good business sense. I run a shop in Somerset that just about breaks even.' She grinned at her own joke.

'But if the ghosts are real, then how can we help them?' Julien asked.

Megan had the answer already. 'Like I said, I'll call on Tom Hocking later and see what we can find out.'

'Can I come too?' Julien asked.

'Of course.'

He was delighted. 'Megan, how can I thank you?'

'Make me a mac and cheese.' She glanced at Claude. 'And then join me for dinner, if you have time.'

'Tuesdays are quiet,' Claude said. 'And Josh is behind the bar tonight. We can try.'

'Then why don't we talk more later? The surfers would love all that smuggling history.' Megan's face shone with excitement. 'You never know – by next summer The Ship could be one of the most popular inns in Cornwall.'

'You're a genius, Megan,' Claude said, holding up the stone. 'The citrine's already working its magic.'

23

A silence had descended on St Mawgen Cove. The rain was falling steadily as villagers went about their business quietly, their heads down. No one knew exactly how Beaten Gilbert had died, but tongues had started to wag. Someone wished her ill. There were several names on people's lips now. She had been found by her brother, floating in the sea. But everyone who knew her swore that although she had been melancholy, by all accounts she was recovering well, thanks to Susanna's help. The skin on her hands and face was healing. Certainly, no one believed she'd taken her own life.

Merryn was heartbroken and would speak to no one but Katel. He went about his fishing work in silence, refusing to talk about what had happened. He had lost his mother and now his sister. But Hedyn took himself to The Ship Inn, explaining earnestly to everyone that he was sure someone had killed his daughter with magic, and he knew who it might be.

Susanna opened the door to Samuel early in the morning. He was standing outside, looking troubled. She waved him inside. 'Come in. Sit down. It's nice to see you.' She placed a cup of warm ale on the table in front of him. 'How fares Annie, and how's little Bartholomew?'

Samuel drank thirstily. 'They're well although the baby cries a lot.'

'I'll go to see him today with something that will soothe him.'

'Hedyn and Merryn need your assistance too, I fear. The funeral will be this afternoon. Everyone in the cove will be there.'

'I know. Hedyn asked me to prepare Beaten last night.' Susanna closed her eyes, remembering how she had bathed the body.

'Poor Hedyn has no idea how to keep house. Beaten did everything for her father and brother.'

'I'll call on him and take him some pottage.'

Samuel's brow clouded. 'He talks of Beaten often. Susanna, I don't like what he's saying. It can only bring trouble to the cove.'

'What does he say? He's mourning, Samuel. Perhaps he needs the company of other men.'

'He believes that Beaten's death was no accident and the fishermen agree with him. They're looking to point the finger of blame.'

'Hedyn knew his daughter better than anyone. She didn't harm herself, I'm sure of it. Beaten was in better spirits. I saw her that very morning. I changed the binding on her hands and applied salve to her face. She even managed a small smile. Although it hurt her to speak, she'd started to feel better.' Susanna was puzzled. 'So what happened? Did she go for a walk, become weak and fall into the water?'

'It's much worse than that,' Samuel said. 'Hedyn has told the fishermen that after you'd left her, Beaten fell asleep. She slumbered for most of the afternoon, then Tedda Lobb called round to the house to offer some herbal potions. Hedyn sent her away; he told her that he had no need of her medicine. Tedda said some bad things to Hedyn in the old language. An hour later, Beaten stood straight up from her bed, her eyes wide, and held her hands in front of her, saying, "My fingers burn. I need to cool them." Hedyn says she wandered from the house in a daze, chattering as if someone was talking to her and telling her what to do.'

'What does this mean?' Susanna asked anxiously. Poor Beaten's death was already causing rumours to spread.

'She was speaking all the time to an invisible companion. Hedyn heard her say something like, "I'll do as you command. I'll bathe my wounds and I'll be whole again." He's telling everyone in The Ship that the same devil who pushed her into the fire forced her into the ocean.'

Susanna caught her breath. 'Does Hedyn think his daughter was enchanted?'

'He does. He was too afraid to run after her because he believed invisible magic surrounded her,' Samuel said firmly. 'And he tells everyone who'll listen.'

Susanna could easily imagine Tedda visiting the Gilberts' cottage, talking to Hedyn, crossing the threshold of the door to work her magic. Tedda had let herself into Susanna's cottage while she had been at Eliza's. Later, Susanna had seen the poppet floating in the bowl of water, the same poppet she'd now buried beneath a rosemary bush in her herb garden. She shivered.

Samuel asked, 'Where's Katel?'

'She's already left for the salt cellar. I believe she intends to seek out Merryn.'

'Is she sweet on him?'

'I think not, Samuel, but his heart is sad and she'll give him cheer. She feels troubled about Beaten.'

'Tedda should stay away from the Gilberts' home. And she shouldn't come to the burial this afternoon. Many people will shun her. They are saying that it was Tedda who charmed her. As Hedyn sent her away, she whispered a curse beneath her breath and spat tobacco on his floor. It made the shape of a chawk.'

Susanna shivered. 'She did the same here.'

'I fear something bad has come here,' Samuel said quietly. 'Although we had a big catch of fish recently, I hear Yowann is looking to make even more money. The word among the fishermen is that he and his friends have their eye on the biggest haul yet.'

'What does that mean?' Susanna asked.

'A ship. It's best not to ask more.' Samuel drank the dregs of ale from the cup. 'And I'm late for the boats. But I pray you, call in on my Annie. If you can stop the baby's cries, I'd be most grateful.'

'I'm sure Bartholomew and Annie would be glad of it too,' Susanna said. 'I'll see you later at the cemetery, when poor Beaten is put in the earth.'

'Indeed.' Samuel walked outside into the fresh air, a breeze blowing straight in from the sea. 'The sun's up and the ground's warming in readiness for her.'

'Poor Beaten – she had too much warmth – and yet not enough of it,' Susanna said.

* * *

The passing bell tolled from the church tower, a hollow note. A large crowd had gathered around the graveside as Beaten, swathed in black cloth, was lowered into the ground. Susanna stood at a distance, remembering how the night before she had washed Beaten's body and wrapped it in the plain sheet. She had prayed that Beaten would rest in peace as she treated her gently, washing the red blotches, the swollen flesh. She had wept as she worked.

Now, as she stood next to her brother, she recognised many sombre faces. Hedyn Gilbert's head was bowed, alongside Merryn, both wearing sprigs of rosemary in their hat bands and pinned to their sleeves. Katel had taken a place at Merryn's side, holding fresh flowers to throw in a maiden's grave, as was traditional. Anne stood on Samuel's other side, baby Bartholomew hidden beneath her shawl. There were groups of fishermen, their wives, children. Colan and Joan Stephens stood side by side, their heads bowed. Yowann Hicks placed himself next to the priest: the talk was that he had paid for the burial. Eliza was not there. Susanna wondered if she was still unwell.

There were people from nearby villages who had come to pay their respects, farm-workers and miners. Several men in fine clothes stood behind Yowann. Susanna didn't recognise any of them but Samuel pointed them out. They were from the nearest town, friends of Yowann's – a shopkeeper, a merchant, a miller, a shoemaker, a weaver, a blacksmith, a carpenter and a mercer.

The sun had come out, illuminating the circle of people in black clothes who watched as Beaten's coffin, draped with a cross of folded linen strips, was lowered into the ground, the grave then covered in more black cloth. The priest said a quiet prayer. Samuel whispered, 'No expense has been spared. A penny has been put in her mouth, to give to St Peter at the pearly gates.'

Susanna kept her voice low. 'How can she be buried in hallowed ground?'

Merryn, then Hedyn, threw flowers into the grave. Hedyn stood back in silence, his face bewildered, but Merryn fell to his knees and began to sob.

Susanna said, 'Does the priest not believe she took her own life?'

'No one thinks it,' Samuel said. 'Yowann has paid the priest for customary prayers; he's asked for a Christian burial. The poor maid suffered enough in this life. It's not right that she's troubled in the afterlife.'

Katel dropped her flowers gently in the grave as Merryn keeled forward, his sobs loud against the silence. A jackdaw flew onto the church roof and cawed, a harsh, eerie sound. Susanna gazed over towards the sea. 'It's dark yonder. Is the rain coming in?'

'A storm perhaps?' Samuel wondered. 'But it won't trouble Beaten now. And the rest of us are invited to The Ship when the burial's done. Yowann's paid for it all. Joan Stephens has baked funeral cakes and Colan will provide ale, claret and brandy.' He glanced towards the inn. 'It's good that Hedyn can drink to the memory of his daughter among friends.'

'And all Yowann's companions are here for the drink too,' Anne said cynically. 'I doubt Hedyn Gilbert has ever met any of them.'

'Yowann wants to feast with his friends,' Samuel said quietly. 'I heard that the visitors brought gifts for Hedyn: a coat, a pair of shoes, grain.'

'I don't know how they'll manage without Beaten,' Anne muttered.

The priest spoke his last words and the gravedigger, a man in thick brown clothes, shovelled soil into the grave. It landed on the body with a low thud.

Yowann raised his voice. 'On behalf of Hedyn, I invite you to The Ship Inn. Come, let us remember Beaten with good cheer and eat and drink.'

Susanna saw Merryn stand slowly. Katel whispered a quiet word and hurried to her mother, taking her arm. 'I won't go to the feast. If you wish, we'll think of Beaten at home quietly, by ourselves.'

'We should join the Gilbert family in The Ship for just a few moments,' Susanna replied, but she felt uneasy being near Yowann and Colan for long. 'We must show our respect. Then we can slip away unnoticed.'

People had started to move from the graveside. Then a cry went up: Hedyn pointed a finger, a sharp jab of accusation, and shouted. 'She's here. Look where she stands watching. But you'll not come near me, Tedda. You'll not be under the same roof with me while I drown my sorrows for the daughter you drowned with your magic.'

Susanna reached for Katel's hand, holding it in both of hers. Tedda Lobb, draped in a black shawl, was standing at a distance, watching. Susanna took in her dark clothes, her folded arms and bowed head. She gazed up towards the top of the church where the jackdaw sat watching, its wings furled. She looked back to Tedda and saw the resemblance, the hunched body, the sharp eyes.

'You can't put what happened to Beaten at my door,' Tedda rasped. 'It wasn't I who gave her the simples and potions. It wasn't I who sat at her bedside feeding her soup. Who knows what charms she was given then?'

'You're not welcome here, Tedda.' An authoritative voice boomed. It was Yowann, the smartest dressed mourner in dark breeches and jacket, ribbons, neck ruffs, gloves and stockings. 'Go home.'

But Tedda stayed where she was. Susanna gazed into the distance. The sky was overcast now, a brooding darkness that sucked warmth from the air. Clouds hung low over the sea, the waters turbulent. A wind was whisking in; it ruffled the mourners' hair and lifted their clothes. Tedda raised a finger.

'I knew Beaten Gilbert, Yowann. She always spoke me fair. I'll say goodbye to her with everyone else in St Mawgen Cove and you'm can't refuse me.'

Katel touched Susanna's arm; pearls of tears appeared in her eyes. Susanna knew why. She could see the fear in her daughter's face. She was thinking about the poppet, how Tedda had persuaded her to sink pins in the doll's face. It had been the beginning of poor Beaten's end. A tear slid down her cheek.

'I don't want to linger.'

'We'll leave now,' Susanna said soothingly as the first drops of rain spattered on faces.

Merryn bent down and seized a clod of earth, hurling it hard in Tedda's direction. 'Go away, Tedda. I know what you did to my sister.'

Hedyn copied, throwing a piece of earth at the old woman. 'Stay away.'

The rain was teeming now as other men flung hard pieces of earth and stones towards the old woman, who cowered at a distance and seemed to shrink. Susanna watched in shock as Samuel hurled a pebble with all his might. It hit Tedda on her arm and she yelped in pain.

Tedda raised her shoulders and turned to go, pausing once to point a long finger and mouth something over the noise of the pelting rain. Susanna heard the faint words: 'You'm going to regret this hour.'

She scurried away down the hill as pebbles and clumps of soil flew after her. There was a low rumble of thunder in the distance. Susanna hugged her daughter and shivered as rain drenched them to the skin, mud forming underfoot.

The jackdaw on the church roof cawed once, flapped its oily wings and flew up towards the black clouds.

Then someone said the word 'Witch'.

24

Megan didn't mention anything about ghosts to her parents on the phone; she thanked her mother for sending the parcel, saying how delighted Julien and Claude had been. She'd wanted to talk about how much fun she'd had surfing, but Jackie was keen to tell her that Amy had been into the shop – business had been really slow – she'd bought a Baltic amber teething bracelet for baby Leo, who was suffering with sore gums. They'd had a long chat about babies. Jackie went on to say that there was plenty of time for Megan to think about all that, but Megan could hear the disappointment in her mother's voice, the longing for her daughter to settle down.

Jackie had handed the phone to Bill for a catch-up, and Megan had mentioned cryptically that she was getting to know some of the community quite well and would report on any new discoveries before the end of the week. Right now she was having fun surfing and her father reminded her that a holiday was a priority.

Later, on the way to Tom's cottage, Julien was chattering excitedly about advertising ideas. 'We could call the website The Ship: Smugglers and Spirits. Or we could change the names of the rooms – no more numbers – we could have The Watery Man room.'

'The Drenched Man,' Megan reminded him, although she couldn't ignore the wriggling discomfort in her stomach. She had heard both the ghosts.

'The Sad Woman room.'

'Weeping Woman.'

'Or maybe we could make each room about smugglers – The Cabin Boy, The Captain. I was telling Claude, if we're ready by Halloween, we could have a haunted evening. Light the big fire, fill the place with strings of lights like little white ghosts.' Julien was excited.

'It's all good.' Megan gazed down the hill towards Tom's cottage. 'Do you think he's home? There might be some lights on inside the undertaker's parlour.'

Julien looked suddenly nervous. 'You don't think we're rude, interrupting him to talk about ghosts?'

'Perhaps he'll enjoy telling us.' Megan lowered her voice as they walked up to the door and knocked.

The door opened and Tom Hocking was standing in the hall in a bright T-shirt and colourful shorts. He seemed unperturbed by the chilly sea breeze as he called a cheery greeting.

'Hello. How can I help? If you're here to hire a limo, you really should see me at the business premises tomorrow.'

'Tom, isn't it? Do you remember me? I'm—'

'Megan Hammond. I never forget a face, or a name. Besides' – he leaned against the doorpost, as if ready for a long conversation – 'Megan, St Mawgen – it's almost the same. It's as if you're meant to be here.'

'Right.' Megan tried again. 'This is Julien from The Ship.'

'I know,' Tom said. 'You're one of the French guys who've taken it over and can't get guests to stay the whole night.'

'That's true.' Megan seized her chance. 'We were talking about the history of the inn and decided it would be a good idea to find out some facts. I heard you'd know all about its history.'

'Oh, I don't know so much.'

'When might be a good time to talk about it? I could buy you a drink in the bar later,' Megan said.

'There's no time like the present, especially in my business,' Tom said. 'But I'll drop by for that drink. Never turn a free one down. Rum's my tipple.'

'So.' Megan took a deep breath, framing her question. 'Do you know anything about the Drenched Man? There's a story that he moves around in the room above me, room four.'

'Have you heard him?' Tom asked.

'I think so, yes,' Megan replied, and Julien shot her an anxious look.

'You'd better come in.' Tom left the door wide and led the way into a small room crammed with furniture, two pale sofas, a chest of drawers covered in ornaments. There were photos of Tom over many years. In some he had short hair, in others, long hair, a beard, beardless, but in all of them he was carrying a surfboard.

A fire crackled in the tiny hearth, a little at odds with Tom's shorts and T-shirt. He plonked himself down and patted the seat. 'So, sit. What do you want to know?'

Megan sat down next to him and Julien took the chair opposite, leaning forward, all ears.

'St Mawgen,' Megan began. 'It has a lot of history.'

'It does,' Tom agreed. 'I'd like to say I could tell you about it, but I can't go back more than a few generations.'

'Have you lived here long?' Julien asked.

'Man and boy. My father was undertaker here, and his father before him. Mind you, it was a different sort of business when they ran it. But there you are. I've read a few history books about the cove and I've heard the tales.'

'Are they just tales or are the stories real?' Megan asked.

'The fact is, St Mawgen was always a fishing village. The cove kept many families alive through the ages. Pilchards mainly, but other fish too: hake, a few skate, cod, ling. The pilchards were cured in layers of salt – they called it baulking – and that's what kept the people fed. A lot of the fish was sent elsewhere in Britain and abroad. There was some smuggling business too, by all accounts, but I'm not an expert on that.'

'It all sounds the perfect backdrop for ghost stories,' Megan said, trying to bring the conversation back to the subject of the inn.

'There are many spirits here,' Tom agreed. 'Anchor Cottage by the seafront is haunted by a young girl who drowned herself years ago. The owners can't sell the place. And the voices of sailors who perished at sea can be heard down by the rocks on a moonless night.'

Megan thought that sounded like a fisherman's yarn. 'Really? And what about the ghosts at the inn?'

Tom folded his arms. 'The Drenched Man came to a bad end a few hundred years ago. A sailor who's been drowned at sea and brought from the waves can never find rest on either land or ocean. This cove has known so much misery, and that's the truth of it. The Weeping Woman died of a broken heart. They are both connected to the Waiting Witch, who stands on the clifftops when the moon comes out, watching. She's really bad news.'

'I've heard people sing about her in the shanties,' Julien began.

Megan asked, 'Why does she stand on the cliffs?'

'Ah, she did something dreadful, by all accounts.' Tom shook his head. 'The cove was rampant with witchcraft in the seventeenth century. The Drenched Man died in the cottage next to The Ship – that's why he can't leave. And the Weeping Woman cries for the Waiting Witch.'

'Have you seen the witch?' Megan asked quickly.

'I wouldn't be here if I had,' Tom replied.

'Why?' Julien asked.

'She comes down from the clifftops on the cold air and kisses them.' Tom's expression was serious. 'My father and grandfather buried many a man she kissed on the lips as they walked home. I've buried three myself, the last one just a few months back.'

Megan felt a shiver go through her body. She leaned closer to the fire. 'That can't be real.'

'I assure you it is,' Tom said quietly. 'She watches for people who are out late at night. Then when a man comes past – and it's always a man – she comes down from the clifftop for revenge. She calls his name.'

'Why is it always a man?' Julien asked.

'Many a woman has heard her whisper while walking on the cliffs. But she doesn't have a grudge against women. Only men. I believe it was a man who called her a witch and that's why.' Tom shook his head. 'She puts her lips against his, and the kiss stops his breath. The next day he's found on the ground. His heart has failed.'

'Could the deaths just be natural causes?' Megan was sceptical. 'I mean, plenty of people die from heart attacks.'

'I know the rhyme well. All kids in St Mawgen were taught it from childhood.' Tom lowered his voice and began to recite:

> *If she walk behind ye, fear*
> *In case she should come too near.*
> *If ye ever hear her call*
> *Then that same moment ye shall fall.*

'I just felt a chill go through me,' Megan said honestly. 'Is there anything that can be done to help her? I mean – can't she be laid to rest?'

'I've heard that the answer lies at the bottom of the ocean,' Tom said gravely. 'The Waiting Witch has a long-standing grudge against the men of St Mawgen.'

'You know some people this has happened to?' Megan asked.

'I do.' Tom took a deep breath. 'A few months back, just before the past owners of The Ship left, a man I knew well, John, went for a drink after work. He left at closing time to go home to his wife. He never got there. He was found in the morning in the road, stone cold. His heart had stopped.'

'I heard about this.' Julien seemed terrified. 'How do you know it was the witch that killed him?'

'He was forty-four years old, a fisherman, healthy as you and me,' Tom explained. 'And perhaps if the ghost of a witch kissed you on the lips, you'd have a heart attack too. But that's not how I knew the witch had kissed him. I could tell by the look on his face.'

'The look?' Julien asked.

'His eyes were wide open, as if he'd had the shock of his life,' Tom said firmly. 'I've seen it three times in all my days as an undertaker. I never want to see it again.'

'And was she a real witch?' Megan asked.

'There's a history of witchcraft in the cove, as I said. Cunning women practised here with herbs and potions; they were midwives who delivered babies and healed the sick. But there were also women who did other things, by all accounts – dolls and charms and bad magic.'

Megan was unsure. 'Do you really believe all that?'

'I do.' Tom nodded slowly. 'You can feel it sometimes in the air. Something really chilling. Not just in The Ship, although bad things happened there. People hear her voice on the clifftop, or down by the cove at night, when the moon comes out. You can feel she's not far away.' He paused for a moment and then forced a dry chuckle. 'And if she catches me, there's no one to put me in the ground. I'm the only undertaker for ten miles.'

'So where can we find out more?' Megan asked. 'It'd be nice to bring her some peace.'

'No one will talk about her.' Tom's eyebrows came together. 'But if you want to research the history, there's a chap who's been living here for the past few months from the university over at Falmouth. He does a bit of teaching there, and the rest of the time he's here messing about in the ocean, looking for shipwrecks. If the truth lies at the bottom of the sea, he might know something.'

'Poseidon,' Megan said. She knew exactly who Tom was referring to. He'd walked straight past her this morning without a word. It didn't seem likely that he'd be keen to tell her much about the cove but she could at least try. 'Yes, I'm told he lives in the little cottage right at the end, before you get to the seawall: Surf's Up!'

'That's right.'

'I might pay him a visit,' Megan said. It would be fun to see if she could get him to talk to her. 'He knows about smugglers and shipwrecks then?'

'He might have facts behind the stories,' Tom said. 'Certainly, you'll get scientific evidence from him. But he probably doesn't know anything about the Waiting Witch. I've heard he's mucking about in the sea at all hours.'

'Oh?' Megan was already fascinated.

'But a word of advice.' Tom lowered his voice again. 'It's considered bad luck even to mention the witch in passing, except in the singing of shanties. I mean, a few months ago, John Davey was well and fit and hearty. Now he's six feet under.'

'John Davey?' Megan repeated, her mouth open.

'I heard this too.' Julien looked uncomfortable.

'Yes, he was here one minute, then he was gone,' Tom said, shaking his head. 'The local people believe the witch stopped his breath with her kiss. It was bad luck for him. And for his poor wife, Emma.'

'Emma?' Megan shuddered.

It was as if someone had walked over her grave.

25

Late that night, Susanna was fast asleep on her straw mattress when a loud knocking woke her. She sat up and listened. It was there again: a hard rapping of knuckles, insistent.

She called, 'Wait while I come,' and pulled a skirt over her shift, wrapping herself in a shawl and hurrying downstairs. By the fire, Katel was stirring. She sat up slowly, rubbing tired eyes.

'What ails you, Mother? It's not yet time to wake.'

'Hush, Katel. I'll see who it is.'

Susanna pushed open the door to see the shadowy shape of a man outside in the darkness, rain falling hard around him. His eyes gleamed from beneath a broad hat, glancing at her.

'Yowann?' She was puzzled. 'What brings you here at this time?'

'You must come with me, Susanna. Bring your basket of simples and potions. It's Eliza.'

'What's wrong?' Susanna was already reaching for her basket. 'I thought the influenza had subsided. Does she still cough? I gave her honey and ginger, marshmallow root.'

'The cough has grown serious. She makes a hacking sound, and she can't breathe.'

'Shall I come?' Katel called from the hearth.

'Stay and rest, child.' Susanna grabbed a shawl and followed Yowann into the rain, as he led the way up the path to his house. They reached the door quickly and he ushered her inside. She was about to rush upstairs to the room where she knew Eliza slept but he caught her arm.

'Help her. If she should die, Susanna...'

'We mustn't think of that.' Susanna's gaze held his for a moment, then she rushed up the wooden steps towards the smallest bedroom. She heard Eliza coughing, a deep rasping that sounded inhuman.

Eliza was in bed, almost bent double, retching into her lap. Susanna called, 'Fetch water, for the love of God,' then she reached into her basket and tipped oil from a jar onto her palm, hiking up Eliza's shift to rub it onto her back. 'I have lavender oil here, Eliza. Breathe it in deeply.'

Eliza was still coughing as Yowann returned with a pewter cup filled with water, holding it to Eliza's lips, forcing her to drink. She began to hack furiously, spluttering water, her eyes filling with tears. Then she made a muffled sound, between a cough and a cry, and she spat something onto the bedcover. Yowann lifted a small piece of metal, his eyes wide. 'It's a nail. Eliza has coughed up a nail.'

Eliza spluttered, gasping for air. Then she began to calm down. 'I thought I should die.'

'All may be well now,' Yowann said to himself.

'Here.' Susanna placed a cup to Eliza's lips. 'Drink this liquor. It will help your cough and calm your lungs. It's made from liquorice, sage and willow.'

Eliza sipped slowly and then fell back onto the bolster. She closed her eyes. 'I feel a little better.'

Yowann's eyes met Susanna's. 'My wife has coughed a nail.' He held it up. 'Look.'

'What does it mean?' Susanna lowered her voice.

'Someone meant to do her ill. It's a charm made to kill her.' Yowann moved closer to Susanna. 'Thank goodness you were here to stop it.'

Susanna leaned over Eliza, touching her cheek with a gentle hand, covering her shoulders with blankets. 'Can you sleep now?'

'I can,' Eliza said. 'I feel better. Thank you, Susanna.'

Susanna turned to Yowann. 'We'll talk of this downstairs.'

They sat in the largest room by the fire. Yowann poured two cups of brandy, warmed them by the flames and placed one in her hand. Susanna sipped slowly. It was strong and soothing, but she was not used to the sharp taste of the spirit. He reached over and took her hand. 'You saved Eliza's life. How can I thank you?'

Susanna allowed his hand to cover hers for a moment, then she moved it away and shuffled back in her seat. 'I hope she'll be well.'

Yowann said nothing for a moment, then he showed her his palm: the tiny nail was still in his hand. 'This came from her mouth when she coughed. You know what this is, Susanna?'

Susanna shook her head. 'I've never seen the like of it before. How did it come to be there?'

'A curse has been put upon me and someone sought to harm her to spite me,' Yowann said seriously. 'You were there at the burial of Beaten Gilbert. You saw Tedda Lobb. You heard her words.'

Susanna nodded. 'I did.'

'I accused her of – what she did to Beaten,' Yowann said quietly. 'I told her she was not welcome at the church. Then she cursed all of us who were present. Do you recall her words, that we would live to regret the hour?'

'I do.' Susanna could not deny it.

'Then she summoned the rain and the storm. But she wasn't wet. The rain came down and drenched all who stood at the graveside, but she was not troubled by it.'

'I don't remember seeing that,' Susanna said.

'Many of the men who drank to Beaten's memory in The Ship remarked upon it,' Yowann said. 'Tedda Lobb caused the maid to die. She's capable of such bad magic. People say she's told them that she changes her shape into that of a chawk and she whispers to young maidens in the cove. She tells them what to do.'

Susanna wondered at his words. There was some truth in them. Tedda had befriended Katel; she had coaxed her to learn her old ways. She had told her that the chawk would speak to her, that a prince would come to marry her. And Tedda had given Katel the poppet and told her to put in the pins.

Now Eliza Hicks had coughed up a nail. Susanna shuddered. 'What will happen now?'

'I can't allow Tedda to practise her evil in St Mawgen.' Yowann took a deep breath. 'I have some standing in the community. People listen to me.'

'That's true.'

'Today, I'll speak to a man I know in Bodmin. Tedda must be stopped. I fear she practises witchcraft.'

Susanna remembered talking to Tedda in Bylen woods, her wicker basket full of belladonna. She said slowly, 'Perhaps she does.'

'And will you testify, if asked, that she has tried to bewitch Katel, that she bewitched Beaten and made her drown herself in the sea?'

'But what if Tedda is innocent?'

'Don't concern yourself with that. The man I know will discover whether she's true or false. He has ways to prove if a witch lies.'

Susanna sighed. 'I don't like it.'

'Nor I.' Yowann deliberately misunderstood her meaning. 'We're none of us safe while Tedda lives in the cove. I'll send a message tonight. I'll have her removed. There are some who say she brought the haul of pilchards to us through her cunning.'

Susanna was thoughtful. 'I've seen her on the clifftops.'

'As if summoning the seas, or the devil.'

Susanna was trembling again.

'Are you afraid?' Yowann removed the cup from her hands and brought them towards his lips. 'You need someone to care for you.'

Susanna felt the warm brandy on her tongue and closed her eyes. She heard Yowann say, 'We loved each other, once.'

'That was many years ago.' Susanna felt him lean towards her and his lips brushed hers. The tender feelings surrounded her and she felt weak again. Then she sat upright. 'It's late, Yowann. I must go home to Katel. But I'm glad we've been able to help Eliza.' She stood up. 'I'll bid you good night.'

Yowann was on his feet, reaching in his pockets. He slipped a coin in her hand. 'Here's payment for your pains. You saved Eliza's life.'

She gazed at the coin glinting in her palm. 'It's too much.'

'No, it's the first of many more. I'm grateful to you, Susanna. And I'll care for you and Katel in the manner you both deserve.'

Susanna began to back away as quickly as she could. 'Thank you, Yowann. I'll come back later today to see how Eliza fares. But all will be well.' She reached the door and tugged it open, stepping out into the rain.

'I think of you often.' Yowann's voice was light on the night air. 'You know my feelings won't change.'

'Good night,' Susanna said hastily as she scurried down the path towards her cottage. She hugged her shawl tightly, her thoughts rushing.

Eliza Hicks had coughed up a nail. But it did not happen until Yowann brought her water to drink from a cup. Susanna was puzzled. It was not possible for a woman to cough nails, not even by magic. She thought of Tedda and what might befall her and, as she pushed the door to her cottage open, she was still shaking with fear.

* * *

Two days later, a warm, fresh day, Susanna sat with Anne and Bartholomew in their cottage, the door wide. The baby nestled in the crook of her arm. His face was flushed as he slumbered like a cherub.

Anne said, 'Thank you for the water of crushed fennel seeds. It has helped him.'

'I'm glad,' Susanna said. 'Many cunning women like to use poppy extracts, but I fear they're too harsh. It's better to use gentle herbs with the child, not subdue him.'

Anne gazed at Bartholomew and stroked his soft cheek with her finger. 'I love him more than I thought possible.'

Susanna agreed. 'I remember my first few years with Katel. I was alone, but I felt strong with her in my arms. I would do anything in the world to keep her safe.'

Anne's eyes filled with tears. 'When I hear about Beaten, my heart aches for the family. How that poor maid must have suffered.'

'I liked Beaten. She was a kind soul.'

Anne's expression clouded. 'Shame on Tedda for what she has done.'

'She's a foolish woman,' Susanna admitted.

'You were at the church. You saw what happened.'

'I saw people throw stones at her.' Susanna remembered Yowann's expression as he'd thrown the clod. It was the same cruel face he'd had as he held the nail in his hand. 'Perhaps she is just lonely and unwise in what she says.'

'I believe it's true that she enchanted Beaten and led her to the sea where she drowned. I'm afraid of Tedda. What if she harms my child? She curses whoever she wishes.'

'But she's frightened, Annie,' Susanna said. 'I must admit, she's as prickly as a thistle and I don't trust her, but that doesn't mean that the name they are calling her is true.' She took a breath. 'I recall my mother's wise words: "Tittle-tattle is the curse of every village. For who knows what a wagging tongue in the morning will bring home to roost by nightfall?"'

Anne pulled her baby close. 'Who knows, indeed? All I want is for my baby to be safe.'

'Amen to that,' Susanna whispered. Then she leaned forward, peering towards the door. 'Here comes Samuel, and at a lick too.'

Anne stood quietly and laid baby Bartholomew gently in the box that Samuel had fashioned as a cradle, and tucked him up tightly. Then Samuel burst into the room, shouting excitedly. 'Annie, come quickly. It's all happening at the harbour.'

'What's amiss?' Anne whispered, putting a finger to her lips to bid Samuel to be quieter.

'Come and see.' He was still talking too loudly. 'There is an uproar by the seawall. A man has come from Bodmin to take Tedda Lobb. She's tied in a cart, and they are threatening to put a scold's bridle on her.'

'For shame,' Susanna began.

'No – she's shouting and cursing for everyone to hear. Come, it's sport to see her screaming.'

'I will not,' Anne replied. 'Bartholomew's asleep. And if Tedda sees him there, who knows what curses may fly?' She knelt by the cradle protectively.

Susanna stood up. 'Poor Tedda. I'll come with you.' She followed Samuel out into the street. He had begun to run.

'I don't want to miss it. The man from Bodmin has a horse and cart to take her to the jail. He says he'll make her admit her wrongdoing.'

Susanna hurried after him. They arrived at the harbour where a tall man in a black hat had thrust Tedda into a wagon and tied her hands. A crowd had gathered – fishermen, children, other villagers – all watching the scene. Susanna saw Merryn Gilbert, Hedyn next to him. Yowann was standing nearby, with his hands on his hips.

'And she stands accused of bewitching Beaten Gilbert, causing her to fall in the sea, whereby she drowned. And she made my wife cough up a nail.' He caught sight of Susanna. 'Here's Mistress Boram, who is a good pellar. She nursed my beloved wife back from near death. She'll swear that my words are true.'

Susanna stared down at her hands. She had never heard Yowann speak fondly of Eliza and she wondered at the strength of his words. 'I hope Eliza's better now, Yowann. I can only say that she was plagued with the cough.'

'She speaks true.' Yowann behaved as if she had agreed with him. He turned directly to the man in the black hat. 'Take the old woman at once, before she does any more damage. And stop her tongue.'

'Stop her tongue,' a man yelled from the crowd and there was loud cheering.

'I'm not what you call me.' Tedda wriggled away from the man, who had her by the wrist. 'But you'm all cursed, all of St Mawgen Cove will be blighted. Trouble brews like a storm and when it breaks, you'm all be hit by the lightning that follows.' Her eyes blazed. 'And there are others where you should point the finger of blame – one who stands nearby, and her daughter, who may appear an innocent maid but she'll become that which you all call me today, you mark my words. I taught her all.' Her eyes glinted. 'And I tell you, she'll cause many of you men to perish until Judgement Day arrives, when her soul will be deemed black as hell.' She spat at the man in the hat as he threw her to her knees. She cried out, '*Gas dhymm yn kres!*' but he ignored her pleas for mercy and turned her to the baying crowd for all to see.

Susanna looked for Katel and saw her standing at the back of the crowd, her shawl pulled tightly. Their eyes met and Susanna saw the fear in her daughter's face. She had seen it there when Katel had been a child and soothed her nightmares. But now, Katel was frozen with a new terror.

The man in the black hat pushed a scold's bridle on Tedda's face and dragged her to her feet. She was shrunken now, quaking and sobbing. The man urged the horse and cart forwards. 'I'll take her to Bodmin Jail,' he announced to Yowann. 'There she'll admit to her sins and be punished.'

Someone in the crowd said, 'Hang the witch.' Another fisherman crossed himself quickly as the cart pulled away. Susanna had seen enough. She wrapped her shawl across her body and set off back towards her cottage.

There was someone at her side, speaking in a low voice. 'May I walk with you?'

Susanna gazed into Colan's eyes. 'Where's Joan?'

'She's busy in The Ship. I came down to see the commotion.'

Susanna hurried ahead. 'I think you came to see poor Tedda brought to her knees.'

'What do you think of it? Is Tedda what they call her?'

'Truly? I think not,' Susanna replied. 'I think her no more than a lonely, frightened woman. Beaten was confused and wandered from her bed. Eliza's cough was just the result of influenza. I cannot believe she coughed up a nail. Men are ready to blame an innocent old woman when they want to explain unnatural things.'

'And women are quick to cast doubt too.' Colan kept pace with her. 'I agree. You have a kind heart, Susanna. You see the best in all people.'

'I believe we all must,' Susanna said sadly. 'Poor Tedda. I don't like her and, in truth, I feared her a little. But she's no witch.'

'She sought to accuse you and Katel too, a moment ago.' Colan moved protectively towards her. 'But no one will believe that. Everyone in St Mawgen admires your skills.'

'I do my best.' Susanna paused; they had reached the top of the hill. 'I must go in, Colan. I have much to do and so do you. I'm sure your wife waits.'

'Susanna.' Colan did not move. 'I don't believe in enchantment. But I can't sleep at night for thoughts of you. It's always been this way. I can't change. And sometimes I wake in a fever.'

'Go to Joan,' Susanna said gently.

'One soft word from you, and I'd be happy.'

'You and I have always been close, since we played as children. You know there's a place in my heart that belongs to you.' Susanna gave a long sigh. 'But we may not look backwards. You have a wonderful wife. One day, God willing, you'll be the best of fathers to happy children. Go.'

She left him where he was and rushed into the cottage, pausing to gulp a breath. She wondered why, after all these years, standing so close to him made her tremble. He was the best person she knew. She loved him more than any man. But she'd chosen to put him from her after Katel was born. Only she knew why. And she wouldn't change her mind.

There was no tomorrow for her and Colan, no today. Only yesterday and sweet, secret memories.

26

Megan was still thinking about the phone call she'd just made to her parents as she dressed for dinner. She was enjoying surfing and meeting new people so much, she'd almost forgotten to mention Emma Davey, but when her father had asked her if there was 'any news', she knew who he was referring to. She told him she was working on it – she'd find out more tomorrow. She left it at that. For now, she knew that she was a widow, that her husband had died of a heart attack, and he was called John.

But tonight she was in a party mood as she stood in her room deciding what to wear. The evening would be a celebration. Claude was cooking special macaroni cheese for four, and he and Julien wanted to open a bottle of Prosecco to thank her for her support with their plans for the future. Megan had invited Carly from the surf shop to join them. Megan had visited the shop that afternoon to buy swimwear, a red bikini and a black swimsuit. She'd also selected a snorkel mask, telling Carly she might try a bit of diving. She'd free-dived several times with Jay years ago, and she'd become a good scuba diver, although her skills were a bit rusty. So she wasn't worried about the risks, and in truth, she was imagining bumping into Poseidon, the grumpy Greek god, while she was in the water. Perhaps she'd find a way to ask him about the history of the cove. He intrigued her. Yes, he'd been rude and had just about acknowledged her when she'd spoken to him, but it hadn't put her off. He was very good looking. Megan hoped that didn't make her shallow.

Her thoughts moved to Emma Davey. Megan felt sorry for her. Whatever had happened to her husband was apparently linked to the spooky story of the Waiting Witch and her kiss of death, although she wouldn't tell her father that part. Megan wasn't sure she believed Tom's words. An unexplained heart attack was a much more logical reason for John Davey's death. She was definitely on the way to discovering more about her half-sister, and that gave her mixed feelings of empathy, warmth and, at the same time, apprehension.

For now, tonight's dinner was a celebration. Megan picked a favourite dress that she'd brought with her on the off-chance she might be going somewhere smart and she felt cheerful as she stepped into the hall.

The smell stopped her in her tracks. It was heavy, acrid, like brine, the deep ocean. A rancidity stuck in her throat, like rotting flesh. Megan was surprised: the cleaner had been in earlier and the space had smelled fresh after breakfast. And, to the best of her knowledge, there were no new guests in either of the upstairs rooms who might have returned from an afternoon's fishing.

She looked up. The stairs that led to rooms two and four twisted into darkness. The stench seemed to be lingering there and the air was even colder, making her shiver inside the thin dress. She decided to go up, just step by step. Of course, there would be nothing there. And if anything... jumped... from the shadows, she'd run back to the safety of her room. Curiosity made her determined to check that the horrible smell came from stale, empty old rooms.

She made her way to the top, following the sour odour. Around the corner there was a narrow landing with room four at the end. The door was ajar. The stink was coming from the room.

Megan crept towards the door but she couldn't see inside. She could hear a faint, muffled sound, a slow wheezing. It could be anything: the ancient central heating system, an old radiator. Her skin was gooseflesh. She wondered if she should call out, if anyone might reply, but the idea of her own voice breaking the silence made her nervous. She stuck out a hand and pushed the door. It opened slowly with an agonising creak.

Megan took a single pace inside the room. The heavy curtains were pulled together, stifling the light. Only a diamond chink of brightness filtered from outside. She tried the light switch but it didn't work. The furniture was shrouded in darkness; it was less modern than in her room, and the space felt eerie, as if something was waiting. A tall wardrobe loomed in the corner and a wooden rocking chair had been placed against the far wall. She took another step forward.

The stink of rotten fish filled her nose as she stood blinking in the darkness. Megan was becoming accustomed to the gloom. There was an etching on the wall in black and white, an old ship perched on rough seas, its sails billowing. She approached it and read the inscription beneath: *Bonaventure*, 1625. She edged further into the room, her legs like jelly, narrowing her eyes in the shadows to examine the rigging, the masts, the decks.

Then the rocking chair began to move.

Megan turned quickly, her pulse jumping in her throat. The chair creaked, forward and back, forward and back. It was empty, but still it swayed, as if propelled by an invisible energy. The reek of fish was intense as the chair gathered speed, groaning as it swung to and fro.

Megan rushed to the door and ran downstairs, her heart thudding. She bolted outside into the cool, fresh air, leaning against the wall, catching her breath in gulps. Her legs almost gave way beneath her.

* * *

Megan decided that she wouldn't allow the image of the rocking chair to spoil her evening, but she was badly shaken. Nothing would make her go upstairs again. The creaking sound of the rocking chair was still with her. Making her best effort to look as if nothing had happened, she met Carly at the entrance to the inn. 'I hope you're hungry. It's mac and cheese.'

'My fave,' Carly said. 'And I've just seen a fisherman come in with a squeezebox thing under his arm. We're in for some music tonight.'

Megan thought briefly about her conversation with Tom. 'Carly,' she said, 'do you know what happened to John Davey?'

Carly frowned. 'Is he the man who died of a heart attack by the harbour?'

Megan wasn't sure how to say what was in her mind. 'Did you know him? Or his wife?'

'They weren't surfers,' Carly said simply. 'So I never met them. Shall we get some food?'

'Let's.' Megan decided she'd leave things where they were for now and led Carly to the table set for four.

Julien poured fizz into glasses and Claude rushed from the kitchen in chef's whites, placing a huge dish on the table. He glanced into the bar area where a well-groomed young man wearing a crisp white shirt served drinks. 'Josh is getting busy, Julien. If we get more customers, you'll have to go behind the bar.'

The inn was crowded now, and a woman with a violin was tuning up. There would definitely be shanties this evening.

'I can't complain, Claude. It's business.' Julien lifted a fork. 'Let's eat while we can. Then, if we have to leave the ladies to finish off the cheesy mac, at least we've celebrated.' He looked pleased. 'We found out lots of useful things today.'

Megan thought so too. 'Tom told us about the Waiting Witch.'

'I heard something about her,' Carly said. 'People say she's linked to the man who was found dead in the street. But that's just superstition, right?'

'It must be superstition,' Claude said. 'But if a good story helps make this place popular, isn't it useful?'

Megan wasn't so sure. 'We ought to avoid upsetting anyone. A man died. He has a widow in the cove.'

'Of course, I know. You're right, it troubles me too.' Julien held up his hands. 'We won't mention the woman on the cliffs. But what if we can make people excited about the idea of ghosts?'

'Excited isn't a word I'd use.' Carly pulled an unimpressed face. 'I've heard people in the surf shop talking. Apparently, the rooms here are creepy as hell.'

'Mm.' Megan was still thinking about the creaking chair.

'Yes, but,' Julien protested, 'I like what Megan suggested at breakfast. We sell T-shirts with the slogan, "I just slept with the Drenched Man".'

'I just saw him.' Megan couldn't help herself.

'Who?' Claude raised an eyebrow.

'The Drenched Man,' Megan said. 'Not exactly *saw*. He was in a rocking chair in room four. It rocked back and forward by itself.'

Carly placed a hand on her shoulder. 'You saw him?'

'I smelled him. The chair moved by itself.'

'That's horrible.' Julien wrinkled his brow. 'Were you afraid?'

Megan hugged herself. 'I wouldn't spend a night in there.'

Julien exhaled nervously. 'When we first came here to look round, I thought the inn had a bit of an atmosphere. I just kept hoping things would be all right once we got the business going. But the guests don't want to stay.'

'It's worse than that. We can't ask anyone to sleep in a room where rocking chairs move by themselves.' Claude placed a hand over Julien's. 'We can't open the inn to the public if...'

Julien cringed at the thought. 'The last owners were glad to leave. I should've known it was too good to be true when we bought it for such a low price.'

'There has to be a way to make it work,' Carly said.

'I think there is.' Megan was thoughtful. 'We can be upfront about the ghosts. But I think the best way is...'

'Yes?' Julien asked.

'We have to find out everything we can. We make the inn a kind of museum, or at least a place where people who stay here have the facts.'

'So the knowledge of the ghosts makes them less scary?' Carly asked. 'Or at least the guests are forewarned.'

'It means we're honest,' Claude said.

Julien agreed. 'But we just don't mention the Waiting Witch at all. Because people believe she's bad luck.'

'I wish there was a way of bringing her some peace. Think how badly she must've been treated, being called a witch. So many women were wrongly accused. And that poor woman who weeps—' Megan looked up. A man had just come in and was waving, leaning on the bar. 'Oh, it's Tom.'

'I'll buy him a drink.' Julien called out, 'Tom.' He jumped to his feet, hurrying towards him. 'Thank you for your help today. You were most kind. Josh, get this man a double rum.'

'Cheers,' Tom said. He accepted a glass and immediately put it to his lips.

'Come and join us,' Julien said.

'I might come over dreckly,' Tom said slowly. He indicated a small case that he'd deposited on the floor. 'I brought my concertina. We'll sing first and talk later.' Tom emptied his glass. 'Is that champagne you've got there?'

'Prosecco,' Julien said.

'I'll definitely join you.' Tom raised his glass in Megan's direction. 'Nice to see you again, Megan.'

'You too.' Megan lifted her glass in reply.

Julien came back to the table and sat down. 'So, how do we lay our ghosts to rest?'

'I have a few leads. Tom said the answer lies at the bottom of the ocean,' Megan said cryptically, hoping that Julien wouldn't mention Tom's idea of seeking the advice of the Greek god in front of Carly.

'And I can ask people who come in the shop if they've got the bottle to stay overnight in a local pub with a really spooky atmosphere.' Carly spooned more macaroni cheese onto her plate. 'This is delicious.'

'It is,' Megan agreed. 'It's a good job we're surfing at dawn again.'

'Oh – no, sorry – count me out tomorrow,' Carly said, chewing. 'A friend of mine in St Austell has got two kids and she's on her own. I usually take Wednesdays off and we go out somewhere.'

'No problem,' Megan said. 'I'll just hit the barrels by myself.'

'I'll see you on Thursday, though, bright and early.' Carly held up her glass. 'More Prosecco, please, Claude. I'm buying, mind. No more "on the house" this evening.'

'Of course,' he said, rushing to the bar for a bottle.

A melancholy chord sounded, the strains of a violin, and a woman started to sing. She was dark-haired, serene-faced, wearing a long velvet dress. Her voice was sweet, filled with emotion. Everyone in the room listened intently as she performed a song about a sailor who broke her heart. For a while, Megan was transfixed: it amazed her how such a beautiful voice could tug at her heartstrings and evoke feelings of loss and anguish. The people in the bar applauded and Megan clapped too. Then a man with an accordion sang about smugglers on the high sea. Most of the audience joined in the chorus, slapping the table with open palms.

'We have a full house,' Julien said.

'Maybe this is the way forward,' Claude agreed. 'We give our guests the proper Cornish experience.'

Megan glanced towards the bar. Tom Hocking stood up, gave a little bow and started to play his concertina. Then he began to sing.

> *Early in the morn, on the clifftop, all alone*
> *A Cornish maid stands waiting, her locks all long and blown*
> *Her face is wet with tears, me boys, and I can tell you true,*
> *She's searching for a fishing boat lost in the ocean blue.*

Megan sat up, listening to the words. It was a slow song, and his voice was sorrowful. The crowd in the bar joined in the chorus.

> *Let's hear it for the Cornish boys who sail the salty brine.*
> *And for the maid who waits alone upon the dark shoreline...*

Megan leaned forward, all ears, as the tale unfolded of broken hearts, sailors lost at sea, a woman who waited in vain. Tom raised his gravelly voice and everyone in the bar was silent, hanging on to each note. Then, with a flourish of his squeezebox, Tom sang the final verse.

> *So when you walk the cliffs, me boys, and stand upon the beach*
> *She'll be watching there behind you, better pray you're far from reach*
> *Her lips will brush against your face and rest assured of this*
> *No man has never lived who felt the Waiting Witch's kiss...*

Everyone in the bar raised their voice for the final chorus.

> *Let's hear it for the Cornish boys who sail the salty brine.*
> *And for the maid who waits alone upon the dark shoreline...*

Tom squeezed a few more bars from the concertina and then there was silence. No one clapped. It was as if everyone was lost in thought.

Megan shuddered. It was the song of the Waiting Witch. Everyone in St Mawgen believed she was out there, on the clifftop, watching.

At that moment, it felt like she was no myth. She was real.

27

Several days had passed since Tedda Lobb had been taken away in the horse-drawn cart. Susanna and Katel sat by the fire one evening, eating pottage. Katel was lost in thought; she'd been in low spirits for a while and Susanna was anxious. The death of Beaten and the subsequent arrest of Tedda had made everyone in the cove edgy. She reached out a hand, placing it tenderly on Katel's wrist.

'You're quiet.'

Katel made a low sound, as if thinking. Then she said, 'I haven't heard the chawk since Tedda was taken away.'

Susanna nodded. 'You won't hear it again. I think she sought to fill your head with false hope.'

'And now I have no hope at all.' Katel turned her face to Susanna and it was streaked with tears. 'I set my heart on a prince.'

'This is how people ensnare us, by promising things that won't come to pass.'

'She told me I could become a great pellar, and that she'd teach me.'

'Her ways are not ours. I'll teach you, Katel. You already know much about the powers of simples and stones.'

'But what of Beaten? What of her?' Katel wiped her face. 'It was my fault, what happened. The doll. I took it freely because my heart was full of foolishness and now I regret it.'

'We must not talk of the poppet that Tedda gave you. I've buried it. We must forget what she bade you do.' Susanna's hand gripped her daughter's wrist. 'Don't speak of it again.'

Tears brimmed in Katel's eyes. 'But I could have prevented it. Had I not been mean-spirited, Beaten would be alive.'

'Tedda saw a weakness in you, child. You're young and impressionable, and she used it for her own evil,' Susanna whispered. 'You mustn't think of her again.'

Katel pointed to the hag-stones, still scattered in the hearth. 'And what of these little stones? The cord broke.'

'I'll thread them and hang them back in the chimney. I hope they'll keep evil at bay. But we can't undo what has already been done.'

'I'll make amends to the Gilbert family.' Katel took a breath. 'Merryn has asked me if I'll walk with him sometime, just for a while after we finish work. I said I would ask you if I may. And if he wishes, perhaps I can give him good cheer.'

Susanna frowned. 'Do you love Merryn?'

'I'll try to like him.' Katel gazed towards the chimney again, as if listening. 'Perhaps liking can become a sort of love. After all, I owe his family.'

'No, Katel,' Susanna said quietly. 'You owe yourself the best life you can have. Be a good person. Be honest with yourself and with this young man.'

'He loves me, Mother.' Katel looked sad. 'May I walk with him tomorrow? Just to please him, and to see if it pleases me a little?'

'You may,' Susanna said. 'After this sad time with poor Beaten, and with Tedda, we all need some happiness.'

'I don't believe I'll ever be happy,' Katel said. 'But I'll be good. Perhaps, Mother, I'll become like you.'

'Like me?' Susanna was troubled by her words.

'Loved by many but giving your heart to no one. I think you're lonely. Whoever fathered me changed your life for ever.' Katel leaned forward. 'I long to know who he is.'

'I understand. But I'll never speak of it.' Susanna stared into the fire. She saw an image there, a man and a woman in each other's arms. The licking flames became their bodies in the crackling heat of passion, quick to burn, quickly over. It had been a costly mistake that would be with her all her days.

Her thoughts were interrupted by a knocking on the door. Katel met her eyes and Susanna noticed the fear there. She knew at once that her daughter's guilt was uppermost in her mind at all times: Katel expected those who came for Tedda to come for her and she was constantly on edge. Susanna put her bowl of pottage down, stood silently and placed a hand on Katel's head, smoothing her long hair. 'Fear nothing,' she said. 'I'll take care of you – you know that.'

Katel's round eyes met hers and she nodded. 'Thank you.'

Susanna opened the door to see Yowann Hicks blocking the last light of dusk, his arms folded. Behind him, a horse trudged by pulling a cart and Susanna was reminded of Tedda Lobb's last day in the cove. Beyond, the hill to the harbour stretched away to a tossing crinkled sea and a dappled mauve sunset.

Susanna asked politely, 'What can I do for you, Yowann?'

'May I come inside?'

'Of course.' Susanna stepped back. 'Would you like some ale?'

'No, I won't stay long, thank you,' Yowann said quickly. He glanced towards Katel and nodded.

She looked at her fingers to avoid his eyes and said, 'Good evening, Yowann.'

Susanna asked, 'How's Eliza? When I saw her this morning, she seemed much cheered.'

'She's recovering well. I thank you for the care you have shown her. And you too, Katel. You'll soon learn your mother's craft. St Mawgen Cove has much need of it.'

'Thank you,' Katel said quietly.

Yowann turned back to Susanna. 'I bring news of Tedda Lobb. She's in Bodmin Jail still, but I believe she won't be there long.'

'Oh?' Susanna felt her pulse quicken.

'She's admitted to her evil ways. Under examination, she's told us how she sought to harm Beaten Gilbert and how she caused Eliza to cough up a nail.'

Susanna shook her head. 'It's hard to believe it.'

'She's evil,' Yowann said simply. 'And we'd all do well to forget her.'

'Well, thank you for telling us this,' Susanna said, hoping Yowann would leave.

'There's one more thing.' He stood his ground. 'Tedda said she was not acting alone.'

'Oh?' Susanna suddenly found it difficult to breathe.

'She named many women from the cove.'

Susanna lowered her eyes in an attempt to appear humble. 'Perhaps you shouldn't believe her, Yowann.' She glanced towards Katel, who was watching, wild-eyed, like a cornered animal. 'A frightened woman may easily lie to save herself.'

'I don't believe her, but her talk is dangerous for those who are innocent.' Yowann pressed his lips together. 'I've paid the jailer for his silence. When Tedda's dead, she'll speak no more lies.'

'I thank you,' Susanna said, her eyes full of gratitude.

Yowann shrugged as if it was nothing. 'The jailer won't speak of it. But Tedda told him that there were others who practised dark magic. She spoke of Katel as if she'd learned evil ways from her. She mentioned you and Anne Boram. She even named Joan Stephens, whom she said sought her help to get with child.'

'Tedda's telling lies. Katel did no such thing. And many women seek help from pellars who offer herbs and plants. But Joan wouldn't go to Tedda.'

'I agree. Tedda's methods were steeped in bad magic,' Yowann said. 'She assumed the shape of a chawk – she confessed to it – and spoke to people in that form to confuse them. She admitted that she cursed Eliza and Beaten. She made poppets, and potions from nightshade, and she sought to harm people.'

'I'm sorry to hear these things.' Susanna did not know what else to say. 'I thought of her only as a woman who went too far with her old ways.'

'She's sentenced to hang at Exeter in two weeks' time,' Yowann said. 'She'll be watched night and day until then. She wears a scold's bridle at all times to stop her tongue. Given the chance, she'll speak more evil. I've had her locked in chains to prevent her from changing her shape into a jackdaw and flying away.'

Susanna couldn't help it. 'I feel sorry for her.'

'You mustn't,' Yowann said gently. 'She sought to blame you in her place, and Katel too. She even said it was Katel who caused Beaten to drown.'

'That's not true,' Katel said too loudly.

'Don't concern yourself with her accusations,' Yowann replied. 'No one else will hear what she has said.'

'I'm grateful,' Susanna said quietly.

'I'm pleased to hear it.' Yowann met her gaze meaningfully and Susanna examined his face. There was satisfaction in his expression; he believed she was indebted to him now and it gave her an uncomfortable feeling.

He gave a polite bow. 'Good evening to you, Susanna, Katel.'

'God be with you,' Susanna said quietly. She watched him go, closing the door crisply.

Silence filled the room along with many anxious thoughts. Then Katel leaped up and rushed into Susanna's arms. 'Mother, I'm afraid of what may happen.'

'Don't worry, Katel. All will be well.' Susanna held her tightly, smoothing her hair.

'But Tedda said—'

'Tedda's words don't concern us. Yowann has bought the jailer's silence. He has been kind.'

'Why would he do that, Mother?'

'Because he's a powerful man; he can do as he wishes.' Susanna was thoughtful. 'It suits him well that the cove is a place of calm. He will profit best from people working hard with nothing else on their minds but their pay and filling their bellies each evening. Talk of evil practices and bad magic make for a troubled community, and that is not good for his business.'

Katel understood. 'I hear that on dark nights Yowann brings goods from wrecked ships and sells them for profit.'

'He smuggles brandy.' Susanna closed her eyes, her child warm in her arms. 'Once, when I was helping Eliza with her influenza, Yowann gave me brandy to drink. It was strong and warm, unlike anything I've ever drunk.'

'Strong and warm, like a man's kisses,' Katel said quietly.

Susanna held her at arm's length. 'What do you know of a man's kisses, child?' She tugged her next to the fire, huddling close to the warmth.

'I know nothing yet but'– Katel's eyes shone – 'it must be wonderful. Sometimes I dream of my prince coming across the seas. He's dark of countenance and his embrace is strong, and he whispers sweet things in his own tongue.'

'It's a dream,' Susanna said gently. 'We all dream.'

'Beaten will dream no more.' Katel closed her eyes.

'No, she won't,' Susanna said firmly. 'And may her soul rest in peace. But you have a future, Katel. You can become a great pellar, you can know the love of a real man, not one who fills your imagination. You can share the joy of children in your home and a man whose touch makes your heart leap like a hare.'

'Did you know that joy? With my father?'

'I knew the love that comes with holding my child in my arms and looking into the sweetness of a trusting face. There's nothing like it, Katel, believe me.'

'Then I shall pray for it,' Katel said. 'I'll try to think no more on Tedda.'

'That's wise.'

'Even though I'm afraid of what Yowann said, that she mentioned our names and those of Aunt Annie and Joan Stephens.'

'No one will know of it now,' Susanna said quietly. 'Thanks to Yowann.'

'But it reminded me, Mother, of what you said about the place in the north country. You told me it happened years ago, in a place called Pendle: that Old Demdike and Mother Chattox and many other women confessed to selling their souls to the devil, creating clay figures.'

'Don't concern yourself with the past. It's sad what happened to those women, but we can do nothing.'

'I imagine it may have been the same as with Tedda. One woman spoke a single word and many other women were accused. Then everyone in the community was jangling about it and agreeing.'

'Jangling and gossiping spread like fire. People wish to believe the worst,' Susanna said. 'I beg you, Katel, put it far from your thoughts. It is almost bedtime and tomorrow will be a beautiful long day of sunshine. You may walk with Merryn, get to know him, listen to him as he shares the secrets of his heart.'

'I will, Mother.'

Susanna collected the dishes to wash them. 'Be at peace in your thoughts and your heart. Think only of the future.'

'I will. Each night I pray for Beaten, for forgiveness, and that she may now know peace. May I too remember Tedda in my prayers?'

'It may do some good. Don't think of her otherwise. She has gone now. She won't come back.'

'She won't,' Katel agreed. She leaned closer to the fire, stretching her palms, warming them. Then there was a loud, throaty screech and she jerked back.

A jackdaw flew down the chimney and swirled into the room. It flapped its wings hard on the air, squawking a loud cry. Then it settled on the table, next to a jug of water, and looked around.

Its beady eyes moved from Katel to Susanna, back to Katel, then it opened its beak and cawed again.

28

Megan fell asleep quickly thanks to the Prosecco, but all night she was tossed by dreams. She imagined herself as a sailor in the black-and-white etching of the ship she'd seen in room four. Sea shanty chords rattled in her head, storms rolled in, dark clouds threatening on the horizon, lightning flickering over turbulent waves. She woke just before dawn and sat up in bed to listen for signs of movement overhead. But there was no banging, no rocking chair. Her room was in shadow, the furniture huddled like ghosts in the darkness. She switched the bedside lamp on. All was quiet and calm. The air smelled fresh and clean: today was just another day of her holiday. She crept from bed, reached for the clothes she'd laid out for surfing and tugged them on.

Outside, it was not yet light, but Megan was happy in the chugging Beetle as she drove down to the beach, the first rays of sunlight a dappled red over the sea. She enjoyed the familiar clanking and churning of the engine, the faulty heater blowing a cold jet in her face. She shivered and thought of the breakfast Claude would make later. There would be hot coffee and the chance to talk more to Julien about his plans for the inn's future.

Today was Wednesday: that gave her four more days to surf and swim with Carly and to find out information about Emma Davey. She was more intrigued than ever now she'd heard Tom's terrifying story of the Waiting Witch and how John Davey was found dead. She didn't believe he'd been touched by a witch – the poor man had simply suffered a heart attack. The rest was St Mawgen Cove tradition, gossip and superstition.

Half an hour later, the sky was a snaking line of blue, orange sunshine dispelling cobalt clouds as Megan paddled her board towards the surf. It was breathtaking to be alone, feeling the swell and the tug of the waves, conscious of each movement beneath her body. Her heart thudded, adrenalin pumping, and her mouth was wide open, gasping for more air. The water cracked around her like the loud crash of a tree trunk snapping as a huge wave approached. Megan paddled as fast as she could, clawing herself under the lip to match the speed of the rising wave, trying her best to catch it.

Spray blinded her eyes as she leaped to her feet, popping up on the board, a steep ramp of water beneath her, shifting and taking shape. Megan accelerated down the wave, whooping with joy – she couldn't help it – using all her strength, feeling the thrill of the ocean's lift. She'd caught the wave perfectly: it must be seven, eight feet high. Then someone was close by, sharing it with her. Megan was aware of a black wetsuit, the flash of damp blond hair.

Poseidon.

He was closest to the curl, the breaking part of the wave, so she raised her thumb, giving him priority. He moved to the left and she to the right. A surfboard's nose could kill, and Megan was well aware of the importance of surf etiquette. Then he was gone.

The lip of the wave folded over: a barrel, the biggest thrill of all. Megan found herself in her own private room of water. It was like being held still, a precious moment inside Mother Nature's silent womb. Suddenly, all sound was muffled, she felt totally at peace and the water was illuminated as it rotated through the face of the wave.

The paddle back to shore was both exhilarating and exhausting. Megan stood on the beach dripping, breathing heavily, but she couldn't stop smiling. The muscles in her limbs ached but the whole experience felt delicious. She picked up the towel she'd left and wiped her face, squeezing water from her hair. Then someone was beside her, holding up a surfboard, his face serious. It was the surfer, Poseidon.

'I'm sorry. I owe you an apology. That's twice I've done that now,' he said.

'What?' Megan's ears were still full of surf, her mind filled with the excitement of getting barrelled.

'I should've asked you pre-drop if I could share a party wave. I didn't mean to burn you. I'm sorry.'

'No damage done. You're an experienced surfer and so am I. I wasn't worried.' Megan rubbed saltwater from her eyes. 'It was no more disrespectful than blanking me yesterday when I said good morning.'

'Ah.' The surfer seemed momentarily confused. Megan noticed his blue eyes, made bluer by the harsh spray of surf on his tanned face. Her eyes flicked to the gold chain around his neck, a little engraved bell, a symbol of good luck. His grin broadened, showing perfect, even teeth. 'I'm sorry. I was lost in thought. I often do that before a dive – it's no excuse, I know. It was only when I'd passed you that I realised I hadn't said good morning back.'

Megan had started to feel cold. 'No problem.'

'I've seen you here a few times surfing. Are you on holiday?'

'Yes.' Megan nodded. 'I'm staying at The Ship.'

'That's great,' he replied, sounding as if he had no idea about its reputation. They stood, waiting for the other to say something. Then the surfer said, 'I often bring the board down first thing, then dive later in the day.'

'I've seen you scuba diving. I'd like to dive while I'm here.' Megan thought of the mask she'd bought, and here was an opportunity to use it. 'What are you looking for?'

'Evidence of old wrecks, any relics. Information, really. The cove's history is beneath the ocean.'

'That sounds awesome.' Megan was intrigued. She remembered Tom's words about the witch's secret lying beneath the waves. She couldn't help the words that flew from her mouth next. 'Could I come with you?'

Poseidon didn't seem to know how to respond. Then he said, 'Maybe.'

'So, when do you go next?' Megan was trying to tie him down. She wanted to be there herself, beneath the ocean. She wasn't so sure that he'd be a good diving companion, though. There was something distant and self-absorbed about him, as if he was not quite sure what he might be doing next.

'I don't know,' the surfer said.

There, just as she'd thought, he was looking for an excuse not to take her with him. He clearly preferred diving solo. Megan almost changed her mind:

if he wasn't interested in sharing his knowledge, if he wasn't interested in her, then so be it.

'I came here to surf and to do some scuba diving. I'm pretty good at it.' She turned to go. 'But no worries. I'll go by myself. Well, it was nice meeting you.'

He let her get five paces away. 'Wait.'

She looked back, a half turn, giving him the smallest of chances, and paused. He called, 'Can I get you a coffee later and we'll talk about a dive? That way I can gauge what sort of diver you are. How much you've done before, what you want to get out of it.'

'Sure.' Megan put on her best uninterested look. She had no idea why, but she was deliberately mirroring his indifference. 'There's a café on the other side of the car park.'

'Afterdune Delight. We could meet there.'

'This afternoon?' Megan helped him – he'd never make his mind up otherwise.

'What about at eleven, this morning?'

'Right. I'll be there at eleven,' Megan said. She spun on her heel and hurried back to the Beetle. She was cold now. She needed a shower, a change of clothes and breakfast. But her heart was thumping. She'd got her dive.

Then she realised she hadn't introduced herself to the surfer, and she couldn't call him Poseidon. He was gorgeous, certainly, but quite eccentric. She wasn't sure if that put her off him a little. Jay had been passionate, spontaneous, full of enthusiasm. She'd loved that about him. The idea of a cold-fish diver who couldn't make his mind up and was so self-absorbed he couldn't manage a hello wasn't really exciting her at all.

* * *

'So, what will you do with yourself today?' Julien asked as he poured coffee.

'Well.' Megan tucked into beans on toast. 'It's funny you should ask. I've been talking to the surfer who lives in the cottage by the harbour. He might take me diving.'

'Oh?' Julien paused, holding the jug. 'Then you might find out something about the history of The Ship?'

'I hope so,' Megan said. 'He seems a strange sort of person. A bit distant.'

'I suppose he's in love with his work. I've spoken to him a couple of times.'

'Oh? Has he been in here?'

'Twice. Once for a meal.'

'By himself?' Megan wondered if he had a partner.

'No, he was with friends from the university in Falmouth. They were from the same faculty. I remember him telling me.'

'What faculty?'

'I've no idea, but he teaches there, I think. And the rest of the time he researches, but I don't know what.'

'And the other time you saw him?'

'That was early in the summer. We had a barbecue outside and there was music and singing. He came with his parents. He introduced them. I remember he brought a guitar and they did a couple of songs.'

'Is he any good?' Megan asked.

'He's a talented guy.' Julien gave her a knowing look. 'And hot. Claude thinks so too.'

'But he has no personality.' Megan waved a hand. She felt a little disloyal to be dismissing him. She didn't know him. 'He's a great surfer, though, and I hope he can tell me about the cove's history and what's at the bottom of the ocean. Then...' She held out her coffee cup for a top-up. 'I can come back here and tell you all about it.'

Julien flourished the jug of coffee. 'Perfect. Claude and I will join you later for a chat. Would you like pan-fried salmon for dinner?'

'I'd love it,' Megan replied.

'And I hope you slept well last night. No dripping men? No moving rocking chairs?'

'It was fine,' Megan said, taking in his anxious expression.

Julien was still hovering. 'Sometimes guests give us wonderful reviews and say how much they've enjoyed it here because they've slept well and other times, people refuse to pay.'

'Maybe you should keep some sort of record,' Megan suggested. 'Perhaps the spirits only come when there's a full moon or on Tuesdays and Saturdays?' She saw Julien's expression become even more troubled. 'No, don't worry.'

'I must go. Our barman isn't in this lunchtime and our cleaner has gone to see her midwife. Will you be all right if I do your room later today?'

'It's OK. It was cleaned yesterday.'

'I'll change the towels,' Julien said. 'I'm – what is the English expression? – the Jack of all trades.'

'I think you do a great job,' Megan said encouragingly. 'And yes to the towels, please. I'm off for a shower now. After all, I have to look my best to meet the enigmatic diver.'

She pushed her chair back, collecting her phone and keys. As she hurried away, Julien called, 'You never know, he might turn out to be fascinating.'

Megan's voice travelled back through the air. 'If he can take me on a dive to see a wrecked seventeenth-century ship at the bottom of the sea, I'll be totally delighted.'

29

The next weeks passed quietly. At the end of August, news reached the cove that Tedda Lobb had died in jail before she could be hanged. No one spoke about her now. In the second week of September, the huer's dawn cries brought in another huge haul of pilchards and everyone was busy each waking hour, salting and smoking the fish. The word among the fishermen was that now Tedda had gone, good luck would prevail.

October brought in the rains. Samuel Boram bought his wife a new dress made from the best linen and a new bed with a straw mattress. Baby Bartholomew had started to crawl. Joan Stephens served ale in The Ship with a secret smile on her face – only Susanna knew the reason for it – and Colan busied himself each evening as Yowann and his friends crowded around a round table, drinking wine and brandy, hunched over a map in candlelight, their voices low.

Katel walked down to the ocean each evening before dusk with Merryn Gilbert, her arm through his, speaking quietly. The latest rumour in St Mawgen was that they would marry the following year, although Katel lowered her eyes when asked, as if they had never discussed it. She was working hard during the day, salting fish, and accompanying her mother in her free time to visit people in the cove, treating children with coughs, helping pregnant women prepare for birth with raspberry teas for the womb and ginger root, mint and balm to help with sickness. Several times a week they called in on Eliza Hicks, who had pains in her hands and feet and was in a perpetual state of melancholy.

The jackdaw had not returned since Susanna let it fly out of the door on the evening that it had come down the chimney and it had disappeared into the skies. She'd convinced herself that it was the last time she'd hear from Tedda.

Then, one evening in late November, the storms came. Susanna lay on the straw mattress and listened to the whirling winds. Outside, the sea would be rough, the sky starless, the darkness stifling as the moon glided behind a cloud. It was a turbulent night, the sort of raging weather that signified change. She felt instinctively that something was coming, something new and dangerous, and she could not sleep.

As she often did, Susanna rolled on her back and closed her eyes. To calm her mind, she thought about the people she loved. Katel was becoming fond of Merryn; she was calmer, more settled. Tedda's influence had gone now and her daughter had grown into a lovely young woman with the kindest heart and the sweetest nature. Susanna whispered a thankful prayer for Katel, for her beloved brother, Samuel, his sweet wife and baby. She added gratitude for friends and neighbours, asking for Eliza's pains to leave her, for Hedyn Gilbert to be comforted and for Beaten to rest in peace. Tedda too. Then she whispered for a blessing for Joan, who was with child, that she might safely deliver a healthy baby. Colan did not speak to her much now, or beg her to offer him a kind word. Hopefully, Joan and the baby filled his thoughts.

Susanna opened her eyes. The wind wailed through the rafters like a ghost and she sat up straight, wide awake. It was raining heavily outside. She decided to go downstairs in her shift and make a drink from valerian root. It would help her to sleep. She stood up, shaking her hair loose from its plait and picked up a tallow candle. The smoky flame cast long shadows on the cobb walls. Downstairs, Katel was sitting bolt upright, staring into the fire.

'Can you not sleep?' Susanna's voice was hushed.

Katel did not turn round. 'I heard his voice. He spoke to me.'

Susanna knelt beside her, kissing her head. 'Whose voice did you hear?'

There was no reply as Susanna cradled her daughter in her arms. She felt an anxiety creeping over her skin. Katel's eyes were glassy. 'Whose voice?'

'The man who speaks in a different tongue. He's searching for me.'

'It's a dream, Katel.'

'No.' Katel was listening for the voice again. 'I heard him again. He's calling.'

Susanna frowned. 'I hear nothing.'

'It is to me he calls. Only I can hear him. He's afraid. He's shouting over and over in his language, "*Ay-day mwah – mon Dew*".'

'What does that mean?' Susanna gathered Katel closer in her arms. 'It's surely a dream?'

'It's real. I hear him now. He says, "*jay purr...*"'

'Katel, this is just the workings of a tired mind. I'll fetch you a drink and then you can sleep.'

Katel turned round and Susanna caught her breath. She had never seen her daughter look so wild, her face set in an expression of fear. 'Listen. Listen.'

Susanna was silent. She could hear noises outside: hammering rain, the sound of feet squelching in mud, the single cry. She pushed open the door and stared into the street. Teeming rain blinded her vision. There were lights in the harbour, flaring flames, and the cry of voices drifted from the sea. Then she saw them: two men, one with the other in his arms, urging him forward. They were soaked to the skin and moved awkwardly, spectres from the darkness. Susanna reached for her shawl, lifting the candle. 'Who's there?'

Samuel's cottage door scraped open – he too had heard the noise. The two young sailors lurched towards him, one talking in a breathless voice in a language Susanna had never heard before. The other was coughing violently, slipping from his grasp.

Samuel noticed Susanna and called to her, 'Help me. They're hurt.'

'Who are they? Where have they come from?' Susanna asked.

'I don't know. But they need our help. Let's get them inside.' He called over his shoulder, 'Annie, take Bartholomew and come into Susanna's house for a while. She and I need to tend them.'

Katel was behind her mother, wrapped in her shawl. 'I'll come.'

Susanna grabbed her basket and rushed to the sailors. Anne and her baby passed her on the threshold, hurrying towards Susanna's hearth. She and Samuel helped the tallest into Samuel's house. He was drenched and half-conscious. Katel was guiding the other man to the fireside, urging him to sit.

She called, 'Mother, he's bleeding.'

'Where from?' Susanna called over her shoulder as she and Samuel helped the taller one upstairs. He was wheezing, his breathing jagged. He smelled of the sea, a stench of salt water.

'From his shoulder, I think.'

'Clean the wound with vinegar and bind it tightly,' Susanna panted. The taller man was at the top of the step now. Samuel hauled him towards a chair in the bedroom, but it rocked several times under his weight and he slumped to the floor. Samuel eased him onto his back and stood away.

Susanna knelt over him. 'This one's shivering. He's swallowed a lot of ocean – it leaks from him. He's bleeding from his head. Bring blankets, Samuel, we must warm him. And fetch some ale.' She leaned over. His clothes were wet. She unlaced his shirt, attempting to ease it from him. His teeth chattered as she wrapped blankets around him. His eyes were glassy and he groaned once, then he vomited copiously.

Susanna turned him over on his side. Samuel knelt next to her, holding a cup. The man slumped over towards the floor and was still. Susanna put her fingers close to his mouth and felt no warm air. He had stopped breathing. With all her might, she rolled him onto his chest and began to pummel his back. 'He's drowned, Samuel. Perhaps...' She was breathless from the effort. 'I can force the water from his lungs and make his heart beat again.'

Samuel's face held tension. 'Who are they? Where did they come from?'

'I know not, but...' Susanna rolled the sailor over on his back again. His mouth was open, water seeping from it, and his eyes stared. 'I can do nothing.'

'He has died?'

'He swallowed too much water. I can't save him.' Susanna met her brother's eyes. 'You know what this means?'

'A sailor who perishes at sea and is brought back to land will know no peace.'

'His spirit will stay here in this room for all time, forever seeking a place of rest.' Susanna crossed herself quickly.

'It makes no sense. Who is he?' Samuel began.

'We must look to those who are living. Go down to the harbour and see what's happening. I saw lights.' Susanna urged him to go with a flap of her hand. 'Perhaps there are fishermen who can help us understand what has befallen and where they have come from.'

'I think I know.' Samuel was on his feet. 'I heard whisperings among the fishermen. In the storm, a ship has been wrecked in the cove.'

'Wrecked?' Susanna knew such things happened, and that Yowann Hicks's name was associated with it.

'A ship is sometimes guided aground with lanterns. When it founders, the men will use pickaxes and hatchets to dismember it, and any goods are carried away. But you haven't heard it from me, and you must never speak of it.'

'And the sailors on board? What happens to them?'

'They're thrown into the sea, or killed, or drowned as they try to escape.' Samuel indicated the sailor who lay still on his back, clothes drenched. 'I'll go to the harbour now and see what's amiss.'

'And the other, by the fireside with Katel?' Susanna asked. 'What will become of him?'

'I don't know.' Samuel was already rushing down the steps, reaching for a lantern, his hat and jacket. 'I'll see what I can discover. I won't be long.'

Susanna followed him but the downstairs room was empty. Katel and the other young sailor had gone. She rushed back to her own cottage and stood in the doorway.

Anne was seated at the table, suckling her baby, and Katel huddled by the fire, the young sailor lying on her lap, his shirt torn open, his upper arm bandaged. He was staring into her eyes as if hypnotised while she helped him to sip ale from a cup.

Susanna asked, 'What has happened?'

'His name is Jack.'

The sailor looked up and spoke weakly. 'Jacques.'

'Have you bathed his wounds?' Susanna asked. 'Do you want me to look at them?'

'He has a cut on his shoulder, a large gash as if he caught it on a rock. I cleaned it and bound it as you told me. And he's cold, but I'm warming him by the fire.' Katel pointed into the chimney. 'The little hag-stones are threaded and hanging on the side. I pray they'll keep him safe from evil.'

'He'll need to sleep soon. He must be exhausted,' Susanna said. 'I'll find him some food. There's still a little pottage and bread.'

'I'll feed it to him,' Katel said, touching his face with tender fingers.

Anne asked, 'How's the other sailor, the one who was soaked to the skin? He must have been dragged from the depths by the look of him.'

'He was filled with seawater, his clothes, his lungs,' Susanna said. 'I tried, but I couldn't save him. He's gone.'

Jack turned his face towards Susanna, aware of the sadness in her tone. He was still shivering, but behind large brown eyes and damp dark hair, Susanna could see that he was handsome, probably only a few years older than Katel. He spoke breathlessly. Susanna thought she recognised the word 'mercy' but she had no idea what he was saying. He was clearly upset, his face wet with tears, his clothes damp. Then he asked her a question hurriedly, his face tense. Susanna could not understand him, but he repeated the word *frayer* several times.

Susanna said, 'Annie, can you give me the baby and fetch Jack some dry clothes of Samuel's? He shivers with cold and he'll surely catch a chill.'

'I will, and I'll bring extra blankets. Perhaps Colan is out there, and I can ask for a little brandy too.' Anne slipped little Bartholomew into Susanna's arms and hurried into the night.

Katel said, 'Jack will be well now. But I fear he's restless and worried about the other sailor. I think his name's Gillyam.'

'Guillaume.' The sailor struggled upright, then sank back into Katel's embrace and said something unintelligible.

Susanna looked down at Jack and shook her head slowly. 'He has died.'

Jack studied her expression for a moment, then he understood. His face crumpled and he began to sob. Katel pulled him close. She pressed her lips against his forehead. Then she looked up, meeting Susanna's eyes, her own round with trust.

'He has come to me from across the seas. He speaks in a tongue I do not understand, but I love him. It's just as the chawk told me. He has come to me. He's my prince.'

30

Megan sat in the Afterdune Delight café, drinking a latte, staring at her phone. It was ten minutes past eleven. She would have finished her drink by quarter past: she'd give him until then. She was already making decisions about what she'd do if he stood her up. There was the Museum of Cornish Life in Helston. She wondered if someone there might be able to tell her about the history of St Mawgen. Or there was a good beach at Porthleven: she could surf or swim, and there were interesting cafés and shops. There would be plenty of photo opportunities, pictures to send back to her parents and to Amy, who was asking every day for photographic evidence of her holiday.

She'd just reached for her coffee to take the last mouthful when the bell on the door clanged. She looked up and saw the surfer strolling towards her as if he had all the time in the world. He looked good, wearing shorts, a T-shirt, his blond hair gleaming, sunglasses on his head. She wondered if he was late on purpose to make an entrance, or if he was arrogant. It wouldn't be difficult to change her mind about going on a dive. The idea of spending time with a self-obsessed diver wasn't her idea of fun.

He sat down. 'I'm sorry I'm a bit late. I had a call from uni. I couldn't get off the phone and there was no way of contacting you. Let me buy you another coffee? Something else?'

Megan changed her mind at once. She'd misjudged him, and she was horrified at how easily she'd jumped to the wrong conclusion. The reason came to her instantly: it was all about her relationship with Jay. The way it had ended had left her bruised and she lacked trust now. She was judging this man by Jay's past behaviour, and that wasn't fair. She resolved to do better. It wasn't his fault – whoever he was. She held out a hand to shake. 'I didn't introduce myself. I'm Megan Hammond.'

'Patrick Penrose.' He took her hand.

Megan thought that at least she could stop calling him after a Greek god now.

A waitress was hovering. Patrick said, 'Can I get a cranberry juice, please, Linda? And...' He turned to Megan.

'I'll have the same.'

Patrick leaned forward on his elbows, all interest. 'So, you're on holiday and surfing every morning on the dawn patrol. That's real commitment.'

'I love it. I live in Somerset. I don't get the chance to surf there, so I'm making the most of my time. I own a shop with my family. I sell crystals, do aromatherapy.'

Patrick smiled. '*Earth is both life's mother and life's tomb, and thus many different plants are born from nature.*'

'Pardon?'

'Shakespeare.' Patrick raised an eyebrow. 'People have always believed in the power of herbs and stones.'

Megan was suddenly excited. 'Are you a historian? I mean, do you know anything about the history of the cove?'

'I started off as a marine biologist,' Patrick explained. 'But I got into diving, took a photography course and became a member of the Professional Association of Diving Instructors. So I spend a lot of the time beneath the water looking at old wrecks as well as sea life.' His eyes twinkled. 'I'm writing a book on it at the moment.'

'On what?'

'The expansion of the south-western fisheries in late medieval England. But I've got a bit distracted. I discovered that a ship had been wrecked by smugglers and I want to find out if any of it's still on the seabed.' He noticed her excited expression. 'It sounds much more romantic than it is.'

'Have you found anything?'

'I'm still looking.' Patrick frowned. 'So, what makes you want to dive deep?'

'Well, at first it was just the thrill of it, but...' The waitress arrived with two drinks on a tray. 'How much do you know about life in the cove hundreds of years ago?'

'Apart from the shipwrecks and the fishing industry? Not much,' Patrick said. 'I can tell you about pilchards and hake, how they caught them in seine nets in the sixteen hundreds.'

'Do you know anything about the ghosts in The Ship Inn? The inn was built around that time.'

Patrick shook his head. 'I had a chat to the undertaker, Tom. He goes surfing sometimes. He told me ghost stories were a big part of the culture here. I didn't really follow it up.' He reached for his glass. 'I took my parents to the pub when they came for a visit, and some of the faculty, and I dived off the coast to photograph dolphins. But I don't get involved much in the local community. I've been here since April. My main aim's to research the book and take pictures.'

'I get that,' Megan agreed. 'It's a lovely place to live. You have the ocean, the surf.'

'I lecture at Falmouth two days a week. Marine and Natural History Photography, and I do field trips, take students out on location. That's my social life, pretty much. The rest of the time, I'm writing and researching.'

Megan was sympathetic. 'It must be very easy to lose yourself in your work.'

'It is.' Patrick seemed delighted that she understood. 'I make sure I go surfing at dawn to wake myself up. Then I work all day, maybe dive in the afternoon or surf in the evening, then I eat and sleep.'

'Have you always been a loner?' Megan couldn't help herself.

'I don't think of myself as a loner. I'm a bit of a workaholic,' he admitted. 'And right now I'm stuck into a project that's taking up every minute. I have to find evidence of this wreck.' He pushed a hand through his hair and Megan realised that he was completely unaware of his good looks. 'You're on holiday by yourself?'

'Yep.' Megan wondered how to explain. 'I came here to do some research about my family.'

'Do you have family in Cornwall?'

'I'm not sure. I might have.' Megan didn't think it was the right time to tell him about Emma Davey. 'But it's interesting, staying at The Ship. There's a real atmosphere, a history to the place.'

'Tell me about these ghosts.'

'Legend is that they haunt three of the four rooms. One cries in the dark, one smells of the sea. Do you believe in ghosts?'

'No.' Patrick didn't hesitate. 'I get atmospheres, though. Sometimes when I'm diving deep where there's evidence of the past, there's a definite feel to the water. An absence of fish or simply a strange feeling that I have no right to be there.'

Megan decided that the deep sea-blue of his eyes when he spoke passionately was incredibly appealing. She forced the thoughts away and said, 'The ghosts at The Ship are absolutely real.'

Patrick looked unsure. 'I'd take some convincing.'

'I've heard them; I've felt presences. The Weeping Woman in rooms one and two, and the Drenched Man in room four.' Megan noticed he was staring at her. 'And they're not helping The Ship's business.'

'Perhaps it's the same thing I experience underwater, residual vibrations. I believe there's always a scientific explanation, though.'

'There may be. But what about the Waiting Witch?'

'Tom mentioned her. It's a local tradition to explain people having heart attacks.'

'A man died a few months ago, and Tom swears that the witch took his life.' Megan met Patrick's level gaze. 'She watches men from the clifftops and, if they see her, she comes down and they're found dead in the street the next day. I mean, it could be coincidence.'

'It's probably a local myth. The origin of it is the place to start. Does she have a grudge, or a broken heart, this witch, or is there a reason for her being a man hater?'

'It would be good to know. It's a bit of a far-fetched idea that a kiss can kill,' Megan said. 'But apparently, that's the story. And that she's linked to the Drenched Man and the Weeping Woman.'

'That could work. A sailor dies at sea, a wife is left poverty stricken, and the witch caused it to happen? Perhaps she loved the man – or the woman – or perhaps they were related in some way?'

'How could we find out?' Megan was suddenly excited. 'It might be a way to help the spirits to rest. I've heard some of the strange goings-on at the inn first-hand and it's terrifying. I'd love to understand.'

Patrick drained the glass. 'Do you fancy a walk up the cliff?'

'Now?'

'Why not? We can always dive later.'

'Don't you have to work?'

Patrick thought for a moment. 'I owe myself some down time.'

'In which case, yes, let's go and see what we can find out. But why up the cliff?'

'So we can see the world from the witch's perspective. It makes sense.' Patrick stood up, his eyes shining. 'And we can see what she's looking at when she's up there.'

* * *

'The *Bonaventure*, on its way from Brittany in France to Bristol with a cargo of silk and brandy, was wrecked in the storm last night.' Yowann Hicks's voice boomed as he stood in the harbour, hands on his hips. 'All the crew were lost apart from one young man who is staying with Samuel Boram until he's well. Then he'll join our fishermen here to earn his living. He doesn't understand our language but nevertheless, we'll make him welcome.'

Susanna hugged her shawl and glanced up at her brother. 'Katel doesn't want to let him go, Samuel.' She frowned. 'It's as if she's bewitched again. I believed she and Merryn were close to marriage, but this young man Jack has captured her heart and changed everything.'

Samuel moved closer. 'Yowann spoke to me earlier and told me I must keep my mouth closed about last night. His wrecking crew led the *Bonaventure* into danger, and it crashed against rocks. I helped him to carry the brandy and silk to The Ship. It's now hidden in Colan's cellar. Yowann owns the place. Colan daren't speak of it.'

'So all those young men died for Yowann's greed?' Susanna said. 'Including the one in your upstairs room?'

Samuel looked uncomfortable. 'The drowned sailor will be fetched from my cottage this morning and buried at sea.'

Susanna crossed herself quickly. 'But sailors buried at sea will become ghosts, as their burial ground is unhallowed.'

'Then it's good that he was brought here before he died.'

Susanna's face paled. 'No, Samuel. He was filled with sea water, half dead, far from home. He died in misery. How can he ever rest? His spirit will be imprisoned in the walls of your house for all time.'

'I fear that may be true, but what can I do but bear it? Yowann has his group of men around him, and they'll make sure his wishes are carried out. I wouldn't cross him,' Samuel said quietly.

'He believes he owns every man and woman in the cove.' Susanna glanced towards Yowann, who was now ordering the fishermen back to work. 'Can Jack stay with you?'

'He can sleep by my hearth,' Samuel said. 'Annie will feed him. We have enough to go round since the last haul of pilchards.'

Susanna exhaled, a long breath filled with anxiety. 'It's been a difficult summer, with what befell Tedda and Beaten. Now the ship has come aground and all but one of the men lost. It seems there's bad luck in the cove. Who knows what will happen this winter?'

She turned away from the sea wind that blew her hair free of her cap and scurried back to the house. Her heart was heavy. It was as if Tedda's curse still hung on the air.

31

The winds brought in a harsh wet winter, and the fish drifted sparsely to the cove. There was much activity in The Ship, men drinking into the night, then later flaring lanterns coming and going in the darkness, voices whispering. By the first day of March, the raw wind became a lighter, sweeter one and the seas were calm. Susanna went out at every opportunity, seeking fresh new herbs in Bylen woods or on the cliffs, taking Katel with her. Yowann strutted around the harbour in new breeches of the best cloth and Eliza was seen in pretty dresses and ribboned bonnets, although she walked around with her head down and coughed frequently, rubbing aching fingers. Joan moved slowly in the kitchen; her child would be born any day. She made food in The Ship for the hungry fishermen, her belly tight as a drum behind her apron. Joan would need a new assistant to help with the cooking soon. Colan stayed behind the bar, serving wine and ale with watchful eyes.

Samuel took Jack out to sea fishing each morning. The young sailor was healthier now, although his left arm was weakened by his injury. He was a cheerful man, keen to do his best, and he had learned enough English to explain that his brother, Guillaume, and he had attempted to escape from the wrecked *Bonaventure* and had got into trouble in the water. He was becoming fond of Katel; they spent every spare moment in each other's company.

It was a bright morning as Susanna returned from Bylen woods with a basket full of pennywort, chickweed, dandelion and hawthorn. She had carefully picked a bunch of young nettles for Eliza, to treat her joint pain. The sun was high in the sky and Susanna's spirits lifted. She hoped with all her heart that there would be a wedding this summer, that Jack and Katel would marry and he'd move into their cottage. It would be good to have a man living with them. There were repairs that needed doing: the door creaked, the windows let in water when the rain came in a certain direction. And it was always tiring, bringing in firewood; another pair of hands would be useful. Katel and Jack could make the upstairs room their own. Susanna would be content to sleep on Katel's straw mattress by the fire.

She imagined their happy lives, a family together, eating around the table at night. Then babies would come in time, grandchildren for her to dote upon. The boys would grow to be strong fishermen, friends for Bartholomew and Joan's new baby, who, Susanna was sure, would be a boy. The girls would be of an age to play with their new cousin who would be born in the summer. Anne was expecting another baby and she had experienced constant, intense heartburn this time: the child would be a girl and she would be born with a full head of hair.

Fleetingly, Susanna thought of Tedda, of how she'd often meet her in Bylen woods collecting nightshade, how Tedda would talk to her in the old Cornish language. It was a great shame, what happened, but it was in the past now and Susanna hoped that she could put it behind her. The little hagstones still hung in the chimney; the poppet was buried beneath the rosemary bush in the garden. Life was back to normal.

As Susanna trod the hard dirt track towards the cove, she was aware of someone running towards her, hair flying, skirts blowing. She knew her daughter, her every movement, the cry of her voice. She stopped as Katel drew level.

'What's amiss?'

'You must come. Colan sent me. Joan has fallen. She's clutching her belly and moaning like a beast.' Katel's eyes were wide with fear. 'Colan fears she's hurt herself.'

'Let's hurry.' Susanna lifted her basket and she and Katel broke into a run.

When they reached The Ship, Colan was standing outside, his face troubled, his shoulders hunched. 'Susanna?'

'How's Joan?' Susanna caught her breath. 'Let's go in, Colan.'

'I won't go inside.' Colan's voice was low. 'Joan's on the kitchen floor. She was cooking at the hearth, then she dropped a sack of flour and fell down. She cries that she'll die.'

Susanna met his eyes, her own gentle with compassion. 'I'm sure she will not. It's just the baby making his way into the world.'

'I'm afraid. I ran to your cottage and knocked for all the world to hear, but you were out.' He reached out, grabbing Susanna's wrist. 'Please, I beg you, don't let her die.'

'Let me go to her, Colan.'

He spoke quietly. 'I never thought it possible that I'd love another, but Joan's my best friend in the world. She's as dear to me as my own heart. I can't lose her.'

'I understand,' Susanna said gently, pushing past him, moving into the shadows of the inn. She rushed into the kitchen where Joan had fallen onto the dirt floor. She lay on her back moaning, flour spilled all around her. Susanna knelt beside her, aware of the roar of the fire in the hearth, the orange glow. Moments later, Katel was at her shoulder.

'Can you stand, Joan?' Susanna's voice was gentle, full of encouragement. 'Can we get you to your upstairs room?'

'I'm afeared to move,' Joan whispered between dry lips. 'The pains come and I'm clutched by them.'

'It's nature's way. It won't last,' Susanna said as she and Katel eased Joan to her feet, moving her gently to the wooden staircase. Halfway up, Joan stopped, gripping Susanna's hand tightly, catching her breath. Then they were at the top and Susanna helped Joan to lie on the bed.

Katel was wide-eyed. She whispered, 'Mother, will Joan die?'

Susanna shook her head. 'I think not. The baby will come soon. Can you help? I need you to go back to her kitchen and make sure I have hot water. Fetch some here, and as much clean linen as you can find. Then go back to the cottage and collect my eagle birthing stone, some sweet almond oil and some herbal tinctures. Then you must make some caudle from warm ale mixed with bread, eggs, sugar and spices to nourish her.'

'I'll go now.' Katel gazed quickly at Joan, who was seized with another pain, then hurried downstairs.

Susanna went to Joan's side and spoke quietly. 'It's time for us to work together to bring this little one into the world, Joan. You must trust me and do exactly as I say.'

'I will.' Joan turned desperate eyes on Susanna.

'I'll rub your belly with an eagle stone to hasten the baby's birth and the herbal tinctures will keep you calm.'

Joan said, 'I've much need of it.'

'Firstly, I'll find out how the baby is progressing and then we'll know how soon he'll take his first breath.' Susanna placed a hand on Joan's damp brow. 'Have you decided on a name for him?'

Joan nodded. 'We'll call him Thomas. It was the name of Colan's father.'

Susanna remembered Thomas Stephens. As children, she and Colan had sat outside The Ship, chattering, when his father was innkeeper there. Thomas was a kindly man who'd often come outside to give them a cup of buttermilk from his wife's kitchen. She said, 'It's a good name.'

Joan made an unintelligible sound, then rolled on her side and groaned. The light sound of feet padded on the stairs and Katel was back, holding a basket. She stared at Joan for a moment, then at Susanna. She whispered, 'Is Joan in a lot of pain?'

'There's no need to be afraid. Now do as I bade you, Katel, and fetch me water and linen, then prepare some caudle.'

'I will.' Katel rushed away. Susanna noticed the fear in her eyes, the way she looked at Joan as if worried for her life. Helping with a birth was a new experience for Katel. Susanna wondered how well she would cope. Joan made a low sound of suffering and Susanna mixed a tincture, held it to her lips and talked gently.

* * *

After a long night, the new dawn dappled the sky grey and mauve. Joan sat on the edge of the mattress, moaning. Susanna frowned. There was still no sign that the baby would arrive soon. Katel stood in the corner, not knowing how to help as Joan laboured. Susanna gave Joan a little more tincture and rushed to her daughter's side. 'Stay with her. Feed her a little caudle. I'll be back in five minutes.'

'Don't leave me alone, I pray,' Katel said.

'I'll be downstairs a short while, just to tell Colan that all's well here. I'll return before Joan has two more pangs.'

'But what will I do?'

'Hold her hand and tell her that soon she'll be suckling her firstborn.' Susanna gathered her skirts and hurried downstairs. The room was empty now. Colan leaned against the bar, a half-empty cup of brandy in his hand. His face held the exhaustion of a man who had not slept. His eyes were frightened as Susanna approached.

'What news of Joan?'

Susanna spoke reassuringly. 'She's in the throes of it. Pray she'll not be long now.'

'But it's been hours. All day I waited and then all night, hoping for news.'

Susanna took his hand. 'Have courage.'

'I can't lose her. Or the child. I couldn't bear it.'

'Try not to fret.'

'She's the best of wives, Susanna. She works without complaint, she always has a good word for everyone and she loves me with all her heart. She's bringing forth this child to please me.'

'It's true.'

Colan placed his head in his hands, ruffling his hair. Then he looked up, tears in his eyes. 'I didn't treat her well at first. I thought only of you. Yet she wanted nothing but my happiness. And now I realise how lucky I am, the most fortunate of men.'

'Drink your brandy and be patient.'

'But it's been one day, almost two.' Colan seized her hand. 'What if she dies? What if the child dies?'

'Don't speak of it. It may bring bad luck.'

'Many babies die during birthing. My mother birthed two sons before me and both died.'

'Colan.' Susanna gripped his fingers hard. 'Your wife needs you to be a husband.'

She turned her back on him and rushed back upstairs. She could hear

Joan's screams before she entered the upstairs room. Katel was kneeling at her feet, a bowl of water to one side beside a folded pile of linen. She panted, 'The baby's coming.'

'That's good, Joan,' Susanna soothed. 'We're ready to meet the little one. Now breathe lightly and listen. When I say it, you'll push him out and he'll take his first breath.'

An hour later, Joan was propped up on the mattress with a bolster and baby Thomas was swaddled in her arms, suckling contentedly. Her eyelids were heavy with tiredness.

'Thank you, Susanna, from the bottom of my heart.'

'You must stay here. There will be no more baking in The Ship for a while.'

Joan sighed. 'When will Colan be able to greet his son?'

'Soon.' Susanna busied herself with clearing up after the birth. 'Katel, feed Joan a little more caudle. She has need of it.'

Katel looked almost as exhausted as Joan. She whispered, 'What do you have there?'

'The caul. It follows the baby into the world. This one was wrapped around the baby's head.'

'What will you do with it?'

'Don't concern yourself,' Susanna replied quickly. 'But some sailors believe a baby's caul will bring its bearer good luck and protect them from drowning. They're highly prized and can bring large sums of money if dried and sold.'

'I've heard that.' Katel put her hand out. 'May I have it to give to Jack? For the world, I'd keep him safe at sea.'

'Find another good luck charm. There are others, more powerful,' Susanna said. 'I'll take this away.'

'Will the hag-stones protect him?'

'Many believe they have that power.' Susanna kept her voice low. 'I've also heard that they can calm a troubled soul, such as the one that still walks in Samuel's bedroom. Annie cannot sleep for the smell of him.'

'Can you help Jack's brother to rest?' Katel asked, round-eyed.

'I'm not sure anyone can.'

'I'll help you tidy away. In truth, I didn't enjoy watching the birth,' Katel said. 'But next time, I'll be less frightened. May I help at Aunt Annie's birthing in the summer?'

'You may. It's good for you to learn.'

'I want to have children with Jack, even though what I've seen frighted me. I've talked to him of it, Mother. I speak slowly and he understands what I say to him, and he's learning. He loves me and I'm sure he wants us to wed.'

'And do you wish it too?'

'With all my heart,' Katel said. 'I love him more than my own life.'

'Then I wish you many happy years.' Susanna glanced at Joan and little Thomas. Mother and baby were fast asleep. She stood up, packing things into her basket. 'Come, Katel. We must perform the last task for Joan now.'

'What is that?'

'We must go to the happy father and tell him that his wife and baby are well. Then we'll bring him up here to greet his new son.'

32

The last part of the climb to the clifftop was a struggle up the steep path, and Megan panted lightly, pushing herself forward. But the view was worth it. She and Patrick stood among rough gorse and craggy rocks, looking down on the curve of the seawall, at the small fishing boats bobbing in the harbour, the deep turquoise sea beyond. The wind lifted her hair and she shivered beneath her light jacket.

Patrick asked, 'Are you warm enough?' He seemed quite comfortable in T-shirt and shorts.

'I'm fine,' she said, grateful for his concern. 'This is an incredible view.'

'Isn't it?' Patrick agreed. 'You can see the cove from here, stretching from The Ship at the top of the hill' – he pointed a finger – 'all the way to the surrounding cliffs and, beyond, to the English Channel.'

'And you dive down there? It looks so good.' Megan felt the thrill of wanting to submerge herself beneath the ocean. 'I'd love that.'

'Then let's dive tomorrow,' Patrick suggested. 'If you like, I can meet you after you've finished surfing and we'll see how you get on.'

She felt a pang of disappointment. 'You could come surfing too, dawn patrol?'

'Oh, I'll be there, but you usually go with Carly from the surf shop. I don't want to get in the way. I've already done the party wave twice without asking.'

'You'd be welcome to join us.'

'Thanks.' He smiled, and Megan wanted to reach out and take his hand. It was too early; she wasn't sure about the signs yet, although she was convinced there was chemistry between them.

Patrick met her eyes and she wondered if he was thinking the same thing. 'So, we'll dive around eleven thirty? You'll need time for breakfast, then a rest. You can't dive straight after a meal.'

'Of course.' Megan understood. 'Anything else I should know?'

'You're an experienced swimmer and diver. But there are a few things we'll go through first dive.'

Megan was suddenly excited. First dive? There might be more?

'We'll just keep it simple,' Patrick continued. 'A look around, to see what might be down there.'

Megan gazed at the view again. 'Thanks for bringing me up here.'

'So, let's think about your witch.' Patrick looked round carefully. 'Why is she here? What can she see?'

'Everything. But what's she looking for?' Megan asked. 'It's an amazing view. Maybe she feels powerful, being so high.'

'Good point,' Patrick said. 'She can see the cottages, so she's watching... Who? What? Victims to prey on, or for something in particular?' His expression was doubtful.

'If what Tom said is correct, the man leaves The Ship after a couple of drinks and starts to wander home. She'd certainly see him from here,' Megan said. 'So how's she linked to the two ghosts at the inn?'

'Let's think what her life might have been like.' Patrick stared out to sea.

'It was a simple time.'

'Poverty. Superstition.'

'Witchcraft?' Megan's voice was hushed.

'Fishing boats, cargo ships, smuggling. I wonder if this myth of her haunting is linked to the shipwreck I'm looking for.'

Megan looked down to the sea. 'It could be. She'd be able to see all the boats below in the harbour.'

'She'd see everything that happened too: the fishing boats out at sea... sailors, storms.'

'I wonder if she was looking for a particular boat. Or a particular person?

I wish she'd give me some sort of sign,' Megan began, then she shivered, as if icy fingers had touched her neck.

'You're getting chilly. Shall we head off?' Patrick asked.

'I think so.'

'We can always come back,' Patrick said, and Megan was delighted. 'Would you like to come to my cottage for a drink? I could show you some info I've collected about the shipwreck.'

'Perfect,' Megan said. She'd have a lot to tell Julien later, and Patrick was good company.

A thought crossed her mind. 'I'm just going to stand here for a few seconds. I want to imagine how the witch felt all those years ago, up here. I'll follow you down.'

'Right,' Patrick said, heading towards the path.

Megan turned into the wind and felt the sudden rush of it as it blew her hair across her face. She closed her eyes and tried to visualise how it might have been to be a young woman in Cornwall four centuries ago. She'd have expected to marry and have children. Round here, her husband would probably have been a fisherman. She'd be poor, living hand to mouth, but there would be plenty of fish to eat after a catch. She'd have worn a shift, a cap, a long skirt, a neckerchief and a shawl. Her hands would have been roughened by hard work.

She took a deep breath and imagined the young woman – for some reason, Megan visualised a woman in her late teens with a long, silky coil of fair hair – standing on the clifftop, gazing out to sea. She would be watching, waiting. But what for? Megan's heart began to beat faster. She'd be waiting for her lover to return. Where had he been? Fishing? Or overseas? It was unlikely that he'd travel that far if he was a local man, a fisherman.

Something touched her face, light fingers.

'I'm here.'

Megan heard a voice on the wind. She opened her eyes and looked around. Patrick was on his way down the path. She ought to follow him. But she had no idea where the voice had come from.

She closed her eyes again, remembering she'd asked for a sign. Was this it? Was the witch trying to tell her something?

The young woman would have been waiting – but why? Because

someone was due to come home. She missed someone. They were overdue, delayed. She was anxious, heartbroken.

'*I watch each night...*'

Megan heard the voice again. Or perhaps she imagined it. She asked, 'Tell me. What happened to you?'

'*My story is deep as oceans, wide as skies.*'

It was like the whisper of the sea, but it could have been a voice. Megan stared out across the ocean, then towards the village, The Ship Inn. She said quietly, 'What do you want?'

The sea was rough, waves crashing, surf spattering against the rocks.

'*He will come back to me.*'

Megan concentrated hard. 'Who are you waiting for?'

She imagined a fisherman had been lost at sea, his ship sunk beneath the ocean for centuries. It must have been a dangerous life. Her mind travelled to the wreck that Patrick was searching for. She envisaged a ship like the one in the black-and-white etching in room four. She could see it clearly, tossing on rough seas. Of course: the answer was at the bottom of the ocean.

Then the voice whispered in her ear, each word clear.

'*One breath, one kiss... for what he did to me...*'

Megan tensed, catching her breath in fright. It was as if someone was standing behind her. She trembled, whirling round, but no one was there.

Then she heard Patrick shout from below, 'Are you OK?'

'I'm just coming,' she called back, as she hurried down the path behind him as fast as her feet would move.

* * *

Megan recovered her composure as quickly as she could and by the time she had reached the harbour, she and Patrick were talking excitedly about tomorrow's dive. They reached his cottage at a pace; Megan caught her breath as soon as she stepped inside Surf's Up! There was very little furniture, just floor cushions, and bookshelves stuffed with countless books. In the corner there was a desk with two huge monitors and a keyboard. It was the focal point of the room and clearly where Patrick worked. Then, on the far side where the living room led to the kitchen, surfboards and diving equipment – regulators, bottles, fins, a wetsuit, masks, eight belts and a knife – were stacked against the wall. There were cameras in boxes on a table to one side. It reminded Megan of Carly's surf shop. Patrick didn't seem at all troubled by how unconventional his home was.

'What would you like to drink?'

'What have you got?' Megan asked.

'Juice – cranberry, or tomato. Coffee – decaff or ordinary. Tea – builder's, matcha, green, lemon and ginger. Water, sparkling or not sparkling. I have a machine that fizzes it,' Patrick said, and she immediately warmed to his humour. 'I might even have some hot chocolate and soya cream.'

'Hot chocolate would be a treat.'

'Coming up.'

While Patrick clanked about in the kitchen, Megan looked around for clues about his past – photos of graduations, ex-girlfriends or partners, family, baby photos. There was nothing at all. Just books everywhere, all to do with marine biology, shipwrecks, Cornwall, underwater photography. Here was a man who was completely focused on his work.

Megan decided he might be happy to have a little distraction while she was on holiday. Tomorrow, after they'd been diving, she'd invite him to The Ship for dinner.

Patrick emerged with two mugs, handing the chocolate-filled one with a swirl of cream to Megan. He sat at the two giant monitors, indicating the chair next to him. 'I want to show you something.' He wiggled the mouse and a black-and-white picture appeared on the screen. It was a ship with three masts, not unlike the one Megan had seen in room four at The Ship. 'The *Bonaventure*.'

'Is that the ship you're looking for?' Megan asked.

'Mm. What remains of it, if anything. The ship is a carrack, called *caraque* or *nef* in French.' Patrick brought up a document, a paragraph highlighted in yellow. 'It was on its way from Brittany to Bristol with a cargo of brandy, silk, salt and tea in September 1625 when it was lost, wrecked by smugglers not far from here. It would be a perfect haul. In the seventeenth century, import duties were high to finance Britain's wars. Local people profited from smuggling.'

'So what do you want to find on the seabed?'

'Well, I was part of a dive in the Med a few years ago and we discovered treasure. I'm not joking: a gold chalice, an amphora and a two-handed cup known as a kylix. Real evidence of the past. It was incredible. I want to know how people lived then, what their lives were like. There's so much history waiting to be found, that explain the harsh lives of the working people, how they existed from day to day, how they traded. The rich and poor, men and women. It's incredible. And smuggling is key in this part of the world. There's so much evidence on the seabed, waiting to be discovered and analysed. Just to photograph bits of a wrecked vessel would be brilliant. And it might shed light on your ghosts. I think we're talking about the same time period.'

Megan was fascinated. 'Tom Hocking mentioned voices calling from the sea at midnight. Sailors who drowned.'

'Many men would have lost their lives in shipwrecking,' Patrick agreed.

'I wonder if a sailor's calling from the depths to his beloved?' Megan thought of the witch, waiting on the clifftops, and the voice she thought she had heard.

'We might get some clues from the dive, then we can research the old logs and muster books and the parish registers, and see what comes of that. I don't know how deep we'll be able to go tomorrow or what we'll find. But' – Patrick's eyes shone – 'if we can find something, anything at all, it would be amazing.'

'It would.' Megan sipped her hot chocolate, wiping the moustache of cream from her top lip. 'A smuggler's tale, a lost ship – it would be perfect for Julien and Claude's website.'

'I've met them both a couple of times. They seem cool.'

'Oh, they're lovely,' Megan enthused. 'Imagine if we could give some kind of closure to their troubled ghosts.'

Patrick looked at her levelly. 'How long are you staying here?'

'Until Sunday, in theory.' She wondered what he was really asking her: if they'd have time to get to know each other, if a relationship was a possibility. She added, 'But Minehead's only a few hours away and my work in the shop is pretty flexible.'

'Right.' Patrick's thoughts were back in the water. 'So we'll dive around half eleven tomorrow. You could come here first, and we'll go through a few things, equipment, basic safety.'

'I'm looking forward to it. Uncovering the past...' She wondered whether she could confide in him. The words came out easily. 'And the present. I'm actually hoping to bump into someone in the cove. Her name is Emma Davey. Do you know her?'

'No, but I'm not the best person to ask,' Patrick said.

'She's the wife of the man who died, the one who Tom said was visited by the Waiting Witch.' She took a breath. 'I think she's my half-sister.'

'Oh?' Patrick raised an eyebrow. 'When did you find that out?'

'Just over a week ago. She's my father's first child. She wrote him a letter.'

'Because she's alone now?'

'I guess,' Megan said. 'But it would be good to make contact with her before I go back.'

'I can see why you'd want to meet her, but it could be traumatic. I mean, does she know you're here?'

'No. My mum doesn't even know about her yet. Dad's really nervous. I hope I'll be able to help.'

'Well, this is an amazing week of discovery.' Patrick took her empty mug. 'Old wrecks, ghosts, long-lost sisters. I think I'll enjoy tagging along. That is, if you'd like me to.'

'Oh, definitely.' Megan grinned. She pushed the idea of the ghosts to one side and thought about her holiday. 'I think that might be just what I need.'

33

It had been a blustery March day, bitterly cold, the wind whipping the grey sea into froth against the rocks. Now it was a wild, stormy night. Katel and Jack sat by the blazing fire in the hearth of the little cottage toasting their cold fingers; the candles flickered and the shutters shook.

Susanna stood with her hands on her hips. 'Katel, it's time for that young man to go next door now.'

Katel clutched Jack's hand in both of hers, keen to hold on to him. 'Can he stay just a little longer, Mother? His company makes my heart glad.'

Jack's brown eyes were round and serious. 'It will not be for a long time, chèrie. Soon you are my wife and we are happy for ever.' He kissed Katel's hand as if it was precious. 'I fall from the *Bonaventure* into the seas and lose my beloved brother, but this summer I shall have a beautiful wife.' His expression was filled with gratitude. 'I thank you forever for your kindness, Madame Susanna.'

It warmed Susanna's heart to see Katel and Jack so happy. She had been working hard to teach him English and he hung on her every word. 'You need to go to Samuel's cottage now, Jack, and get your sleep. The boats may be out early tomorrow. Perhaps the storm will bring in some fish.'

'I like to fish with Samuel,' Jack said happily. 'And Merryn. But he says me nothing. I think he is not my friend.'

Katel and Susanna exchanged glances. They knew that Katel had broken Merryn's heart when she'd turned to Jack. But he was a good-natured young man – he kept his thoughts to himself.

Jack kissed Katel's hand again. 'I must go, my love. But tomorrow, I see you in the harbour before we fish.'

'Please take care, Jack. I worry so.' Katel glanced towards her mother.

Susanna said, 'It's how a woman's heart is, when she truly loves a man. We suffer for our feelings.'

'I wish I could give you something to keep you safe at sea. Is there a potion, Mother? I remember you told me about the caul, how it can be dried as a charm. Maybe when Aunt Annie has borne her child.'

'Perhaps.'

'Or.' Katel's eyes travelled to the chimney. 'What about the little hag-stones on the cord?' She reached up and held them out, like a necklace. 'Jack, you could wear them around your neck.' With gentle hands, she draped them over his head and they hung over his shirt. 'To keep you from harm. Forever.'

'*Mon amour.*' Jack's voice was husky as he touched the stones for luck.

'These stones will always bring you back to me,' Katel said.

'Enough of this,' Susanna teased. 'Tomorrow begins early.'

Jack stood, pulling Katel tenderly into his arms, his lips brushing her cheek. 'Until tomorrow.'

'My Jack.'

Susanna watched Katel's eyes close, her face tender with love. She was reminded of when she had been Katel's age, how she had felt when lifted into strong arms, her knocking heart pressed against another's.

She was tugged from her dream by a harsh pounding at the door. A voice called urgently, 'Susanna, are you there? Your help is needed.'

She opened the door to Colan, wet with rain, his face crumpled in anxiety. 'Susanna, can you come now?'

'What is amiss?'

'Baby Thomas coughs and his forehead is burning. Joan, too, has a fever.'

'Wait while I grab my basket and shawl,' Susanna called.

'May I come?' Katel asked. She ushered Jack out into the night where he rushed to Samuel's cottage. Susanna followed Colan as he sped towards the inn. He called over his shoulder, 'Tonight's busy, I'm alone and I haven't even eaten. Moments ago, I slipped upstairs to take Joan a little food. Her face was damp and pale, and she and Thomas are racked with coughing.' He pushed the door open and hurried into the darkness, candles burning on tables and in wall sconces. 'I must go down to the cellar to bring up more barrels. The men call for ale, wine, brandy. I can't satisfy their thirst.'

Susanna gazed at the men huddled at tables, draining tankards, wet lips swigging until the cups were empty, then clanking them down on the wooden tables. She heard someone call, 'More wine here, Colan, and be quick about it.' It was Yowann, seated among his friends. They were all clearly the worse for drink.

'Don't fret,' Susanna said. 'Katel and I will go to Joan and little Thomas. I believe I can help their fever. Hopefully, it's one I can cure, caused only by damp weather and draughts. You go about your business.' She turned to Katel. 'I'll treat the baby and you must help Joan. Give her coriander to reduce fever. Ease her lungs with the medicine made of honey, ginger, liquorice and comfrey. I'll burn a little lavender oil to make the air better for them.'

'I can do that,' Katel said, then stopped as someone grasped her wrist. One of Yowann's friends, a large man with his hat pulled low over his eyes, leered in her direction. His lips were moist. 'And who's this sweet lambkin? She looks ripe for my bed.'

Katel froze. She turned to her mother for help. Susanna glared at the man. 'Leave her. We're here to administer herbs to a sick woman.'

'How about a kiss?' The man held Katel fast. He rolled to one side as he sat, clearly drunk. His voice was slurred. 'Sit upon my knee, pretty maid.'

'I pray you, let me go.' Katel's voice was a whisper.

'Leave her,' Susanna said, louder.

The man tugged Katel and she fell against him, landing in his lap. He guffawed, 'That's better. Now a kiss...'

'Mother, help me.' Katel tugged away as the man laughed. He clearly thought this was good sport. He hoisted her against him, kissing her neck, and she gasped with fear, hissing, 'May you burn in hellfire.'

'Let go,' Susanna said, grasping the man's hand to prise it from Katel's waist. He was attempting to lift her skirt and Katel cried out as the man's other hand reached for her breast.

Susanna grabbed the man's cup of wine and threw it hard in his face, hauling Katel to her, pulling her towards the stairs. The man's face dripped with tawny-coloured liquid as he shouted, 'Shrew – whore,' but Susanna clutched her basket in one hand and guided Katel with the other.

'I'm sorry you had to endure that.'

Katel's eyes were full of tears. 'I'm glad you helped me.'

'I'll speak to Yowann about his friends.' Susanna was quietly furious. She hurried upstairs, Katel at her heels, and rushed towards the straw mattress. 'Joan, how are you? How's the baby?'

She prised Thomas from Joan's arms, inspecting his glassy eyes, touching the flushed forehead. The baby whimpered, too exhausted to cry. Susanna watched as Katel propped Joan up with a bolster behind her. She poured liquid from a jar in the basket and brought the cup to her lips. Then she gave her full attention to Thomas, finding a jug of water, soaking linen and placing the damp cloth against the baby's brow to bring the fever down. She made him a concoction of coriander, cumin and fennel, pushing small amounts of it into his mouth with a tiny wooden spoon. She felt the baby relax in her arms, his breathing slowly becoming less laboured. She turned to Joan, placing damp linen on her heated brow.

'How do you feel?'

'Tired.' Joan's mouth was dry. Katel offered her a cup of water and she gulped desperately, then she tried again. 'Thomas and I have been coughing since last night. My throat is sore and my head pains me. Then tonight I felt the fever begin to take me. But I worry about my child.'

'You and Thomas will be well soon,' Susanna said soothingly. 'I'll leave you this mixture. Thomas may have a little bit from a spoon often, and you must take some too. Then tomorrow morning, I'll return early to see how you progress. But you should both sleep well tonight now.'

'Thank you,' Joan said, her eyes closing.

'I'll place the baby in his crib next to you, Joan,' Susanna said quietly, then she gestured to Katel that they should leave.

Downstairs, Colan was nowhere to be seen, but the door to the cellar was open. He was clearly busy, bringing up more barrels for the thirsty drinkers.

The men were still making a lot of noise, shouting and laughing raucously. Susanna noticed Hedyn and Merryn Gilbert in one corner, drinking together, their heads down, but the men at Yowann's table were banging tankards, shouting, swearing, calling for more drinks. Susanna grasped Katel's arm in an attempt to hurry past the man who had accosted her earlier, but he was waiting, his face furious.

He grabbed at Katel as she passed. 'Where's my kiss, little maid?'

Katel dodged out of the way and clung to her mother. Susanna was incensed. She would not let him accost Katel again.

'You're nothing but a foul swill-belly,' Susanna hissed as she pushed past.

He lunged for her. 'You crone. You threw sack in my face.' He gritted his teeth. 'I'll order you to be whipped. I'm a mercer, a man of importance.'

'Yowann.' Susanna lifted her voice. 'If you must associate with this barrel of fat, you'll tell him to leave my daughter alone.'

'I'm sorry, Susanna.' Yowann stood up, staring around in an attempt to assert himself, and the other men were suddenly quiet. 'Charles, you'll not trouble this woman and her daughter. I forbid it.'

'But the scold threw wine in my face,' the large man shouted. 'I demand that she be punished as the law allows.'

'Leave it,' Yowann said angrily. 'Susanna's a friend of mine. You'll let her pass safely.'

'I need a drink.' The mercer stood up, his belly protruding, his face sulky. 'And there's no innkeeper here to get me one in this stinking place.' He moved towards the cellar, grabbing a candle. 'So I'll get one for myself.' He tottered on the top step, swaying, falling against the wall as he descended. Several of the other men at the table laughed scornfully.

Someone said, 'Charles can't hold his wine – or a woman.'

Another replied, 'He's too fond of the sweet sack we brought from Spain. He should content himself with weak ale for his weak humours.'

Yowann reached Susanna, taking her hand, his expression tender. 'I apologise. I hope he didn't cause you pain.'

Susanna wrapped an arm around Katel. 'We came here to tend Joan and little Thomas. I won't have Katel accosted by a swill-belly.'

'Charles is in his cups tonight,' Yowann said as an excuse. 'But I'm sorry for his rudeness.' He touched Susanna's face with the tips of his fingers and she smelled the brandy on his breath. He had clearly been drinking all evening. 'I would not for the world have him offend you.'

Susanna gently moved his hand away, full of gratitude. 'Thank you, Yowann. I bid you a good night.'

She turned, but he held her wrist and whispered into her hair, 'You might stay, have a drink with me?'

'It's late.'

'Then perhaps you could come to my home later? Eliza will be asleep. She slumbers in the back room now. And I yearn for your company, sweet Susanna.'

'Yowann.' Susanna tried to pull away. She felt his breath against her cheek and her eyes closed as the old feelings she tried so hard to deny came flooding back.

'Do you still feel for me as you used to?'

Susanna's lips were almost against his. She struggled away. 'Please don't speak like this in front of Katel. I must go.'

'You don't realise the power you have.' Yowann brought the cup of brandy to his mouth and swigged. 'Even after all these years, I think of you often.'

'Good night.' Susanna had almost regained control of her emotions. She reached the door, pushing past a fisherman who tottered in from the rain, his face and shoulders wet from the downpour. Colan was coming up from the cellar, a barrel on his back and, as he closed the door, he caught her eyes, his questioning. She turned away. 'Come, Katel, let us go home. I long for my bed.'

'Me too. And to dry myself by the heat of the fire.' Katel reached for her mother's hand.

'Let's leave these drunken men to their ale,' Susanna said with a final glance towards Yowann. 'We won't think of them or their foolish words again.'

34

Susanna and Katel stood in front of the roaring fire in their shifts. They had removed their damp skirts, caps and kerchiefs, and were drying their hair in front of the blaze. Katel gazed towards the chimney.

'I hope the hag-stones will bring my Jack luck.'

'They will.' Susanna shook out the length of her hair and Katel did the same, her fair coil tumbling.

'Do you think we're free of Tedda now?'

'I doubt she meant us harm, Katel.'

'But sometimes the chawk still talks to me. He was called Master Jack, and the man I'll marry is Jack. Do you not think it strange?'

'I doubt it's anything other than coincidence.' Susanna couldn't help the tremor that passed through her. 'And the chawks sit on the roof to warm themselves all day and night, so you'll hear them chatter.'

'Mother.' Katel was wide-eyed as she took Susanna's hands in hers. 'I love Jack more than I can say.'

'That's what love is,' Susanna said. 'It's strong as the winds and the sea and as beautiful as the dawn sunshine.'

'Before, when we were in the inn, Yowann spoke to you from his heart. I heard him. And I noticed how Colan looked on sadly.'

'Both men have good wives.'

'But they both love you. Even though Colan loves Joan, you were the first to steal his heart.'

'All that's in the past.'

'I truly believe one of them is my father. They're both fair-haired. They both have blue eyes. Perhaps Colan's hair curls a little less than mine does.'

'Stint, Katel. You know that the name of the man who fathered you will never pass my lips. I've told you many times.'

'Do you hate him?'

'No, but I love you more. My future is yours and Jack's, and the babies you may have.'

'I wish for a wonderful future for us all, Mother. I dream of it.' Katel shuddered. 'How can it be that I am so happy when Jack puts his arms around me, but when the mercer pinched my flesh, I thought I would faint away with fear?'

'He was drunken and foolish. Such men attract ill luck.'

'I cursed him as we left,' Katel said. 'Tedda showed me how.'

'Don't curse,' Susanna said, her voice low. 'And tell no one of it. We should take ourselves off to our beds. It's soon morning.'

She paused, lifting her head, sniffing the air. She could smell burning. An acrid stench of smoke reached her throat, the heavy smell of wood on fire. Katel had recognised it too. She was suddenly afraid.

'What's happening? Something's on fire, Mother. Is it the chimney?'

Susanna grabbed her damp shawl, pulling it round her shift, and rushed to the door, feeling the cold air and rain against her skin. The stench of burning was stronger outside and smoke billowed from The Ship in clouds through the door. Samuel was already outside, followed by Anne, the baby in her arms, and Jack. Yowann's voice could be heard, barking orders. Men spilled from the inn, then Joan and baby Thomas, wrapped in blankets, followed by Colan.

Susanna asked, 'What's amiss?'

'The inn's on fire,' Samuel shouted.

Jack was next to Katel, his arm around her to keep her warm.

'Everyone's outside now,' Anne said. 'Praise God that Joan and Thomas are well enough to get out quickly.'

Yowann came over to talk to Samuel. 'The mercer's in there, Charles

Rowe. He's a fool. He went to the cellar to get more sack and took a tallow candle with him. Colan didn't know he was there.'

'Is he trapped?' Susanna asked anxiously.

'It's all ablaze. My men are trying to salvage what they can. I had cargo in the cellar – silks, brandy – it'll all go up in smoke.'

'And the mercer?' Susanna asked.

'I fear no one can help him now. Look how strong the blaze is.' Yowann's face was illuminated by the orange furnace. 'The men will have it under control soon. The cellar can be rebuilt, the inn can be restored – but my possessions will be lost in the flames.' He turned back to Susanna. 'The mercer can't survive. The door was closed behind him, and his movements were slowed by drink. He has a wife and two boys living in the next town.'

'He intended me harm,' Katel said.

Susanna shot her a warning look. 'Yowann, I'm sorry for the loss of your goods and very sad for the mercer. No one would wish—'

A cry went up from The Ship and Yowann shouted, 'I'm coming now.' He turned to Susanna. 'My men are busy and I need to help them. There's no threat to you or to Samuel's cottage now. It's cold out here, and damp. Go inside. I have work to do.'

His eyes met hers, a fierce expression. Susanna nodded. She knew Yowann and his men would be inspecting the damage to their smuggled goods and dealing with the mercer's body.

'Katel, let's leave. I fear there's little we can do to help.' She beckoned to Joan. 'Come inside and bring the baby. You are welcome to stay overnight while the men work on. You have a fever and I fear the wind and rain will not help you recover.'

She ushered Katel inside, urging Joan, with her baby, to follow quickly, then she shut the door on the blaze, blocking the image of the burning inn from her mind.

She whispered to Katel, 'Yowann has lost money and a great deal of contraband. A man has lost his life. This doesn't bode well.'

* * *

Megan tucked into salmon and sipped Chablis. Her day had been much better than she'd expected. Julien refilled her glass.

'So you'll dive tomorrow and look for wreckage?'

'Before lunch. I'm surfing with Carly first thing. I'm so excited.' Megan was genuinely looking forward to it. 'What if we find out that there were smugglers in the cove? That could really be used to market the inn.' She glanced around the dining area, and into the bar. 'You're busy tonight.'

'We are, and usually Wednesdays are quiet,' Julien agreed. He leaned over and lowered his voice. 'Do you see the two couples on the table just across from you? They're staying in rooms one and two.'

'Where the Weeping Woman is?' Megan whispered back.

'I hope they'll be all right,' he said nervously. 'I can't wait to hear more about your walk up the cliffs and the sunk ship. What was it called?'

'The *Bonaventure*.'

'I'll be back as soon as I can.' Julien whirled away, pausing by the opposite table to make small talk. Megan heard him asking the four guests if all was well, if their rooms were comfortable, if the fish was good. The guests seemed happy enough. One of them, a woman about her own age with short red hair, was full of praise. Julien hurried back into the kitchen to help Claude.

Megan leaned forward, looking into the bar but there was no one she recognised. A few couples sat at tables and some groups of men were drinking, leaning against the bar. There were no musicians tonight. She'd hoped to see Tom Hocking, but he wasn't there. She stuck her fork into her food, deep in thought.

She had three days left – four, if she counted Sunday and she left St Mawgen Cove late. In truth, she didn't have much time at all, especially if she was thinking seriously about Patrick. She liked him, that much was certain. He gave her a warm feeling. But there was no doubt he was very work obsessed. He was obsessed with diving too. And being alone didn't seem to bother him. It was too early for her to draw any conclusions about a romance. There mightn't be one; they may be incompatible. She'd noticed the absence of reminders of the past in his house. There were no photos of family or friends. Megan thought of her own flat full of pictures of her parents, her and Amy and Leo; photos of friends' hen nights and pictures of herself surfing and various holidays. There was even one of her and Jay that she didn't have the heart to take down.

'Excuse me.'

Megan was suddenly conscious that someone was talking to her. The red-haired woman from the opposite table was leaning over. Megan glanced around to see if she was addressing someone else.

'Hello,' Megan said tentatively.

'Are you staying here?'

'Yes.'

'I thought it was you. The owner said someone was staying here all week to surf.'

'That's me. I'm in room three.'

'It's a nice place,' the red-haired woman said and Megan wondered what she was leading up to. There was clearly something on her mind.

'I love it here,' Megan said loyally.

'The thing is,' one of the men, tall and bearded, chipped in, 'we're here for just one night. We're walking the South West Coast Path.'

'Lovely,' Megan enthused. 'The views are to die for.'

'But apparently,' the other woman, lean, with a serious face, said, 'the owner said that the rooms have a reputation for smugglers and ghosts.'

'Oh, I do hope so,' the bearded man enthused. 'That would be something to tell the lads in my rugby team.'

'Is it true?' the red-haired woman asked.

'There are certainly local stories.' Megan sipped her wine, waiting. She wasn't sure how they'd react.

'Have you seen a ghost?' the bearded man asked.

'I heard some banging about upstairs in room four.' Megan wondered whether to tell them about the Drenched Man and the chair that rocked.

The serious woman shivered. 'Oh, that's made me go all cold, Joey.'

'You're in rooms one and two?' Megan asked.

'One above the other. It used to be a fisherman's cottage, apparently,' the man without the beard answered. He wore a T-shirt with the slogan 'More Trees, Less People'.

Megan leaned forward. 'There's a story about the Weeping Woman who lived in those rooms.'

'Oh, how exciting,' the red-haired woman said. 'We should take a bottle back and wait up to see if she comes.'

'Great idea,' the bearded man agreed. 'We might get to see some ghosts of pirates, too. Thanks.' He picked up his fork and continued to eat.

The woman drained her glass and called over, 'We'll let you know at breakfast if we see anything.' She turned to the bearded man. 'Do you think we can buy a bottle of wine at the bar and take it back to the room?'

Megan hoped Julien would have some satisfied customers this time. She hoped they wouldn't wake her up or leave in the middle of the night, as the last guest in room one had.

Julien rushed from the kitchen and was soon by her side, offering more wine. Megan winked. 'The other guests seem unfazed about the ghosts.'

'I thought I'd try being upfront about it, like we said,' Julien whispered in her ear as he took her plate. 'It feels like our luck's changing.'

'They're really excited,' Megan agreed.

'Plus, I've found a replacement for Josh: a new barman by the name of Steve. He seems really nice. He rides a motorbike. He'll come in from Gunwalloe.'

'That's where I went swimming. There was a great beach and a café.'

'That's right.' Julien nodded. 'So, to celebrate – pudding or a coffee?'

'Just a coffee, and please don't make it strong. I don't want to be awake all night.'

'Coming up.' Julien beamed. 'I just need to find a replacement for my cleaner while she's on maternity leave and everything will be tickety-boo.'

'When does her leave start?'

'October. The baby's due in December. She's a single parent, and she's having to do it all by herself.'

'That must be tough,' Megan commented.

'It's horrendous. Do you remember Tom saying her husband died of a heart attack, not far from this pub, just before we took it over.' Julien was already on his way back to the kitchen. 'We're doing our best to help, but most of the time I don't know what to say to her. I mean, imagine being on her own and pregnant. Poor Emma's had a really hard time of it.'

35

The September air was salty and fresh, straight from the sea. Megan stood on the beach with Carly after surfing at the crack of dawn, her board dripping. She was exhausted and happy, but as she set off across the sand towards the car park, her mind drifted back to Emma Davey – to her half-sister. So, she was the cleaner at The Ship. Megan had been talking to her for several days without realising who she was. Getting to meet her properly, to introduce herself, would be so easy now.

Her plan was to go back to the hotel, shower, have breakfast and wait for Emma to turn up for her shift, then she'd introduce herself. It was Thursday – the holiday was rushing by – she had no time to lose. In truth, she was nervous – she had no idea what she'd say – but today was finally the day she'd meet Emma properly, take the first steps to their being a family, whatever that meant.

She wondered how her father would take the news.

Carly was rubbing her fringe dry. 'Penny for them?'

Megan wasn't sure she should divulge what was in her mind, not yet. It was silly, but she didn't want to jeopardise a positive meeting with Emma by saying too much too soon. So she said, 'I've got a busy day today, lots to do. I'm researching Julien and Claude's ghosts at the inn. It's become a bit of an obsession.'

'Enjoy,' Carly said. 'I'm buying my ticket for Portugal today. We'll both be off to different places soon. Shall we get together in The Ship before you go? Saturday night's good.'

'Yes, let's. That would be great,' Megan said, but she was distracted by a blond man in a wetsuit strolling towards her, a surfboard beneath his arm. She thought Patrick was a little late this morning. As they passed, he said, 'Hi.'

'Hi,' Megan replied.

Carly gripped her arm and hissed, 'Did you just wink at him?'

Megan pressed her lips together so she wouldn't smile too widely. 'I met him yesterday when I was surfing and we were talking about the history of the inn. We're going diving later.'

'You're a sly one.' Carly nudged Megan gently. 'I'm away in St Austell for one day and you're arranging dates with men. No wonder you said you were busy.' Her eyes followed Patrick as he walked away. 'He's hot, though. I've always thought so.'

'He's very – knowledgeable,' Megan said, and Carly burst out laughing.

'So you just like him for his brain, Megan? It didn't look that way.'

Megan feigned innocence. 'We're diving for shipwrecks.'

'Right,' Carly said. 'I mean, look at him.'

'What do you mean?' Megan wasn't sure if Carly was joking.

'He's gorgeous. Look at that toned bod. And he's so brainy. And a little bit weird. What's not to like?'

'I don't know much about him,' Megan admitted. 'He dives, he's a photographer and a biologist, he loves the water, he works a lot. And yes, he's eccentric.'

'And fit as hell.' Carly made an exaggerated growling noise that Megan found funny. Then she was suddenly serious.

'He might have a partner somewhere. I'm not pinning my hopes.'

'I've never seen him with anyone. He's been in the shop a few times for surfboard wax and ding repair kits, and he's friendly enough, but he's always by himself.' Carly flourished her keys. They had reached the car park. 'Text me. Let me know how the hot date goes.'

'It's not a date.'

'Then make it one.' Carly hugged her. 'Your holiday's running out but there's still time for a fling.' She hugged her again. 'Leap in with both feet. And text me all the juicy bits.'

'I will,' Megan promised, wondering what on earth she'd have to report later. She wriggled into the Beetle and started the clanking engine. Patrick was not on her mind now. Her heart had started to thump as she planned what to say when she met Emma.

As soon as she arrived at her room, the opposite door opened and the bearded man emerged, the red-haired woman behind him. Megan hesitated, wondering what they'd have to report.

'Hello.' She wondered how to phrase the question. 'Did you sleep well? Did you see any ghosts?'

'No, none at all.' The woman was visibly disappointed. 'The four of us sat up until two in the morning. We even did all that ghosty hunting stuff, you know, "If you can hear us, please reveal yourself…" Nothing.'

'Oh?' Megan did her best to look sympathetic. 'That's a shame.'

'I wonder if Mark and Bella saw anything. They're on their way down.'

'You'll have to come back and try again,' Megan said optimistically. 'The breakfasts here are great. The chef is French.'

'Oh, I'd certainly come back,' the man enthused.

'We shouldn't be late, Joey – we've got to get started on the route,' the woman said, tugging the man's hand impatiently.

Megan hurried inside her room, showering, drying herself, tugging on warm clothes as fast as she could. She felt her pulse racing: the idea of introducing herself to Emma properly made her nervous. She thought of Patrick and wished she'd asked him for his phone number. It would have been nice to text him and ask him if he enjoyed his morning surf.

Once she was dressed warmly, she tugged open the door and paused in the hall. A muffled noise came from room one, opposite. The door was closed, but she was sure she'd heard a sound. It wasn't a radio left on or a phone ringing. Megan approached the door, leaning closely against it. There it was again: a sob, a human sound of grief. Megan listened. There was nothing for a while, then it came again, a drawn-out breath that might have been a sigh, or a barely audible cry. But she was sure it was a woman.

Megan tugged herself away, shivering with cold, filled with a sudden feeling of emptiness. The sound went right through her, as if the pain of suffering was too much to bear. It was the saddest, most tragic cry she had ever heard.

She hurried on to breakfast. The other guests would be there already and Julien would be delighted that they were enjoying their stay, that they might come back. She wanted to talk to him briefly to explain that she might invite a guest for dinner tonight. She wasn't sure if Patrick would accept: he could have other plans. Or perhaps he'd have too much work to do.

Megan spotted someone walking across from the inn car park, a woman in a loose coat. As Emma approached, Megan caught her breath: she was starting work early. Megan hesitated a moment. What if it all went wrong? What if Emma was upset or angry? She forced herself forward with no idea what to say, but she had to say something now or she'd lose her nerve.

Emma waved as she recognised her. They paused outside the dining room. 'Are you off for breakfast? I can smell bacon cooking.' She made a face. 'I just had a slice of toast and peanut butter. But that smell's making me feel hungry.'

Megan examined Emma's face. She had her father's dark hair, his brown eyes – Megan's eyes. How had she not noticed before?

'So how's the baby doing?'

'Oh, I think I must be having a footballer.' Emma laughed. 'This one kicks all the time now.'

'My dad played football a bit when he was younger,' Megan blurted, and Emma looked confused.

'That's nice.'

'My dad, Bill. Bill Hammond.'

'Bill?' Emma didn't move. 'Bill Hammond is your father?'

Megan thrust out a hand eagerly. 'I'm Megan. I...' How could she explain that she'd come to the cove to find out about her half-sister?

'I thought you were here on holiday.'

'I am.' Megan took another unsteady breath. 'But then I found out who you were and – I hope it's OK—'

Emma's face was frozen. Megan couldn't tell if it was shock, annoyance or happiness. She waited.

'You're Bill's daughter? He has a daughter?'

Megan nodded. She was shaking. 'I know it must be weird, but I'm so glad to meet you. And Dad sends his love.'

'How did you find me?' Emma was still staring, stunned. A tear gleamed on her cheek. 'Megan?'

Then, in one movement, she threw her arms around Megan and hugged her. A huge sob shuddered through her body, then another. 'I'm so pleased to meet you,' Emma said, then she burst into tears.

* * *

The huer waved branches from the summit of the cliff as dawn broke. He yelled 'Hevva, hevva!' then a trumpet blew a blasting note to alert everyone in the cove that the seas were full of pilchards ready to be netted.

Susanna handed plates of bread and cheese to Katel and to Joan, who was sitting by the fire with Thomas on her knee, her eyes almost closed with exhaustion. Her fever had broken and the baby was suckling contentedly. Susanna sprinkled some lavender flowers onto the fire to help their breathing, then she scurried to the door and opened it wide, letting the cool air of the day and its brightness flood the room. The sky was wide and bright, all traces of the storm now gone. Susanna thought the clouds held the silver grey of fish scales. The tide was crashing in, surf splashing against rocks.

The huer called again; the seine nets were already being laid out. The fishermen were needed to take the boats out into the ocean and net the shoals of fish. Susanna gazed towards The Ship. From the outside, she couldn't tell there had been a fire – it had been contained in the cellar – but the salt air still carried a heavy stench of smoke. She thought again about the mercer and her heart was heavy.

Then Samuel burst from his cottage, followed by Anne, her belly round, baby Bartholomew in one arm. She hugged her husband and kissed his lips. 'There's a good frumenty pottage for supper. Don't you spend too much time in The Ship.'

Samuel pulled her to him fondly. 'I'll have one ale. And I'll ask Colan if he needs any help with clearing the cellar.'

Then Jack appeared, his hair tousled as if he had just woken. As he pulled his boots on, Katel appeared from under Susanna's arm and threw herself into his embrace. Jack kissed her lips, his eyes closed. He said, 'We'll be late.'

Katel busied herself with arranging his shirt, his neckerchief, his jacket, the small stones around his neck. Then she kissed him again. 'This evening, you must eat with me and Mother. Then you and I will walk to the harbour.'

Jack's eyes darted to Susanna, then he kissed Katel again. '*Mon amour.* The summer cannot come quickly for me.'

'Nor for me.' Katel clung to him until he pulled himself away reluctantly. Samuel had already started to run towards the harbour.

Jack broke into a trot, turning round to wave. '*Je t'aime...*'

Katel put her hands to her flushing cheeks. 'He says that to me often in his language.'

Susanna wrapped an arm around her daughter. 'It does my soul good to see you so happy, Katel.' She waved to Anne, who was on her way inside. 'I'll call round this morning to see how you are and how the growing baby fares. Young Bartholomew, too.'

'I'll bake a custard tart for us both and I have some good honey bread. This baby's giving me a taste for sweet food.'

Susanna waited until the door clicked, then she turned to Katel. 'You'll have plenty of fish to salt for the next few weeks. The huer's trumpet and bushel marshal the movement of boats around the shoal. Look, Samuel's there with them.' She wrapped a hand around Katel and kissed the softness of her head. 'It will be a good summer. And then you'll be married.'

'I wish it would come soon.' Katel turned huge eyes on Susanna and a sigh shuddered through her small frame. 'He's my prince, just as the chawk told me. And he's so dear to me, more than I believed possible. I swear I love that man more than I love my own life.'

36

Megan grabbed Emma's hand and tugged her towards the dining room. The four guests looked up from their breakfast and met her eyes briefly in recognition. Julien rushed over, his expression perplexed. 'Hi, Emma. I didn't expect to see you here.'

Megan said, 'Julien – I hope it's OK – I'd like Emma to have breakfast with me. We have a lot to talk about.' She glanced at Emma's tear-stained face. 'We've just found out we're related.' She pulled out a seat, urging Emma to sit as Julien poured tea into one cup and coffee into another.

Megan lowered her voice. 'I'm going to ring Dad.'

'I ought to explain why I contacted him after all these years,' Emma said awkwardly. 'I'd often thought about it, but then I lost my husband a few months ago. I'm on my own now and with the baby on the way.' She took a breath and tears gleamed in her eyes. 'John and I thought we couldn't have children. We gave up trying and then, at the ripe old age of forty-two, I suddenly found out that I was pregnant. We were so looking forward to...' Emma paused, waving a hand in front of her face, trying not to cry. 'I-I never knew my real dad. My adopted parents live in France now – they're retired – so I searched for him and sent the letter.'

'He's keen to meet you.' Megan couldn't stop smiling. 'He's very nervous.'

'So am I.' Emma reached for her tea. 'I'm still shaking. Oh, I can't believe it – my baby will have a new family.'

'I'll be an aunt.' Megan was delighted. Everything was happening so quickly, it was hard to believe it was real. 'Right, let's have a calm, quiet breakfast – if I can get my heart to stop bumping. You and I have loads to talk about. Then we'll ring Dad and tell him we've found each other. I'm sure he'll be over the moon.'

'What about your mother? What does she think about it?'

Megan didn't know what to say. 'I hope she'll be over the moon too. We'll talk to Dad first. Mum'll be in the shop. Let's just tell him by himself. After all, he's your dad.'

'Megan.' Emma looked tearful. 'All I wanted was a family. Now John's died, I thought there would just be me and the baby. The thought terrified me. Are you sure Bill wants to meet me? I mean, I won't disappoint him? You said he was a teacher. Is he strict? Really intelligent? What if he doesn't like me?'

Megan grabbed her hand. 'Dad's exactly like you – he's warm and sweet, and he'll worry that you won't like him.' Julien appeared at her elbow with two plates of mushrooms on toast. 'Let's have breakfast, then we can go back to my room and catch up.'

'I hope I'm not taking up your time. You're on holiday.'

'I certainly am. Oh my goodness, I nearly forgot. I'm going diving at half eleven.' Megan remembered Patrick and her smile widened. 'This is going to be a really lovely day.'

* * *

'What a lovely day it is turning out to be.' Susanna stood in the doorway to her cottage, looking up at the sky, the silver grey turning deep blue, clouds fluffy as lambs' tails. 'I'll come with you, Katel, as you walk down to the salt cellar. The men are busy in the harbour and it would be good to see them bring the fish in.'

'There's a sharp breeze from the sea.' Katel wrapped herself in her shawl and came to stand next to her mother. 'And my hands will be rough from all the salting I must do today. I pray, make me some marigold cream to soften them. Tonight, before I walk with Jack, I'll bathe so that I smell sweet.'

Susanna's eyes were gentle with affection. 'Of course I will.' She turned to look over her shoulder. Joan and her baby were asleep in the chair by the fire. Their breathing was less ragged as they slept peacefully. She kept her voice low. 'Joan can go home and rest in her bed soon. Her strength is returning. Soon she'll be back at The Ship, cooking for the fishermen.'

'How can she bear it there?' Katel whispered. 'As we passed through there last night, when the mercer grabbed me, I was so afraid. If you hadn't been there, I shudder to think what might have happened. Do men behave like that to Joan, too?'

'She's Colan's wife and he's a respected innkeeper. He would not permit it. He was busy in the cellar last night, or he would have prevented the mercer from accosting you. Colan's a good man with a kind heart.' She shuddered. 'But the mercer will trouble a passing woman no more.'

'I'm glad,' Katel said. 'Although I'm sorry that he died. It's sad for his family.'

'What happened in the cellar was unfortunate,' Susanna said quietly.

'Yowann will be angry about losing his plunder.' Katel stared towards the seashore. 'He's not down at the harbour this morning. I wonder where he is.'

'Perhaps he's with Eliza.' Susanna frowned. 'Despite her bright new clothes, she didn't look well when I last saw her. Her cough hasn't gone as I hoped it would.'

'Everyone knows she's unhappy,' Katel said. 'All the women gossip when we're together in the cellar salting the fish. It's good to hear their chatter sometimes – it makes the time pass quickly. And they all say that Yowann Hicks married his wife because her father was rich. He doesn't love her. And she hasn't brought him a son, so he loves her even less.'

'It's not good to listen to tittle-tattle, Katel.'

'But it gives everyone good cheer, and sometimes there's much mirth when people talk about Yowann. He's handsome, and there are many stories of how he likes to choose from the young women of the cove after he's been drinking late at night. Eliza knows nothing of his merry ways.'

A loud scream came from behind them inside the cottage. Susanna and Katel whirled round.

'What's amiss?' Susanna stepped inside the room, Katel at her shoulder.

Joan leaped from her chair, clutching baby Thomas to her chest, screaming. 'Look – look! It's perched over there.'

Thomas had started to whimper. Joan was shaking, her eyes wild with fear as she glanced towards the table, then back to Susanna. 'I was asleep. Then I heard its cry. It swooped down the chimney, its wings beating, and it landed. See how it looks at us, with its mouth open.'

It took Susanna a few moments to work out what had happened. Then she saw it. There, on the table, a jackdaw was perched on a pitcher of water, its beady black eyes fixed on her.

It opened its mouth and cawed, a low warning screech.

* * *

Megan and Emma sat on the edge of her bed in room three, looking at each other nervously. Megan picked up her phone from the bedside table.

'I can't believe that I'm about to ring my real dad.' Emma gripped Megan's hand.

'Are you ready?'

'I don't know. What shall I say?'

'He'll be so excited about the baby.'

'And should I tell him I'm on my own now?'

'Yes, I suppose so,' Megan said gently. 'John died of a heart attack?'

'He did. I try to believe that. But he was so fit.' Emma shook her head quickly. 'You know what people say around here? That it was the witch's kiss?'

Megan pretended not to know. She wanted to hear it from Emma. 'Tell me.'

'Well, the story goes that the witch watches from the cliffs. She sees a man late at night and she comes down and kisses his lips. It's the kiss of death.'

'Do you believe that?'

'I was brought up around here.' Emma's expression didn't change. 'St Mawgen's full of ghost stories. I've heard the lost sailors who whisper down by the seafront at night. It's a low wail, like the wind, but different. And the

Drenched Man's upstairs. He drowned in a shipwreck and he can't rest. And I've heard the Weeping Woman.'

'I've heard her too.'

'They say she's weeping for the witch.'

Megan caught her breath. 'Why? What happened?'

'Who knows? People say the witch was punished for her crimes and the Weeping Woman will cry for ever.'

Megan remembered the heart-wrenching sound. 'I wish there was something we could do to help them rest.'

Emma pulled herself from her thoughts. 'I always think the Weeping Woman must be a mother. Her crying is so sad, as if she's torn in two. Since I've been pregnant, I've thought that she must be crying for a child. I know how that kind of love feels, even before the baby's born.'

Megan nodded sympathetically.

'And I've often wondered about my own mother – she was called Christine Ahearne – but I couldn't find anything out about her. She might have a married name now.'

Megan recalled that her father had said Chrissie had moved to Yorkshire, that Emma had been named Sarah Jane at birth. She thought it best not to say anything yet. They had only just met and it was going so well. She took Emma's hand. 'It's almost half ten. Shall we do it?'

'I'm so nervous.' Emma's voice was hushed.

'Me too. Well...' Megan took a breath. 'Dad'll be desperate to talk to you. I think it's time to ring.'

Megan pressed the button on her phone. A low voice crackled, 'Hello' and Emma gripped her hand.

Megan launched in, trying to keep it cheerful. 'Dad, it's me.'

'Hello, holiday girl – how's it going?' Her father sounded nervous.

'Really well. And I've got Emma with me. Emma works here, at The Ship, Dad. She's dying to talk to you.'

There was a pause, then Bill said, 'Hello, Emma.'

'Hello—' Emma didn't know what to call him. She was suddenly formal. 'I'm very pleased to meet you.'

'You too,' Bill said. Megan heard him take a deep breath. He tried again.

'So, it's such a coincidence you work in the pub, that you were there all along.'

'Yes,' Emma said.

'It seems a nice part of the world, Cornwall,' Bill replied. Megan knew it was difficult for him to explain what was in his heart after so long.

'It is,' Emma said.

'It's nice to talk at last, after so long.' Bill gulped and Megan knew her father was crying.

Emma was sobbing too, her face wet. 'I always wondered what this moment would be like.'

'Me too.'

Neither Bill nor Emma could speak now: it was too much.

Megan took over. 'Dad, would you and Mum like to come down here on Saturday and meet Emma? It's her day off and—'

'I'd love to,' Bill said straight away. 'I'll need to talk to your mother, though.'

'Of course,' Megan said knowingly. 'But she can close the shop for the day and you can drive down first thing.'

'I'd like that,' Emma said, sniffing into a tissue.

'Yes.' Bill swallowed audibly. 'Yes, we'll be there.'

'Let's talk again this time tomorrow, shall we?' Megan suggested cheerfully. 'Emma, come and have breakfast with me again. You and Dad must be completely emotionally worn out but maybe by tomorrow we can sort out where we're going to meet. And then we can spend the day together.'

'Yes, please...' Emma's voice trailed away.

'We'll call you tomorrow, Dad,' Megan said.

'Right, yes, thanks, Megan.' Bill gave a muffled laugh. 'It seems the bracelet did its trick. Until tomorrow. Bye.' The phone clicked and he was gone.

'Bracelet?' Emma asked, wiping her face.

'Crystal beads, from my shop,' Megan said, taking her hand.

Emma rubbed her stomach. 'I don't suppose you can cure heartburn?'

'As a matter of fact,' Emma said, 'I've got some meadowsweet capsules that prevent stomach acid. When my friend Amy was pregnant, I gave her some wheatgerm oil with mandarin for stretch marks. They both worked wonders. I'll get Mum to bring some down.'

* * *

Susanna and Katel walked down to the harbour to see the haul come in: crowds had gathered. Hedyn Gilbert was watching from his cottage, looking melancholy. Many of Yowann's friends had arrived from neighbouring villages, but Susanna could not see Yowann. Colan was in the crowd as the seine nets were laid out. The huer was waving and shouting from the clifftop, organising boats to gather in the pilchards.

As Susanna and Katel approached the seawall, the jackdaw followed them, flying overhead before landing on the pavement, screeching and flapping its wings, then fluttering to another distant place to caw again.

Katel tucked her arm through her mother's nervously. 'What does the chawk want?'

'It's springtime. He's searching for his mate,' Susanna said hopefully.

Katel snuggled closer for comfort as she walked. A stiff breeze rushed from the sea and she shivered. It blew her hair across her face as she pointed. 'Look at all the fishing boats. There's Jack, Mother, with Samuel and Merryn. They're so far out I can hardly recognise my uncle. See how he leans over to haul in the net.'

'Your uncle Samuel has been fishing since he was fourteen years of age. He has much experience. Can you see how Jack watches and learns from him?'

'As we must all learn from those we love and trust,' Katel said. 'I've never thanked you, Mother, for the care and love you've shown me. It must have been hard to bring up a child by yourself. I'm sorry I let Tedda turn my head with her promises and her tales of magic. I'm ashamed of it now. But I'll learn only from you. I'll be a good pellar.'

'And you'll be a happy wife and mother,' Susanna said. She felt her heart expand with joy; her child's happiness was her own. There could be no greater love than she had for Katel.

Katel leaned her head against Susanna's shoulder. 'I've never been happier.'

'Nor I.'

At that moment, the raw wind rose from the ocean, buffeting them hard, pushing them back as if with strong hands. The jackdaw flew over their heads, the sudden pounding of wings making them shiver, and it landed on the harbour wall, its beak wide. It cawed raucously three times.

A huge wave crashed in from the sea, a barrel of water, hurtling towards the little fishing boat as Samuel hauled in a full net. He was shouting instructions to Jack and Merryn, who stood either side of him, tugging in the catch. Samuel's words were lost in the roar of the ocean as the wave rose high and smashed against the wooden boat, forcing it over in a single movement. The three men tumbled into the water.

Samuel surfaced first, swimming against the tossing waves, trying hard to stay afloat, thrashing furiously before he was sucked beneath. Merryn's arm appeared, as if waving or begging for help, then he disappeared.

Only Jack remained visible. His words were lifted on the wind, shouting in his own language, and his eyes met Katel's. He called again, reaching a hand to her, then another wave hit him and he was gone.

The jackdaw took to the air, shrieked once more and flew upwards into the sky.

37

It was almost twelve. Megan was running late as she knocked on the door of Surf's Up! When she'd dropped Emma off, she'd been invited inside her little cottage to see the newly painted nursery, and it had cost her twenty minutes. She knocked again, wondering briefly if Patrick had already left for the dive.

The door opened and he stood there, his wetsuit rolled down to his waist, and Megan took in the tanned skin, the taut muscles on his body and the careless way he leaned against the door frame, oblivious of how good he looked. She found her gaze lingered too long. 'Sorry I'm late.'

'Oh, no problem.' Patrick seemed to have no idea that she was late – or that she was staring at him. 'I'm still getting organised. Come in.'

'Thanks.' She followed him, smiling at his indifference to being half dressed and wearing shoes with holes in them. She told herself it was another lesson: unlike when she'd sat in the Afterdune Delight café counting the minutes, Patrick trusted her to arrive in her own time. Unlike her, he wasn't making judgements based on a past relationship that hadn't worked.

In the living room he flopped down on the cushions. She sat beside him as he asked, 'How's it going? How's the search for your half-sister?'

'Brilliant.' Megan suddenly wanted to gush, to tell him the whole story of Emma and how they had spoken to her father. 'We met. We had breakfast. She's a really lovely person.'

'That's great news,' Patrick said.

Megan was observing him again. He was devastatingly handsome, and refreshingly unaware of the effect he had on her. She was suddenly nervous. She hadn't had a relationship for so long that it would be easy to allow herself to rush in, to be bowled over by his good looks. But Patrick was calm, laid back: everything happened in its own time. Megan wished she had his easy-going disposition.

'Have you always been so relaxed?'

'I suppose so,' Patrick said. 'It annoys some people, I know.'

'Oh, no, it's really cool. I'm the opposite. I'm too impetuous. I don't think things through, and then when I do, I put them off.' Megan was gabbling. 'Mum always said I was late with everything, walking, talking, then whoosh! I caught up. That's me all over. I came here on a mission to find my sister and all I did was surf!'

'Yes, but you're spontaneous and great to spend time with. I think you're lovely.'

Megan caught her breath. He'd paid her a compliment. She tried to brush it aside. 'My mum thinks I procrastinate. Or jump in with two feet.'

'It's nice to talk to someone with so much energy. Sometimes people think I'm a cold fish, because I'm so focused on one thing.'

'I think that's impressive.'

'It's because I have hyperfocus, a kind of intense concentration.' He shrugged as if it wasn't important. 'It's normal for me. I've never known anything else.'

'Oh?' Megan racked her brains to try to remember what she knew about hyperfocus. Was it a symptom of ADHD? 'Does that make life difficult? Relationships?'

'No, not really.' Patrick ran a hand through his hair. 'I just carry on as normal, do my own thing. I decided long ago that a relationship would come to me when it was the right time and I wouldn't seek it out or try too hard.'

'Oh, so,' Megan couldn't help herself, 'no girlfriend then?'

'Not yet,' Patrick said enigmatically. 'Anyway, I want to hear about what you've been up to, about the half-sister, and about the ghosts in The Ship. And I want to talk to you about all sorts of other things but...' He leaped up and held out a hand. 'Shall we go diving first?'

'On one condition.' Megan allowed herself to be helped up. 'Will you have dinner with me tonight? At The Ship? I owe you... for letting me come with you.'

'I'd love that,' Patrick said brightly. 'Are we going ghost hunting afterwards?'

'Who knows?' It was Megan's turn to be enigmatic. 'Let's see what we find on the dive.'

Megan had expected to be nervous, diving for the first time with Patrick, but her overriding emotion was one of excitement. As they walked into the water, Patrick was steady and calm: if he was in any way concerned about diving with a novice, he didn't show it.

They swam out a little, side by side. Then he said, 'We'll just go down as far as we can and see what we find. Let me know if you want to come back up. We won't stop down too long. OK?'

'OK.'

'Stay relaxed. Don't hold your breath. Don't fight nature. If you feel a surge then go with it. If you need to go up, signal.'

'Right. I remember all that. I'm ready.'

'First, let's check releases are secured and that buoyancy devices are working.'

'Right.'

Patrick went through procedure quickly and calmly. Then they dived beneath the water. Megan's emotional memory kicked in straight away. She remembered how much she enjoyed the sensation of weightlessness, how easy it was to move beneath the waves, and she felt free and light. Her diving skills weren't as rusty as she'd thought. The water felt colder the deeper they went. Despite their carrying lamps, visibility was poor and the sea became darker. But instead of feeling anxious, she was filled with a feeling of peace. She concentrated on breathing steadily as Patrick had coached. He swam beside her and, as they descended, Megan relaxed into being held by the ocean. It almost felt like being in space, and she forced herself not to laugh at the absurdity of floating.

Time passed, and they dived deeper, eyes keen for a sign of something interesting. Then, all of a sudden, Patrick waved an arm to convey the direction he wanted to go in, and they swam towards a murky-looking place on the ocean bed. He pointed below as she hovered horizontally, feeling suspended in air. He had seen something. She followed him as he swam lower and lower, doing her best to stay calm. Her heart had started to pound. What if it was some sort of evidence?

Patrick was transfixed. He descended further into the foggy deep towards the seabed. Megan watched through her mask as he took some photos. He pulled a little sack from his weight belt and reached out, plucking something from the sea floor and pushing it in the bag. Then he turned to Megan and gave a thumbs up. It was time to surface. She was glad to be going up again.

They took off their masks and regulators as soon as they broke water, Megan blinking in the brightness, Patrick beside her, reaching out a steadying hand. They swam for shore and waded out, sliding off their flippers, standing on the beach. Megan's legs felt wobbly, but she wanted to whoop for joy, she'd loved it so much. She said breathlessly, 'Can we do that again?'

'We certainly can,' Patrick said. 'Was it good?'

'Our first dive? Too right.'

'You did well.' Patrick was full of enthusiasm. 'I can't wait to get back down there. I saw some strange bits on the seabed. I think there were fragments, metal fittings, a bit of rotten wood. And look what I found. You'll be interested in these.' He pulled out the little bag from his belt and took out a stone. 'There are eleven of them, all the same.'

Megan took one in her hand. 'They've got small holes, like they were linked in a chain, or a necklace.'

'Exactly.' Patrick frowned. 'Do you think someone was wearing them?'

Megan shuddered. 'When they drowned?'

'Shall we go back to the cottage?' Patrick suggested. 'We can do a bit of research and see if we can find out what they are.'

'Maybe they were worn for protection – for good luck. They remind me of these.' She held out her wrist, showing him her crystal bracelet.

'I wear this.' Patrick's fingers touched the chain around his neck. 'A guardian bell for good luck. It's about as superstitious as I get.' He held out a hand. 'Come on. Let's see where this takes us.'

Megan wasn't sure whether he meant the research or holding his hand. But she reached for his fingers gratefully.

* * *

They were still talking excitedly about the stones Patrick had found on the seabed as they sat together in The Ship that evening. Julien hovered, taking orders.

'So, Megan, the dish Claude has prepared for you tonight is a seafood risotto, and can I get you a glass of Chablis to accompany it?'

'That's great. Yes, please,' Megan said.

'Is there a vegetable option?' Patrick asked. 'And can I get a tomato juice?'

'We can make you a veggie risotto,' Julien said affably. 'Oh, and while you're both here, I've been working on the website and I can't wait to hear what you find out about shipwrecks. I'm going to really push the smuggler angle in our marketing. I've already had two bookings for Saturday night.'

'That's great,' Megan said, genuinely thrilled. 'I love this place.'

'I need to sort out the heating, though.' Julien rubbed his hands together. 'I can't get used to the intense cold in here. Risottos coming up.'

Megan watched him walk away, then she leaned forward. 'So let's go through what we know about the stones.'

Patrick took one of the stones from his pocket and placed it in her palm. 'Well, according to what we found on the internet, they are called hag-stones.'

Megan spoke quietly. 'Yes, they had magical properties, even able to heal a snake bite. People thought they could see through a witch's disguise by looking through the hole.'

Patrick was thoughtful. 'They'd have been on the beach for years, but then someone came along and chose them and made them into a necklace. They're worn for luck.'

'People used to believe the stones could help a lost soul to rest,' Megan said.

'How could they? They're just pebbles.'

'Some people believe they resonate at the same frequency as the human body,' Megan went on. 'They're very tactile.' She held the stone in her hand and turned it over. 'I'm drawn to this one.'

'You should keep it then.'

'Thanks. What do you think happened to the person who wore them?'

'I found bits of broken wood. A fishing boat broke up a long time ago. Perhaps one of the fishermen wore the stones on a cord for luck.'

Megan felt sad. 'It didn't help him much.'

'It's our connection with the past, though,' Patrick said. 'If that really is the site of a sunken fishing boat, there will be other stuff down there. I'm going to keep looking until I find the *Bonaventure*.'

'I loved our dive today.'

'I'd love you to be there when I find the sunken ship.'

Megan caught her breath. 'I have my shop to run. And you're such an experienced diver. I'd get in the way.'

'Not at all. You're the perfect companion,' Patrick said, and Megan wondered what he meant. 'It was great diving with you today.'

Megan's heart sank. He rarely thought of anything but work. She smiled to cover her disappointment.

'I'd like to get better at it. Count me in. When can we go again?' She hoped he'd say tomorrow.

'Maybe at the weekend, before you go home? I'm working first thing tomorrow. I'm off to Falmouth, giving a nine o'clock lecture.' He paused. 'And I had something planned for afterwards.'

Megan was disappointed, but Patrick had his own life, and she shouldn't expect to be a central part of it, certainly not yet anyway. She said, 'The weekend would be great.'

'And I thought—' Patrick picked up his fork and examined it. 'Maybe you'd be free tomorrow afternoon for a date. Of sorts.'

Megan didn't understand. 'A date?'

'A first date.' He gave her a hopeful look. 'If you like, we could go somewhere interesting, spend time.'

Megan's mouth was open with surprise. Then she was smiling before rearranging her expression, trying to make herself look less ridiculously keen. 'I'd like that.'

'Where would you like to go? Walking? We could drive somewhere?'

'Surprise me,' Megan said.

'I'll do that,' Patrick said cheerily as Julien arrived with their drinks, rushing off again to come back straight away with two steaming plates of risotto. Megan looked at the single stone in her palm. Until today, the stone had spent centuries on the ocean bed.

'Perhaps this will bring me luck.'

She met Patrick's gaze and felt a warmth pass between them, a sense of hope. And something else she wasn't sure of yet, but it was filled with promise.

38

Katel cried herself to sleep. It was pitch dark outside as Susanna sat beside her daughter by the fireplace, stroking her hair, whispering soothing words. But in truth, there was nothing she could say that would help. Her own face was damp with tears. She had lost a dear brother; her daughter had lost the man she loved. Anne had shut herself in her cottage, the door firmly closed, refusing to speak to anyone as she cried alone, clutching Bartholomew above her rounded belly. She was inconsolable.

Katel was wretched too. She sobbed as she slept, still in her clothes, lying by the fire. Susanna had secretly mixed a little valerian root in her warm ale to help her find some solace in sleep. But as Susanna stared into the firelight, the events of the morning were still with her. She could see the barrelled wave that broke the boat; she could hear the loud cries of the men. In the flames, the image was there: Samuel sinking, Merryn lost, and finally, with one last look to Katel, Jack drowned beneath the rough seas.

Susanna wondered what to do. Katel was broken-hearted. She had refused food. Her eyes were red from crying, her hair unkempt like a wild woman's. She'd sobbed until Susanna thought she'd faint. Susanna felt helpless, filled with anxiety, weighed down by her own grief. She had no idea how to comfort her daughter. She was gripped with sadness, not just for Katel's suffering, but for Anne, an expectant mother, now a widow. And she couldn't imagine life without Samuel, her beloved brother. Susanna felt the tears come again.

There was a muffled knock on the door. Susanna touched Katel's fevered brow with tender fingers and stood up slowly, moving aimlessly towards the soft rapping sound. She opened the door to see Colan Stephens standing outside in the cold darkness. She ushered him in.

'Colan? Aren't you busy in the inn?'

'Joan sent me. She's serving in my place, the baby in her arms. But she bade me come to you.'

'Why? What's amiss?'

Colan glanced at Katel. 'How's the poor little maid?'

'Heartbroken. I fear she may never recover.'

'My heart's heavy too. I'm almost afraid to tell you.'

'Why, what has happened?' Susanna clutched his arm.

'The men are talking among themselves. They're talking about Tedda Lobb.'

'But Tedda's long gone.'

'They believe she came back today in the shape of a chawk. Three times it was heard to crow. And three men were drowned.'

'That's folly,' Susanna said. 'How can Tedda come back?'

'Hedyn Gilbert said that Katel summoned her.'

'Katel? That's nonsense, Colan. How could she do that?'

'That's why Joan sent me to warn you. Hedyn believes that Katel caused the ship to sink with Merryn in it. Now his children have died, Merryn and Beaten both, he looks to point the finger of blame.'

'How can that be her doing? Katel has lost the man she loves.'

'I believe you and Joan does too. But there's talk that Katel made the fire happen that killed the mercer and burned Yowann's silk and brandy in the cellar. I know it was an accident – I closed the door – but Katel was overheard.'

'Overheard?'

'As Charles was trying to steal a kiss from Katel, someone heard her telling him to burn in hell.'

'He was being rough with her. She was afraid she'd be harmed.'

'I know that,' Colan said, his brow twisted in anxiety. 'But the men talk.

And Katel's name's on everyone's lips. They're using the word that I don't like to repeat, the one they used about Tedda.'

'That's enough. Katel would never hurt Jack or Samuel. She loved them. And she was fond of Merryn.'

'I know. There are those who say she brought Jack here by magic that night, that she killed his brother by drowning him. The men say his ghost has started to walk in the upstairs room at Annie's house. You know well that the sailor was brought from the sea almost dead, killed by the wreckers, so his soul can never rest. Joan and I were talking together.' Colan held out his hand. 'Here are some coins.'

'What would I do with them?'

'Take Katel and all the things you can pack in a bag. There's a man I know with a horse and cart. He'll ride with you to Bodmin, and from there you can go to Plymouth, then north. Go as far as you can, and quickly.'

'But why should we?'

'Susanna, I've heard what Hedyn Gilbert says to everyone about Katel. I fear you're both at risk. Joan thinks so too.'

'I won't run away.'

'I beg you to do it. As much as I love your friendship, I cannot bear what will happen if the men's anger turns from words into deeds.'

'What will they do?'

'Don't wait to find out. Go, please.'

Susanna was confused. 'Why would you do this for me, Colan?'

'Because, although I love Joan very much, I've always loved you.' He grasped her hand, pressing the coins in it. 'Because I'm afraid. Because I believe Katel's my child.'

'Surely the men are only gossiping because the news is fresh.' Susanna stared at the coins. 'Tomorrow will be a new day. Their thoughts will be more reasonable.'

'I doubt it.' Colan was serious. 'Please, Susanna. I'll ask my friend to come here tonight with his horse and cart.'

Susanna looked at Katel by the hearth, still sobbing as she slept. 'I can't disturb her.'

'Then tomorrow, first thing?'

'I'll think again about what to do. Thank you, Colan, but I can't take your money, and Joan's. You have baby Thomas.' Susanna pushed the coins back into Colan's hand.

Colan moved towards the door. 'I'll see you tomorrow, Susanna. We'll talk more then. I'm sorry for your loss. I liked Samuel.' He made a low sound of sadness. More words would not come. He disappeared in the darkness.

Susanna looked at Katel, curled in a ball, her hair unkempt, her cheeks damp. She heard her whisper, 'Why does he not come back to me?' and she thought her heart would break.

* * *

Megan sat on the bed in her room, Emma next to her clutching the phone, her face covered in tears.

'Then I'll see you tomorrow, Bill.'

'I'm looking forward to it.' Bill's phone crackled. 'Jackie is, too. You heard what she said. She can't wait to meet you.'

Emma sniffed. 'Me too.' She handed the phone back to Megan.

'I'll book you a room at The Ship, Dad,' Megan said. 'It'll be great to see you and Mum. And I'll book us a table for the evening. I'll invite Carly. She's been my surfing partner. We were up with the dawn patrol this morning – the waves were magical. And you'll love Julien and Claude.' Megan wondered if she should invite Patrick too. 'So, we'll catch up on Saturday afternoon, you'll be able to spend some time with Emma and then we'll go home on Sunday.' The thought made her heart sink and she knew why, but Megan kept her voice cheery. 'See you then. Bye, Dad.'

Bill said something, then the phone went quiet. Emma sniffed once, and caught her breath, wiping her face with the back of her hand. 'I have a proper dad. I can hardly believe it. And your mum was so nice.'

Megan wrapped an arm around her. 'Dad's really nervous about meeting you tomorrow.'

'I'm nervous too,' Emma said. 'I've never been fazed by anything before, then John and I found we were expecting this little one, and we were so excited. Not long after, I lost him – you know the story.' She rubbed the bump tenderly. 'You've no idea how much having a family means, Megan. We both wanted this for so long.'

'It means a lot to me too,' Megan agreed. 'I bet my mother starts crying tomorrow. And my dad. I'll get hold of Julien and book a room.' She frowned. 'The Drenched Man's available but the other rooms are booked. Do you think they'll be all right in there?'

'Who knows when he'll come?'

'Perhaps I'll let them have my room, and I'll go upstairs.' Megan shuddered at the thought.

'Won't you be nervous by yourself?' Emma asked.

'Of course,' Megan said, taking a breath. 'But I can't let my mother sleep in there.'

'That's true. But what about you?'

'I'll be fine,' Megan said, wondering how she'd manage a whole night wide awake, waiting for the rocking chair to creak. 'Let's book the room and Mum and Dad can have mine. I'm so excited.'

A shiver caught her like an embrace: she remembered the whispered words she'd heard on the clifftop. She wondered if Emma's husband had heard them too, before he died.

* * *

Katel stood by the fire, trembling and sobbing. Her eyes were wild, and red with crying.

'I won't leave him.'

'Colan thinks it's wise. He thinks it may be better to go far from the cove.' Susanna was doing her best to explain.

'Jack's at the bottom of the sea but the hag-stones will protect him and one day they'll bring him back to me.'

'Katel, this is grief talking.'

'It's the truth, Mother. The chawk told me so. The stones will come back to me, then Jack and I will be together forever. When I gave them to him, he promised never to leave me. I must wait for him.'

'Colan says it's not safe for us here.'

'I won't leave.' Katel rushed to the door and pushed it wide. The spring sunlight flooded in as she whirled into the street, still in her shift.

'Katel, come back.'

'Jack won't fail me. If I stand on the clifftop, I'll see him when he swims to shore. The magical stones will bring him back to my arms.'

'Katel.'

Katel was running down the hill towards the seawall, her hair flying, her shift loose around her ankles. Susanna watched as people in the street stopped to stare as she hurried past them, not noticing. Then she was lost from sight.

Susanna scurried back into the room for her shawl. She would have to chase after her daughter and persuade her to walk back calmly to the cottage. She had already packed their things in two bags. Then she'd accept the coins from Colan and find the man who could take them both to safety. Susanna whirled towards the door to find the light blocked. Yowann was standing in the doorway, his arms crossed, looking serious.

'Susanna, I need to talk with you about Katel. There's trouble in the cove, much talk from the men, and I'm expected to deal with it. And what I have to say brings me much sadness.'

39

Everything about the date surprised Megan. It had been a lovely afternoon, but she'd had no idea what to expect beforehand. Every moment in St Ives had been glorious. She sat in Patrick's bright red car on the return journey, amazed at his choice of vehicle: she'd imagined him to own an old surf banger.

'I didn't think you'd drive one of these. It's nothing like my Beetle. It's just so cool.'

'It's a Jeep Renegade Hybrid,' Patrick said, looking handsome in sunglasses, T-shirt and cut-off jeans. 'I need something to take me to and from Falmouth for lectures, and to get around Cornwall when I'm diving. Plus it's a great car to drive off road when I visit my parents.'

'Are your family Cornish?'

'With a name like Penrose, how could we be from anywhere else? My parents have a smallholding in North Somerset now. They've retired. They live in the middle of nowhere, completely off-grid,' he said. 'They're eccentric, but I love them for it.'

'Are you an only child?'

'I've got a sister, Lottie. She's in London, works in finance. We aren't at all alike. She does stand-up comedy at the weekends.' He took the narrow road back towards St Mawgen. It was almost six o'clock. 'Have you had a good afternoon? I mean – was it a nice first date?'

'It's been wonderful. I don't know what I expected – a walk in the woodlands, maybe. Then you said to bring my swimming stuff, but I had no idea where we were going.' Megan leaned back in her seat. 'St Ives is incredible. Porthmeor Beach is fantastic for surfing. I could have stayed for ever.'

'I knew you'd love the big waves. Then the Tate's the perfect place to wind down.' Patrick braked to allow a pheasant to saunter across the road before driving on. 'The gallery's lovely – it was built on an old gasworks site. I wish we'd had more time there.'

'Yes, the light in St Ives is quite incredible.'

'I mean I wish there was more time left of your holiday. You've only got a couple of days.'

'I have.' Megan wasn't sure what to say.

'But we're diving again tomorrow.'

'Mum and Dad are coming down to meet Emma, so I'm going to leave them to it in the afternoon and come with you.' She resisted the inclination to snuggle closer to him. 'If that's OK?'

'It's perfect,' Patrick said.

'Then afterwards, I've booked a table for us all at The Ship. I've asked Carly to come and... I wondered if you'd like to come too.'

'I'd love to,' Patrick said. 'Are your parents staying over?'

'Yes. Julien said all four rooms are booked. Mum and Dad got the last one. I'm moving my stuff up to room four tomorrow. I couldn't let my parents have that room, so they'll have mine.'

'You're staying in room four? Isn't that where you said the Drenched Man is?'

'Yep.' Megan tried to sound confident.

'Do you want me to stay with you?' Patrick realised what he'd said. 'I mean, I could bring a sleeping bag.'

'I might.' Megan had to admit to feeling relieved. 'Half of me is scared to death. The other half, I'm just telling myself not to be so silly. I'll be fine.'

'I'll leave the offer with you then. Whatever you decide. So, what do we do now?'

'I'm quite hungry,' Megan said. 'But I don't think Julien's expecting me at The Ship for dinner tonight.'

'So, given that this is our first date, can I take you to dinner?'

Megan looked down at her jeans and hoodie. 'I'm not dressed for it.'

'Nor am I, but they won't mind us turning up as we are,' Patrick said. 'There's this lovely little clifftop café on the way home where we can sit and watch the sun set.' He turned the Jeep round a corner, and they began to ascend a steep path. 'The road's a bit bumpy on the way up, but the view's spectacular.'

* * *

Susanna hurried up the stony path to the cliff, Yowann on her elbow. He hadn't stopped talking since they'd left her cottage. Her face was covered in tears. She couldn't look at him as she spoke.

'The things the men are saying are gossip. You know yourself how people talk in the cove. Poor Katel is distracted – the man she loved was drowned. And Samuel, too, my own brother, her uncle.'

'And Merryn Gilbert,' Yowann added emphatically. 'Hedyn feels there's a grudge against his family. That there have been foul deeds, dark magic.'

'That's foolish and you know it.'

'Listen to me, Susanna. Beaten died, then Merryn.'

'And my brother, and Jack.' Susanna pushed ahead of him, refusing to listen to him. She was halfway up the cliff path and she could see Katel now, at the edge, looking towards the sea.

'But that's not all.' Yowann grabbed her arm, forcing her to stop. 'Eliza's sick.'

'She's not a well woman. Her hands pain her. And her cough was bad. She had influenza.' Susanna faced him.

Yowann looked behind him. A group of people were following, on their way up the path, not far away. Susanna looked over her shoulder too. She could see Hedyn Gilbert, Colan, many of Yowann's friends from local villages – the blacksmith, the shopkeeper, the merchant, the miller – hurrying towards them. Behind them, she could see Anne, moving heavily, her baby in her arms.

She faced Yowann angrily. 'What's happening?'

'This morning, Eliza coughed up a nail.'

'She did not.'

'You know well that she did, Susanna. Just as she coughed up a nail when Tedda Lobb cursed her.'

'That's nonsense. I saw it with my own eyes. You put it in her cup and she almost swallowed it by mistake.'

His face flushed; he was furious. 'How dare you?'

'You're a liar, Yowann. You don't love Eliza. And you're angry because your mercer friend died in a fire that burned your smuggled goods.'

'Someone must pay,' Yowann said, his voice a cold whisper. 'The men are demanding it.'

'Not I. Not Katel. She's done nothing.' Susanna stopped, facing him. 'You're a coward.'

'What can I do now?' Yowann gripped her wrist. 'There are men who'll swear that Katel cursed the mercer – and you saw how he died. She summoned the chawk and it cried out, then three men drowned. Katel befriended Tedda. People are saying that she learned enchanted ways from the witch.'

'Then they're wrong, and you know it.' Susanna dragged herself free from Yowann's grasp and broke into a run, her skirts impeding her movement, although she reached the top quickly.

Katel stood at the edge of the cliff, pointing with her finger to the place where the waves crashed against the rocks. 'Jack will come soon.'

Susanna took a breath. 'Come down with me, Katel, back to the cottage. I'll make peace with the people of the cove. You mustn't speak to them. Allow me to deal with this.'

'But the stones he wore around his neck will bring Jack back to me. Then we'll be together.'

'Shush, child.' Susanna hugged her tightly, as if she might pull her to safety by the sheer force of the embrace. She felt the softness of her hair beneath her palm, the cool cheek against hers, damp with tears.

'Katel Boram,' a low voice shouted and Susanna whirled round, her daughter in her arms, 'you stand accused of dark deeds.'

'Leave her alone, Yowann,' Susanna hissed. There was a crowd of people from the cove standing behind him. She looked at their angry faces – she knew most of them. Colan was there, his expression tense, and Anne, holding the baby, panting heavily. Then Hedyn Gilbert pushed forward.

'Katel killed my son. She caused my daughter to die. She cursed my family.' He pointed a shaking finger. 'We cannot suffer her to live among us.'

'Then I'll take her away with me,' Susanna called out. 'She's innocent. But if you wish it, we'll leave the cove and you'll never see us again.'

Colan raised his voice. 'I have a man waiting with a horse and cart. He'll take Susanna and Katel safely to a distant place.'

'But what about justice for those among us who have been harmed?' one man called. 'What about Charles, the mercer? The girl cursed him.'

'And the fire started, just as she bade it,' another man shouted.

Another voice hissed, 'And she cursed the *Bonaventure*. All the men on board died but one, and he was the one she would have to herself, the whore.'

A voice from the back said, 'She must be punished for her wickedness. Or more evil will come to the cove.'

'You're all wrong,' Susanna said quietly. 'Let us leave. We've harmed no one.'

'She killed my boy Merryn, because she'd had enough of him,' Hedyn yelled furiously, spittle flying from his lips. 'She cursed poor Beaten and made her fall into the fire.'

There was silence, just the low wail of the sea breeze, an eerie whisper. Then Katel seemed to notice everyone around her. Her voice was a whisper in the wind.

'I'd never harm anyone. I'm waiting for my Jack to come back. I've summoned him with the stones.' All eyes were on her, the mob hunched together as one. 'The chawk told me how. He prophesied it.'

'Hear what she says?' Hedyn looked around for support.

Katel took a breath. 'And as for Beaten, it was the poppet that killed her, the one buried beneath the rosemary bush in our garden.'

* * *

Megan couldn't take her eyes off Patrick throughout the meal. They talked the whole time, laughing, sharing stories, but she found herself staring at the curve of his lips, her gaze straying constantly to the blue of his eyes. She wanted to reach out a hand, touch the tanned cheek, clasp his fingers in hers. But he seemed oblivious to her thoughts and there was no sign that he felt the same. He was happy in her company, enthused by whatever she said, but he didn't touch her arm, reach for her hand. She wondered if he would kiss her later, if he'd ask to come to her room for coffee when he dropped her off. And how would she respond if he did? Her pulse started to quicken.

They had finished their food; Megan had enjoyed the crab cakes and the chocolate fudge brownie with a glass of wine. Patrick had a veggie burger, ice cream, mango juice. He waved his card towards the waiter and leaned over. 'Do you want to walk down to the cliff edge and see the sun set?'

'I'd love to.' There was nothing Megan wanted more.

They set off from the café across cropped grass and loose rocks. He took her hand as they stood at the brink of the drop, gazing across to the sea and beyond, more cliffs and rolling land. Patrick pointed. 'There's St Mawgen Cove. The twinkling lights are The Ship Inn. The bay is where we dived yesterday and that cliff' – he indicated the jagged rock opposite – 'that's where we climbed, where the Waiting Witch is supposed to be.'

A gust of wind blew hard and it was suddenly cold. Megan was grateful for the dry warmth of Patrick's hand.

'It's eerie.' She felt she could confide anything to him now. 'You know, I thought I heard her voice when I was standing there.'

'Perhaps you did.' Patrick didn't flinch at her words. 'I was talking to one of the lecturers about paranormal sightings this morning. She said it could be autosuggestion – you expect to see a ghost, so it happens. It could be imagination. Or it could be real. Who knows?' A thought occurred to him. 'The offer's still on. I'll bring my sleeping bag tomorrow, if you're worried.'

Megan stared into his eyes as his hair blew across his face and he made no effort to smooth it. He was still in T-shirt and shorts, oblivious to the cold. She had never met anyone like him. He was honest, unpretentious. There was no game playing: if he brought a sleeping bag to her bedroom, he'd intend to sleep in it all night. She was grateful for his simple trustworthiness. He was lovely.

'Thanks. I'll think about it.' The sun had dipped behind the sea, an orange flickering glow. The sky was stippled with crashing colours, vivid red light darkening into mauve, merging with the ocean.

Megan said, 'This is glorious.' She turned to face him.

'Beautiful,' he whispered. She hoped he meant her.

'I've had a great time.' Megan felt a little sad. The holiday would soon be over. She wondered how it would end, if she and Patrick would keep in touch. She could go to Cornwall for weekends or he'd drive to her flat in Minehead. She pictured them together, arms wrapped around each other, sharing glorious moments such as this one.

'Me too.' Patrick reached out a hand to touch her hair. Megan's eyes flickered and closed; he was about to kiss her. She held her breath, waiting.

'The thing is,' Patrick said slowly. Megan opened her eyes: he was shifting his feet, about to say something important. 'I need to explain how things are.'

Megan met his gaze. He was about to tell her he had a wife and three children in Falmouth.

'I'm not like most guys, Megan. I don't drop in and out of relationships one after the other.'

He wasn't going to kiss her. He was going to end the relationship there and then, before it had even started. Megan nodded as if she understood, but she feared the worst.

He said, 'I want to kiss you.'

Megan waited for the 'but'. It didn't come. Neither did the kiss. She decided, nothing ventured nothing gained, so she said, 'I want to kiss you too.'

Patrick put his arms round her and placed a finger tenderly on her lips. Megan was confused. 'You're going back home on Sunday.'

Ah, Megan thought, he doesn't want a long-distance relationship. He said nothing, so she tried to help. 'So does that feel like a problem?'

'Yes and no.' Patrick was choosing his words carefully. She waited patiently, although her heart thumped.

'The thing is, Megan, I can't just be in this relationship a little bit. That's not the sort of person I am.' His eyes were glued to hers: he was serious. 'I'm in a hundred per cent, or I'm not in at all, even if we are apart most days. It's the same with my work.'

'Hyperfocus?'

'Exactly.' He couldn't help smiling. 'I won't kiss you now if on Sunday you're going to go home and then we text a couple of times, and after that, I don't hear from you again.' He shrugged. 'A kiss is more than a kiss. It's a pact, that we go for it and see what happens. We give it the best chance. I like you a lot – and if we can make it something good, then that's agreed, sealed with a kiss.'

'I get that.' Megan wrapped an arm around his neck but Patrick was still explaining.

'I know it's early days and anything can happen, but I want you to think about it.'

Megan had already thought about it. The sunset was glorious, her arms were around Patrick; he was gorgeous. 'I'm thinking now.'

'Good. Then that's sorted. We'll meet tomorrow for the dive and that gives you some time to make your mind up and, decide if you'd like a relationship with me.'

Megan took a step back. 'Then we'll kiss?'

'Definitely.'

'What if I've already made up my mind?'

Patrick took both her hands. 'Then we can move tomorrow forward a bit.'

'To now?'

She was in his arms and their lips met. Megan closed her eyes. All thoughts of the Waiting Witch and going back home on Sunday had gone. All that mattered was the deliciousness of the moment. As far as she was concerned, it could go on and on and on.

40

They had been huddled on the clifftop for a long time, Katel clutched in Susanna's arms, both shivering in the cold. The crowd of people were gathered behind Yowann, their eyes filled with hatred: there was no way to escape. The only sound was the low breath of the wind. Susanna heard an approaching footfall. A man was running up the stony path, one arm in the air. Hedyn reached them, shouting furiously, brandishing a piece of grubby cloth as if he'd found treasure.

'It was where she said it was, hidden beneath the rosemary bush in their garden. It's a poppet – look – it's had pins pushed in its face. And see here. It's been burned. It was made for Beaten.'

There was an intake of breath from the mob and Yowann stepped forward. 'Then it's true.' He took the doll from Hedyn and held it out to Katel, thrusting it beneath her nose. 'Do you recognise this?'

Katel looked at Susanna for guidance. Susanna pulled her even closer and met Yowann's eyes boldly. 'It was given to me by Tedda. It has nothing to do with Katel.'

Yowann frowned, turning to Katel. 'Is that true?'

Katel was too afraid to speak. She clung to her mother, trembling.

'Then you're both wicked women and will be treated according to the law, as you deserve. The judge in Bodmin will decide your fate. And he'll be harsh on you both.' Yowann looked around for approval from the crowd and was greeted with cheers and shouts of support.

Colan stepped forward. 'This is foolish. You all know Susanna. Most of us have known her since she was a child. She's a pellar, a healer, a woman who understands the power of herbs and stones. But she's no witch. She delivered my Joan of our baby, staying with her for hours until she brought Thomas into the world. She tended Beaten when she was burned. You know that well, Hedyn. She cared for her with all the knowledge she has. She's sweet, filled with grace – she has tended us all when we have been sick. Her touch is gentle.' He paused, thinking about his words, closing his eyes for a second, remembering. Then he glanced at the crowd, at each face. 'You all know it to be true. Susanna's the kindest person. She wouldn't harm any of you.'

'But what of the child? Katel was fond of Tedda. Many times we saw them by the harbour, their heads together.' Yowann placed his hands on his hips. 'Someone must take the blame. And this morning, Eliza coughed up a nail, exactly as she did when Tedda Lobb was here, cursing us all.'

'You know that's a lie.' Susanna raised her voice. 'I was with you when you found the first nail. You slipped it into your wife's cup.'

'Be quiet,' Yowann shouted. He looked around quickly to gauge the reaction of the crowd, but they just cheered, encouraging him.

Hedyn pushed himself forward, his face creased in fury. 'It's Katel we must punish, not Susanna. She bewitched Merryn. She made Beaten fall into the fire and then she spoke in her ear and told her to throw herself in the sea. Katel Boram can turn herself into a chawk. You all saw the chawk by the harbour when the huge wave crashed into the fishing boat and killed Samuel.'

There was a gasp from Anne: she was sobbing. Hedyn continued, pointing a finger in anger, performing to the crowd now.

'Annie Boram has been made a widow, with one child in her arms and another in her belly. Katel caused the wave to swell and to smash the boat that killed Samuel and my Merryn and her own young man. I tell you, she's heartless. She's a murderer and a witch.'

Katel wriggled from Susanna's grasp. 'I wouldn't harm my Jack. He was my truest love.'

'See,' someone in the crowd hissed. 'She's admitted to murdering the others, Samuel Boram and Hedyn's son.'

'She has not,' Susanna shouted. 'You know she's innocent.'

'Everyone here has made their views clear. And we're all agreed.' Yowann's voice was low, but it carried the tone of a death sentence. 'She's a witch.'

Susanna rushed forward, grasping Yowann by his shirt. 'You know that Katel wouldn't harm anyone. She's innocent.'

Yowann clutched her wrist. 'The law is the law, Susanna. My hands are tied – I can't help now. Katel must be punished. The crowd are howling for it.'

'She's done nothing.' Susanna pulled Yowann towards her urgently. 'I beg you, please let her go.'

'My men will take her to Bodmin Jail as we did with Tedda, and she'll stand trial there for her crimes.'

'Where's Jack?' Katel asked, her voice a whisper. 'Why has he not come for me?'

'Do you deny that you enchanted Merryn and Jack? That you hated Beaten and lured her to her death?' Yowann asked.

'I love my Jack.' Katel had grown pale; she was shaking visibly.

Yowann took a step forward and Katel reached out her arms. 'Mother.' She rushed to Susanna, wrapping her arms around her. 'Help me, please.'

Susanna clung to Katel as several men hurtled towards her, prising her daughter from her arms, tugging her towards the cliff edge. She flung herself towards Katel again but was hauled back by her hair, lifted from her feet. She hit the ground hard and tasted the bitterness of blood on her tongue. On all fours, she looked up. 'Yowann, please, I beg—'

Yowann ignored her. 'Katel, we here assembled find you guilty of witchcraft.'

'You're wrong.' Susanna leaped to her feet and tried to run forward but hands gripped her firmly and held her back. She struggled, screaming.

Yowann continued, 'You stand accused of the murders of Beaten Gilbert, Merryn Gilbert, Charles Rowe, Samuel Boram, Jack of the *Bonaventure* and the crew of the aforesaid ship.'

'No,' Susanna cried out again. 'It was me, Yowann. You won't say it was Katel.'

Katel looked around bewildered, from Yowann to the crowd and then to Susanna. 'When will he come, Mother? When will my Jack come? He promised me.'

A voice in the crowd shouted, 'She talks of the devil. Listen, she calls upon him to help her.'

Someone else called, 'She's guilty.'

'Guilty as sin.' The cry came from Hedyn Gilbert.

'Where's Jack?' Katel shouted. 'Mother, help me.'

Susanna struggled to free herself. 'Yowann, stop this.'

'It can't be stopped,' Yowann said quietly. 'She'll be taken to Bodmin.'

'But she's yours, Yowann,' Susanna cried. 'Yours and mine. We made her together. Katel is your child.'

Yowann turned to Susanna, his face frozen. His words were barely audible. 'Mine?'

'She is.' Susanna's voice was a whisper.

'But I lay with you once. Just once.'

'And I loved you, Yowann. I turned to you. Afterwards, I swore I would love no one but my child.'

A woman's voice gave a curdling scream. 'Witch.'

A clod of earth flew through the air towards Katel as Anne Boram hurled it as hard as she could, her baby clutched tightly in her other arm. 'You heard it. She killed my Samuel. She deserves to die.'

She threw another, a hard pellet. It hit Katel full in the face and she stared around, confused, as if entreating someone to help. There was blood on her mouth.

A rock pelted her in the chest. Hedyn threw a second, a third, shouting with all his might. Katel cried out in pain, wrapping her arms across her body to stop the missiles from hitting her. She called out, 'Help me, Mother.'

'Katel.' Susanna tried to rush towards her child, but a strong arm held her back.

'You're a witch,' Hedyn yelled. 'You'll be punished.'

'Am I? Am I what you say I am?' Katel's eyes wide with terror as she shrieked, 'Then if I am, I curse you all. One by one, I'll come for you until you're all gone. Until the day my Jack returns to me, I'll be waiting for you, all of you. Tedda taught me how. Tedda told me how to make a curse. How to make it stick.'

The whole crowd bent down, one after the other, lifting small rocks, stones, clumps of earth, hurling them towards Katel, screaming, shouting. Yowann moved to Susanna, as if to hold her in his arms, then he twisted towards the baying mob. 'Stop, stop – there's been a mistake.'

'It's no mistake.' Hedyn threw another rock, which hit Katel full in the face and she staggered backwards.

'You must stop,' Yowann shouted, but no one was listening. Voices were raised over his cries.

'Witch,' Anne yelled as she flung another stone with all her might.

Katel was stunned, confused. She wrenched herself around, looking towards Susanna, her mouth open as she cried out. The wind blew her hair across her face, her shift billowed. Then time slowed, Susanna saw each moment as it happened. Katel's foot slipped and she fell backwards over the cliff, stumbling. A few stones dropped with her as she tumbled away and was gone from sight.

The crowd was silent, statue still. Then baby Bartholomew gave a piercing cry.

A quiet voice said, 'She got what she deserved.' Hedyn rushed towards the edge of the cliff. 'There's no sign of her now. She's disappeared completely. Into thin air, like the witch she was.'

A few other men joined him. One said, 'Drowned in the sea, I expect – where she belongs.'

'Or flown away,' another voice added.

Susanna stared, horrified. Her child had gone. She couldn't move.

Yowann was by her side. 'Susanna, I'm sorry for this. I tried. If only I had known' – he placed a hand on her arm – 'I swear, if only—'.

There was a resounding slap, her palm against the skin of his face, and Yowann put a hand to the pain. Susanna's eyes were small with anger.

'I will not speak to you again. I will not speak.'

Colan made a move towards her. 'Susanna, I...'

'Because of you, my daughter will never know peace. I lay all this on you, Yowann. And until the moment she rests, nor will I. I swear it on Katel's name. She did no wrong, but St Mawgen Cove will suffer because of this day. My heart is broken for ever. No. There will be nothing more for me. Nothing but weeping.'

Tears glistened on Susanna's face. She swallowed hard, incapable of another word. Her throat was swollen with grief. She lifted her skirts and ran down the path as fast as she could towards her cottage. It was the only place she could be alone to cry.

* * *

Megan rushed in from the darkness where Patrick had dropped her off, hurrying into the hall towards her room, keys in her hand. She was smiling. How could she not be smiling? It had been a perfect day. A perfect evening. She and Patrick had found something wonderful in each other, something unique – she could tell already; she understood him, she liked everything about him. He was special.

She pushed the key into the door of room three and asked herself if she was being impulsive, if she was plunging in too quickly. She wondered if having had no relationship for so long had left her needy, a bit desperate. But the answer came straight back to her: she'd never felt like this before. Being with Patrick was completely right. As he had said, they had made a pact to try, to see what would come of their relationship.

As she pushed the door open, the air around her turned colder. She could hear a sound from the opposite room, although it was muffled. Room one across the hall was empty tonight but she'd heard a low noise behind the door, like a sob. She froze, holding her breath, almost afraid to make a sound. It was there again, a whimper, a cry.

Megan crept across to the door, as if whoever was behind it might hear her. Her whole body was shaking, but she placed her ear close to the wood. Inside the room, someone was weeping, such grief-stricken anguish that Megan felt tears prick her own eyes.

Then she heard the rise and fall of breath, wrenched sobbing, too many tears, the agony of loss.

Megan was terrified and trembling. She was about to hurry away to the safety of her own room when the woman cried out again. A strangled whimper rose on the air, rising to the fullness of a heart-aching moan.

There was silence, a moment of quiet, then a single word.

'Katel.'

Megan heard the name clearly. Two broken syllables splitting the air, as if a soul had been torn in two.

41

'Katel.'

Susanna bolted the door and sat in the hearth in the exact place where Katel used to sit; she curled up on the straw mattress, watching the flames flicker weakly as the fire died. As darkness crept into the corners, the heat left the room as if sucked away, but she didn't move. There was bread on the table, pottage in the cooking pot, barely warm over the dying embers, but she didn't think about it although her stomach growled. Her face was wet with tears.

She continued to stare into the fire, the final image of her daughter filling her mind. The moment that Katel stumbled backwards and was lost for ever would not go away. The fear in her child's eyes flashed before her again and again.

Exhausted, Susanna wrapped her arms around herself: they would always be empty now.

Katel had gone.

Her life was over.

She breathed in deeply and smelled the sweetness of her daughter on the mattress; the faint aroma of lavender in the hand cream, the sweet mint and thyme that she used when she washed her hair, the light scent of her skin. Susanna sobbed, one heaving sound followed by another. Then the tears came faster and she cried out, her wail filling the absolute darkness. She would never see her child, never touch her cheek with a tender finger – she'd done that since Katel was in the crib, the light touch of a mother's devotion – but she would do it no more.

The sadness of loss tore through her until she thought she'd break. The injustice of Katel's treatment at the hands of the people in the cove hit her like a hurled stone. Again and again, the image of each person in the angry crowd rose up in her mind. Yowann had blamed Katel for his own ends; Hedyn had encouraged the mob to respond with blind hatred. Even Anne had thrown clods of earth, her face twisted in spite. The unfairness made Susanna weep again, a sob for each stone that hit her child. Her heart was split open.

Even in sleep, Susanna cried. She called out for her child. The loss would never go away. Then dawn came and she opened her swollen eyes, but she could not move. Tears came back almost at once, then she was silent again, staring into cold ashes. There was no reason to move, nothing to live for.

She leaned her head against her knees and exhaled, thinking of Katel. But fond images of her daughter would not come; she could not remember happy times. She could not even bring the image of Katel's smile from her memory. All that remained was the final image of her face, her eyes wide with terror before she was lost for ever.

She had no idea how long she stayed in the same position. Time stuck. There was no more time, not now. The room was cold, but Susanna didn't notice it. Someone was at the door. She was vaguely aware of a distant knocking and a woman calling, at first asking if she was all right, if she needed anything, then the voice rose, anxious, and cried, 'Who'll deliver my child if you don't help me, Susanna? I meant no harm. I was angry because of what happened to Samuel. Please, I beg you, forgive me.'

Susanna didn't listen. She couldn't hear the words; she couldn't recognise the speaker. There was nothing now, only the loss of her child in every breath.

Darkness sat in the room and the ash in the fire swirled and settled as the wind funnelled down the chimney. Susanna closed her eyes and Katel's face filled the space behind them.

Much later, there was a louder knock at the door. Susanna was unsure whether it was her own heart knocking. She was weary with weeping, but still she sobbed.

A man's voice called her name many times. She was aware of the tone, entreating her to let him in, using the reasoning of a man who believed he knew what was best. He said that she needed food, water, the help of others. He talked about unfortunate mistakes, then he said he would care for her in his house – there were plenty of rooms. The noise became the low buzzing of flies in her ears and she covered them with fists. Her eyes closed and Katel was there again, standing on the edge of the cliff, her face frozen in terror.

Sometime later, another voice hummed in her head. Susanna wondered if her own thoughts were berating her now. She couldn't be sure. Or perhaps someone else stood behind the door, talking of love, of wanting to care for her, all apologies, all promises. But she didn't hear him; he was nobody. He was not there.

Time dragged. Once Susanna thought she could hear her daughter's voice, a muffled sweetness, the snatches of a song, and Susanna cried out Katel's name as if the two syllables were wrenched from her soul.

She collapsed on the mattress and heard a single, distant sound. It might have been her own tired voice. It might have been the throaty caw of a jackdaw. Susanna didn't know. It didn't matter.

She had lost her child. Her arms were empty.

Nothing mattered now.

* * *

At eleven o'clock that morning, as arranged, Megan sat in the bar of the inn with Emma, Bill and Jackie. Her mother's grin had never been wider but Bill was awkward, fiddling with his tie. Megan was moved by the fact that her dad had worn a suit to meet his daughter for the first time. Emma clutched a glass of orange juice, looking nervously from Bill to Jackie and then to Megan for support. She said, 'Well, it's not every day that this happens.' As she placed a hand on her belly, Jackie watched, smiling with delight.

'I think it's wonderful, Bill. We've found a daughter. And there will be a grandchild.'

Bill shook his head. 'Steady on, Jackie. Emma might not want us pushing our noses in yet.'

Bill was talking about Emma in the third person, as if she was not there. Megan had never seen her father look so terrified.

'No – no, I'm really pleased to meet you,' Emma protested, and Jackie said at exactly the same time, 'I'm so happy to be here.' Then there was a moment of silence.

Megan broke the tension. 'Well, I'm going to leave you to it. I'm off scuba diving.'

'Diving?' Jackie was aghast. She turned her attention to the daughter she knew and began behaving normally. 'On your own?'

'I'm going with Patrick.' Megan left his name hanging in the air teasingly.

Jackie couldn't resist. 'Is he an instructor?'

'He's my boyfriend,' Megan said quietly, watching her mother's perplexed reaction. 'So.' She beamed encouragingly at her father, who was still fiddling with his tie, to Jackie and Emma, who held the glass of juice as if she'd throttle it. 'I'll see you all for dinner later.'

'Well – what – what will we do with ourselves in the meantime?' Bill stammered.

'I thought you could come to my house. You could see the baby's nursery and I could show you some of my old photos so that you can find out what I've been doing over the years and... I've prepared lunch.' Emma took a breath. 'I hope you like quiche and salad – it's not much.'

'Oh, no, that's so kind of you,' Jackie said, 'and then perhaps, afterwards, we could all go shopping somewhere. I'd love to look at baby clothes. We could buy whatever you need for the little one.' She was positively thrilled. 'It's been nearly thirty years since I shopped for a new baby.'

Emma was visibly relieved. 'That sounds wonderful.'

'Well.' Bill stood up. 'We'll make a start, and leave you to your diving, Megan.'

Jackie offered Emma an arm. 'I'm just so happy to meet you.' She had almost reached the door when she turned round to Megan, a familiar look of mixed excitement and admonishment on her face. 'And I can't wait to hear all about this new boyfriend, love.'

'You can meet him tonight.' Megan laughed. 'He's coming to dinner. And

Carly, my surfing buddy, will be there too. But don't let me keep you, Mum,' Megan said mischievously. 'I'll see you in here, around seven. Claude's making something special.'

She rushed back to room three, lifted by a delicious feeling of independence. There were definite positives to having a sister.

* * *

Megan was still excited about her parents' visit as she stood on the beach in her wetsuit with Patrick. They were strapping on gas bottles and weight belts as they chatted, wading into the water, flippers on their feet.

Patrick was busy wetting their masks. 'I'm looking forward to meeting them.'

'It was so cute this morning, Emma and Dad looking at each other nervously. I can see so much of Dad in Emma now. And Mum was bowled over by the baby.'

'The perfect outcome,' Patrick said. 'And you went surfing earlier?'

'Carly and I had a great time. She's off to Peniche in two weeks until next spring. What a life she has.'

'Everything's working out,' Patrick agreed. 'Things feel good, don't they?'

Megan took his hand. 'They do.'

'Maybe the hag-stones we've found will bring us luck?'

'The one you gave me is still in my jacket pocket,' Megan said. 'I know you don't really believe in good-luck charms, but Mum and Dad have met Emma. I've met you.'

'It's meant to be.' Patrick's lips brushed hers. 'I'll take the other stones into uni on Monday morning, show them to a few people. But now let's dive. I have a funny feeling we'll find something interesting today.'

Megan took the face mask from him. 'Such as?'

'No idea. But I've been looking at maps and currents. Let's go and see what's down there.' Megan felt suddenly nervous but Patrick's expression was completely reassuring.

Once they were in the sea, diving side by side, Megan felt completely at ease. She breathed easily and consciously, sucking and blowing on the regulator. Patrick was close by, extending his thumb, rotating his wrist: that was the sign they were going down. The water quickly became darker and colder, as Megan kicked her legs deliberately to descend. She felt her heartbeat slowing, a sense of deep relaxation taking over as she focused entirely on breathing. She could hear nothing else.

Patrick turned to check that all was well, bubbles rising from his regulator, and Megan felt a rush of gratefulness. It occurred to her briefly that if things went wrong underwater, she would die. Patrick had warned her that the thought would come, and she pushed her worries away, smiling beneath the mask: they had a trust that went beyond diving together, and she felt completely safe.

Patrick indicated himself with the left index finger, then pointed down, suggesting that he was about to lead the way and Megan should follow him. She dived lower, the ocean becoming a deep foggy green colour, eerily dark. Patrick swept his flat hand from side to side – they were levelling off.

Then Megan saw it. There wasn't much of it, just a few bits of wood, debris on the seabed, but she was sure what it was. She hung vertically as Patrick swam down, watching him take out his underwater torch, then his camera. He was busy working, taking photos, then he tugged at something, wriggling it free from the sand. He came towards her, a piece of ship's timber in his hand and gestured with his thumb that they were going up.

Megan swam upwards slowly, Patrick by her side, regulating the steady pace of their ascent towards the light. They swam underwater towards shore and broke the surface, standing slowly. They took the regulators off, slipped the masks back onto their heads. Megan saw Patrick was smiling.

In his fist he gripped a piece of wood, holding it aloft in triumph. She could see three letters had been carved into it; they were now faint, but she could make out them out: AVE.

The *Bonaventure*.

42

Megan and Patrick sat together at the laptop in Surf's Up! staring at the screen.

'Let's consider the facts,' Patrick said. 'The *Bonaventure* sailed to Bristol from France in 1625. It was wrecked just off the cove here.'

'Have a look at the crew list.' Megan was excited. 'Did all the sailors die?'

'There was one survivor. His name's in the records. Jacques Beaufoy, from Saint-Pol in Brittany.'

'These old records you've found are incredible. Muster books, log books...' Megan pointed at the screen. 'And the parish records – here, look – Jacques Beaufoy had an older brother, Guillaume. He was brought from the shipwreck to the cottage of a man called Samuel Boram, near The Ship Inn, where he died.'

'The Drenched Man.' Patrick glanced at Megan.

'I wonder if it was.' Megan held her breath in excitement as Patrick moved the mouse, a frown between his eyes as he concentrated hard.

'The following spring, Samuel Boram and Jacques Beaufoy and another man – Merryn Gilbert – were drowned at sea in a fishing boat just off the cove. Their deaths are recorded as lost at sea.' He turned to Megan. 'I wonder if that's where we found the stones on the dive.'

'There's more here, look.' Megan pointed to the screen again. 'A woman,

Katel Boram, believed to be eighteen years of age, died not long afterwards. It records her death as accidental, falling from a cliff. It says here that she was accused by the residents of the cove of witchcraft.' She caught her breath. 'Patrick, that's her.'

'I bet it's the same cliff where she's said to watch now.'

'Look at this.' Megan pointed excitedly, hardly able to believe what she saw. 'Three weeks later, her mother, Susanna Boram, passed away in her home. It says there was no known cause. And read what happened afterwards. Over the next twelve months, a long line of men from the cove died, one after the other, with no explanation. Here are all the names, and dates. In 1626, Yowann Hicks, aged forty-one, found dead by the harbour. In 1626, Hedyn Gilbert, forty-one, found dead outside Anchor Cottage. In 1627, Colan Stephens, thirty-eight, found dead outside The Ship Inn.'

Patrick met her gaze. 'There's definitely a pattern.'

'She killed them.' Megan's voice was low. 'Katel Boram must be our witch. And was the French sailor, Jacques Beaufoy, her lover? Do you think she gave him the hag-stones to protect him?'

'It makes sense.' Patrick took her hand. 'And Susanna Boram would have been her mother. She lived in the cottage.'

'So she's the Weeping Woman?'

'But what can we do about it?' Patrick asked.

'There must be something,' Megan said. 'I've a feeling the answer lies in the stones.'

* * *

The restaurant was busy on Saturday evening, the whole area dimly lit by pretty lanterns, the air smelling of delicious cooking. Julien was rushing around with trays of food as strains of sea shanties trickled from the bar. He paused just behind Bill, who sat with his legs stretched, Emma between him and Jackie, to unload four plates of pan-fried scallops. He placed the dishes on the table. 'Claude's made his best food tonight. Scallops all round – Bill, Megan, Jackie, Carly – and beetroot gnocchi for Patrick and Emma.'

Emma made a mock-sad face. 'I loved scallops before I was pregnant but now I get heartburn.'

'Oh, scallops are a treat,' Jackie gushed, patting her hand. 'And the main course sounds delicious, Julien. I can hardly wait.'

'Cod fillet, with proper twice-fried French frites and purée of cauliflower. And for Patrick, portobello tacos.' Julien glanced towards Patrick, then back to Jackie. 'I hope you'll sleep well tonight. You're our special guests.'

Only Megan noticed the moment of anxiety in Patrick's eyes: she knew he was worrying about her being alone upstairs. Carly waved her glass of Prosecco. 'I always sleep well after a few of these.'

Jackie glanced towards Patrick's glass of tomato juice, with a brief questioning look at Megan. She was clearly interested in her daughter's new partner. 'So, Patrick, don't you drink?'

'I dive most days,' Patrick explained philosophically. 'I think it's better if I steer clear of alcohol.'

Megan said, 'I dived today, Mum, and I think I'm getting really good at it.'

'Definitely,' Patrick agreed.

Megan raised her glass of Chablis. 'It's been a good week. I've really enjoyed being here. Thanks, Julien.'

'No, thank *you*, Megan. You've helped us so much – more than you realise. You must come back soon,' Julien said. 'Claude and I are finishing the new website. We've really gone for the smuggler angle, the dark secrets.'

Bill clutched his pint. 'Is that true? Were there smugglers here?'

'Apparently,' Julien said proudly. 'The inn was the centre of it all.'

'The Ship certainly has history,' Emma said quietly. The jolly chorus of a sea shanty drifted from the bar. A man was singing about drinking an entire bottle of rum. Julien scurried back to the kitchen with an empty tray.

'Talking of history,' Megan chimed, 'we've made some real discoveries while we were diving.'

'Did you find treasure?' Carly asked, draining her glass.

'We did.' Megan beamed.

'Anything interesting?' Bill tucked into scallops.

'A piece of an old seventeenth-century French ship,' Megan said.

'It was probably wrecked by people in this cove for its haul,' Patrick added. 'It was a *caraque* – a three-masted one. The *Bonaventure*. It sank in 1625.'

'Patrick's writing a book about Cornish fishing and the history of the cove,' Megan said proudly. 'And we found hag-stones on our first dive, which were near a wrecked fishing boat.' She produced the stone from the pocket of her denim jacket. 'Here's one.'

'It's a pebble with a hole.' Jackie frowned. 'I'm not sure we'd sell many of those in the shop.'

'They were a big thing in the days of witchcraft.' Megan saw Emma stiffen, her face troubled. She gave her a warm smile and pushed the stone back in her jacket pocket, changing the subject. 'Mum, did you bring the things from the shop?'

'I did,' Jackie said with a flourish, reaching into her bag and handing Emma a brown parcel. 'We have wheatgerm oil and mandarin for your skin, meadowsweet capsules for your heartburn, raspberry leaf tea. And a present from Megan.'

Emma gave her a look of gratitude as Jackie presented her with a little box. Emma opened it eagerly. 'A necklace. How pretty.'

'It's moonstone, the crystal of sisterhood,' Megan said. 'And the herbal remedies will really help.'

'Thanks. I need them more than you can imagine,' Emma said, her voice thick with emotion. She turned to Bill as if it was the most natural thing in the world. 'Can you help me put this on?'

Bill fiddled with clumsy fingers as Emma lifted her long hair so that he could fasten the necklace around her neck. Megan saw tears in his eyes. She longed for a few moments alone with him, to ask him how he was feeling. It had been an emotional day.

A familiar sound came from the bar, a wheezing concertina, a rich male voice lifted in song. Megan clapped her hands. 'It's Tom.'

'Tom?' Jackie asked.

'He's a local expert on just about everything,' Carly said with a brief look towards Megan. With Emma at the table, she wouldn't mention undertakers.

The song continued and everyone sat still at the table listening, forks poised. Megan had heard the tune before.

> *The years have gone and much is changed, the fishing boats*
>   *still roam*
> *And in the wind they say, some nights, you still can hear her moan.*

Oft times you'll see her on the shore, pale in the gliding moon
Weeping for the boy who stole her heart, but he will ne'er return.

Let's hear it for the Cornish boy who sails the salty brine.
And for the maid who waits alone upon the dark shoreline.

So when you walk the cliffs, me boys, and stand upon the beach
She'll be watching there behind you, better pray you're far from reach.
Her lips will brush against your face and rest assured of this
No man has never lived who felt the Waiting Witch's kiss.

Let's hear it for the Cornish boy who sails the salty brine.
And for the maid who waits alone upon the dark shoreline.

'What a sad song,' Jackie said.

'It is,' Emma said quietly, examining her fingers.

Megan thought she should try to lift the mood. 'It's so nice to be celebrating tonight. Mum, Dad, should we have a toast?'

'We should.' Jackie raised her glass. 'What shall we drink to? Friends and family?'

'Maybe, Emma, you'd like to do it,' Megan suggested.

'I'd like to, very much,' Emma said slowly. She raised her glass of orange juice, her expression hesitant. 'A year ago, I was working here in the pub with the old owners, and I still had my John. Then I found out I was expecting a baby and we were over the moon.' She took a deep breath. 'I lost him and I thought I was alone. It was hard, especially in the evening, at night. Well, I knew I'd been adopted and – on a whim – I contacted my parents who are retired and live in France. I wanted to find my real parents.' She raised her glass higher. 'I met Megan; I met you and Jackie, Bill, and I'm so glad I did. I'd been a little bit scared about the future, but now I have another family. So, I'd like to toast – my new family.' She turned to Bill. 'My new dad.'

Carly said, 'Aww,' and everyone's glasses chimed. Megan met Patrick's eyes and a look of understanding passed between them. She reached for his hand beneath the table and it was there, palm open, fingers waiting to clasp hers.

Bill finished his food and said, 'The main course will be here in a minute. I'll just pop to the Gents.'

'I'm so glad you like the pendant.' Jackie was oblivious to Bill's effort to cover his emotion. She was deep in conversation with Emma and Carly as Julien came in to collect plates. 'You must come and see Earthbound Essentials, Emma. You too, Carly.'

Carly was delighted. 'I must get something for extra energy for Portugal.'

'Megan's a very good herbalist,' Jackie said.

Julien hovered between Megan and Patrick, his voice low as he said, 'Will you be all right sleeping in room four, Megan?'

'I'll probably be fine,' Megan reassured him.

'I've brought my sleeping bag, just in case you need solidarity,' Patrick whispered. At that moment, Megan wanted to kiss him, despite the fact that her mother was watching her. He understood her completely, and the affinity between them made her heart expand. Instead, she leaned in close and pecked his cheek. 'You're special.'

'You too.' Patrick looked around suddenly. 'Megan, where did your Dad go? He's been gone a while.'

'The loos,' Megan replied.

'I saw him go outside.' Julien frowned. 'I'm bringing in the main courses now.'

'Shall I...?' Patrick asked.

'Oh, I'll go and tell him the food's on its way.' Megan stood quickly, shrugging on her denim jacket. She hurried through the bar, waving a hand towards Tom Hocking as she passed the throng who surrounded him. He was in the middle of a sad song, all minor chords, as his audience swayed and joined in the chorus:

And this is my Cornwall, I'll tell you all why,
For here I was born and here I shall die.

Megan found her father outside, beneath the fuzzy glow of an orange lamp. He was standing in hazy darkness, shivering in the sea breeze, staring towards the harbour wall. She placed a hand on his arm. 'Dad, are you all right?'

'I needed a moment.' Bill took a deep breath. 'It's been quite a day.' Megan waited for him to speak. 'It's been lovely – but tough. Your mother's wonderful. I'm amazed just how supportive Jackie is.'

'She seems to like Emma.'

'They get on like a house on fire,' Bill said. 'I think Emma's lovely, but I feel like I've let her down, Megan.'

'You haven't, Dad. It starts now, being the parent of two daughters.'

'But I feel dazed. My heart's been going like the clappers all day.'

'How's the blood pressure?' Megan asked.

'You sound like your mother. She's got me on all sorts of herbal remedies.'

'I know: hawthorn, fish oil, garlic.' Megan hugged her father. 'And you're doing well.'

'What about you?' Bill asked. 'I mean, I don't want you to feel that I'm giving Emma all the attention.'

'Oh, not at all, Dad.'

'Your mother's a bit obsessive about the baby.'

'That's fine. It's good for Emma and good for Mum.'

'You don't feel left out?'

'No,' Megan replied. 'I'm delighted for us all.'

'Thank you.' Bill wrapped an arm around her. 'And this boyfriend, Patrick. You seem fond of him.'

'I am,' Megan said earnestly. 'We've just met, but he's so easy to get on with and...' She paused. Her father was staring into the distance, not listening. 'What is it, Dad?'

'There's a woman.'

'What woman?'

'Up there. On the cliff. She's just standing, above the harbour, staring out to sea.'

'Where?' Megan felt the rush of cold. 'I can't see her.'

'There she is. Right at the edge. In a pale dress.'

'Are you sure?'

'She's there.'

Megan looked at her father's face. Bill's eyes were glazed, as if hypnotised. 'Dad?'

His voice was the lightest trace of a whisper. 'She's gone now.'

'Come on.' Megan grabbed his arm. 'Let's go inside.' Bill stood like a statue. 'Dad?' She hugged him close. 'Dad.'

Then she heard the voice behind her, a breath on the wind.

'*I'm here.*'

'Dad, let's go in the warm.' Megan tugged her father's arm but he was transfixed. 'Come on.'

Bill didn't move. He was staring at something. Then Megan saw something. A shadow of a woman, her fair hair over her face.

A sensation of the most intense cold went through her. 'Dad.'

The voice came again. '*I watch each night...*'

Megan felt a light wind circling, a whisper in her ear. The woman was standing behind her. There was a new coldness, ice on her neck. She pulled her father's sleeve urgently. 'Dad.'

Bill inhaled loudly and held his breath. His hand moved to his chest. He couldn't exhale.

Megan heard another voice, the lightness of a sigh.

'*One breath, one kiss... you are mine...*'

The Waiting Witch.

Megan jerked her father's arm hard. He was frozen, mouth open. She whirled round. The shadow was inches away, hovering.

Megan called out desperately, 'Are you Katel Boram? I know what happened to you. I know about Jacques Beaufoy. I know about his brother, Guillaume, the Drenched Man.'

The shadow had disappeared. Megan glanced at her father and he hadn't moved. His hand was clutching at his throat. He was gasping, unable to breathe out.

There was another low sound and Megan reeled round again. The shadow was there, a pale face with glistening eyes. Megan tried again. 'Katel.'

The shadow seemed to shift, to hover.

'Are you Katel? Was Susanna Boram your mother? Is she the Weeping Woman?'

The shadow didn't move. Cold eyes glistened through the tangled mass of hair. Megan noticed the pale dress shift like mist in the breeze. She called, 'Katel, please don't hurt my father.'

The voice came again, faintly, rustling like dead leaves.

'*One kiss...*'

Megan delved into her jacket pocket, pulling out the hag-stone, holding it up high. 'Please. Please go away. I don't know why you are so angry. Did Jacques drown in a fishing boat? Were the hag-stones his? We found them at the bottom of the ocean. Please, take this one. It's yours. I hope it brings you peace.'

Megan lifted the stone higher. Hag-stones protected against witches, didn't they? And weren't they supposed to help a wandering spirit to find peace? She hugged her father, squeezing her eyes closed, cringing, waiting for the worst. There was a sound like the long sucking in of breath.

She heard a heavy beating of wings, and something fluttered in front of her face. Megan wasn't sure what happened next. There was a rush of cold air, as if a bird had descended sharply. Perhaps a beak or a claw looped through the hole of the hag-stone, or a gust of wind whisked it away, but the stone was tugged from her fingers. There was a low sound, an exhalation. She heard her father breathe out as if released from a spell.

She opened her eyes. The witch had gone.

'Dad?'

Bill turned to her. 'Megan.'

'Dad.'

'What happened? I just seemed to lose track of time.'

'Are you all right?'

'Yes, I'm...' His face was mystified. '...a little dizzy, I feel a bit odd. Do you think it was stress?'

'No, it's been a bit of a... strange day.' Megan stared towards the harbour. The icy breeze had calmed. The air somehow felt gentle, warmer. She searched the dark skies for any sign of the bird. A crow or a jackdaw might have taken the hag-stone: didn't they have a reputation for stealing treasure? But there was nothing.

A lone cloud drifted across the face of the moon. The street was deserted.

'Shall we go in?' Megan took her father's arm. 'Our main course is ready.'

'Yes.' Bill was still shaken and confused; he let himself be shepherded inside.

It was surprisingly warm in the bar. Tom was leading the singers in a jolly song about a drunken pirate climbing a mast and falling down. The crowd was clapping, stamping their feet.

Megan and her father walked into the restaurant and sat down. Her mother was fanning her face with a menu. 'I swear the temperature has just gone up in here. I was cool before, but now...' Julien arrived with a tray, placing plates of food. Jackie's brow was damp. 'I was just saying, have you turned up the heating?'

'No, we always have it on a high setting.' Julien lifted an eyebrow. 'Claude said the same thing in the kitchen. It's usually chilly in the corners, but the whole room's too hot.'

'Patrick was telling us while you were gone' – Jackie beamed at Bill – 'that you've been to St Ives. We should go to the gallery there, Bill. Apparently, there's a lovely little café on top of a cliff just a short drive away.'

Emma said, 'Oh, I know the one.'

'We'll all go, next time we're down here,' Bill said. He looked more alert now.

'We could take the baby,' Jackie said.

'I'd love that,' Emma said.

Julien hovered between Megan and Patrick. 'So, enjoy your meal.' He put the final dishes down with a flourish and was gone.

Patrick looked at Megan inquisitively. 'Are you OK?'

'Never better.' She put her lips against his ear.

'Did something happen outside, with your dad? You were gone a long time.'

'Yes.'

'He looked a bit dazed when he came in.'

'It was incredible,' Megan began. She reached for Patrick's hand beneath the table. 'I'll tell you about it later.'

* * *

It was past eleven. Emma had gone home. Tom had insisted on walking her and Carly through the cove. Back in the hotel accommodation, Bill and Jackie were comfortably installed inside room three. Bill was exhausted and ready for bed, although Jackie was still talking about Emma and the baby.

Megan and Patrick stood at the bottom of the stairs with her holdalls and surfboard and his sleeping bag. They looked up into the grainy gloom. It was time to make a decision. Megan leaned closer to him. 'Room four beckons.'

'Right.' Patrick was in no hurry 'So, what happened when you were outside with your dad?'

'The witch made an appearance. I think it was Katel Boram.'

'You actually saw her?' Patrick was concerned. 'Are you all right?'

'I'm fine.' Megan wrapped an arm around his neck. 'And so's Dad. She... she came down from the cliff. She had some sort of hold over Dad for a while. I offered her the hag-stone. I think she took it. Then something changed – something really changed. I think she's gone.'

At that moment the door to room one opened, and a young woman rushed out, her hair flying, talking quickly into her phone. She ran past breathlessly. 'Yes, that's great news. You can tell Hugh yourself. He's in the car park, unloading the cases. I'll get him now – hang on. We just arrived in St Mawgen.'

Megan watched her rush out. The door to room one was ajar. She glanced at Patrick. A breeze snaked past them, the raw night wind. At first they thought it was a draught from the door.

Then they heard a soft sound coming from inside the empty room.

A single sob.

Patrick reached for Megan's hand and they approached the door uncertainly, peering in. The room was dim, lit by a red glow, like the last flames of a hearth. A woman was hunched in the centre by the embers, dishevelled, her head down. She looked broken.

She gave a heartbreaking cry and the whole of her body shook with sorrow. Patrick's hand tightened around Megan's as her voice rose in a loud keening, as if her heart was broken in two.

Another figure appeared from the shadows. It was a young woman wearing a pale dress, her hair over her face. Megan recognised her at once.

There might have been a third shape beside her, the silhouette of a young man: Megan wasn't sure. The Weeping Woman looked up and the image froze for a moment. Something unsaid had passed between mother and daughter. She stood hesitantly and stretched out a hand. The young woman reached out and placed something in her palm.

The two women's fingers linked and held. Time seemed to stand still. Megan waited, her heart in her mouth. She heard a hollow, drawn-out sound, like the rattle of a final breath. The figures became dark and hazy around the edges, like crushed velvet; the red glow of the room faded into nothing and it was all light and shadows again.

Room one was just an ordinary hotel room, empty, the gleam of a bedside lamp illuminating a double bed, a single suitcase on top.

Megan was still holding Patrick's hand tightly as she led the way up the stairs. Her voice was a whisper. 'The Weeping Woman has gone, hasn't she?'

Patrick exhaled. 'I can hardly believe what I saw.'

'But it's all over. They've found peace. Do you think Katel gave her mother the hag-stone, the one I had in my hand?'

'Perhaps she did.'

'Then things will be all right now.'

'It's hard to make sense of it.'

'But something's changed. The air's warmer, like everything's somehow... normal again. So.' Megan paused at the top of the landing. 'Do you think the Drenched Man will make an appearance tonight?'

'I don't know. Let's go inside.'

Patrick pushed the door open, flicked on the light and they both glanced around. Room four was cosy, warm. There was a light scent of salt on the air, but the space was fresh and welcoming. Patrick said, 'I'll help bring your things in.'

They placed her holdalls and surfboard in the room, next to the etching of the *Bonaventure*. She put her handbag on the rocking chair.

The room was calm. Welcoming. Peaceful.

Megan said, 'I think he's gone too.'

They stood for a moment, looking at each other.

'Right.' Patrick broke the silence, kissing her lightly. 'You don't need me to stay.'

'No, I don't.' Megan leaned forward. 'But I'd like you to.' Her voice was a whisper. 'We have a lot to talk about.'

'I want to hear everything that happened while you were outside. I need to make sense of what I've seen.'

'Or we could talk about us instead,' Megan said.

'OK.' Patrick took a deep breath: a new thought had come to him. 'You're going home tomorrow. Perhaps I could drive up next weekend? Or if you'd like to come down here, we could dive and surf.'

'We could,' Megan whispered as she wrapped an arm around his neck. 'There are so many things I want to say to you, though, about us... We've got so much to talk about, and it could take a long time.'

'We have all the time in the world.'

'We have.' She tugged him towards her and closed the door with a click.

EPILOGUE

It was the last day of the year. Megan and Patrick clambered up the cliff in warm hats and jackets, wearing sturdy boots, their gloved hands clasped. They stood at the top and looked down into rough frothing waves, the wind in their faces. Megan leaned against Patrick and he wrapped an arm around her.

She rested her head against his shoulder. 'It's a good job Mum and Dad didn't come up with us. It's a tough climb.'

'Especially in the cold,' Patrick agreed.

'Mum's totally obsessed with baby Jack, though,' Megan said. 'At least Emma's getting a break while she fusses. It's been her best Christmas ever.'

'Your mum and dad look really happy,' Patrick said quietly.

'Emma's delighted they're staying over New Year. And there's the big fancy dress party in The Ship tonight. Everyone will be in smugglers' costumes.'

'It'll be packed out in there.'

'Mm. I'm happier staying with you at Surf's Up!' Megan said.

'Me too.' Patrick kissed her forehead. 'I wish you didn't have to keep going back to Somerset.'

'Well, I'm thinking about making some changes.' Megan examined Patrick's face, watching his expression. 'You know Carly's not coming back this spring, thanks to the big romance with José in Peniche? So I'm going to take over the surf shop. Mum's retiring. Amy's mum will mind Leo while Amy works in Earthbound Essentials, and I've got her an amazing assistant. They'll keep everything going while I'm down here. I want to turn Unravel the Ocean into the best surf and herbal remedy hub in Cornwall.'

Patrick was smiling. 'So we can be together all the time.' He stared out to sea. 'What a perfect way to start the new year.'

'I want to be with you.'

'That's what I want too,' Patrick said.

Megan followed his gaze, out across the ocean. They were quiet for a while. Then she said, 'It still feels strange to be up here. This is where the witch used to look out from. She must have been here when Dad saw her.'

'I wonder if she was watching for her sailor. Or maybe she'd lost her mind. Do you think she was a real witch?'

'Who knows? The stones connected her to Jacques. I think she gave them to him for protection.' Megan felt sad at the thought.

'It's very strange.'

'Patrick, I really did see her outside The Ship. I heard her voice. The hagstone was whisked from my hand.'

'It might have been a gust of wind.'

'It might. But you saw what happened in room one. We both saw it. Julien says the Weeping Woman hasn't been heard since that night,' Megan said. 'You heard her sobbing. Her heart was broken. She must have been crying for centuries. But after we saw her with Katel, she stopped.'

'The inn certainly feels warmer,' Patrick agreed.

'Everyone's noticed it. That atmosphere's totally different. But I'll never forget the Weeping Woman,' Megan said sadly. 'I've honestly never heard anything so heartbreaking.'

'I hope they're at peace.'

'Me too.' Megan was suddenly animated. 'Right. Now we're here, let's do what we promised we'd do. For Katel and her mother and Jacques.'

'I brought the stones.' Patrick pushed his hands into his pockets. 'It's the proper thing, to give them back.'

'It is.'

Megan held out her cupped hands as Patrick placed the small hag-stones in them, one by one. She noticed the soft gleam of light on the smooth surface, the tiny holes. 'Where should we put them?'

'Katel stood here, on the edge of the cliff. If this is where she tumbled into the sea, let's place them where her feet might have been,' Patrick said.

Megan laid the small stones side by side, Patrick moving them so they were equally spaced. They stood back to survey their work.

Megan felt a sigh rise in her chest. 'I so hope she can rest.'

'I hope they can all rest. We can look to the future now. Our future,' Patrick said. 'Shall we go back?'

They walked away down the path towards the harbour, hand in hand. The wind gave a hollow sigh, and the grass shuddered.

* * *

A jackdaw landed on the edge of the cliff. It stared around, its eyes shining like beads, unblinking. It gave a harsh croak.

In a single sharp movement, it lifted one of the smooth stones in its beak. For a while, it remained motionless, as if deep in thought, then it stretched its wings and flew over the ocean and away, until it was lost in the sky.

* * *

MORE FROM ELENA COLLINS

Another book from Elena Collins, *The Wicked Lady*, is available to order now here:

https://mybook.to/WickedLadyBackAd

ACKNOWLEDGEMENTS

Thanks to Kiran Kataria and Sarah Ritherdon, whose professionalism and kindness I value each day.

Thanks to the wonderful team at Boldwood Books; to Amanda and Marcela and Emma and Wendy and Nia, to designers, editors, technicians, voice actors. You are magicians.

Thanks to Rachel Gilbey, to so many wonderful bloggers and fellow writers. The support you give goes beyond words.

Thanks to, Shaz, Gracie, Mya, Frank, Martin, Cath, Avril, Rob, Tom, Emily, Tom's mum, Erika, Rich, Susie, Ian, Chrissie, Kathy N, Julie, Martin, Steve, Rose, Steve's mum, Jan, Rog, Jan M, Helen, Pat, Ken, Trish, Lexy, Rachel, John, Nik R, Pete O', Chris A, Chris's mum, Dawn, Beau CC, Slawka, Katie H, Fiona J and Jonno.

Thanks to Peter and the Solitary Writers, my writing buddies.

Also, my neighbours and the local community, especially Jenny, Laura, Claire, Paul and Sophie, Niranjan and all at Turmeric Kitchen.

Much thanks to Ivor Abiks at Deep Studios and his friend Tony for their work on the sea shanty with me. It's always a blast working with you, Ive.

Thanks always to Darren and Lyndsay at PPL.

Thanks and love go to Ellen, Hugh, Jo, Jan, Lou, Harry, Chris, Norman, Angela, Robin, Edward, Zach, Daniel, Catalina.

So much love to my mum and dad, Irene and Tosh.

Love always to our Tony and Kim, to Liam, Maddie, Kayak, Joey.

And to my soulmate, Big G.

Warmest thanks always to you, my readers, wherever you are. You make this journey special.

I initially researched *The Cornish Witch* on The Lizard Peninsula in Cornwall and in the Museum of Witchcraft, Boscastle. There are so many people I'd like to thank, including the staff of The Old Inn in Mullion, residents of the cove whom I met in St Mellanus Church, and the many experts on Cornish language, history and fishing who kindly offered their expertise.

Special thanks to:

- Bernard Deacon
- Sian Wheeler, Archives and Special Collections Assistant, Falmouth University
- Michelle, The Old Inn, Mullion
- Richard, Colin, Alyson, Mullion residents

Additional Research:

- Boorde, Andrew, *First Book of the Introduction of Knowledge*
- Carew, Richard, *The Survey of Cornwall*
- Kowaleski, Maryanne, 'The expansion of the south-western fisheries in late medieval England', *Economic History Review* 53 (2000)
- https://www.thegypsythread.org/wortcunning/
- https://www.cornwallheritage.com/
- https://en.wikipedia.org/wiki/List_of_Cornish_dialect_words
- https://museumofwitchcraftandmagic.co.uk/
- https://bernarddeacon.com/the-blog/

ABOUT THE AUTHOR

Elena Collins is the pen name of Judy Leigh. Judy Leigh is the bestselling author of *Five French Hens*, *A Grand Old Time* and *The Age of Misadventure* and the doyenne of the 'it's never too late' genre of women's fiction. She has lived all over the UK from Liverpool to Cornwall, but currently resides in Somerset.

Sign up to Elena Collins' mailing list for news, competitions and updates on future books.

Visit Elena's website: https://judyleigh.com

Follow Elena on social media here:

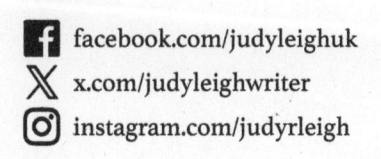

facebook.com/judyleighuk
x.com/judyleighwriter
instagram.com/judyrleigh

ALSO BY ELENA COLLINS

The Witch's Tree

The Lady of the Loch

Daughter of the Mists

The Wicked Lady

The Cornish Witch

ns from
the past

Discover page-turning historical novels from your favourite authors and be transported back in time

Join our book club Facebook group

https://bit.ly/SixpenceGroup

Sign up to our newsletter

https://bit.ly/LettersFromPastNews

Boldwood

Boldwood Books is an award-winning fiction publishing company seeking out the best stories from around the world.

Find out more at www.boldwoodbooks.com

Join our reader community for brilliant books, competitions and offers!

Follow us
@BoldwoodBooks
@TheBoldBookClub

Sign up to our weekly deals newsletter

https://bit.ly/BoldwoodBNewsletter